OPAL

A LUX NOVEL
BOOK THREE

OPAL

A LUX NOVEL
BOOK THREE

JENNIFER L. ARMENTROUT

Entangled Publishing, LLC
2614 South Timberline Road
Suite 109
Fort Collins, CO 80525
Visit our website at www.entangledpublishing.com.

Edited by Liz Pelletier
Cover design by Liz Pelletier

ISBN   978-1-62061-009-1
e-ISBN 978-1-62061-010-7

Manufactured in the United States of America

First Edition December 2012

The author acknowledges the copyrighted or trademarked status and trademark owners of the following wordmarks mentioned in this work of fiction: Expedition, Google, Wikipedia, WWE, Popsicle, Lite Brite, Costco, Nintendo, Wonder Woman, Tinker Bell, IHOP, Coke, He-Man, Kool-Aid, Ghost Investigators, Starbucks, Texas Chainsaw Massacre, Hostel, MacBook Air, Jurassic Park, Pop-Tart, Smurfs, Energizer, The X-Files, Highlighter, Walmart, Lucky Charms, Taser, Happy Meal, Tiffany's, Predator, Jetta, Gorilla Glue, Prius

This book is dedicated to the winning Daemon Invasion team.
You ladies rock!

Janalou Cruz
Nikki
Ria
Beth
Jessica Baker
Beverley
Jessica Jillings
Shaaista G
Paulina Zimnoch
Rachel

Chapter 1

I wasn't sure what woke me. The howling wind from the first hardcore blizzard of the year had calmed last night and my room was quiet. Peaceful. I rolled onto my side and blinked.

Eyes the color of dew-covered leaves stared into mine. Eyes eerily familiar but lackluster compared to the ones I loved.

Dawson.

Clenching the blanket to my chest, I sat up slowly and pushed the tangled hair out of my face. Maybe I was still asleep, because I really had no idea why Dawson, the twin brother of the boy I was madly, deeply, and quite possibly insanely in love with was perched on the edge of my bed.

"Um, is...is everything okay?" I cleared my throat, but the words came out raspy, like I was trying to sound sexy and, in my opinion, failing miserably. All the screaming I'd done while Mr. Michaels, my mom's psycho boyfriend, had me locked in the cage in the warehouse was still reflected in my voice a week later.

Dawson lowered his gaze. Thick, sooty lashes fanned the tips of high, angular cheeks that were paler than they should be. If I'd learned anything, Dawson was damaged goods.

I glanced at the clock. It was close to six in the morning. "How did you get in here?"

"I let myself in. Your mom's not home."

With anyone else, that would've creeped the hell out of me, but I wasn't afraid of Dawson. "She's snowed in at Winchester."

He nodded. "I couldn't sleep. I haven't slept."

"At all?"

"No. And Dee and Daemon are affected by it." He just stared at me, as if willing me to understand what he couldn't put into words.

The triplets—hell, *everyone*—was coiled tight, waiting for the Department of Defense to show up as the days ticked by since Dawson escaped their Lux prison. Dee was still trying to process her boyfriend Adam's death and her beloved brother's reappearance. Daemon was trying to be there for his brother and to keep an eye on them. And though storm troopers hadn't busted up in our houses yet, none of us were relaxed.

Everything was too easy, which usually didn't bode well.

Sometimes…sometimes I felt like a trap had been set, and we'd galloped right into it.

"What have you been doing?" I asked.

"Walking," he said, glancing out the window. "I never thought I'd be back here."

The stuff that Dawson had been put through and made to do was too horrific to even think about. A deep ache filled my chest. I tried not to think about it, because when I did, I thought of Daemon being in that same position, and I couldn't bear it.

But Dawson… He needed someone. I reached up, wrapping my fingers around the familiar weight of the obsidian necklace. "Do you want to talk about it?"

He shook his head again, shaggy wisps of hair partially obscuring his eyes. It was longer than Daemon's—curlier—and probably needed a trim. Dawson and Daemon were identical, but right now, they looked nothing alike, and it was more than the hair. "You remind me of her—Beth."

I had no idea what to say to that. If he loved her half as much as I loved Daemon… "You know she's alive. I've seen her."

Dawson's gaze met mine. A wealth of sadness and secrets were held in its depths. "I know, but she's not the same." He paused, lowering his head. The same section of hair that always fell on Daemon's forehead toppled onto his. "You…love my brother?"

My chest hurt at the desolation in his voice, as if he never expected to love again, couldn't really even believe in it anymore. "Yes."

"I'm sorry."

I jerked back, losing my grip on the blanket as it fell lower. "Why would you apologize?"

Dawson lifted his head, letting out a weary sigh. Then, moving faster than I thought he was capable of, his fingers brushed over my skin—over the faint pink marks that circled both wrists from fighting against the manacles.

I hated those blemishes, prayed for the day when they completely faded. Every time I saw them, I remembered the pain the onyx had caused as it pressed into my flesh. My ruined voice was hard enough to explain to my mom, not to mention Dawson's sudden reappearance. The look on her face when she'd seen Dawson with Daemon before the snowstorm was sort of comical, though she seemed happy that the "runaway brother" had returned home. But these babies I had to hide with long-sleeved shirts. That worked during the colder months, but I had no idea how I'd hide these in the summer.

"Beth had those kinds of marks when I saw her," Dawson said quietly, pulling his hand back. "She got really good at escaping, but they always caught her, and she always had these marks. Usually around her neck, though."

Nausea rose, and I swallowed. Around her neck? I couldn't... "Did...did you get to see Beth often?" I knew they'd allowed at least one visit between them while imprisoned in the DOD facility.

"I don't know. Time was messed up for me. I kept track in the beginning, using the humans they brought to me. I'd heal them and usually if they...lived, I could count the days until everything fell apart. Four days." He went back to staring out the window. Through curtains that had been drawn back, all I could see was the night sky and snow-covered branches. "They hated when everything fell apart."

I could imagine. The DOD—or Daedalus, a group supposedly within the DOD—had made it their mission to use Luxens to successfully mutate humans. Sometimes it worked.

Sometimes it didn't.

I watched Dawson, trying to remember what Daemon and Dee had said about him. Dawson was the nice one, funny and charming—the male equivalent of Dee and nothing like his brother.

But this Dawson was different: morose and distant. Besides not talking to his brother, from what I knew, he hadn't said a word to anyone about what had been done to him. Matthew, their unofficial guardian, thought it was best no one pushed for more.

Dawson hadn't even told anyone how he escaped. I suspected Dr. Michaels—that lying rat bastard—had led us on a wild goose chase to find Dawson to give himself time to get the hell out of Dodge and had then "released" Dawson. It was the only thing that made sense.

My other guess was much, much darker and more nefarious.

Dawson glanced down at his hands. "Daemon... He loves you, too?"

I blinked, brought back to the present. "Yes. I think so."

"He told you?"

Not in so many words. "He hasn't *said it*, said it. But I think he does."

"He should tell you. Every day." Dawson tipped back his head and closed his eyes. "I haven't seen the snow in so long," he said, almost wistfully.

Yawning, I glanced out the window. The nor'easter everyone predicted had hit this little speck of the world and had made Grant County its bitch over the weekend. School had been canceled on Monday and today, and the news last night said they'd still be digging everyone out by the end of the week. The snowstorm couldn't have come at a better time. At least we had an entire week to figure out what in the hell we were going to do with Dawson.

It wasn't like he could just pop back up in school.

"I haven't seen it snow like this ever," I said. I was originally from Northern Florida, and we'd gotten a couple of freak ice storms before but never the white, fluffy stuff.

A small, sad smile appeared on his lips. "When the sun comes up, it'll be beautiful. You'll see."

No doubt. Everything would be encased in white.

Dawson jumped up and suddenly appeared on the other side of the room. A second later I felt warmth tingle along my neck and my heart rate pick up. He looked away. "My brother is coming."

No more than ten seconds later, Daemon was standing in the doorway of my bedroom. Hair messy from sleep, flannel pajama bottoms rumpled. No shirt. Three feet plus of snow outside, and he was still half naked.

I almost rolled my eyes, but that would've required I take my eyes off his chest…and his stomach. He really needed to wear shirts more often.

Daemon's gaze slipped from his brother to me and then back to his brother. "Are we having a slumber party? And I'm not invited?"

His brother drifted past him silently and disappeared into the hallway. A few seconds later, I heard the front door close.

"Okay." Daemon sighed. "That's been my life for the last couple of days."

My heart ached for him. "I'm sorry."

He sauntered over to the bed, his head cocked to the side. "Do I even want to know why my brother was in your bedroom?"

"He couldn't sleep." I watched him bend down and tug the covers. Without realizing it, I'd grabbed them again. Daemon pulled once more, and I easily let them go. "He said it was bothering you guys."

Daemon slipped under the covers, easing onto his side and facing me. "He's not bothering us."

The bed was way too small with him in it. Seven months ago— heck, four months ago—I would've run laughing into the hills if someone said the hottest, *moodiest* boy in school would be in my bed. But a lot had changed. And seven months ago, I didn't believe in aliens.

"I know," I said, settling on my side, too. My gaze flickered over his broad cheekbones, full bottom lip, and those extraordinarily bright green eyes. Daemon was beautiful but prickly, like a Christmas cactus. It had taken a lot for us to get to this point, being in the same room with each other and not overcome by the urge to commit first-degree murder. Daemon had to prove his feelings for me were real and he did...finally. He hadn't been the nicest person when we first met, and he had to really make up for that. Momma didn't raise a pushover. "He said I remind him of Beth."

Daemon's brows slammed down. I rolled my eyes. "Not in the way you're thinking."

"Honestly, as much as I love my brother, I'm not sure how I feel about him hanging out in your bedroom." He reached out with a muscular arm and used his fingers to brush a few strands of hair off my cheek, tucking them behind my ear. I shivered, and he smiled. "I feel like I need to mark my territory."

"Shut up."

"Oh, I love it when you get all bossy-pants. It's sexy."

"You're incorrigible."

Daemon inched closer, pressing his thigh against mine. "I'm glad your mom is snowed in elsewhere."

I arched a brow. "Why?"

One broad shoulder shrugged. "I doubt she'd be cool with this right now."

"Oh, she wouldn't."

More shifting and our bodies were separated by a hairbreadth. The heat that always rolled off his body swamped mine. "Has your mom said anything about Will?"

Ice coated my insides. Back to reality—a scary, unpredictable reality where nothing was what it seemed. Namely Mr. Michaels. "Just what she said last week, that he was going out of town on some kind of conference and visiting family, which we both know is a lie."

"He obviously planned ahead so no one would question his absence."

To disappear was what he needed, because if the forced mutation worked on any level, he'd need some time off. "Do you think he'll come back?"

Running the back of his knuckles down my cheek, he said, "He'd be crazy."

Not really, I thought, closing my eyes. Daemon hadn't wanted to heal Will but his hand had been forced. The healing hadn't been on the level required to change a human at the cellular scale. And Will's wound hadn't been fatal, so either the mutation would stick or it would fade away. And if it faded, Will would be back. I would bet on it. Although he conspired against the DOD for his own gain, the fact he knew it had been Daemon who mutated me was valuable to the DOD, so they'd be forced to take him back. He was a problem—a huge one.

So we were waiting… Waiting for both shoes to drop at once.

I opened my eyes, finding Daemon hadn't taken his off me. "About Dawson…"

"I don't know what to do," he admitted, trailing the back of his knuckles down my throat, over the swell of my chest. My breath caught. "He won't talk to me, and he barely talks to Dee. Most of the time, he's locked up in his bedroom or out wandering in the woods. I follow him, and he knows." Daemon's hand found its way to my hip and stayed. "But he—"

"He needs time, right?" I kissed the tip of his nose and pulled back. "He's been through a lot, Daemon."

His fingers tightened. "I know. Anyway…" Daemon shifted so fast, I didn't realize what he was doing until he'd rolled me onto my back and hovered above me, hands braced on either side of my face. "I've been remiss in my duties."

And just like that, everything that was going on, all our worries, fears, and unanswered questions, simply faded into nothing. Daemon had that kind of effect. I stared up at him, finding it hard to breathe. I wasn't 100 percent on what his "duties" were, but I had a very vivid imagination.

"I haven't spent a lot of time with you." He pressed his lips against my right temple and then my left. "But that doesn't mean I haven't been thinking about you."

My heart leaped into my throat. "I know you've been occupied."

"Do you?" His lips drifted over the arch of my brow. When I nodded, he shifted, supporting most of his weight on one elbow. He caught my chin with his free hand, tipping my head back. His eyes searched mine. "How are you dealing?"

Using every ounce of self-control I had, I focused on what he was saying. "I'm dealing. You don't need to worry about me."

He looked doubtful. "Your voice…"

I winced and uselessly cleared my throat again. "It's getting much better."

His eyes darkened as he ran his thumb along my jaw. "Not enough, but it's growing on me."

I smiled. "It is?"

Daemon nodded and brought his lips to mine. The kiss was sweet and soft, and I felt it in every part of me. "It's kind of sexy." His mouth was on mine again, taking it deeper and longer. "The whole raspy thing, but I wish—"

"Don't." I placed my hands on his smooth cheeks. "I'm okay. And we have enough things to worry about without my vocal chords. In the big scheme of things, they're nowhere near the top of the list."

He arched a brow and wow, I did sound kind of uber-mature. I giggled at his expression, ruining my newly discovered maturity. "I have missed you," I admitted.

"I know. You can't live without me."

"I wouldn't go that far."

"Just admit it."

"There you go. That ego of yours getting in the way," I teased.

His lips found the underside of my jaw. "Of what?"

"The perfect package."

He snorted. "Let me tell you, I have the perfect—"

"Don't be gross." I shivered, though, because when he kissed the hollow of my throat, there was nothing flawed about that.

I would never tell him this, but beside the...*pricklier* side of him that reared its ugly head from time to time, he was the closest thing to perfect I'd ever met.

With a knowing chuckle that had me squirming, he slid his hand down my arm, over my waist, and caught my thigh, hooking my leg around his hip. "You have such a dirty mind. I was going to say I'm perfect in all the ways that count."

Laughing, I wrapped my arms around his neck. "Sure you were. Completely innocent, you are."

"Oh, I've never claimed to be *that* nice." The lower part of his body sank into mine, and I sucked in a sharp breath. "I'm more—"

"Naughty?" I pressed my face into his neck and inhaled deeply.

He always had this outdoorsy scent, like fresh leaves and spice. "Yeah, I know, but you're nice under the naughty. That's why I love you."

A shudder rolled through him, and then Daemon froze. A stuttered heartbeat passed and he rolled onto his side, wrapping his arms around me tightly. So tightly I had to wiggle a little to lift my head.

"Daemon?"

"It's okay." Voice thick, he kissed my forehead. "I'm okay. It's… early still. No school or Mom coming home, yelling your full name. Just for a little while we can pretend that crazy doesn't wait for us. We can sleep in, like normal teenagers."

Like normal teenagers. "I like the sound of that."

"Me, too."

"Me, three," I murmured, snuggling against him until we were practically one. I could feel his heart beating in tandem with mine. Perfect. This was what we needed—quiet moments of being normal. Where it was just Daemon and me—

The window overlooking the front yard blew apart as something large and white crashed through it, sending chunks of glass and snow shooting onto the floor.

My startled scream was cut off as Daemon rolled, springing to his feet as he slipped into his true Luxen form, becoming a human shape of light that shone so brightly I could only stare at him for a few precious seconds.

Holy crap, Daemon's voice said, filtering through my own thoughts.

Since Daemon hadn't gone ape wild on someone, I scrambled to my knees and peered over the edge of the bed.

"Holy crap," I said out loud.

Our precious moment of being normal ended with a body lying on my bedroom floor.

Chapter 2

I stared down at the dead man, dressed like he was prepared to join the rebel alliance on the Hoth system. My thoughts were a little hazy at first, which was why it took me a few seconds to realize, dressed like that, he'd really blend in with the snow. Except for all the red streaming from his head…

My already pounding heartbeat skyrocketed. "Daemon…?"

He pivoted, slipping back into his human form as he wrapped an arm around my waist, pulling me back from the carnage.

"He's a-an Officer," I stuttered, smacking at his arms to get free. "He's with the—"

Dawson suddenly stood in the doorway, his eyes glowing much like Daemon's were. Two bright white lights, like polished diamonds. "He was sneaking around outside by the tree line."

Daemon's arm loosened. "You…you did this?"

His brother's gaze flickered to the body. *It*—because I couldn't really think of *it* as a human being—lay in a twisted, unnatural heap. "He was watching the house—taking pictures." Dawson held up what looked like a melted camera. "I stopped him."

Yeah, Dawson had stopped him right through my bedroom window.

Letting go of me, Daemon made his way over to it. He knelt and pulled back the insulated white down jacket. There was a charred spot on the chest that smoked. The smell of burned flesh wafted into the air.

I climbed off the bed, pressing my hand to my mouth just in case I started to hurl. I'd seen Daemon hit a human with the Source—their power based in light—before. Nothing but ashes had remained, but it had a hole burned through its chest.

"Your aim is off, brother." Daemon let go of the jacket, the thick cords of muscles in his back bunched with tension. "The window?"

Dawson's eyes drifted to the window. "I've been out of practice."

My mouth dropped open. Out of practice? Instead of incinerating it, he'd knocked it into the air and through my window. Not to mention he'd *killed* it. No, I wouldn't think of that.

"My mom's gonna kill me," I said, feeling numb. "She's really going to kill me."

A broken window—of all the things to focus on, but it was something, something other than *it* lying on my floor.

Daemon stood slowly, eyes sheltered and jaw set like stone. He didn't take his gaze off his brother, his expression a blank mask. I turned to Dawson, our gazes colliding, and for the first time, I was scared of him.

• • •

After a quick change and bathroom visit, I stood in the living room, surrounded by aliens for the first time in days. A perk of being made of light, I guessed—the ability to go just about anywhere in a blink of an eye.

Since Adam's death, everyone had pretty much given me a wide berth, so I was unsure what was about to go down. Probably a lynching. I knew I'd want one for whoever had been responsible for the death of someone I loved.

Hands shoved into his pockets, Dawson pressed his forehead against the window by where the Christmas tree had once stood, his back to the room. He'd said *nothing* since the bat signal had been sent out and the aliens had come a-running.

Dee sat perched on the couch, her eyes fixed on her brother's back. She looked wired, her cheeks flushed with anger. I think it bothered her being in this house. Or just being near me. We hadn't had a chance to really talk after…everything.

My gaze slid to the other occupants. The evil wonder twins, Ash and Andrew, were seated beside Dee, their gazes locked onto the spot where their brother, Adam, had last stood…and died.

Part of me hated being in the living room since it reminded me of what had happened when Blake finally fessed up to his true purpose. When I had to come in here, which wasn't often since I moved all my books out of the living room, I looked right at the spot to the left of the throw carpet under the coffee table. The pine floors were bare and shiny now, but I could still see the pool of bluish liquid that I'd mopped up along with Matthew on New Year's Eve.

I wrapped my arms around my waist to try to suppress the shudder.

Two sets of footfalls came down the steps, and I turned, finding Daemon and his guardian, Matthew. Earlier, they'd gotten rid of… *it*, incinerating it outside, deep in the woods, after doing a quick run of the area.

Walking to my side, Daemon tugged on the edge of my hoodie. "It's been taken care of."

Matthew and Daemon had gone upstairs no more than ten minutes ago with a tarp, a hammer, and a bunch of nails. "Thank you."

He nodded as his gaze slid to his brother. "Did anyone find a vehicle?"

"There was an Expedition near the access road," Andrew said, blinking. "I torched it."

Matthew sat on the edge of the recliner, looking like he needed some liquor. "That's good, but it's not good."

"No shit," Ash snapped. Upon a closer look, she wasn't the picture perfect ice princess today. Her hair hung limply around her face, and she wore sweats. I didn't think I'd ever seen her in sweats. "That's *another* dead DOD Officer. How many does that make it? Two?"

Well, actually, that made it number four, but they didn't need to know that.

She tucked her hair back, her chipped fingernails pressing into her cheeks. "They're going to wonder where they are, you know? People don't disappear."

"People disappear all the time," Dawson said quietly without turning around, his words sucking the oxygen from the air.

Ash's bright sapphire eyes slid to him. Well, everyone pretty much looked at Dawson, since that was the first time he'd spoken since we all gathered. She shook her head but wisely remained quiet.

"What about the camera?" Matthew asked.

I picked up the melted thing, turning it over. Warmth still radiated from it. "If there're pictures, they're gone now."

Dawson turned around. "He was watching this house."

"We know," Daemon said, moving closer to me.

His brother tilted his head to the side and when he spoke, his voice was empty. "Does it matter what was on the camera? They were watching you—*her*. All of us."

Another shudder rolled through me. It was his tone more than anything that got to me.

"But next time, we need to kind of…oh, I don't know, talk first and then throw people through windows later." Daemon crossed his arms. "Can we try that?"

"And we can just let killers go?" Dee said, voice shaking as her eyes darkened, flashing with fury. "Because that's apparently what should happen. I mean, that Officer could've killed one of us, and you would have just let him go."

Oh, no. My stomach sank.

"Dee," Daemon said, stepping forward. "I know—"

"Don't 'I know, Dee' me." Her lower lip trembled. "You let Blake go." Her gaze moved to me, and it felt like a kick in the stomach. "Both of you let Blake go."

Daemon shook his head as he unfolded his arms. "Dee, there was enough killing that night. Enough death."

Dee reacted as though Daemon had hit her with his words, wrapping her arms around her waist for protection.

"Adam wouldn't have wanted that," Ash said quietly, sitting back against the couch. "More deaths. He was such a pacifist."

"Too bad we can't ask him how he really feels about it, isn't it?" Dee's spine stiffened, as though she was forcing herself to bite out her next words. "He's dead."

Apologies bubbled up in my throat, but before they could break free, Andrew spoke. "Not only did you guys let Blake go, you lied to us. From her?" He gestured at me. "I don't expect loyalty. But you? Daemon, you kept everything from us. And Adam died."

I whipped around. "Adam's death isn't Daemon's fault. Don't put that on him."

"Kat—"

"Then whose is it?" Dee's gaze met mine. "Yours?"

I sucked in a sharp breath. "Yeah, it is."

Daemon's body went rigid beside me, and then, always the referee, Matthew jumped in. "All right, guys, that's enough. Fighting and casting blame isn't helping anyone."

"It makes us feel better," Ash muttered, closing her eyes.

I blinked back tears and sat on the edge of the table, frustrated that I was even close to crying because I didn't own the right to those tears. Not like they did. Squeezing my knees until my fingers dug in through the soft material, I let out a breath.

"Right now, we need to get along," Matthew went on. "All of us, because we have lost too much already."

There was a pause and then, "I'm going after Beth."

Everyone in the room turned to Dawson again. Not a single thing had changed in his expression. No emotion. Nothing. And then everyone started talking at once.

Daemon's voice boomed over the chaos. "Absolutely not, Dawson—no way."

"It's too dangerous." Dee stood, clasping her hands together. "You'll get captured, and I won't survive that. Not again."

Dawson's expression remained blank, like nothing his friends or family had said made any difference to him. "I have to get her back. Sorry."

It looked like a dumbfounded stick had smacked Ash in the face. I probably looked the same. "He's insane," she whispered. "Freaking insane."

Dawson shrugged.

Matthew leaned forward. "Dawson, I know, we all know, that Beth means a lot to you, but there's no way you can get her. Not until we know what we're dealing with."

Emotion flashed in Dawson's eyes, turning them forest green. Anger, I realized. The first emotion I'd seen from Dawson was anger. "I know what I'm dealing with. And I know what they are doing to her."

Prowling forward, Daemon stopped in front of his brother, legs spread wide, arms crossed again, ready for battle. Standing together like that, it was surreal seeing them. They were identical, with the exception of Dawson's thinner frame and shaggier hair.

"I cannot allow you to do that," Daemon said, voice so low I barely heard him. "I know you don't want to hear that, but no way."

Dawson didn't budge. "You don't have a say over it. You never did."

At least they were talking. That was a good thing, right? Somehow I knew that the two brothers going toe-to-toe was oddly comforting as much as it was distressing. Something Daemon and Dee thought they'd never experience again.

Out of the corner of my eye, I saw Dee moving toward them, but Andrew reached out, catching her hand and stopping her.

"I'm not trying to control you, Dawson. It's never been about that, but you just got back from hell. We just got *you* back."

"I'm still in hell," Dawson replied. "And if you get in my way, I will drag you down with me."

A look of pain shot across Daemon's face. "Dawson…"

I jumped to my feet, reacting to Daemon's response without thinking. An unknown urge propelled me to do so. I guess that urge was love, because I didn't like the pain flickering across his face. Now I understood why my mom got all Mama Bear sometimes when she thought I was threatened or upset.

A wind blew through the living room, stirring the curtains and flipping the pages of Mom's magazines. I felt the girls' eyes on me and their surprise, but I was focused.

"All right, the alien testosterone right now is a little too much, and I really don't want to have an alien brawl in my house on top of the broken window and the dead body that came through it." I took a breath. "But if you two don't knock it off, I'll kick both of your asses."

Now everyone was staring at me. "What?" I demanded, cheeks flushing.

A slow, wry smile teased Daemon's lips. "Simmer down, Kitten, before I have to get you a ball of yarn to play with."

Annoyance flared deep inside me. "Don't start with me, jerk-face."

He smirked as he focused on his brother.

Beside him, Dawson looked sort of...amused. Or in pain—one of the two, because he really wasn't smiling or frowning. But then, without saying a word, he stalked out of the living room, the front door slamming shut behind him.

Daemon glanced at me, and I nodded. Sighing deeply, he followed his brother, because there really was no telling what Dawson would do or where he would go.

The alien Kumbaya fell apart after that. I followed them to the door, my attention fixed on Dee. We so needed to talk. First off, I had to apologize for a lot of things, and then I had to try to explain myself. Forgiveness wasn't expected, but I needed to try to talk.

I clenched the door knob until my knuckles bleached. "Dee...?"

She stopped on the porch, back straight. She didn't face me. "I'm not ready."

And with that, the front door tore free from my hand and swung shut.

Chapter 3

Already treading on thin ice with my mom, I decided not to mention the whole window thing when she called later in the evening, checking in. I was hoping and praying the roads were cleared enough to get someone out here to fix the window before Mom could make her way home.

I hated lying to her, though. All I'd been doing lately was lying to her, and I knew I needed to tell her everything, especially about her supposed boyfriend, Will. But how would this kind of conversation go? *Hey, Mom, our neighbors are aliens. One of them accidentally mutated me, and Will is a psycho. Any questions?*

Yeah, that was so not going to happen.

Right before I hung up, she pushed the whole going-to-see-a-doctor-for-my-voice thing again. Telling her it was just a cold worked now, but what was I going to say in a week or two from now? God, I really hoped my voice healed by then, although a part of me knew this might be permanent. Another reminder of… everything.

I had to tell her the truth.

Grabbing a package of instant mac and cheese, I started to pop it in the microwave but then stared down at my hands, frowning. Did they have microwave powers like Dee and Daemon did? I turned over the bowl, shrugging. I was too hungry to risk it.

Heat wasn't my thing. When Blake was training me to handle the Source and tried to teach me how to create heat—i.e. fire—I'd caught my hands on fire instead of the candle.

As I waited for the mac, I stared out the window over the sink. Dawson had been right earlier. It really was beautiful now that the sun had risen. Snow blanketed the ground and covered the branches. Icicles hung from the elms. Even now, after the sun had set, it was a beautiful white world out there. I kind of wanted to go out and play.

The microwave dinged, and I ate my unhealthy dinner standing, figuring at least I would burn off calories that way. Ever since Daemon had mutated me into this human-alien-hybrid-mutant-freak, my appetite was out of this world. There was almost nothing left in the house.

When I finished, I quickly grabbed my laptop and sat at the kitchen table. My brain had been scattered the last week, and I wanted to look up something before I forgot. Again.

Pulling up Google, I typed in DAEDALUS and hit enter. Wikipedia served up the first link and since I wasn't expecting a "Welcome to Daedalus: Secret Government Organization" website, I clicked.

And I got all acquainted with Greek myths.

Daedalus was considered an innovator, creating the labyrinth the Minotaur resided in, among other things. And he was also the daddy of Icarus, the kid who flew too close to the sun on wings fashioned by Daedalus, and then drowned. Icarus got giddy from flying and, knowing the gods, it was probably a form of passive punishment, leading to Icarus losing his wings. That and a punishment for Daedalus, who'd outfitted Icarus with the contraption that gave the boy the godlike ability to fly.

Nice history lesson, but what was the point? Why would the DOD name an organization overseeing human mutation after some dude—?

Then it struck me.

Daedalus created all kinds of things that bettered man, and the whole godlike-abilities angle was kind of like humans who were mutated by the Luxen. It was a leap in logic, but come on, the government *would* be so full of themselves they'd name their organization after a Greek legend.

Closing the laptop, I stood and found myself grabbing my jacket and going outside. I really didn't know why. Who knew if there were more Officers sneaking around? My overactive imagination formed the image of a sniper hiding in the tree and a red dot appearing on my forehead. Nice.

Sighing, I dug out a pair of gloves from the pockets of my jacket and high-stepped it through the mounds of snow. Needing some form of physical exercise to keep my brain from going into overdrive, I started rolling a ball of snow across the front yard. Everything had changed in a matter of months and then again in a matter of seconds. Going from shy, book-nerd Katy to something impossible; someone who had changed on more than a cellular level. I no longer saw the world in black and white and deep down I knew I didn't operate on basic social norms anymore.

Like thy shalt not kill or whatever.

I hadn't killed Brian Vaughn, the Officer who had been paid off by Will to turn me over to him instead of the Daedalus as I could be used as leverage to ensure that Daemon mutated him instead of killing him outright, but I had *wanted* to and I would have if Daemon hadn't beaten me to it.

I'd been totally okay with the idea of killing someone.

For some reason, killing the two evil aliens, the Arum, hadn't affected me as much as the idea of being totally kosher with killing a human did. Not sure what that said about me, because like Daemon had said once before, a life was a life, but I didn't know how to process adding the words 'okay with killing' to the bio section on my book blog.

My cotton gloves were soaked by the time I finished with the first ball and moved on to rolling the second lump of snow. This whole physical-exertion thing wasn't doing anything other than causing my cheeks to burn in the frosty, snow-scented air. Fail.

When I was done, my snowman had three sections, but no arms or face. It kind of mirrored how I felt inside. I had most of the body parts but was missing vital pieces to make me real.

I really didn't know who I was anymore.

Stepping back, I ran the sleeve of my arm over my forehead and let out a ragged breath. Muscles burned and skin ached, but I stood there until the moon peeked out behind thick clouds, sending a slice of silvery light over my incomplete creation.

There'd been a dead body in my bedroom this morning.

I sat down in the middle of my front yard, right in a pile of cold snow. A dead body—another dead body, just like Vaughn's dead body that had fallen near the driveway, just like Adam's dead body that had lain in the living room. Another thought I'd tried to ignore wormed its way through my defenses. Adam had died trying to protect me.

Wet, cold air stung my eyes.

If I had been honest with Dee, telling her from the start about what really happened in the clearing that night we fought Baruck and about everything thereafter, she and Adam would have been more cautious about bum-rushing my house. They would've known about Blake and how he was like me, capable of fighting back on a souped-up alien level.

Blake.

I should've listened to Daemon. Instead, I wanted to prove myself. I wanted to believe that Blake had good intentions when

Daemon had sensed something off about the boy. I should've known when Blake had thrown a knife at my head and left me alone with an Arum that there was something very demented about him.

Except was Blake demented? I didn't think so. He'd been desperate. Frantic to keep his friend Chris alive and trapped by what he'd become. Blake would've done anything to protect Chris. Not because his life was joined with the Luxen, but because he cared for his friend. Maybe that's why I hadn't killed him, because even in those moments where everything was pure chaos, I saw a part of me in Blake.

I'd been okay with the idea of killing his uncle to protect my friends.

And Blake had killed my friend to protect his.

Who was right? Was anyone?

I was so caught up in my thoughts, I didn't pay much attention to the warmth skipping across my neck. I jumped when I heard Daemon's voice.

"Kitten, what are you doing?"

I twisted around and lifted my head. He stood behind me, dressed in a thin sweater and jeans. His eyes glimmered under thick lashes.

"I was making a snowman."

His gaze drifted beyond me. "I see. It's missing some stuff."

"Yeah," I said morosely.

Daemon frowned. "That doesn't tell me why you're sitting in the snow. Your jeans have to be soaked." There was a pause and damn if that frown didn't turn upside down. "Wait. That means I'd probably get a better look at your butt, then."

I laughed. Leave it to Daemon to always take things down a level or two.

He glided forward as if the snow moved out of the way for him and sat beside me, crossing his legs. Neither of us said anything for a moment, and then he leaned over, pushing me with his shoulder.

"What are you really doing out here?" he asked.

I'd never been able to hide anything from him, but I really wasn't ready to go *there* with him yet. "What's going on with Dawson? Has he run off yet?"

Daemon looked like he was going to push the subject for a moment but then just nodded. "Not yet, because I followed him around today like a babysitter. I'm thinking about putting a bell on him."

I laughed softly. "I doubt he'll appreciate that."

"I don't care." A little bit of anger flashed in his voice. "Running off after Beth isn't going to end well. We all know that."

No doubt. "Daemon, do you…"

"What?"

It was hard to put into words what I thought, because once I said them, they became real. "Why haven't they come after Dawson? They have to know he's here. It would be the first place he'd come back to if he had escaped. And they've obviously been watching." I gestured back at my house. "Why haven't they come for him? For us?"

Daemon glanced at the snowman, silent for several heartbeats. "I don't know. Well, I have my suspicions."

I swallowed past the lump of fear growing in my throat. "What are they?"

"You really want to hear them?" When I nodded, he went back to staring at the snowman. "I think the DOD was aware of Will's plans, knew he was going to arrange for Dawson to be released. And they let it happen."

I drew in a shallow breath as I picked up a handful of snow. "That's what I think."

He glanced at me, eyes hidden behind his lashes. "But the big question is why."

"It can't be good." I let most of the snow slip through my

gloved fingers. "It's a trap. Has to be."

"We'll be ready," he said after a few seconds. "Don't worry, Kat."

"I'm not worried." Such a lie, but it seemed like the right thing to say. "We need to stay ahead of them somehow."

"True." Daemon stretched out his long legs. The underside of his jeans was a darker blue now. "You know how we stay under the humans' radar?"

"By pissing them off and alienating yourselves?" I gave him a cheeky grin.

"Ha. Ha. No. We pretend. We constantly pretend like we're not different, that nothing's happening."

"I'm not following."

He flopped onto his back, his dark hair splashing against the white. "If we pretend like we've gotten away with Dawson being released, that we don't think anything's suspicious or that we know they're aware of our abilities, then it may buy us time to figure out what they're doing."

I watched him throw his arms out to his sides. "You think they'll slip up then?"

"Don't know. I wouldn't put money on it, but it kind of gives us the edge. It's the best we have right now."

The best we had kind of sucked.

Grinning as if he didn't have a care in the world, he started sliding his arms through the snow, along with his legs, moving them like windshield wipers. Really nice-looking windshield wipers.

I started to laugh, but it got stuck in my throat as my heart swelled. Never in my life did I think Daemon would be into the snow-angel-making business. And for some reason, that made me all warm and fuzzy.

"You should try it," he coaxed, eyes closed. "It gives you perspective."

I doubted it could give me perspective on anything, but I lay down beside him and followed suit. "So I Googled Daedalus."

"Yeah? What did you find out?"

I told him about the myth and my suspicions, which Daemon smirked at. "It wouldn't surprise me—the ego behind that."

"You'd know," I said.

"Hardy har-har."

I grinned. "How is this giving me perspective, by the way?"

He chuckled. "Wait for a couple more seconds."

I did and when he stopped and sat, he reached over, grasping my hand, and pulled me up with him. We brushed the snow off of each other—Daemon taking a little longer than necessary on certain areas. Finished, we turned to our snow angels.

Mine was much smaller and less even than his, like I was top heavy. His was perfect—show-off. I folded my arms around me. "Waiting for the epiphany to happen."

"There isn't one." He dropped a heavy arm over my shoulder, leaned in, and pressed a kiss against my cheek. His lips were so, so warm. "But it was fun, wasn't it? Now..." He steered me back to the snowman. "Let's finish with your snowman. It can't be incomplete. Not with me here."

My heart tripped up. There were so many times I wondered if Daemon could read minds. He could be amazingly spot-on when he wanted. I tilted my head back against his shoulder, wondering how he'd gone from douchebag extraordinaire to this...this guy who still infuriated me but also constantly surprised and amazed me.

To this guy I'd fallen madly in love with.

Chapter 4

When the plows came out, clearing a path through town and down the back roads, Matthew got a glass repair company here in the nick of time. They'd left minutes before Mom arrived home on Friday, looking like she'd ate, slept, and saved lives in her polka-dot scrubs.

She threw her arms around me, nearly taking me to the floor. "Baby, I've missed you!"

I hugged her back just as tightly. "Same here. I…" I let go, blinking back tears. Looking away, I cleared my throat. "Have you actually showered in the last week?"

"No." She tried to hug me again, but I jumped back. She laughed but I caught a flash of sadness in her eyes just before she turned toward the kitchen. "Just kidding.. There're showers at the hospital, honey. I'm clean. I swear!"

I followed behind her, wincing as she went straight to the raided fridge. Mom threw open the door and then stepped back, looking over her shoulder. Wisps of blond hair sneaked out of her bun.

Her delicately arched brows lowered and her perky little nose wrinkled. "Katy…?"

"Sorry." I shrugged. "I was snowed in. And I got hungry. A lot."

"I can tell." She closed the door. "It's okay. I'll run to the store later. The roads aren't bad now." She paused, rubbing her brow. "Well, some look like you'd need a snowmobile to get down, but I can make it into town."

Which meant there'd be school on Monday. Boo. "I can go with."

"That would be nice, honey. As long as you plan not to put stuff in the cart and then throw a fit when I take it out."

I gave her a bland look. "I'm not two."

Her saucy smile was cut off by her yawn. "I've barely had any down time. Most of the nurses couldn't make it in. I covered the ER, prenatal ward, and my favorite," she said, grabbing a bottle of water, "the detox floor."

"That blows." I trailed behind her again, feeling incredibly Mommy needy.

"You have no idea." She took a sip, stopping at the base of the stairs. "I've been bled on, peed on, and thrown up on. In that order and sometimes not."

"Ew," I said. Mental note: nursing was now placed with school administration in the Not Going To Happen Possible Job list.

"Oh!" She started up the stairs, twisting halfway around and teetering on the edge of the step. Oh, dear. "Before I forget, I'm changing shifts next week. Instead of working at Grant on the weekends, it will be Winchester. Busier in the city and more action on the weekends than doing the shift around here, and Will works weekends anyway, so it works out better."

Which also meant more time away— *What*? My heart stuttered and there was this falling, spinning-down feeling. "What did you say?"

Mom frowned. "Honey, your voice… I really want to look at

your throat. Okay? Or we can get Will to take a look. I'm sure he won't mind."

I was frozen. "Have…have you heard from Will?"

"Yes, we've talked while he's been out west attending an Internal Med conference." She smiled slowly. "Are you okay?"

No. I was not okay.

"Here," she said. "Come upstairs, and I'll take a look at your throat with the scope—"

"When…when did you talk to Will?"

Confusion flickered across my mom's pretty face. "A couple of days ago. Honey, your voice—"

"Nothing's wrong with my voice!" It cracked halfway through, of course, and Mom stared at me like I was telling her I was considering making her a grandma. This was my chance to tell her the truth.

I went up a step and stopped. All the words—the truth—got tangled up somewhere between my vocal chords and my lips. I hadn't cleared telling my mom the truth with anyone—or at least given any of them a heads-up. And would she believe me? Worst yet, Mom… She loved Will. I knew she did.

Stomach twisting into raw knots, I forced the panic out of my voice. "When is Will coming home?"

She watched me closely, her lips pressing into a pinched line. "Not for another week, but Katy… Are you sure that's what you wanted to say?"

Was he really coming back? And if he was talking to Mom, did that mean he'd gone through the mutation successfully and Daemon and I were now linked to him? Or had it faded?

I needed to talk to Daemon. Now.

My mouth was so dry I couldn't swallow. "Yes. Sorry. I have to go…"

"Go where?" she asked.

"See Daemon." I backpedaled, heading for my boots.

"Katy." She waited until I stopped. "Will told me."

Ice drenched my veins as I turned around slowly. "Told you what?"

"He told me about you and Daemon—that you two had decided to start seeing each other." She paused and got that *Mom* look. The one that said, *I'm so disappointed in you.* "He said you mentioned it and honey, I just wish you would've told me instead. Finding out through someone else about my daughter's boyfriend isn't how I wanted to learn."

My jaw hit the floor.

She said something else, and I think I nodded. Honestly, she could've been telling me that Thor and Loki had a battle royale down the street. I wasn't hearing her anymore. What was Will up to?

When Mom finally gave up on trying to hold a conversation with me, I hurried to my boots and hauled butt to Daemon's house. When the door swung open, I already knew it wasn't Daemon answering. I hadn't experienced the freaky alien connection thing, the warmth on the back of my neck whenever he was near.

But Andrew's blazing ocean-colored eyes weren't what I was expecting.

"You," he said, contempt lacing his tone.

I blinked. "Me?"

He folded his arms. "Yeah, you—as in Katy, the little human-alien-hybrid baby."

"Um, okay. I need to see Daemon." I started to step in, but he moved quickly, blocking me. "Andrew."

"Daemon's not here." He smiled, and there wasn't an ounce of warmth in it.

Folding my arms, I refused to back down. Andrew never liked me. I don't even think he liked people in general. Or puppies. Or bacon. "And where is he?"

Andrew stepped out, shutting the door behind him. He was so

close that the toes of his boots touched mine. "Daemon took off this morning. I assume he's following Rain Man."

Fury flashed through me. "There's nothing wrong with Dawson."

"Is that so?" Andrew cocked an eyebrow. "I think he's said three coherent sentences a day and that's about it."

My hands curled into fists against my sides. A soft breeze picked up my hair, stirring the strands around my shoulders. I so wanted to hit him. "He's been going through God knows what. Have some compassion, ass. Anyway, I don't know why I'm talking to you. Where's Dee?"

The smirk faded from his face, replaced by cold, hard hatred. "Dee is here."

I waited for a little more detail. "Yeah, I figured that much." When there was still no response, I was two seconds from showing him what a little human-alien-hybrid baby could do. "Why are you here?"

"Because I was invited." He leaned down, close enough to kiss, and I had no other option but to take a step back. He followed. "And you're not."

Ouch. Okay, that stung. Before I knew it, my back hit the railing and I was trapped. There was nowhere for me to go, and Andrew wasn't budging. I felt the Source, the pure energy that the Luxen—and now I—could harness building inside me, spreading over my skin like static electricity.

I could make Andrew move.

Andrew must've seen something in my eyes because he sneered. "Don't even think about pulling that crap with me, because you push? I'll push right back. There won't be any lost sleep over it."

Fighting my body's response to lay it on him was the hardest thing. My human side and the other side, whatever it was, wanted to tap into that power and use it—exploit it. It was like an unused muscle flexing. I remembered the dizzying rush of power, and the release.

A part of me, a teeny, tiny part of me liked it, and that scared the crap out of me.

Good for Andrew, because the fear coiling tightly inside had knocked the wind right out from underneath me. "Why do you hate me?" I asked.

Andrew cocked his head to the side. "It's the same thing as it was with Beth. Everything was fine, and then she came around. We lost Dawson and you know damn well we haven't gotten him back, not really. And now it's happening with Daemon, except this time around, we lost Adam in the mess. He's gone."

For the first time, something other than arrogant disdain peered through his crystalized eyes. Pain—the kind of suffering I was well familiar with. The same shattered, hopeless look I'd worn after my dad passed away from cancer.

"He's not going to be the only one we lose," Andrew continued, voice hoarse. "You know that, but do you care? No. Humans are ultimately the most selfish life-form there is. And don't try to pretend you're any better. If you were, you would've stayed away from Dee in the beginning. You would've never gotten attacked, and Daemon would've never had to heal you. None of this would've happened. It's your fault. It's on your head."

· · ·

Yeah, the rest of my day sort of sucked. I was worried about what Dawson had done that required Daemon to chase after him all day and feared the DOD was waiting to bring us all in. On top of that, I was freaking out over whatever Will had up his sleeve, and after that conversation with Andrew, I felt like I needed to crawl under my blankets.

And I did for about an hour. My self-pity always had a time

limit because I usually got annoyed with myself.

Pulling my head out of my rear, I cracked open my laptop and started doing some reviews. Since I'd been snowed in and Daemon had mostly been busy with Dawson, I'd gotten four books read. Not my all-time high score, but pretty good considering I'd been slacking like a mofo on the reviews.

It always felt good typing up a review on a book I enjoyed and I went all out, finding bizarre pictures to emphasize the wow factor. I preferred ones with cute kittens and llamas. And Dean Winchester. Hitting 'publish post' cracked a smile.

One down, three more to go.

I spent the rest of the day spewing out reviews and then stalking a few of my favorite bloggers. One of them had a header on their blog I'd do terrible things for. I was never that good at web design, which explained my less than stellar background.

After a quick run to the grocery store with Mom and dinner, I was about to start a manhunt for Daemon when I felt a warm tingle along the back of my neck.

I shot from the kitchen, nearly barreling through a startled Mom. I whipped open the door an instant after Daemon knocked and then threw myself—literally—into his not-so-waiting arms.

Unprepared for my attack, he stumbled back a step. But then he laughed deeply against the top of my head and wrapped his arms around me. I held on, squeezing the hell out of his shoulders, and we were so tightly pressed against each other that I could feel his heart picking up as fast as mine.

"Kitten," he murmured. "You know how much I like it when you say hi this way."

Head buried in the space between his neck and shoulder, which smelled like spice and male, I murmured something unintelligible.

Daemon lifted me clear off my feet. "You've been worried, haven't you?"

"Mmm-hmm." Then I remembered how much I'd been worried

all freaking day. I broke free and smacked his chest. Very, very hard.

"Ouch!" He grinned, though, as he rubbed his chest. "What was that for?"

I folded my arms and tried to keep my voice low. "Have you heard of a cell phone?"

He arched his brow. "Why, yes, it's this small thing that has all these cool apps on it—"

"Then why didn't you have it on you today?" I interrupted.

Leaning down, his lips grazed my cheek as he spoke, sending shivers through me. Not fair. "Going in and out of my true form all day kind of kills the electronics."

Oh. Well, I hadn't thought of that. "You should've checked in, though. I thought…"

"You thought what?"

I gave him a *Do I really need to explain it?* look.

The twinkling in Daemon's eyes faded. Placing his hands on my cheeks, he brought his lips to mine, kissing me sweetly. When he spoke, he kept his voice low. "Kitten, nothing's going to happen to me. I'm the last person you need to worry about."

I closed my eyes, breathing in his warmth. "See, that's possibly the stupidest thing you've ever said."

"For real? I say a lot of stupid things."

"I know. So that's saying something." I took a breath. "I'm not trying to act like one of those obsessive girlfriends, but things… things are different with us."

There was a pause, and then his lips stretched into a smile. "You're right."

Hell froze over. Pigs were flying. "Come again?"

"You're right. I should've checked in at some point. I'm sorry."

The world was flat. I didn't know what to say. According to Daemon, he was right about 99 percent of the time. Wow.

"You're speechless." He chuckled. "I like that. And I also like you all feisty. Want to hit me again?"

I laughed. "You're a—"

Opening the door behind me, Mom cleared her throat and said, "I don't know what it is with you two and porches, but come in; it's freezing out there."

Cheeks flaming an unholy red, I couldn't do anything to stop Daemon. He let go, sauntered inside, and immediately started charming my mom until she was nothing but a gooey puddle in the middle of the foyer.

He loved her new haircut. She got one? I guessed her hair did look different. Like she'd washed it or something. Daemon told her that her diamond earrings were beautiful. The rug below the steps was really nice. And that leftover scent of mystery dinner—'cause I still hadn't figured out what she fed me—smelled divine. He admired nurses worldwide, and by that point, I couldn't keep my eye rolls to a minimum.

Daemon was ridiculous.

I grabbed his arm and started pulling him to the steps. "Okay, well, this has been nice…"

Mom folded her arms. "Katy, what did I tell you about the bedroom?"

And here I thought my face couldn't get any redder. "Mom…" I tugged on Daemon's arm. He didn't move.

Her expression remained the same.

I sighed. "Mom, it's not like we're going to have sex with you home."

"Well, honey, it's good to know that you only have sex when I'm not home."

Daemon coughed as he fought a smile. "We can stay—"

Shooting him a death glare, I managed to get him to come up a step. *"Mo-om."* Whininess ensued.

Finally, she relented. "Keep the door open."

I beamed. "Thanks!" Then I pivoted around, dragging Daemon to my bedroom before he turned my mom into a fangirl. Pushing him inside, I shook my head at him. "You're terrible."

"And you're naughty." He backed up, grinning. "Thought she said leave the door open."

"It is." I gestured behind me. "It's cracked. That's open."

"Technicalities," he said, sitting down on the bed as he raised one arm, curling his fingers at me. A wicked gleam deepened the green hue of his eyes. "Come on…come closer."

I stood my ground. "I didn't get you up here to indulge in wild monkey lust."

"Crap." He dropped his hand to his lap.

Forcing myself not to laugh, because it only encouraged him, I decided to cut to the chase. "We need to talk." I crept closer to the bed, making sure my voice was low. "Will's been talking to my mom."

His eyes narrowed. "Details."

I sat beside him, tucking my legs against my chest. As I told him what my mom had said, the muscle in his jaw started ticking like a heartbeat. The news didn't sit well and there was no way for any of us to find out if the mutation had held or what he was up to, short of asking Will, and yeah right on that.

"He can't come back," I said, rubbing my temples, where a throbbing seemed to be in tune with the muscle in Daemon's jaw. "If the mutation didn't hold, he knows you'll kill him. And if it did…"

"He has the upper hand," Daemon admitted.

I flopped onto my back. "God, this is a mess—a freaking mess of epic proportions." It was like we were damned if we did from every corner. "If he comes back, I can't let him near my mom. I have to tell her the truth."

Daemon was silent as he shifted on the bed until he was leaning against the headboard. "I don't want you to tell her."

I frowned as I tipped my head to the side, meeting his stare. "I need to tell her. She's in danger."

"She's in danger if you tell her." He folded his arms. "I understand why you want to and need to, but if she knows the truth, she's in danger."

Part of me got that. Any human who knew the truth was at risk. "But keeping her in the dark is worse, Daemon." I sat up and twisted toward him, resting on my knees. "Will is a psycho. What if he comes back and picks up where he left off?" Bile rose in my throat. "I can't let that happen."

Daemon ran a hand through his hair, the gesture stretching the thin material of his long-sleeved shirt over his bicep. He exhaled long and hard. "First we need to find out if Will actually has intentions of coming back."

Irritation spiked. "And how do you propose we do that?"

"That I haven't figured out." Daemon flashed a weak grin. "But I will."

I sat up, frustrated. Logically, we had time. Not an endless supply—days or a week if we were lucky—but there was time. I just didn't like the idea of keeping her in the dark.

"What were you doing all day? Chasing Dawson?" I asked, letting the topic drop for now. When he nodded, I felt for him. "What was he doing?"

"He was just roaming around, but he was trying to shake me. I know he wanted to get back to that office building and if I hadn't followed him, he would've. The only reason I feel safe leaving him alone right now is because Dee has him cornered." He paused, looking away. His shoulders stiffened as if a terrible weight had settled on them. "Dawson... He's going to get himself captured again."

Chapter 5

Color me surprised when Daemon swung by early Saturday evening and wanted to go out. Like, brave snow-slick roads and do something normal. A date. As if we had the luxury of doing such a thing. And I couldn't help but remember what he had said to me when I'd been in his bed and so ready to give him the go-ahead.

He'd wanted to do things right. Dates. Movies.

Dee was currently on Dawson-babysitting duty, and Daemon felt confident enough to leave her with him.

I dug out a pair of dark denim jeans and a red turtleneck. Taking a few extra minutes with my makeup, I then bounced down the stairs. It took me about a half an hour to weasel Daemon away from my mom.

Maybe I wouldn't have to worry about her and Will. Maybe I needed to worry about her and Daemon. Cougar.

Once inside the comfy interior of Dolly, his SUV, he kicked on the heat and slid me a grin. "Okay. There are some rules about our date."

My brows rose. "There are?"

"Yep." He eased Dolly around and started down the driveway, careful to avoid the thick patches of black ice. "Rule number one is we don't talk about anything DOD related."

"Okay." I bit down on my lip.

He glanced at me sideways, as if he knew I was fighting a stupid love-struck grin. "Rule number two is that we don't talk about Dawson or Will. And number three, we focus on my awesomeness."

Okay. No fighting my grin. It spread ear to ear. "I think I can deal with these rules."

"You better, because there is punishment for breaking the rules."

"And what kind of punishment would that be?"

He chuckled. "Probably the sort of punishment you'd enjoy."

Warmth infused my cheeks and veins. I chose not to respond to that statement. Instead, I reached for the radio station at the same time Daemon did. Our fingers brushed and static raced down my arm, spreading to his flesh. I jerked back, and he laughed again, but the sound was husky and made the roomy SUV seem way too small.

Daemon settled on a rock station but kept the volume low. The trip to town was uneventful but fun...because nothing crazy happened. He picked out an Italian restaurant, and we were seated at a small table lit by flickering candles. I glanced around. None of the other tables had candles. They were covered with cheesy red-and-white-checkered mats.

But our wooden table was bare except for those candles and two wineglasses filled with water. Even the napkins looked like real linen.

Considering the possibilities as we were seated, my heart did a flip-flop. "Did you...?"

He propped his elbows on the table and leaned forward. Soft shadows danced over his face, highlighting the arch of his cheekbones and the curve of his lips. "Did I do what?"

"Arrange this?" I waved at the candles.

Daemon shrugged. "Maybe…"

I tucked my hair back, smiling. "Thank you. It's very…"

"Awesome?"

I laughed. "Romantic—it's very romantic. And awesome, too."

"As long as you think it is awesome, then it was worth it." He glanced up as the waitress arrived at our table. Her nametag read RHONDA.

When she turned to take Daemon's order, her eyes glazed over—a common side effect of being around Mr. Awesome, I was learning. "And what about you, sweetie?"

"Spaghetti with meat sauce," I said, closing the menu and handing it over.

Rhonda glanced at Daemon, and I think she might have sighed. "I'll bring your breadsticks out immediately."

After we were alone, I grinned at my date. "I think we're going to get extra meatballs."

He laughed. "Hey, I'm good for some things."

"You're good for a lot of things." The moment that left my mouth, I blushed. Whoa. That could be perceived in many ways.

Surprisingly, Daemon let it slide and started teasing me about a book he'd seen in my bedroom. It was a romance novel. Typical barrel-chested alpha male cover model with sixteen-pack abs. By the time our *heaping* pile of breadsticks arrived, I'd almost convinced him that he'd be a perfect cover model for one of those books.

"I don't wear leather pants," he said, biting into the garlicky and buttery goodness.

And that was a damn shame. "Still. You have the look."

He rolled his eyes. "You just like me for my body. Admit it."

"Well, yeah…"

His lashes lifted and his eyes glittered like jewels. "I feel like man-candy."

I busted out laughing. But then he asked a question I hadn't expected. "What are you going to do about college?"

I blinked. College? Sitting back, my gaze dropped to the small flame. "I don't know. I mean, it's not really possible unless I go to one near a buttload of quartz—"

"You just broke a rule," he reminded me, lips forming a half smile.

I rolled my eyes. "What about you? What are you doing for college?"

He shrugged. "Haven't decided yet."

"You're running out of time," I said, sounding like Carissa, who loved to remind me of that every time we talked.

"Actually, we've both run out of time, unless we do a late acceptance."

"Okay. Rule-breaking aside, how is it possible? Do online classes?" He shrugged again, and I sort of wanted to stab him in the eye with my fork. "Unless you know of a college that has...a suitable environment?"

Our meals arrived, staving off the conversation while the waitress grated cheese over Daemon's plate. She eventually offered me some. And the moment she left, I pounced. "So, do you?"

Knife and fork in hand, he started cutting into a piece of lasagna the size of a truck. "The Flatirons."

"The what-a-what?"

"The Flatirons is a mountain just outside of Boulder, Colorado." He cut his meal into tiny bites. Daemon had such delicate eating habits, while I was slopping my spaghetti around my plate. "They are full of quartzite. Not as well-known or as visible as some places, but they are there, under several feet of sediment."

"Okay." I tried to eat my spaghetti in daintier bites. "What does that have to do with anything?"

He peered up through sooty lashes. "University of Colorado is about two miles from the Flatirons."

"Oh." I chewed slowly and then suddenly my appetite vanished. "Is...is that where you want to go to school?"

There was another shrug. "Colorado isn't a bad place. I think you'd like it."

Staring at him, I forgot about the food. Was he getting at what I thought he was getting at? I didn't want to jump to conclusions, and I was too afraid to ask, because he could be suggesting that it was a place I'd like to visit versus living there...with him. And that would be super mortifying.

Hands cold, I set down my fork. What if Daemon did leave? For some reason I'd been operating on the assumption that he wouldn't leave here. Ever. And I'd accepted, on a subconscious level, being stuck here, mainly because I really hadn't considered finding another place that was protected from the Arum.

My gaze dropped to my plate. Had I accepted staying here because of Daemon? Was that right? *He's never said he loves you*, an insidious and annoying voice whispered. *Not even after you've said it.*

Ah, the stupid voice had a point.

Out of nowhere, a breadstick tapped the tip of my nose. My head jerked up. Sprinkles of garlic salt rained down.

Daemon held the stick between two fingers, brows arched. "What were you just thinking about?"

I brushed off the crumbs. A pitching sensation filled my stomach, and I forced a smile. "I...I think Colorado sounds nice."

Liar, said his expression, but he went back to his food. Strained silence descended between us, which was a first. I forced myself to enjoy the food, and the funniest thing happened. With Daemon's light teasing and the conversation turning to different subjects, like his obsession with all things ghost-related, I *was* having fun again.

"Do you believe in ghosts?" I asked, chasing after the last of my noodles.

He cleared his plate, sat back, and sipped from his glass. "I think they exist."

Surprise flickered through me. "Really? Huh. I thought you just watched those ghost shows for entertainment."

"Well, I do. I like the one where the guy yells, 'Dude! Bro!' every five seconds." He smiled when I laughed. "But in all seriousness, it can't be impossible. Too many people have witnessed things that can't be explained."

"Like too many people witnessing aliens and UFOs." I grinned.

"Exactly." He set down his glass. "Except the UFOs are total bunk. Government's responsible for all Unidentified Flying Objects."

My mouth dropped open. Why was I even surprised?

Rhonda appeared with our check, and I was reluctant to leave. The whole date thing was a way too brief moment of normalcy both of us had been sorely lacking. As we headed to the front of the restaurant, I wanted to grab his hand and wrap my fingers around his, but I refrained. Daemon did a lot of crazy things in public, but hand-holding?

So didn't seem up his alley.

There were a couple of kids from school seated by the door. Their eyes got all saucer-sized when they saw us. Considering Daemon and I had this hate-hate relationship for most of the year, I could understand their surprise.

It had started to flurry while we were inside and a thin coating of snow covered the parking lot and cars. The white stuff was still coming down. Stopping by the passenger side, I tipped my head back and opened my mouth, catching a tiny flake on the tip of my tongue.

Daemon's eyes narrowed on me and the intensity in his gaze caused a nervous fluttering low in my stomach. An urge to go forward, cross the distance between us, hit me hard, but I couldn't move. My feet were rooted to the ground and the air expelled from my lungs.

"What?" I whispered.

His lips parted. "I was thinking about a movie."

"Okay." I felt hot even though it snowed. "And?"

"But you've broken the rules, Kitten. Several times. You're owed some punishment."

My heart jumped. "I *am* a rule breaker."

His lips tilted up on one corner. "You are."

Moving lightning fast, Daemon was in front of me before I could say another word, cupping my cheeks, tilting my head back as he lowered his. Lips brushed against mine, sending a shiver down my spine. The initial touch was feather soft, heartbreakingly tender. Then the contact evolved with the second sweep of his lips and mine parted, welcoming him.

I really liked this form of punishment.

Daemon's hands slid down to my hips, and he pulled me against him at the same time we were moving backward, stopping when my back pressed against the cool, damp metal of his car—hopefully his car. I doubted someone would want a couple doing what we were doing on their vehicle.

Because we were kissing, really kissing, and there wasn't a centimeter of space between our bodies. My arms found their way around his neck, fingers sliding through silky locks covered in light snow. We fit everywhere it was important.

"Movie?" he murmured, kissing me again. "And then what, Kitten?"

I couldn't think around how he tasted and felt. How my heart was jackhammering as his fingers slid under my turtleneck, splaying along my bare skin. And I wanted to be bare—completely and only with him, always him. He knew what the "and then what" was. Doing things right…and dear God, I wanted to do those right things right now.

Since I couldn't get my mouth to work between his drugging kisses, I opted to do the show-not-tell thing, sliding my hands down to his jean-clad hips. Hooking my fingers in the belt hoop, I tugged him against me.

Daemon growled, and my pulse pounded. Yeah, he got it. His hand slid up, fingertips brushing against lace and—

His cell phone went off in his pocket, shrilling as loud as a fire alarm. I thought for a tiny instant he was going to ignore it, but he pulled back, panting. "One second."

He kissed me quickly, keeping one hand where it was while he dug out his phone. I burrowed my face against his chest, breathing rapidly. He left my senses spinning in a delicious mess that was out of control.

When Daemon spoke, his voice was rough. "This better be really important—"

I felt him stiffen, his heart rate picking up, and I knew instantly something bad had happened. Pulling back, I peered up at him. "What?"

"Okay," he said into the phone, his pupils becoming luminous. "Don't worry, Dee. I'll take care of it. I promise."

Fear cooled the heat inside me. As Daemon lowered the phone, sliding it back into his pocket, my stomach dropped. "What?" I asked again.

Every single muscle in his body locked up. "It's Dawson. He made a run for it."

Chapter 6

I stared at Daemon, praying I'd misunderstood him, but the keen desperation and the hint of fury in his ultra-bright eyes told me I hadn't.

"I'm sorry," he said.

"No. I completely understand." I tucked my hair back. "What can I do?"

"I need to go," he said, grabbing his keys from his pocket and placing them in my hand. "And I mean I need to go really fast. You should go home and stay there." He then handed me his cell. "Keep that in the car. I'll be back as soon as possible."

Go home? "Daemon, I can help you. I can go—"

"Please." He grasped my face again—his hands warm against my now-cool cheeks. He kissed me, part longing and part angry. Then he backed away. "Go home."

And then he was gone, moving too fast for any human eye to track. I stood there for several moments. We'd had an hour, maybe two, before everything went to shit? My hands tightened around the keys. Sharp metal dug into my flesh.

A ruined date was the least of my problems.

"Dammit." I spun and jogged around the SUV. Climbing in, I readjusted the seat from Godzilla setting to Normal so my feet could reach the pedals.

Go home.

Dawson would've gone to one of two places. Yesterday, Daemon had said Dawson tried to go to the office building, which was the last place he'd been kept. That would logically be his first place to check.

Go home and stay there.

I pulled out of the parking lot, gripping the steering wheel. If I went home and waited like a good little girl, I could curl up on the couch and read a book. Write a review and make some popcorn. Then when Daemon came back, as long as nothing horrific happened, I'd throw myself in his arms again.

Making a right instead of a left, I laughed out loud. The sound was throaty and low, courtesy of my screwed-up vocal chords and anxiety.

Screw going home. This wasn't the 1950s. I wasn't a fragile human being. And I sure as hell wasn't the Katy Daemon had initially met. He was going to have to deal with it.

I gunned the engine, hoping the boys in blue were busy doing other things besides monitoring traffic tonight. There was no way I'd beat Daemon there, but if they ran into any trouble, I could run distraction or something. I could do *something*.

Halfway there, I caught a flash of white light out of the corner of my eye, deep within the wooden tree line crowding the highway. Then it came again—white tinged with red.

Slamming on the brakes, I swerved to the right as the back end of the SUV fishtailed until it came to an uneven stop along the shoulder. Pulse pounding, I flipped on the hazard lights and threw open the door. I bolted across the two-lane highway, half slipping until my feet hit the other shoulder and I gained traction. Tapping into the Source and whatever existed inside me, I picked up speed, running so fast that my feet barely touched the ground.

Low-hanging branches snagged at my hair. Sheets of snow fell as I dipped around a thick tree, disrupting once pristine land. To my left, there was a blur of brown racing away from me. Most likely a deer or, knowing my luck, a chupacabra.

A whitish-blue light flared up ahead, like a bolt of horizontal lightning. Definitely power of Luxen origin but not Daemon's—his was reddish. It had to be Dawson or…

I raced around a cluster of large rocks, kicking up snow as murderous icicles fell from elms, shattering into the ground around me. Flying through the maze of trees, I hung a sharp right—

There they were, two Luxen in full glowworm mode and they were… *What the hell*? I skidded to a stop, gulping in air.

One was taller, pure white with edges dipped in red. The other was a slender, slower form with a bluish glow. The bigger one, which I knew was Daemon, had the other in what looked like a headlock. A glowing, human-shaped headlock I may've seen used in the WWE before.

I'd officially seen everything.

Assuming the other one was Dawson, Daemon's brother was pretty scrappy, breaking loose and pushing Daemon back a foot. But Daemon wrapped his arms around the center of the light, raised it up in the air and *body slamming* it so hard that more icicles fell from the trees crowding us.

Dawson's light pulsed and streaks of blue light rebounded off the trees, shooting back at the two, narrowly avoiding them. He tried to roll Daemon—at least that's what it looked like—but Daemon had the upper hand.

I folded my arms, shivering. "You have got to be kidding me." The two alien hotheads froze, and I really wanted to walk up and kick them both. A second later, their lights flickered out. Daemon's still-incandescent eyes met mine.

"I thought I told you to go home and stay there," he said, voice thin with warning.

"And the last time I checked, you don't get to tell me to go home and stay." I took a step forward, ignoring the way his eyes brightened. "Look, I was worried. I thought I'd come and help."

His lips pulled back. "And how would you have helped?"

"I think I did. I got you two idiots to stop fighting."

He stared at me a moment longer and his look promised lots of trouble later. Maybe punishable trouble. Ah, scratch that. His look didn't promise anything of the fun kind.

"Let me up, brother."

Daemon looked down. "I don't know. You're probably going to run and make me chase you again."

"You can't stop me," Dawson said, voice creepily apathetic.

Muscles bulged under Daemon's sweater. "I can and I will. I'm not letting you do this to yourself. She—"

"She's what? Not worth it?"

"She wouldn't want you to do this," Daemon seethed. "If the situation were flipped, you wouldn't want her doing this."

Dawson reared up, managing to get enough space between them so he could stand. On their feet, they shared wary stances. "If they had Katy—"

"Don't go there." Daemon's hands curled into powerful fists.

His brother was unaffected. "If they had her, you'd be doing the same thing. Don't lie."

Daemon opened his mouth but said nothing. We all knew what he'd do and no one would stop him. And knowing that, how could we ever stop Dawson? We couldn't.

I knew the exact moment that Daemon realized this, because he stepped back and thrust both hands through his windblown hair. Torn between doing what was right and what needed to be done.

Stepping forward, I swore I could feel the weight Daemon carried as if it were my own. "We can't stop you. You're right."

Dawson jerked toward me, eyes a brilliant green. "Then let me go."

"But we can't do that, either." I dared a peek at Daemon. Nothing could be gained from his expression. "Dee and your brother have spent the last year believing you were dead. That killed them. You have no idea."

"You have no idea what I went through." He lowered his gaze. "Okay, maybe you do a little. What was done to you is being done a thousand times over to Beth. I can't just forget about her, even though I love my brother and sister."

I heard Daemon's sharp intake. It was the first time since Dawson's return that he admitted any feelings for his family. I took it and ran with it. "And they know that. I know that. No one expects you to forget about Beth, but running off and getting yourself captured isn't helping anyone."

Wow. When did I become the voice of reason?

"What are the alternatives?" Dawson asked. His head tilted to the side—a mannerism so like his brother.

Here was the problem. Dawson wouldn't stop. Deep down, Daemon knew and understood why and would do the same thing. It was hypocritical to the umpteenth degree to demand someone else do otherwise. There had to be a compromise.

And there was one. "Let us help you."

"What?" Daemon demanded.

I ignored him. "You know rushing the DOD isn't going to work. We need to find out where Beth is, if they are even keeping her here, and we need a plan to get to her. A really well-thought-out plan with low failure potential."

Both brothers stared at me. I held my breath. This was it. There was no way Daemon could keep watch over his brother forever. And it wasn't fair to assume that he could.

Dawson turned away, back straight. Several seconds passed as the wind whipped through the trees, spinning snow. "I can't stand the idea of them having her. It hurts to breathe just thinking about it."

"I know," I whispered.

Moonlight sliced through the branches, carving Daemon's face in a harsh light. He had gone quiet, but anger rolled off him. Did he really think he could keep going after Dawson? If so, then he was insane.

Finally Dawson nodded. "Okay."

Sweet relief flooded me, making my legs feel weak. "But you have to promise to give us time." Everything came down to time we had no ownership of. "You can't get impatient and run off. You have to swear."

He faced me and a shudder rolled through him, taking the fight out of him. As he stood there, tension uncoiled, and his arms fell to his sides limply. "I swear. Help me and I swear."

"It's a deal."

There was a moment of silence, like the wilderness was soaking up his promise and my deal, committing it to memory. And then the three of us headed back to the SUV, the atmosphere silent and strained. My fingers were like Popsicles as I handed the keys over to Daemon.

Dawson climbed into the back, resting his head against the seat, eyes closed. I kept glancing at Daemon, expecting him to say something, anything, but he was focused on the road, his silence a ticking time bomb.

I peeked over the back of the seat. Behind thin slits, he was watching Daemon. "Hey. Dawson...?"

His gaze slid to mine. "Yeah?"

"Do you want to go back to school?" School would keep him busy while we figured out how in the hell to get to Beth. And it matched Daemon's plan of pretending like we'd pulled one on the DOD while enabling us to keep an eye on Dawson just in case he reneged on his promise. "I mean, I'm sure you can. You could tell everyone you ran away. It happens."

"People think he's dead," Daemon said.

"I'm sure some runaways all across the nation are believed to be dead and aren't," I reasoned.

Dawson appeared to consider that. "What do I tell them about Beth?"

"That's a good question." Challenge dripped from Daemon's voice.

I stopped chewing on my finger. "That you both ran away, and you decided to come home. She didn't."

Leaning forward, Dawson rested his chin in the palms of his hands. "Better than sitting around thinking about everything."

Damn straight. He'd go crazy if he did.

"He'd have to get registered for classes," Daemon said, fingers tapping off the steering wheel. "I'll talk to Matthew. See what we can do to get it taken care of."

Thrilled Daemon was finally getting behind this, I settled back and smiled. Crisis averted. Now only if I could fix everything else so easily.

Dee was waiting on the front porch when we pulled into the driveway, Andrew standing sentry beside her. Dawson slid out of the backseat and approached his sister. Words were exchanged, too low for me to hear, and then they embraced each other.

That was an amazing kind of love. Different from what my parents had shared but still strong and unbreakable. No matter what crazy hell they put each other through.

"I thought I told you to go home."

I hadn't realized I was smiling until it faded at the sound of Daemon's voice. I looked at him and felt my heart drop. Yeah, here was the trouble promised earlier. "I had to help."

He looked out the windshield. "What would you have done if it wasn't Dawson you came upon, but me fighting the DOD or whatever the hell the other group is?"

"Daedalus," I said. "And if it were them, I would've still helped."

"Yeah, and that's what I have a problem with." He got out of the SUV, leaving me staring at him.

Drawing in a frustrated breath, I climbed out. He was leaning against the bumper, arms folded over his chest. He didn't look at me when I stopped beside him. "I know you're upset because you worry about me, but I'm not going to be the girl who sits at home and waits for the hero to wipe out the villains."

"This isn't a book," he snapped.

"Well, duh—"

"No. You don't get it." He turned to me, furious. "This isn't a paranormal fantasy or whatever the hell it is you read. There is no set plot or clear idea of where any of this is going. The enemies aren't obvious. There are no guaranteed happy endings and you—" He lowered his head so we were eye level. "You are not a superhero, no matter what the hell you can do."

Wow. He'd really been stalking my blog. But not the point. "I know this isn't a book, Daemon. I'm not stupid."

"You're not?" He laughed without humor. "Because being smart isn't rushing off after me."

"The same could be said about you!" My anger now matched his. "You ran off after Dawson without knowing what you were getting into."

"No shit. But I can control the Source without trying. I know what I'm capable of. You don't."

"I know what I'm capable of."

"Really?" he questioned. The tips of his cheeks flushed with fury. "If I'd been surrounded by human officers, would you have been able to take them down? And live with yourself after that?"

Anxiety blossomed in my stomach, its smoky tendrils wrapping themselves around me. When I was alone and it was quiet, the fact I'd been so willing to take a human life was all I thought about.

"I'm prepared to do that." My voice came out a whisper.

He took a step back, shaking his head. "Dammit, Kat, I don't want you to experience that." Raw emotion filled his expression. "Killing isn't hard. It's what comes afterward—the guilt. I don't want you to deal with that. Don't you understand? I don't want you to have this kind of life."

"But I already have this kind of life. All the hoping, wishing, and good intentions in the world aren't going to change that."

The truth appeared to infuriate him more. "That issue aside, what you promised Dawson was freaking unbelievable."

"What?" My arms dropped to my sides.

"Help him find Beth? How in the hell are we supposed to do that?"

I shifted from one foot to the other. "I don't know, but we'll figure something out."

"Oh, that's good, Kat. We don't know how to find her but we'll help. Awesome plan."

Heat rushed up my spine. Oh, this was grand. "You're such a hypocrite! You told me yesterday we'd find out what Will was up to, but you have no idea how. The same thing with Daedalus!" He opened his mouth, but I knew I had him. "And you couldn't lie to Dawson when he asked what you'd do if they had me. You're not the only one who gets to make brash and stupid decisions."

His mouth snapped shut. "That's not the point."

I cocked a brow. "Lame argument."

Daemon shot forward, his voice harsh. "You had no right to make those kinds of promises to *my* brother. He's not *your* family."

I flinched, taking a step back. Being smacked would've felt better. The way I saw it, at least I talked Dawson off the cliff. Sure, promising to help find Beth wasn't ideal, but it was better than him running off like a crackhead.

I tried to rein in my anger and disappointment, because I understood where a lot of his fury was coming from. Daemon didn't want me to get hurt, and he was worried about his brother, but his inherent, near-obsessive need to be protective didn't excuse his douchebaggery.

"Dawson is my problem, because he's your problem," I said. "We're in this together."

Daemon's eyes met mine. "Not on everything, Kat. Sorry. That's just the way it is."

The back of my throat burned, and I blinked several times, refusing to shed tears even though my chest ached so badly. "If we're not together on everything, then how can we really be together?" My voice cracked. "Because I don't see how that's possible."

His eyes widened. "Kat—"

I shook my head, knowing where this conversation was heading. Unless he was willing to see me as something other than a fragile piece of china, we were doomed.

Walking away from Daemon was the hardest thing I'd done. Made worse by the fact he didn't try to stop me, because that wasn't his style, but deep down, in a place that spoke only the truth, I hadn't expected him to. But I wanted him to. I needed him to.

And he didn't.

Chapter 7

As expected, school resumed on Monday, and there was nothing worse than returning after an unexpected break and having all the teachers buzzing to make up for lost time. Add in the fact that Daemon and I hadn't made up after our major blowout yet and, well, Mondays always sucked.

I dropped into my seat, pulling out my massive trig textbook.

Carissa eyed me over the rim of her burnt-orange glasses. New ones. Again. "You look absolutely thrilled to be back."

"Whee," I said unenthusiastically.

Sympathy marked her expression. "How…how is Dee? I've tried calling her a couple of times, but she hasn't returned any of my calls."

"Or mine," Lesa added, sitting down in front of Carissa.

Lesa and Carissa had no idea that Adam hadn't really died in a car accident, and we had to keep them in the dark. "She's really not talking to anyone right now." Well, besides Andrew, which was so bizarre I couldn't even think about it.

Carissa sighed. "I wish they had the funeral for him here. I would've loved to pay my respects, you know?"

Apparently Luxen didn't do funerals. So we'd made up some excuse about the funeral being out of town and only family could visit.

"It just sucks," she said, glancing at Lesa. "I thought maybe we could go to the movies after school this week. Take her mind off it."

I nodded. I liked the sound of that but doubted we'd get very far with her. It was also time to put Plan A into motion—which was reintroducing Dawson to society. Even though I was on his brother's poo-poo list, Dawson had stopped by yesterday and explained that Matthew was on board. Probably wouldn't happen until the middle of the week, but it was a go.

"She may not be able to do anything this week, though," I said.

"Why?" Curiosity sparkled in Lesa's dark eyes. Loved the girl, but she was such a gossip whore. Which was exactly what I needed.

If people expected Dawson's return, it wouldn't be such a surprise when it did happen. Lesa would make sure word got out.

"You guys are not going to believe this, but…Dawson's come home."

Carissa turned several degrees paler, and Lesa shouted something that sounded an awful lot like *what the duck*. I'd kept my voice low, but their reactions garnered a lot of attention. "Yeah, apparently he's alive. Ran away and finally decided to come home."

"No way," Carissa breathed, her eyes going wide behind her glasses. "I can't believe this. I mean, it's great news but everyone thought…well, you know."

Lesa was just as shell-shocked. "Everyone thought he was dead."

I forced a casual shrug. "Well, he's not."

"Wow." Lesa pushed a section of tight curls out of her face. "I can't even process this. My brain has just shut down. A first."

Carissa asked the one question that was probably going to be on everyone's mind. "Did Beth come back?"

Keeping my face blank, I shook my head. "Apparently they

ran off together, but Dawson wanted to come home. She didn't. He doesn't know where she is."

Carissa stared at me while Lesa kept fiddling with her hair. "That's...so weird." She paused, turning her attention to her notebook. A strange look, one I couldn't decipher, crept across her face, but then again, this was really WTF news. "Maybe she went to Nevada. Wasn't that where she's from? Her parents moved back there, I think."

"Maybe," I murmured, wondering what the hell we were supposed to do if we did free Beth. Wasn't like we could keep her here. Sure, she was eighteen now and legally an adult, but her family was in a different time zone.

Warmth spread over my neck, and I looked to the front of the class. A few seconds later, Daemon strolled in. My stomach tightened, and I forced myself not to look down. If I was arguing that I was capable of handling bad things, I couldn't hide from my boyfriend when we had a fight.

Daemon arched a single brow as he passed by, taking his seat behind me. Before my friends could verbally attack Daemon with all their Dawson-related questions, I twisted in my seat.

"Hey," I said, and then I flushed, because there was nothing lamer than *hey*.

He seemed to think the same thing and showed it as one side of his lip curled up into a trademark Daemon smirk. Sexy? Yes. Infuriating? Oh, yes. I wondered what he would say. Would he yell at me for talking to Dawson yesterday? Apologize? Because if he apologized, I'd probably crawl into his lap right there in class. Or would he go with the ever-faithful "talk in private" comment? While Daemon loved an audience, I knew what he showed the world wasn't really him, and if he were going to open himself up, vulnerable to the core, he wouldn't want people watching.

"I like your hair like that," he said.

My brows rose. Okay. Not what I was expecting. Lifting my

arms, I smoothed my hands down the sides of my hair. The only thing I'd done differently was part it down the middle. Nothing amazing. "Um, thanks…?"

The smirk remained on his face as we continued to stare at each other, and as the seconds passed, the more irritated I grew. Seriously?

"Anything else you want to say?" I asked.

He leaned forward, sliding his elbows across the desk. Our faces were inches apart. "Is there anything you want me to say?"

I took a deep breath. "Lots of things…"

Thick lashes lowered, and his voice was rich as satin. "I bet."

He thought I was flirting? Then he spoke again. "There's something I'd like you to say. How about 'I'm sorry for Saturday'?"

I wanted to clock him. Of all the arrogant nerve, I swear. Instead of being snarky, I shot him an annoyed look and turned around. I ignored him for the rest of class and even left without saying a word to him.

Of course, he was two steps behind me in the hallway. My entire back tingled under his scrutiny, and if I didn't know better, I'd think he was amused by all of this.

Morning classes dragged. Bio was weird, since the seat beside me was now empty. Lesa noticed it with a frown. "I haven't seen Blake since Christmas break ended."

I shrugged, studiously staring at the projector screen Matthew was pulling down. "I have no clue."

"You guys were like BFFs forevah, and you have no idea where he's been?" Doubt clouded her tone.

Her suspicions were totally understandable. Petersburg was like the Bermuda Triangle for teenagers. Many came. Some were never seen again while others resurfaced from the rabbit hole. In that moment, I found myself wanting to spill the beans like I did every so often. Keeping so many secrets was killer.

"I don't know. He mentioned something about visiting fam

back in California. Maybe he decided to stay." God, I was getting frighteningly good at lying. "Petersburg is kind of boring."

"No doubt." She paused. "But he didn't tell you if he was coming back or not?"

I bit my lip. "Well, since Daemon and I are kind of seeing each other now, Blake and I haven't really talked."

"Ha." Her face transformed with a knowing grin. "Daemon seems like the RAWR type. He so wouldn't be cool with another guy being super friendly."

A flush crept over my cheeks. "Ah, he's okay with guy friends…" Just not ones who kill his friends. I rubbed my brow, sighing. "Anyway, how's Chad?"

"My boy toy?" She giggled. "He's perfect."

I managed to keep the conversation on Chad and how close they'd come to doing it. Of course, Lesa wanted to know about Daemon and me, and I refused to go there, much to her dismay. She admitted to wanting to live vicariously through me.

After bio, I stopped by my locker as usual and took my sweet old time changing out books. I doubted Dee wanted to see my face. The seating arrangements in the cafeteria were going to be super awkward, and I was still annoyed with Daemon. By the time I'd finished grabbing books, the hall was empty and the hum of conversation was distant.

I closed the locker door and twisted halfway, closing the flap on the messenger bag my mom had gotten me for Christmas. Something moved at the end of the once-empty corridor, coming out of what seemed like nowhere. A tall and slender form at the end of the hall, obviously male by the quick look, and he was wearing a baseball cap, which was odd, because that was in violation of the school dress code. It was one of those God-awful trucker hats that guys found cool once upon a time.

DRIFTER was written in bold black and behind the words was an oval shape…that looked a lot like a surfboard.

My pulse spiked and I blinked, taking a step back. The guy was gone, but the door to the left was slowly swinging closed.

No...no, it couldn't be. He'd be crazy insane to come back here, but... Holding my bag tightly to my side, I started walking and then I was jogging before I knew it. I hit the door, throwing it open. Rushing to the railing, I peered over it. Mystery Dude was on the bottom level, as if he were waiting at the door.

I could see the trucker hat more clearly. It was definitely a surfboard.

Blake had been an avid surfer when he lived in California.

Then a golden-toned hand, as if the person spent his life under the sun, wrapped around the silver doorknob, and a wave of familiarity raised the tiny hairs on my arms.

Oh, crap.

Part of my brain clicked off. I went down the steps three at a time, my breath locked in my chest. The hallway was more crowded on the first floor as people headed for the cafeteria. I heard Carissa call my name, but I was focused on the top of the trucker hat moving toward the gymnasium and the back entrance, leading to the parking lots.

I darted around a couple totally getting into hallway PDA, slipped between friends talking, and lost sight of the hat for a second. *Dammit.* Everyone and their mother were in my way. I bumped into someone, mumbling an apology, and kept going. When I reached the end of the hall, the only place he could've gone was out the door. I didn't think twice. Pushing the heavy double doors open, I stepped outside. Overcast skies turned everything dreary and cold, and as my eyes scanned the common area and, beyond that, the parking lots, I realized he was gone.

Only two things in this world could move that fast: aliens and humans mutated by aliens.

And I had no doubt in my mind that I'd seen Blake, and he'd wanted me to see him.

Chapter 8

Finding Daemon wasn't hard at all. He was lounging against the painted mural of the school mascot in the cafeteria, talking to Billy Crump, a boy from our trig class. A carton of milk was in one hand and a slice of pizza folded in the other. What a gross-as-hell combination.

"We need to talk," I said, interrupting boy time.

Daemon took a bite of his pizza while Billy glanced down at me. There must've been something in my stare, because his smile faded and he lifted his hands, backing up slowly.

"Okay, well, I'll talk to you later, Daemon."

He nodded, eyes trained on me. "What's up, Kitten? Come to apologize?"

My eyes narrowed, and for a brief moment, I entertained the idea of body slamming him in the middle of the cafeteria. "Uh, no, I'm not here to apologize. *You* owe *me* an apology."

"How do you see that?" He took a drink, appearing naively curious.

"Well, for starters, I'm not an ass. You are."

He chuckled as he glanced to the side. "That's a good start."

"And I got Dawson to heel." I smiled victoriously when his eyes narrowed. "And— Wait. This isn't even important. God, you always do this."

"Do what?" His intense gaze swung back to me without a trace of anger. More like amusement and something really inappropriate, given that we were standing in the lunchroom. Dear God...

"Distract me with the inane. And in case you don't know what that means, it's silly—you always distract me with something silly."

He finished off his pizza. "I know what *inane* means."

"Shocker," I retorted.

A slow, cat-got-the-canary grin pulled at his lips. "I must be really distracting you, because you still haven't told me what you need to talk to me about."

Dammit. He was right. Ugh. Taking a deep breath, I focused. "I saw—"

Daemon cupped my elbow, spun me around, and started down the aisle. "Let's go somewhere more private."

I tried to yank my elbow from his grasp. I really hated it when he went all He-Man on me and ordered me around. "Stop dragging me, Daemon. I can walk on my own, Doofus."

"Uh huh." He led me down the hall, stopping by the gym doors. He placed his hands on either side of my head, caging me in as he leaned down. His forehead brushed mine. "Can I tell you something?"

I nodded.

"I find it incredibly attractive when you're all feisty with me." His lips brushed against my temple. "That probably makes me disturbed. But I like it."

Yeah, it kind of was wrong, but there was something...hot about how quickly he defended me whenever something happened.

His nearness was tempting, especially when his breath was tantalizingly warm and so near my lips. Summoning my willpower,

I placed my hands on his chest and pushed lightly. "Focus," I said, not sure who I was talking to, me or him. "I have something more important to tell you than what disturbing things get you hot."

His lips quirked into a grin. "Okay, back to what you saw. I'm focused. My head's in the game and all that."

I laughed under my breath but sobered up pretty quickly. In no way was Daemon going to respond well to this. "I'm pretty sure I saw Blake today."

Daemon cocked his head to the side. "Say what?"

"I think I saw Blake here, just a few minutes ago."

"How sure are you? Did you see him—his face?" He was all business now, eyes as sharp as a hawk's and his face set in grim lines.

"Yeah, I saw—" I hadn't seen his face. Biting down on my lip, I glanced down the hall. Students piled out of the cafeteria, pushing into one another, laughing. I swallowed. "I didn't see his face."

He let out a long breath. "Okay. What did you see?"

"A hat—a trucker hat." God, that sounded lame. "That had a surfboard on it. And I saw his hand…" And that sounded even worse.

His brows arched up. "So, let me get this right. You saw a hat and a hand?"

"Yeah." I sighed, shoulders slumping.

Daemon smoothed out his expression and placed a heavy arm around my shoulder. "Are you really sure it was him? Because if not, that's okay. You've been under a lot of stress."

I wrinkled my nose. "I remember you saying something like that to me before. You know, when you were trying to hide what you were from me. Yeah, I remember that."

"Now, Kitten, you know this is different." He squeezed my shoulders. "Are you sure, Kat? I don't want to get everyone freaking out if you're not sure."

What I'd experienced was more of a feeling than a true sighting of Blake. God knew that a ton of boys around here broke the dress code with atrocities such as trucker hats. The thing was, I hadn't seen his face and looking back, I couldn't be 100 percent sure it had been Blake.

I looked into Daemon's bright gaze and felt my cheeks burn. There wasn't judgment in his eyes. More like sympathy. He thought I was cracking under the pressure of everything. Maybe I was imagining stuff.

"I'm not sure," I said finally, casting my eyes down.

And those words soured in my stomach.

• • •

Later that night, Daemon and I did babysitting duty. Although Dawson had promised not to do his own search-and-rescue mission, I knew Daemon wasn't comfortable leaving him alone and Dee wanted to get out tonight, go to the movies or something.

I wasn't invited.

Instead, I was sitting in between Daemon and Dawson, four hours into a George Romero zombiethon, with a bowl of popcorn in my lap and a notebook resting against my chest. We'd been making plans to look for Beth, getting as far as listing the two places that we knew to check before deciding to do surveillance this weekend to see what kind of security they had going on now. By the start of *Land of the Dead*, the zombies got uglier and smarter.

And I was having fun.

"I had no idea you were a zombie fan." Daemon grabbed a handful of popcorn. "What is it—the blood and guts or the in-your-face social undertones?"

I laughed. "Mostly the blood and guts."

"That's so un-girlie of you," Daemon commented, brows knitting as a zombie started to use its meat cleaver to break through a wall. "I don't know about this. How many hours do we have left?"

Dawson raised his arm and two DVDs shot into his hand. "Uh, we have *Diary of the Dead* and *Survival of the Dead*."

"Great," Daemon muttered.

I rolled my eyes. "Wussy."

"Whatever." He elbowed me, knocking a kernel of popcorn between my chest and notebook. I sighed. "Want me to get that for you?" he asked.

Shooting him a look, I dug it out and then tossed it in his face. "You're going to be grateful when the zombie apocalypse occurs and I know what to do because of my zombie fetish."

He looked doubtful. "There are better fetishes out there, Kitten. I could show you a few."

"Uh, no, thank you." But I did flush. And there were a lot of images that suddenly polluted my brain.

"Aren't you supposed to go to the nearest Costco or something?" Dawson asked, letting the DVDs float back to the coffee table.

Daemon turned to his twin slowly, face incredulous. "And how would you know that?"

He shrugged. "It's in the *Zombie Survival Guide*."

"It is." I nodded eagerly. "Costco has everything—thick walls, food, and supplies. They even sell guns and ammunition. You could hole up there for years while the zombies are getting their nom nom on."

Daemon's mouth dropped open.

"What?" I grinned. "Zombies got to eat, too, you know."

"Very true about the Costco thing." Dawson picked up a single kernel and popped it in his mouth. "But we could just blast the zombies. We'd be fine."

"Ah, good point." I rooted around in the bowl for a half-popped kernel—my favorite.

"I'm surrounded by freaks," Daemon said, looking dumbfounded as he shook his head, but I knew he was secretly thrilled.

For one thing, his body was completely relaxed next to mine and this was one of the first times that Dawson was acting...normal. Yeah, talking about zombies probably wasn't the biggest step known to mankind, but it was something.

On the flat screen, a zombie took a chunk out of some dude's arm. "What the hell?" Daemon complained. "The guy just stood there. Hello. There're zombies everywhere. Try looking behind you, douche canoe."

I giggled.

"This is why zombie movies are unbelievable to me," he went on. "Okay. Say the world ends in a shit storm of zombies. The last thing anyone with two working brain cells would do is just stand along a building waiting for a zombie to creep up on him."

Dawson cracked a smile.

"Shut up and watch the movie," I said.

He ignored that. "So you really think you'd do well in a zombie apocalypse?"

"Yeppers," I said. "I'd totally save your butt."

"Oh, really?" He glanced at the screen. Then he faded out and something...something else replaced him.

Shrieking, I jerked into Dawson. "Oh my God..."

Daemon's skin was ghastly gray and hanging loose from his face. Patches of decaying brown skin covered his cheekbones. One of his eyes was just...a hole. The other was glazed over and milky white. Clumps of hair were missing.

Zombie Daemon gave a rotted, toothy grin. "Save my butt? Yeah, I don't think so."

I could only stare.

Dawson actually laughed. Not sure what was more shocking: that or the zombie sitting next to me.

His form faded out and then he was back—beautiful, carved cheekbones and head full of hair. Thank God. "I think you'd suck at the zombie apocalypse," he said.

"You...you are disturbed," I murmured, carefully settling down next to him.

With a smug grin, he reached for the bowl and came up empty. Some of it might have been on the floor. Feeling eyes on me, I glanced at Dawson.

He was staring at us, but I wasn't sure if he was even seeing us. There was a reminiscent expression in his eyes, tainted with sadness and something else. Determination? I didn't really know, but for a second, the green hue brightened, no longer dull and listless, and he looked so much like Daemon that I drew in a shallow breath.

Then he gave his head a little shake and looked away.

I glanced at Daemon and I knew he'd noticed. He shrugged. "Anyone want more popcorn?" he asked. "We have food coloring. I can make it red for you."

"More popcorn but minus the food coloring, please." When he grabbed the bowl and stood, I caught him sneaking a relieved glance at his brother. "Want me to pause the movie?"

His look told me no and I giggled again. Daemon sauntered out of the room, stopping at the door when the zombies crested the water. Then he shook his head again and left. He wasn't fooling me.

"I think he secretly enjoys zombie movies," Dawson said, glancing at me.

I smiled at him. "I was just thinking the same thing. He has to, since he's all into ghost stuff."

Dawson nodded. "We used to record those shows and spend all day Saturday watching them. Sounds kind of lame, but it was fun." There was a pause and his gaze flickered back to the TV. "I miss that."

My heart went out to him and Daemon. I glanced at the screen, chewing on my lower lip. "You know, you still can."

He didn't respond.

I wondered if the problem was that Dawson wasn't comfortable alone with Daemon. There was definitely a lot of baggage between the two. "I'd love to watch some of them this Saturday before we check out the buildings."

Dawson was silent as he crossed his legs at the ankles. I was pretty sure he wasn't going to answer, just ignore what I offered, and I was okay with that. Small steps and all.

But then he did speak. "Yeah, that would be kind of cool. I...I can do that."

Surprised, my head swung toward Dawson. "Really?"

"Yeah." He smiled. It was weak, but it was a smile.

Happy about this, I nodded and then turned my attention back to the gore. But I saw Daemon standing just outside the living room. My gaze was drawn to his, and I sucked in an unsteady breath.

He'd heard everything.

Relief and gratitude poured from him. He didn't need to say anything. The thank-you was in his stare, in the way his hands gave a little shake around the fresh bowl of popcorn. He came into the room and sat, placing the bowl in my lap. Then he reached over, took my hand in his, and it stayed that way the rest of the night.

• • •

Over the next couple of days, I came to accept that I probably did have a mini freak-out on Monday. There had been no more trucker hat sightings from hell, and then on Thursday, the whole Blake thing became a nonissue.

Dawson had returned to PHS.

"I saw him this morning," Lesa said in trig, her body practically humming like a tuning fork with excitement. "Or at least I think I did. It really could've been Daemon, but this guy was thinner."

To me, it was easy to tell the two brothers apart. "It was Dawson."

"That's the strange thing." Some of the enthusiasm faded. "Dawson and I were never best buds, but he was always friendly. I went up to him, but he kept on walking like he hadn't even seen me. And hey, I'm hard to miss. My bubbly personality is like its own screaming person."

I laughed. "So true."

Lesa grinned. "But seriously, something…something was off about him."

"Oh?" My pulse picked up. Was there something about Dawson that humans could sense? "What do you mean?"

"I don't know." She looked to the front of the classroom, her eyes traveling over the faded formulas scribbled on the chalkboard. Her curls spilled around her shoulder. "It's hard to explain."

There wasn't much time to dig into what she meant. Carissa arrived to class and then Daemon. He placed a cup of mocha latte on my desk. Cinnamon permeated the air.

"Thanks." I held the warm cup. "Where's yours?"

"Not thirsty this morning," he said, twirling his pen. He glanced over my shoulder. "Hi, Lesa."

Lesa sighed. "I need a Daemon."

I turned to her, unable to hide my grin. "You have a Chad."

She rolled her eyes. "He doesn't bring me lattes."

Daemon chuckled. "Not everyone can be as great as I am."

Now I rolled my eyes. "Ego check, Daemon, ego check."

From across the aisle, Carissa fiddled with her glasses, her eyes serious and somber as she glanced at Daemon. "I just wanted to say I'm glad Dawson's back and okay." Two red spots bloomed on her cheeks. "It must be a huge relief."

Daemon nodded. "It is."

Talk of his brother ended right there. Carissa turned around, and though Lesa rarely let awkward topics detour her, she didn't pick up our conversation. But after class, as Daemon and I navigated the hall, people were almost at a standstill.

Everyone was staring at Daemon and there were a lot of whispers. Some tried to keep it quiet. Others didn't seem to care.

"Did you see?"

"Two of them again…"

"So weird that he'd come back without Beth…"

"Where is Beth…?"

"Maybe he came back because of Adam…"

Gossip mill at its finest, I realized.

I took a sip of my still-warm mocha and peeked at Daemon. The curve of his jaw was hard. "Uh, maybe this wasn't a good idea."

His hand rested on the small of my back as he held open the door to the stairwell. "Now what makes you think that?"

I ignored his sarcasm. "But if he didn't come back, what was he supposed to do?"

Daemon stayed by my side as we headed to the second floor, taking up most of the cramped space. Kids had to squeeze past him. And I really had no idea where he was going. His class was on the first floor.

He leaned down, keeping his voice low. "It was a bad and good idea. He needs to get back into the world. There's going to be fallout, but it's worth it."

I nodded. What he said was true. At the door to my English class, he took a sip of my mocha and handed it back.

"See you at lunch," he said, kissing me briefly before pivoting around.

My lips tingled as I watched the back of his dark head disappear, and then I headed into class. So much was going on that concentrating was pretty much out of the question. The teacher called on me at one point, and I didn't notice. The entire class did, though. Awkward.

Turned out Dawson was in my bio class, and boy did he have a lot of eyes on him. He was seated beside Kimmy when I walked past. He nodded and then returned to flipping through his textbook. His tablemate's eyes were like two moons.

Did he get any sort of education while he was gone? Not that it mattered. The Luxen developed mentally a lot faster than humans. Missing over a year of school probably meant nothing to him.

"See?" Lesa twisted around as soon as I sat behind her.

"See what?"

"Dawson," she whispered. "That's not the Dawson I remember. He was always talking and laughing. Never reading a *bio* textbook."

I shrugged. "He's probably been through some crazy stuff." Not a lie. "And it's probably uncomfortable for him to be back here with *everyone* staring at him." Also not a lie.

"I don't know." She tugged on her backpack as she glanced over at Dawson's table. "He's moodier than Daemon used to be."

"Daemon was moody?" I said a bit dryly.

"Well, just not that friendly, I guess. He kind of stuck to himself before." She shrugged. "Oh! By the way, what the hell is up with Dee hanging out with the Bitch Squad?"

Bitch Squad was a code name Lesa had given Ash and Andrew when I first started at PHS. Once upon a time, I bet Daemon was a part of that group.

"Ah," I said, suddenly wanting to read *my* bio textbook. Whenever I thought of Dee, I wanted to cry. Our friendship had taken a sharp detour to Breakupsville. "I don't know. She's been... different since Adam."

"No. Shit." Lesa shook her head. "Her grieving process is scary. I tried to talk to her yesterday at her locker, and she looked at me, said nothing, and then walked away."

"Ouch."

"Yeah, it actually hurt my feelings."

"Pretty much what I've—"

The door to the classroom opened as the bell rang and the first thing I noticed was the vintage Nintendo shirt worn over a gray thermal. I loved all those old-school screen T-shirts. Then the messy bronze hair and hazel eyes.

My heart stopped; a buzzing started in my ears and picked up to a roar. The air was sucked right out of the room. I'd expected Will to come back, but not...*him*.

"Oh. Look who's here," Lesa said, smoothing her hands over her notebook. "Blake."

Chapter 9

I had to be dreaming because this could not be real. No way. Absolutely not. It wasn't Blake strolling into the classroom like it was any other day. Nor did Matthew drop his stack of notes. I glanced at Dawson before realizing he wouldn't know any better. He'd never seen Blake.

"You okay, Katy? Looking a little wigged out," Lesa said.

My eyes darted to hers wildly. "I…"

A second later, Blake was taking his seat—his seat beside me. The rest of the class blurred out. I was struck stupid by his reappearance.

He placed his book on the table and leaned back in his chair, folding his arms. Casting me a sidelong glance, he winked.

What the holy hell…?

Giving up on waiting for me to finish what I was saying, Lesa turned around, shaking her head. "I have weird friends," she muttered.

Blake said nothing as Matthew gathered up his scattered papers. My heart was now racing so fast I was sure I was going to stroke out any second.

People were staring, but I couldn't pull my eyes off Blake. Finally, I found my voice. "What…are you doing?"

He looked at me, a thousand secrets among the green flecks in his gaze. "Going to class."

"You…" There were no words. And then the shock wore off, replaced with a spike of anger so powerful and so hot I felt static rush over my skin.

"Your eyes," Blake whispered, a grin teasing his lips, "are starting to glow."

Closing my eyes, I struggled to control my swirling emotions. When I was about 40 percent sure I wasn't going to jump on him like a monkey and snap his neck, I reopened my eyes. "You shouldn't be here."

"But I am."

This wasn't the time for evasive comments. I glanced toward the front of the classroom and saw Matthew writing on the chalkboard, his face pale. He was talking, but I didn't hear anything.

I tucked my hair back behind one ear and kept my hand there. Anything to keep me from hitting Blake, because it was a real possibility that I would. "We gave you a chance." I kept my voice low. "We won't do it again."

"But I think you will." He leaned over the small space, coming too close and causing my muscles to lock up. "Once you hear what I have to offer."

A crazed laugh bubbled up my throat as I kept my eyes fixed on Matthew. "You are so, so dead."

Lesa glanced over her shoulder questioningly. I forced a smile.

"Speaking of dead," he murmured once Lesa had turned back around. "I see the long lost twin has returned." He picked up his pen and started writing. "I bet Daemon is so thrilled. Ah, which reminds me, I'm pretty sure he's the one who mutated you."

My hand closest to him curled. A faint white light danced over my knuckles, flicking like the core of a flame. The knowledge of who mutated me was dangerous. Besides the ramifications Daemon would face if it got out in the Luxen community, the DOD could use it against us. Just like they had with Dawson and Bethany.

"Careful," he said. "I can see you still need to work on your anger."

I shot him a dark, promising look. "Why are you here? For real?"

He put his finger over his lips. "Shush. I need to learn about…" He glanced at the board, eyes narrowing in concentration. "Different types of organisms. Yawn."

It took every ounce of my self-control to sit through that class. Even Matthew looked like he was having trouble, forgetting where he was going with his lecture every couple of minutes. I caught Dawson's stare once and wished I could communicate to him…

Wait. Couldn't I communicate to Daemon? We'd done it before, but he'd always been in his Luxen form when it happened. Taking a shallow breath, I lowered my gaze to the blurred lines on my notebook and concentrated as hard as I could.

Daemon?

The space between my ears buzzed like a TV on mute. No discernible sound but a high-frequency hum. *Daemon?* I waited, but there was no response.

Frustrated, I blew out a breath. I needed to find a way to let him know that Blake was back, like, really back and in school. I figured Dawson could get word to him, but there was no telling how Dawson would act if I got up to use the restroom and told him that the douchebag beside me was Blake.

I glanced at said douchebag. No doubt about it, Blake was good-looking. He rocked the whole messy hair and golden skin surfer-boy look. But beneath that easy grin lurked a killer.

The moment the bell rang, I gathered my stuff and headed toward the door, shooting Matthew a look. Somehow he seemed to know, because he waylaid Dawson and—I hoped—would keep Dawson from throwing Blake through a window in front of everyone once Matthew shared who Blake was. Lunch period was next, but I dug my cell out of my messenger bag.

I made it about three steps before Blake stalked up behind me in the hall and cupped my elbow. "We need to talk," he said.

I tried to pull my arm free. "And you need to let go of me."

"Or what? Are you going to do something about it?" His head angled toward me and I caught the familiar scent of his aftershave. "No. Because you know what the risk of exposure is."

I gritted my teeth. "What do you want?"

"Only to talk." He steered me into an empty classroom. Once inside, I tore my arm free as he locked the door. "Look—"

Acting on instinct, I dropped my bag on the floor and let the Source soar through me. Whitish-red light spread over my arms, crackling in the air. A ball of white light the size of a softball built above my palm.

Blake rolled his eyes. "Katy, I just want to talk. You don't need—"

I released the energy. The light shot across the room in a bolt. Blake darted out of the way and the light smacked into the chalkboard. The intensity melted the middle of the green slate and the smell of burning ozone filled the air.

The Source built in me again, and this time I wasn't going to miss. It rushed down my arms to my fingertips. In that moment, I really didn't know if it was powerful enough to kill Blake or just do some serious damage. Or maybe I did and I just didn't want to admit it.

Rushing behind a huge oak desk, Blake raised his hand. All the chairs to the left of me flew to the right, smacking into my legs and crowding me. My aim was off and the energy ball skyrocketed over Blake's head, slamming into the circular clock above the board. It exploded in a hundred dazzling pieces of plastic and glass that rained down…

And then the pieces stopped in midair, hung there as if attached to invisible strings. Below them, Blake straightened, his eyes luminous.

"Crap," I whispered, my gaze darting to the door. There was no way I'd make it there and if he'd frozen those pieces, most likely everything was frozen. The door. People outside the room, I imagined.

"Are you done yet?" Blake's voice was harsh in my ears. "Because you're going to tire yourself out here in a few seconds."

He had a point. Mutated humans didn't have the energy stores like the Luxen did. So when they used their abilities, they wimped out pretty quickly. There was also the fact that even though I whipped up on Blake the night everything went down, Daemon had been there and we were feeding off each other.

But it didn't mean I was going to just stand there and let Blake do whatever he planned.

I took a step forward and the chairs reacted in defense. They launched into the air, forcing me back as they stacked atop one another, forming a circle around me that reached the ceiling.

Raising my hands, I pictured the chairs with little desk areas attached flying apart. Moving stuff was easy to me now, so in theory, those babies should've shot at Blake like bullets. They began to tremble and slid away from me.

Blake pushed back and the wall of chairs shook but didn't budge. I kept the image of them moving away from me, drawing on the static energy inside me until a fierce throbbing sliced through my temples. The pain increased until I dropped my arms. My heart tripped up as I whirled around. Trapped—encased in a tomb of freaking chairs.

"And I bet you haven't been practicing at all?" Through the gaps in chairs, I saw him come around the desk. "I don't want to hurt you."

I paced in a tiny circle, dragging in deep breaths. My legs felt like jelly, skin dry and brittle. "You killed Adam."

"I didn't mean to. You have to believe that the last thing I wanted was for anyone to get hurt."

My mouth dropped open. "You were going to turn me over! And someone did get hurt, Blake."

"I know. And you have no idea how terrible I feel about that." He followed me on the other side of the wall. "Adam was a nice guy—"

"Don't talk about him!" I stopped, hands balling into weak, useless fists. "You shouldn't have come back."

Blake cocked his head to the side. "Why? Because Daemon's going to kill me?"

I mirrored his movements. "Because *I'm* going to kill you."

A brow arched and curiosity marked his features. "You already had your chance, Katy. Killing isn't in your nature."

"But it's in yours, right?" I stepped back, checking the chairs. They shook a little. Blake may have more experience with this stuff, but he was tiring, too. "Anything to protect your friend?"

He drew in a long breath. "Yes."

"Well, I'll do anything to protect mine."

There was a pause. During those seconds, the shattered pieces of the clock fell. I did a little victory dance inside. "You have changed," he finally said.

Part of me wanted to laugh, but the action got stuck in my throat. "You have no idea."

Moving back from the chairs, he ran a hand through his messy hair. "This is good, because maybe you'll understand the importance of what I'm about to offer you."

My eyes narrowed. "There is nothing you could offer."

A wry smile appeared on his lips—lips that I had kissed once. Bile stung the back of my throat. "I've been watching you all for days. At first I wasn't the only one, but you know that. Or at least your bedroom window does."

He folded his arms when he realized he had my full attention. "I know Dawson has been trying to find Beth, but he doesn't know where to look. I do. She's being kept with Chris."

I stopped pacing. "Where's that?"

Blake laughed. "Like I'm going to tell you when it's the only thing that might keep me alive. Agree to help me get Chris free, and I'll make sure Dawson gets to Beth. That's all I want."

Rendered speechless, I blinked. He was asking for our help after everything? That crazy laugh was building again and it came out this time, throaty and low. "You're freaking nuts."

His expression slipped into a scowl. "The DOD thinks I'm their perfect little hybrid. I asked to stay here because of the community of Luxen and the likelihood of another being mutated. I'm their implant. And I can get you into the facility where they're being held. I know where they are, what floor they're on, and what cell. And more importantly, I know their weaknesses."

He couldn't be serious. The chairs at the top wobbled, and I knew I was seconds away from being buried under the damn things.

"Without me, you'll never find her and all you'll do is walk right into Daedalus's hands." He took another step back. Over his shoulder, the air was distorted in waves. The kind of power he was throwing off...

"You need me," he said. "And yeah, I need you guys. I can't get to Chris alone."

Okay, he was being for real. "Why in the world would we trust you?"

"You don't have a choice." He cleared his throat and the chairs rattled. My gaze dropped. The legs of those on the bottom bent toward him. "You'll never find her, and Dawson will end up doing something crazy."

"We'll take our chances."

"I was afraid you'd say that." Blake picked up my bag and

placed it on the teacher's desk. "Either you all help me or I go to Nancy Husher and tell her just how powerful you are." At the sound of her name, I sucked in a sharp breath. Nancy worked for the DOD and most likely Daedalus. "I never reported back to her and since Vaughn was working with Will Michaels, neither did he," he continued. "She thinks your mutation wore off. And handing over that kind of information might save my ass. It might not, but either way, they will come for you now. And before you think getting rid of me fixes this, you're wrong. I have a message that will be delivered to her if anything happens to me, which tells what you're capable of and exposes Daemon as the one who mutated you. Yeah, I've thought of everything."

Anger raged inside me and the chairs really started to shake. In seconds, he'd stripped away whatever power I truly gained, leaving me helpless. "You rat bastard…"

"I'm sorry." He was at the door now, and dear God, I was an idiot, because he looked and sounded sincere. "I didn't want it to come to this, but you understand, right? You even said it yourself. You'll do anything to protect your friends. We really aren't that different, Katy."

Then he opened the door and slipped out. The wall of chairs crumbled, spilling out across the floor. Kind of ironic how they fell upon themselves, just like my whole life was collapsing onto itself.

Chapter 10

In a daze, I stepped out of the demolished classroom and made it halfway through the hall before the stairwell door swung open and Daemon burst through.

His eyes were an incredibly bright green when his gaze landed on me, and he took about four ground-eating steps before he was in front of me, grasping my shoulders. Behind him were Matthew and a slightly-confused-looking Dawson, but Daemon…I'd never seen him so furious, and that was saying something.

"We've been looking everywhere for you," he said, jaw clenched.

Matthew appeared at our sides. "Did you see where he went? Blake?"

Like I needed the clarification. Then I realized they didn't know I'd been with him. How much time had passed in that room? It felt like hours but could've only been minutes. And if Blake had frozen everyone outside the room, the other Luxen would've known, because it wouldn't have affected them. So Blake must not have affected anything out of the room.

I swallowed, knowing Daemon's reaction was going to be epic. "Yeah, he…wanted to talk."

Daemon went rigid. "What?"

I glanced nervously at Matthew. His expression was serene compared to the rage boiling from Daemon's gaze. "He's been watching us. I don't think he ever left."

Daemon dropped his hands and backed off, thrusting his fingers through his hair. "I cannot believe he's here. He has a death wish."

Confusion slipped from Dawson's expression, replaced by curiosity as he inched around his twin. "Why was he watching us?"

And here comes the kicker, I thought. "He wants us to help get Chris."

Daemon whipped around so fast he would've pulled a muscle if he were human. "Come again?"

As quickly as I could, I told them what Blake had said, leaving out the part about turning Daemon and me over to Nancy. I figured that was something best communicated in private. Good call, because Daemon almost went full Luxen mode right there.

Matthew shook his head. "He…he can't think we would trust him."

"I don't think he cares if we do," I said, tucking my hair back. All I wanted to do was sit down and eat a box of sugar cookies, my hands beginning to shake from exhaustion.

"But does he really know where they are keeping Beth?" Dawson's eyes were feverish.

"I don't know." I leaned against a locker. "There's no telling with him."

Dawson shot forward, suddenly in my face. "Did he say anything—anything we can use to find her?"

I blinked, surprised by his sudden animation. "No. Not really. I—"

"Think," Dawson ordered, head lowered. "He had to have said

something, Katy."

Daemon clasped his brother's shoulder, wheeling him away. "Back off, Dawson. I mean it."

He shrugged Daemon's hand away, body coiled tight. "If he knows—"

"Don't go there," Daemon interrupted him. "He was sent here by the DOD to determine if Kat was a viable subject. To do to her what they are doing to Beth. He killed Adam, Dawson. We are not working with—"

My legs had started to wobble, and I swayed a little to the left. I really couldn't even begin to figure out how Daemon knew, but he spun toward me before I could straighten. Strong arms went around my waist, tucking me to his side.

Daemon's brows were dark slashes above his eyes. "What's wrong?"

My cheeks burned. "I'm okay. Really, I am."

"You're lying." His voice dropped low, dangerous. "Did you fight him?" And then his voice went even lower and a chill ran down my spine. "Did he try to hurt you? Because I swear right now, I will tear through this state—"

"I'm okay." I tried to wiggle free, but his arm was like a vise grip. "I used more of the attack first, ask questions later approach. I tired myself out, but he didn't hurt me."

Daemon didn't look convinced, but he turned his attention back to his brother. "I know you want to believe that Blake can help us somehow, but he can't be trusted."

Dawson looked away, a muscle ticking in his jaw. Frustration rolled off him in waves.

"Daemon's right." Matthew planted his hands on his hips. At the end of the hall, the door opened and two teachers entered, carrying steaming cups and papers. "But this is not the place to discuss any of this. After school, your house."

And with that, he spun in the other direction and stalked off.

"I know what you're going to say," Dawson said sharply. "I'm not going to do anything reckless. I promised both of you I wouldn't and I'm keeping my end of the deal. You better keep yours."

Daemon wasn't relieved as he watched Dawson head in the opposite direction. "This isn't good," he said.

"You have no idea." I glanced up at him and waited for the teachers to disappear into their classrooms. "Trusting Blake may be a moot point."

His eyes narrowed as he turned, angling his body as if he was shielding me. "What are you saying?"

I prayed he didn't lose it. "Blake confirmed what Will had said. The DOD and Daedalus believe my mutation wore off. Good news, right? But he's desperate—more so than we realized. If we don't agree to help him, he plans to turn us over."

Daemon's reaction was as expected. There was now a fist-sized indent in the locker beside us, and I grabbed his arm, dragging him into the nearby stairwell before teachers started inspecting the source of the noise.

Helpless anger seeped into the air and settled over him like a blanket. He knew what I wasn't willing to say yet. Like with Will, we'd been blackmailed—trapped again, and what could we do? Refuse to go along with Blake and be turned over? Or trust someone who had already proven he wasn't worthy of such a thing?

God, we were screwed to the tenth degree.

I could tell Daemon wanted to ditch school and search the entire county, but he also didn't want to leave me alone…no matter how hard I worked to convince him that, of all places, I was the safest at school. Because apparently I wasn't, not when Blake was back, acting like a normal student. And Blake knew that as long as he stayed around people, there was nothing we could do.

Throughout the rest of the day, I expected to see Blake again, but I didn't. When the final bell rang, I wasn't surprised when Daemon met me at my locker. "I'm riding home with you," he said.

"Sure." No point in arguing over this. "But how is Dolly getting home?"

He cracked a grin, loving it when I called his car by its stupid name. "I rode in with Dee this morning. Andrew and Ash are riding with her home."

I let that sink in, wondering when Dee had become so close with them. She had never been a big fan of theirs and their human-hating tendencies. So much had changed, and I knew I hadn't even seen the full spectrum yet.

"Do you think he'd really turn us over?" I asked once we were inside my little sedan. Outside, the bare trees surrounding the parking lot rattled like a thousand dry bones.

"He's obviously desperate." Daemon tried to stretch out his long legs, grumbling. "Blake killed already to protect his friend, and the only way for Blake to keep him safe is either by turning you over, as he was originally sent to do, or for us to help him. So, yeah, I believe he'd still do it."

I gripped the steering wheel, welcoming the lava-like anger suffusing my skin. We'd let Blake go, giving him a chance to get as far away as he could, and he came back to manipulate us. How ungrateful was that?

I glanced at Daemon. "What are we going to do?"

His jaw worked. "We have two options: work with him or kill him."

My eyes popped. "And you'd be the one to do that? Not right. It shouldn't always be you. You're not the only Luxen who can fight."

"I know, but I can't expect someone else to carry that burden." He looked at me.

"And I'm not trying to start another argument over whether or not you'd make a good Wonder Woman, but I'd never expect you or my siblings to do that, either. I know you would have done it to... defend yourself and us, Kat, but I don't want that kind of guilt on your shoulders. Okay?"

I nodded. Imagining what I felt already, just magnified, twisted my insides. "I could handle it…if I had to."

A heartbeat passed, and I felt his hand on my cheek. I took my eyes off road for a second. He smiled a little. "You burn bright, to me at least, and I know you could handle it, but the last thing I want is your light to be tainted by something so dark."

Stupid girlie tears burned my eyes and the road became a bit blurry. I couldn't let them fall, because crying over him saying something sweet really didn't help the "I'm A Badass" case. But I gave him a watery smile, and I think he understood.

I pulled into my driveway before the rest of the crew got there. Filled with nervous energy, I followed Daemon into his house and grabbed a bottle of water, then returned to the living room. Before I could begin the agitated wearing of the carpet, Daemon caught my hand and tugged me toward him as he sat, pulling me onto his lap.

Arms wrapped around me, he buried his face in my neck. "You know what we have to do," he said softly.

Dropping the bottle next to us, I wrapped my arms around his neck. "Kill Blake."

He choked on his laugh. "No, Kitten. We're not going to kill him."

I was surprised. "We're not?"

He pulled back, meeting my questioning stare. "We're going to have to do what he wants."

Okay, I was more than surprised. More like dumbstruck. "But…but…but…"

A grin teased his lips. "Use your words, Kitten."

I snapped out of my stupor. "But we can't trust him. This is most likely a trap!"

"We're kind of damned if we do and damned if we don't." He shifted, sliding his hands along my lower back. "But I've given it some thought."

"What? The whole ten minutes it took us to get home?"

"I think it's cute that you call my house *home*." His grin spread to his eyes, deepening their lustrous hue. "By the way, it *is* my house. My name is on the deed."

"Daemon," I said, sighing. "Nice to know, but it's not important right now."

"True, but it's good knowledge to have. Anyway, since you went totally off topic there—"

"What?" How did he figure that? "You're the one—"

"I know my brother. Dawson's going to go to Blake if we don't agree." All his humor was gone in an instant. "It's what I would do if our positions were reversed. And we know Blake better than he does."

"I don't know about this, Daemon."

He shrugged. "I'm not going to let him turn you over."

I frowned. "He'll turn you over, too, and what about your family? Bringing Blake into the fold is going to be dangerous…and stupid."

"The risk outweighs the possible consequences."

"I'm shocked," I admitted, disentangling my arms. "You didn't want me training with Blake because you didn't trust him and that was *before* we knew he was a killer."

"But now we're both going into this knowing what he's capable of. Our eyes are open."

"That makes no sense." At the sound of car doors shutting, I glanced out the window. "The only reason you're going to work with him is for Dawson and me. That's probably not the wisest decision you've made."

"Maybe not." He shifted quickly, clasping my cheeks and laying a deep one on me, and then he unceremoniously dumped me on the cushion beside him. "But my mind's made up. Be prepared. This meeting isn't going to go well."

Half sprawled across the couch, I gaped at him. Damn straight this wasn't going to go well. I dug the water bottle out from underneath my thigh and sat up as the alien pit crew made their way in.

Dee immediately took up pacing in front of the TV. Her long, wavy black hair streamed behind her. An unfamiliar, feverish glint lit her green eyes. "So Blake is back?"

"Yes." Daemon leaned forward, resting his elbows on his knees, watching his sister.

She glanced at me and then quickly looked away. "Of course he would talk to her like nothing happened. They were BFFs."

What the hell was up with the BFF statement? Anger stirred inside me, but I pushed it down. "It wasn't a particularly friendly conversation."

"Then what do we do?" Ash asked. Her cap of blond hair was slicked back into a tiny ponytail. On anyone else it would've looked too severe, but she pulled it off like a model going on a go-see.

"Kill him," Dee said, stopping in front of the coffee table.

At first, I thought she was kidding, because this was *Dee*. Over the summer, I'd once seen her scoop up a pile of dirt full of ants and move them out of the flowerbed so they wouldn't be suffocated under the mulch. But as I stared at her—as the *whole room* stared at her—I came to realize she was serious.

My mouth dropped open. "Dee…?"

Her shoulders squared. "Don't tell me. You're against killing him? I already know that. You convinced my brother to let him live."

"She didn't convince me," Daemon said, fingers curling under his chin.

I jumped in before he could continue. It wasn't his job to always rush to my defense. "I didn't convince him to do anything, Dee. We both agreed that enough people had died that night. We didn't think he'd come back."

"It's more than that," Matthew said. "He's also connected to another Luxen. He dies, his friend dies. We aren't just killing him. We're killing an innocent person."

"Like Katy and Daemon?" Ash asked, her voice lacking the usual venom. Her bitchiness must've transferred to Dee at some point.

Guilt dug in with barb-tipped fingers the second that thought finished and I squirmed, picking at a worn section on my jeans. That wasn't fair. Dee and Adam had a long history—a history spent ignoring what had probably always existed between them. Love and affection. And they'd only gotten to know each other on that level right before he was snatched away from her.

Ash glanced at Dawson. "And like you and Beth?" When the two boys nodded, Ash sat back and glanced at a silent Matthew. "We can't kill Blake knowing it's going to kill an innocent Luxen. That's like killing Katy and it taking out Daemon."

I arched a brow, which earned me a knee nudge from Daemon.

"I'm not suggesting we kill Katy or Beth," Dee reminded everyone. "We don't know who this other Luxen is. For all we know, he could be working with the DOD or whatever that other group is. Blake... He killed Adam, Ash."

"I know that," she snapped, eyes flashing a brilliant blue. "I was his sister."

Dee's spine straightened as she drew herself up. "And I was his girlfriend."

Holy smokes... It was like opposite day or something. I shook my head, stunned. "The group is called Daedalus."

Yeah, Dee couldn't care less what the group was called. She turned to Matthew. "We have to do something before someone else gets hurt."

Matthew looked just as shocked. "Dee, we're not—"

"Killers?" Her face flushed red and then paled. "We have killed before to protect ourselves! We kill Arum all the time. Daemon has killed DOD officers!"

Daemon flinched, and I immediately took offense to this. He may not show how much killing bothered him, but I knew it did. "Dee," I said, and surprisingly, she looked at me. "I know you're hurting right now, but this… This isn't you."

She sucked in a sharp breath and behind her the TV flickered on and off. "You don't know me. And you don't know shit. That… that human freak—whatever he is—was here because of what my brother did to you. In theory, if you never came here, none of this would've happened. Adam…" Her voice caught. "Adam would still be alive."

Daemon stiffened beside me. "That's enough, Dee. It wasn't her fault."

"It's okay." I sat back against the cushion, feeling as if the walls had shifted closer. Andrew had said the same thing days before and even though hearing him say it sucked, coming from Dee's mouth gave it a wasp-sting-like quality. Part of me almost couldn't believe Dee had said it. Not hyper and cute like Tinker Bell Dee. Not the girl who whipped into my life during the summer, feeling just as lonely as I had. This wasn't my best friend.

And then it hit me.

Dee wasn't my best friend anymore.

God, realizing that seemed more important than anything else that was going on. Yeah, that was stupid when the big picture was called into play, but Dee was important to me, and I had failed her.

Beside me, Dawson shifted forward. "If Katy hadn't come here, I would never have been freed. The world works in messed-up ways."

Dee looked like she hadn't even considered that. She pivoted around, playing with a strand of her hair—a nervous habit of hers. Her arm faded out for a few seconds, and then she sat on the coffee table, her back to us.

From the arm of the recliner, Andrew sighed. Every time I

looked at him, he'd had his gaze fixed on Dee. "Guys, whether we like the idea of killing someone or not, we have to do something."

"We do," Daemon agreed. He glanced at me quickly before facing the group. "Arguing about what to do with Blake is a waste of time. If we don't help him free Chris and in turn get Beth back, he's going to turn Kat and me over."

"Wow," Matthew muttered, thrusting his fingers through his hair. And then he did something unheard of, for him at least. He swore.

Dee stood again, her movement abrupt and jerky. "He said that?"

"I don't doubt he's serious," I said, hating that all of them were put in this position because of me. If I had only listened to Daemon in the beginning… So many would've, could've moments. "He's incredibly desperate to free Chris."

"Then it's done," Dawson said, seeming relieved. "We help him, and he helps us."

Dee whirled. "You guys are freaking insane! We cannot help Adam's murderer!"

"Then what do you suggest we do?" Matthew asked. "Let him turn your brother and Katy over?"

Her eyes rolled. "No. Like I said, we kill him. That will stop him from doing anything."

I shook my head, stunned by the ferocity in her voice. I also believed Blake probably had to die, because why should he live when Adam hadn't, but hearing Dee like this cut through me with a dull knife.

Daemon stood, drawing in a long breath. "We are not going to kill Blake."

His sister's hands balled into fists. "Your call. Not mine."

"We are going to help him and we're going to keep an eye on him," Daemon continued sternly. "And none of us are going to kill him."

"Bullshit," she hissed.

On his feet, Andrew took a step forward. "Dee, I think you need to sit down and think about this. You've never killed before. Not even an Arum."

She folded her slender arms and her chin went up a notch. "There's always a first time."

Ash's eyes widened as she slid a look at me that said, *Holy crap*. I wished I knew what to do or say, but there was nothing.

Quickly losing patience, Daemon mirrored his sister's stance. "This isn't up for discussion, Dee."

A faint glimmer of white light shaded the outline of her trembling body. "You're right. There's nothing you can say that will convince me that his life should be spared."

"We don't have a choice. Blake has it set up that if anything happens to him, Nancy will be notified about Katy and me. We can't kill him."

She was undeterred. "Then we find out who he's talked to or working with and take care of them!"

Daemon's jaw dropped. "Are you serious?"

"Yes!"

He turned away, seconds from losing it. My stomach rolled. This whole situation was all wrong.

Beside me, Dawson leaned forward, taking on the same position that Daemon had earlier. "Is your need for vengeance more important than finding and stopping what they're doing to Beth?"

She didn't look away, but her lips pressed into a grim line.

All eyes were on Dawson. "Because, little sister, let me tell you that what Adam went through pales in comparison to what she's experiencing. The things I've seen..." He trailed off and his gaze lowered. "If you doubt what I say, then ask Katy. She's had a taste of some of their methods and she can still barely talk from screaming."

Dee blanched. We hadn't spoken, not really, since New Year's Eve. I had no idea what she knew about my brief capture or the methods Will had used to subdue me. Her gaze flickered to mine, and she looked away all too quickly.

"You ask a lot," she said hoarsely, lower lip trembling. But then her shoulders slumped, and she turned, walking to the front door. Without saying a word, she left.

Andrew was already behind her, shooting Daemon a look. "I'll keep an eye on her."

"Thank you," he said, rubbing his palm along his jaw. "Well, that went wonderfully."

"Did you really expect her or any of us to be okay with it?" Ash asked.

Daemon snorted. "No, but I have a problem with my sister so willing to kill."

"I can't…" I couldn't even finish. Going into this, I knew it wasn't going to be good, but Ash and Andrew were the ones I expected to want to go all serial killer—never Dee.

Matthew directed the conversation back to the present. "How do we contact Blake? It's not something I can or wish to discuss with him in class."

Everyone looked at me…everyone except Daemon. "What?"

"You have his number, don't you?" Ash said, glancing at her naked nails. "Text. Call him. Whatever. And tell him we're ridiculously stupid and plan to help him."

I made a face but reached for my bag and dug out my cell. Sending Blake a quick text, I sighed. A second later he responded. Knots formed in my stomach. "Tomorrow evening—Saturday." My voice sounded weak. "He wants to meet tomorrow evening in a public spot—Smoke Hole."

Daemon gave a quick jerk of his chin.

My fingers wanted to rebel, but I typed out a quick *okay* and then tossed my phone back in the pack like it was a bomb about to go off in my hands. "It's done."

No one looked relieved. Not even Dawson. There was a very good chance that this was going to blow up in our faces like there was no tomorrow. But our choices were limited. Like Daemon had said, Dawson would go to Blake whether or not we did. And working with the enemy we knew was better than the one we didn't.

But something cold and icky opened up in my chest.

Not because we were going to go down this road with Blake and not because Dee wanted Blake to die. But because deep down, underneath the layers of skin, muscle, and bone, hidden away from everyone, even Daemon, I also wanted Blake dead. Innocent Luxen or not... My moral code wasn't at all offended by it. And there was something very, very wrong with that.

Chapter 11

I hung around their house, hoping Dee would come back and I could chat with her, but everyone was leaving and she and Andrew hadn't returned.

Standing on the front porch, I watched Ash and Matthew drive off, my heart heavy with regret and a billion other things. I didn't need to look behind me to know that Daemon had joined me. I welcomed the warmth and strength his arms offered as they circled me from behind.

I leaned back against his chest, letting my eyes fall shut. He placed his chin atop my head and minutes passed with only the sound of a lonesome birdcall and a horn blowing off in the distance. Against my back, his heart beat steady and strong.

"I'm sorry," he said, surprising me.

"For what?"

He drew in a deep breath. "I shouldn't have flipped out over the whole Dawson thing last weekend. You did the right thing by telling him we'd help. If not, God knows what he would've done by now." He paused long enough to kiss the top of my head, and

I grinned. He was so forgiven. "And thank you for everything with Dawson. Even though our Saturday will take a turn into crapsville, Dawson... He's been different since zombie night. Not the old Dawson, but close."

I bit my lip. "You don't need to thank me for that. Seriously."

"I do. And I meant it."

"Okay." Several seconds passed. "Do you think we made a mistake? Letting Blake go that night?"

His arms tightened. "I don't know. I really don't."

"We had good intentions, right? We wanted to give him a chance, I guess." Then I laughed.

"What?"

My eyes opened. "The road to hell is paved with good intentions. We should've blasted his ass."

Daemon lowered his head, his chin now on my shoulder. "Maybe I would've done something like that before you."

I turned my head toward his. "What do you mean?"

"Before you came along, I would've killed Blake for what he did and felt like crap afterward, but I would've done it." He pressed a kiss against my fluttering pulse. "And in a way, you did convince me. Not the way Dee thinks, but you could've taken out Blake, and you didn't."

Everything about that night seemed chaotic and surreal now. Adam's lifeless body and then the Arum that had attacked... Vaughn and the gun... Blake running... "I don't know."

"I do," he said, and his lips spread into a smile against my cheek. "You make me think before I act. You make me want to be a better person—Luxen—whatever."

I faced him completely, peering up at him. "You *are* a good person."

Daemon grinned, his eyes twinkling. "Kitten, you and I both know that's incredibly rare."

"No—"

He placed a finger over my lips. "I make terrible decisions. I can be a dickhead and I do it on purpose. I tend to bully people into doing what I want. And I let everything that had happened with Dawson amplify those...uh, personality traits. But—" He removed his finger, and his grin spread into a smile. "But you...you make me want to be different. That's why I didn't kill Blake. It's why I don't want you making those decisions or for you to be around me if I am choosing those things."

Overwhelmed by what he'd admitted, I didn't know what to say. But he lowered his head and kissed me, and I learned that sometimes when someone says something so devastatingly perfect, there isn't a need for a response. The words said it all.

. . .

I spent Saturday morning with my mom. We had a greasy, artery-killing breakfast at IHOP and then wasted a couple of hours dollar-store shopping. Usually I'd rather pluck my eyelashes out than meander those aisles, but I wanted to spend time with her.

Tonight, Daemon and I were meeting Blake—only us, per his request. Matthew and Andrew were going to play parking-lot spies as backup, since Dee and Dawson, for very different reasons, had been banned from coming within a mile of the place.

There was no telling what was going to happen, though. This could be my last Saturday, my last *anything* with my mom. And that made the whole experience bittersweet and scary. So many times over breakfast and while in the car I wanted to tell her what was going on, but I couldn't. And even if I could, the words probably wouldn't have come out. She was having fun—thrilled to spend time with me—and I couldn't bring myself to ruin it.

But the what-ifs haunted me. What if this were a trap? What if the DOD or Daedalus took us in? What if I became Beth and my mom never heard from me again? What if she moved back to

Gainesville to escape the memory of me?

By the time we got home, I was pretty sure I was going to hurl. My stomach twisted and turned around the food. It was so bad that I went to lie down while Mom got some sleep before her shift started.

About an hour of staring at the wall later, Daemon texted and I responded, telling him to let himself in. No sooner had I hit send than I felt warmth shooting across the back of my neck and I rolled toward the door.

Daemon made no sound as he eased my door open and slid though, a wicked glint in his eyes. "Your mom's asleep?"

I nodded.

His gaze searched my face, and then he shut the door behind him. A heartbeat later, he was sitting beside me, brows drawn tight. "You're worried."

How he knew was beyond me. I started to tell him that I wasn't worried, because I hated the idea of him stressing out over me or thinking I was weak, but I didn't want to be strong right now. I needed comfort—I wanted *him*. "Yeah, a little."

He smiled. "It's going to be okay. No matter what, I'm not going to let anything happen to you."

Daemon ran the tips of his fingers down my cheek, and I realized then that I could have both. I could freak out a little on the inside and need him, but I could still be strong enough to get up at six and meet our fate head-on. I could be both.

God, I needed a little of both.

Wordlessly, I scooted over, giving him room. Daemon slid under the covers, throwing a heavy arm over my waist. I curled against him, resting my head under his chin, my hands folded on his chest. Using my fingers, I drew a heart above his, and he chuckled.

We lay there for a couple of hours. Sometimes talking and laughing quietly, making sure we didn't wake my mom. For a while, we dozed together and then I'd wake, tangled in his arms and legs.

Other times, we kissed and the kissing…well, it took up most of the time.

He was just so damn good at it.

My lips felt swollen as he grinned at me, his lids heavily hooded, but behind those lashes, his eyes were like the color of dewy spring grass. Along the nape of his neck, his hair curled. I loved running my fingers through it, straightening the strands out and watching them spring back into place. And he liked when I played with it. Closing his eyes, he tilted his head to the side so I got better access, much like a cat stretching to be petted.

Ah, the little things in life.

Daemon caught my hand as I slid it around, over the thick muscles in his neck. He brought my palm to his lips. My heart did the flutter thing, and then he kissed me again…and again. His hand moved to my hip, his fingers curling into the denim before slipping under the hem of my shirt, causing my pulse to pound through me. He rolled over me, his weight doing crazy things to my stomach.

As his hand crept up, my back arched. "Daemon—"

His mouth silenced whatever it was that I was going to say, and my brain emptied. There was just him and me. What we had to do later simply disappeared off my worry radar. I moved, throwing a leg over his and my—

Footsteps trotted down the hall.

Daemon faded out above me, reappearing at my desk chair. Grinning shamelessly, he picked up a book as I fixed myself.

"Book's upside down," I taunted, smoothing my hand over my hair.

Laughing under his breath, he turned it over and cracked it open. With seconds to spare, Mom knocked on the door and then opened it. Her eyes shot from the bed to the chair.

"Hello, Ms. Swartz," Daemon said. "You look well-rested."

I shot him a look and then clamped my hand over my mouth, stifling my giggles. He'd picked up one of the historical romance novels with the bodice-ripping, barrel-chested covers.

Mom arched a brow. Her expression basically read WTF, and I almost lost it. "Good evening, Daemon." She turned to me, eyes narrowing.

Codpiece? Daemon mouthed, rolling his eyes.

"Bedroom door, Katy." Mom headed back to the door. "You know the rules."

"Sorry. We didn't want to wake you."

"How considerate, but it stays open."

When her footsteps receded, Daemon chucked the book at my head. I raised my hand, stopping it so that it hovered, and snatched it out of the air. "Nice reading material."

His eyes narrowed. "Shut up."

I giggled.

• • •

There was no laughter as we pulled into Smoke Hole Diner's parking lot a little before six. Looking over my shoulder, I saw Matthew's SUV parked in the back. I seriously hoped he and Andrew paid attention.

"The DOD isn't going to bust up in here," Daemon said, pulling out the keys. "Not in public."

"But Blake could freeze the entire place."

"So can I."

"Oh. I've never seen you do that."

He rolled his eyes. "Yes, you have. I froze the truck. Remember? Saved your life and all?"

"Ah, yes." I fought a grin. "You did do that."

He reached over, flicking me gently under the chin. "Yeah, you better remember that. Plus, I'm not a show-off."

Opening the door, I laughed. "You? Not a show-off? Okay."

"What?" Fake outrage crossed his face as he shut the door and loped around the front of the SUV. "I'm very modest."

"If I remember correctly, you said modesty was for saints and losers." The bantering helped ease my nerves. "*Modest* is not a word I'd use to describe you."

He dropped his arm over my shoulder. "I never said such a thing."

"Liar."

Daemon shot me a roguish grin as we headed in. I scanned the restaurant for Blake, my gaze dipping over the natural rock clusters jutting out of the floors and beside the booths, but he wasn't here yet. The server seated us in a booth near the back, cozied up to the roaring fireplace. I tried to keep myself busy by ripping the napkin into tiny pieces.

"Going to eat that or are you making homemade hamster bedding?" he asked.

I laughed. "Organic kitty litter, actually."

"Nice."

A redheaded waitress appeared, wearing a bright smile. "Daemon, how are you doing? Haven't seen you in ages."

"Good. How about you, Jocelyn?"

Of course I had to give her more than a passing look, since the two were on a first-name basis. Not out of jealousy or anything. Yeah, right. Jocelyn was older than us but not by much. Maybe early twenties, but she was really, really pretty with all that red hair piled up in thick curls, surrounding a porcelain complexion.

Okay, she was beautiful…as in, Luxen beautiful.

I sat straighter.

"I've been real good," she said. "I stepped down from managing since the babies. Working part-time instead, since they're a handful, but you and your family should visit soon, especially since…" She looked at me for the first time, and her smile drooped. "Since Dawson has come back. Roland would love to see both of you."

Total alien, I thought.

"We'd love to do that." Daemon glanced at me and winked slyly. "By the way, Jocelyn, this is my girlfriend, Katy."

I felt a ridiculous surge of pleasure as I extended my hand. "Hi."

Jocelyn blinked, and I'd swear her face got even whiter. "Girlfriend?"

"Girlfriend," Daemon repeated.

She recovered fast and shook my hand. A faint spark jumped from her skin to mine, and I pretended not to notice. "Nice…nice to meet you," she said, quickly releasing my hand. "Uh, what can I get you two?"

"Two Cokes," he ordered.

Jocelyn skedaddled off after that, and I raised my brows at Daemon. "Jocelyn…?"

He slid over another napkin for my pile. "Are you jealous, Kitten?"

"Pfft. Whatever." I stopped tearing. "Okay, maybe a little until I realized she was in the ARP."

"ARP?" He stood, coming to my side while saying, "Scoot."

I scooted over. "Alien Relocation Program."

"Ha." He dropped his arm over the back of the booth and stretched out his legs. "Yeah, she's good people."

Jocelyn returned with our drinks and asked if we wanted to wait until our friend joined us to place our orders. That was a big fat no. Daemon ordered a meatloaf sandwich while I decided to eat half his order. I wasn't sure I could stomach anything more.

He angled his body toward mine as soon as he finished deciding between fries and mashed potatoes—fries won. "Nothing's going to happen," he said, voice low. "Okay?"

Putting on a brave face, I nodded as I looked around the diner. "I just want to get this over with."

Not even a minute later, the bells above the door jingled and before I could glance up, Daemon stiffened beside me. And I knew—I knew right then. My stomach lurched into my throat.

Spiky, bronze-tipped hair—styled messily with a ton of gel—came into view, and then hazel eyes locked on our table from the door.

Blake was here.

Chapter 12

Blake had a confident air about him as he walked up to our table, but it had nothing on Daemon's deadly swagger or the cool and arrogant smile he was wearing that instant. It was a purely predatory look.

Suddenly, I wasn't sure a public place was a good idea.

"Bart," Daemon drawled, his fingers tapping along the booth behind me. "It's been so long."

"I see you still haven't figured out my name." Blake slid into the seat across from us. His gaze dropped to the pile of torn napkins, then to me. "Hey, Katy."

Daemon leaned forward. The smile was still on his face, but his words were like the arctic winds. "You don't talk to her. At all."

There was no stopping He-Man when he came out to play, but I pinched him under the table. Daemon ignored me.

"Well, only talking to you is going to make this conversation real rough."

"Like I care?" Daemon said, placing his other hand on the table.

I exhaled slowly. "Okay. Let's get to the point. Where are Beth and Chris, Blake?"

Blake's gaze slid to mine again. "I—"

A current of electricity coursed from Daemon's hand and shot across the table, shocking Blake. He jerked back with a hiss, his eyes narrowing on Daemon.

Daemon smiled.

"Look, you tool, you can't intimidate me this time." Blake's voice dripped contempt. "So you're just wasting time and pissing me off."

"We'll see about that."

Jocelyn returned with Daemon's massive meal and took Blake's order. Like me, he only requested a soda. When we were alone once more, I focused on Blake.

"Where are they?"

"If I tell you, I'd have to trust that you two, plus anyone else, aren't going to give me a cement swim."

I rolled my eyes at the mafia reference. "Trust is a two-way street."

"And we don't trust you," Daemon threw out.

Blake drew in a long breath. "I don't blame you. I've given you no reason to trust me other than the fact I didn't tell Daedalus about how well the mutation held."

"And I bet either your uncle—Vaughn—stopped you from turning me over, or you thought he was doing his job," I countered, trying not to remember the look of horror that had settled on Blake's face when his uncle betrayed him. He didn't deserve my sympathy. "But he screwed you over for money."

Blake's jaw worked. "He did. And he put Chris in danger. But it's not like I haven't had to convince them otherwise after the fact. They think I'm happy to be an implant. That I've drunk the Kool-Aid and asked for seconds."

Daemon snickered. "To save your own ass, I'm sure."

He ignored that comment. "The fact is, Daedalus doesn't believe you're a viable subject."

"How do you know?" Daemon's fingers tightened on his fork.

Blake shot him a *duh* look. "The only real wild card here is Will. Obviously he knew and used that knowledge."

"Will isn't our biggest or most annoying problem right now." Daemon took a bite, chewing slowly. "You either have a lot of courage or are incredibly stupid. I'm going to go with the incredibly stupid part."

Blake snorted. "Yeah. Okay."

A dangerous look shadowed Daemon's face, and for a moment, no one moved as Jocelyn returned with Blake's drink. The second she was gone, Daemon leaned forward, his eyes starting to shine behind his lashes. "We gave you a chance and you came back here after you killed one of our own. You think I'm the only person you have to look over your shoulder and watch out for? You're so wrong."

A thread of fear finally showed in Blake's churning eyes, but his voice was even. "The same goes for you, buddy."

Daemon sat back, eyes hooded. "As long as we're on the same page."

"Back to Daedalus," I said. "How do you know they're watching Dawson?"

"I've been watching you guys, and I've seen them hanging around." He leaned against the booth, folding his arms. "I don't know how much work Will did to get him free, but I doubt he pulled the wool over anyone's eyes. Dawson is free because they wanted him to be free."

I glanced at Daemon. Blake's suspicions mirrored our own, but that was another problem for another day, it seemed.

Blake's gaze fell to his glass. "Here's the deal. I know where they're keeping Beth and Chris. I've never been there, but I know someone who has and can give us the security codes to get into the facility."

"Hold up," I said, shaking my head. "So you can't really get us in. Someone else can?"

"Go figure." Daemon chuckled. "Biff is virtually useless."

Blake's lips thinned. "I know what level and cell they're being kept in, so without me, you'd just be running around the compound begging to be captured."

"And my fist is begging to be in your face," Daemon shot back.

I rolled my eyes. "Not only are you asking us to trust you but to trust someone else?"

"*That* someone else is just like us, Katy." Blake dropped his elbows on the table, rocking his glass. "He's a hybrid but has gotten out from under Daedalus. And as expected, he hates them and would love nothing more than to screw with them. He's not going to lead us astray."

Yeah, I wasn't liking any of this. "And how does anyone get 'out from under' Daedalus?"

Blake's smile lacked warmth. "They...disappear."

Oh, well that sounded reassuring. I tucked my hair back on both sides, feeling cagey. "Okay, say we do this; how do you get in contact with him?"

"You won't believe anything unless you're there to witness it for yourselves." And he was right about that. "I know where to find Luc."

Daemon's mouth curled. "His name is *Luc*?"

Blake nodded. "He's not going to be reachable by cell or e-mail. He's kind of paranoid about the government tapping cells and computers. We'll have to go to him."

"And where is that?" Daemon asked.

"Every Wednesday night he hangs at a club a few miles outside of Martinsburg," Blake explained. "He'll be there this Wednesday."

Daemon laughed, and I wondered what the hell he found so funny. "The only clubs in that part of West Virginia are strip clubs."

"You would think that." Smugness crept over Blake's expression. "But this is a different kind of club." He glanced at me. "Females don't show up in jeans and sweaters."

I gave him a bland look as I plucked a fry from Daemon's plate. "What do they show up in? Nothing?"

"The closest thing to nothing." His smile was real now, causing the green in his eyes to sparkle, reminding me of the Blake I first met. "Bad for you. Yay for me."

"You really want to die, don't you?" Daemon said.

"Sometimes, I think so." There was a pause, and his shoulders rolled. "Anyway, we go to him, he'll get the codes, and then it's on. We go in, you get what you want, and I get what I want. You guys will never see me again."

"That's pretty much the only thing you've said so far that I like." Daemon's sharp gaze landed on Blake. "The thing is, I'm having a hard time believing you. You say this hybrid is in Martinsburg, right? There isn't any beta quartz near that place. How come he hasn't become some Arum's afternoon snack yet?"

A mysterious glimmer filled Blake's eyes. "Luc can take care of himself."

Something wasn't right here. "And where's the Luxen he's tied to?"

"With him," Blake said.

Well, that answered that question, but still, none of this sat well with me. Crap, this whole situation was looking dicey, but what choice did we have? We were already in deep. Might as well go in over our heads—sink or swim, as my dad would say.

"Look," Blake said, fixing a steady stare on Daemon. "What happened with Adam—I never wanted that. And I'm sorry, but you of all people have to understand. You'd do anything for Katy."

"I would." A faint tremor coursed through Daemon. Static built, raising the tiny hairs on my body. "So, if for one moment I think you're about to screw us, I won't hesitate. You won't get a third chance. And you haven't seen what I'm fully capable of, boy."

"Understood," Blake murmured, his eyes downcast. "Are we on?"

The million-dollar question—were we really going to do this? Daemon's heartbeat calmed, and I felt it in my own chest. His mind was made up. Not only would he do anything to keep me safe, he'd do anything for his brother.

Sink or swim.

I lifted my lashes and met Blake's eyes. "We're on."

• • •

I spent the bulk of Sunday at Daemon's house, watching a marathon of *Ghost Investigators* with the brothers while I waited for—er, stalked—Dee. She had to come home sometime. That's what Daemon said.

It was almost dusk when she returned. I hopped up from the couch, startling Dawson, who had dozed off around hour four of things that go bump in the night.

"Is everything okay?" He was wide awake now.

Daemon scooted over, taking my spot. "Everything's fine."

His brother stared back for a long second and then refocused on the TV. Knowing what I wanted to do without even telling him, Daemon nodded.

Dee started for the stairs without saying a word. "Do you have a couple of minutes?" I asked.

"Not really," she threw over her shoulder as she continued up the stairs.

I squared my shoulders and followed. "Well, if you only have a minute, then I'm taking up that minute."

Stopping at the top of the stairs, she turned around. For a moment, I thought she might push me down the steps, which would totally derail my make-up plans. "All right," she said, and then sighed as if she'd been asked to recite trig formulas. "We might as well get this over with."

Not the way I wanted to start this conversation, but at least she was talking to me. I followed her into her bedroom. Like every time before, I was overwhelmed by the amount of *pink*. Pink walls. Pink bed coverings. Pink laptop. Pink throw carpet. Pink lampshades.

Dee moved to the window seat and sat, crossing her slender ankles. "What do you want, Katy?"

Mustering courage, I took up residency on the edge of her bed. All day, I had planned out this long speech, but suddenly, I just wanted to grovel at her feet. I wanted my best friend back. A look of impatience pinched her delicate features, and my stomach fell.

"I don't know where to start," I admitted quietly.

She drew in a heavy breath. "Maybe start with why you lied to me for months?"

I flinched, but I deserved that question. "The night in the clearing, when we fought Baruck, I don't know what happened, but Daemon didn't kill him."

"You did?" She stared out the window, idly playing with a dark curl.

"Yeah...I connected with him—with you. We...we think it was because Daemon had healed me before. Somehow those healings had already blended us together." Leftover fear from that night surfaced, coiling my insides tightly. "But I was hurt—really badly, I guess, and Daemon healed me after you left."

Her shoulders tensed. "The first lie, right? He told me you were fine, and I was stupid for believing him. You looked...really bad. And afterward, when Daemon was gone, you didn't act right. I should've known something was up." She gave a little shake of her head. "Anyway, you could've told me the truth. I wouldn't have flipped out or anything."

"I know." I rushed to agree. "But we weren't sure what really happened. We thought it would be best not to say anything until we found out. And by the time we realized we were connected somehow, everything…everything else was going on."

"Blake?" She spat out the name, dropping the piece of her hair.

"Him…and other things." I wanted to sit beside her, but I knew not to push it. "Things started happening to me. I would want a glass of tea, and the glass would fly out of the cupboard. I couldn't control it, and I was so afraid of exposing you guys somehow."

She looked at me then, lashes lowered. "You told Daemon, though."

I nodded. "Only because I thought maybe he knew what was happening, since he healed me. It wasn't because I trusted him more than you."

Dee's lashes lifted. "But you stopped hanging out with me."

My cheeks flushed with shame. I had made so, so many poor decisions. "I thought it was the right thing to do. That if I ended up moving something without meaning to around you, I didn't want you to get caught up in it."

She barked a short laugh. "You're so like Daemon. Always thinking you know better than everyone else." I started to respond, but she went on. "The funny thing is, I could've helped you. Water under the bridge now, though."

"I'm sorry." I wished those two words could take back everything I had done wrong. "I'm really—"

"What about Blake?" Her hard stare met mine.

My gaze went to my hands. "I didn't know what he was at first. Honestly, I liked him because he was normal. He wasn't like Daemon and I thought… I thought I didn't have to question why Blake seemed to like me." I laughed, the sound just as harsh as Dee's. "I was an idiot. Right off, Daemon didn't trust Blake. I thought he was jealous or just being Daemon. But then there was this Arum that came into the diner when I was with Blake, and I found out what he was."

Dee faded out and reappeared by her dresser, hands on her

hips. "So, let me get this right. There was an Arum, and never once did you think about telling me or any of the others?"

I twisted toward her. "I did, but Blake killed that one and Daemon knew. And we were watching for them—"

"Sounds like a lame excuse to me." Was it an excuse? It was, because I should've told them. I swallowed the sudden lump in my throat. Her eyes flashed bright. "You have no idea how hard it was to keep everything from you in the beginning! How worried I was that you'd get hurt just being around us and..." Dee stopped, closing her eyes. "I can't believe Daemon kept this from me."

"You shouldn't be upset with Daemon. He did everything to stop this. He didn't trust that Blake just wanted to help control my abilities. It was my fault." And the guilt gnawed away at me, bit by bit. "I thought that Blake could help me. That if I knew how to control my abilities, I could fight—I could help you guys. You would no longer need to protect me or be worried about me. I wouldn't be your problem."

Her eyes snapped open. "You were never a problem to me, Katy! You were my best friend—my first, only real friend. And yeah, I'm a little slow on how the whole friendship thing works, but I do know that friends are supposed to trust each other. And you should've known that I never saw you as being weak or a problem."

"I..." I puttered out, not knowing what to say.

"You never believed in our friendship." Wetness gathered in her eyes, and I felt like the biggest tool ever. "That's the part that kills me. From the beginning, you didn't believe in me."

"I did!" I started to stand, but I froze. "I made stupid decisions, Dee. I made mistakes. And by the time I realized how bad my mistakes were, it was..."

"Too late," she whispered. "It was too late, wasn't it?"

"Yeah." I took a breath, but it got stuck. "Blake was who he was, and everything that happened was because of me. I know that."

Dee came forward, her steps measured and slow. "How long

did you know about Beth and Dawson?"

I lifted my gaze, meeting hers. A huge part of me wanted to lie—wanted to say it wasn't until Will confirmed it, but I couldn't. "Before Christmas break, I saw Beth. And then Matthew confirmed that if Beth was alive, Dawson had to be."

She sucked in a cry and her fingers curled in. "How…how dare you?"

I could tell she wanted to slap me, and my cheek stung even though she hadn't. I kind of wished she would. "We didn't know if we could find him or get him back. We didn't want to get your hopes up only for you to lose him again."

Dee stared at me like she didn't even know me. "That is the stupidest thing I've ever heard. Let me guess, it was Daemon's idea? Because it sounds like him. He'd want to protect me at the same time as he was holding me back—hurting me."

"Daemon—"

"Don't," she said, turning away. Her voice shook. "Don't defend him. I know my brother. I know he has good intentions that usually just suck. But you—you know how much losing Dawson hurt. It wasn't just Daemon who lost his shit. I may not have moved the house off the foundation, but a part of me died the day I was told he was dead. I *deserved* to know the moment you thought he was alive."

"You're right."

Her body shimmered for a second. "Okay. Okay…all of that aside. If you had told me about what was going on with Blake, Adam and I would've known what we were walking into. We still would've done it—believe me, we would've gone into that house to help you—but we wouldn't have been blindsided."

My throat seized up. There was a stain on my soul, dark and cold. I hadn't murdered Adam, but I had a hand in his death. Like an accessory after the fact. People made mistakes all the time, but most of them didn't cause someone's death.

Mine did.

My shoulders sagged under the weight. Saying sorry wasn't going to smooth that over, not for her or me. I couldn't change the hand of time. All I could do now was move forward and try to make up for it.

The anger seeped out of Dee as she watched me. Walking back to the window seat, she sat, tucking her legs against her chest. She rested her cheek on her knees. "And now you guys are making another mistake."

"We don't have a choice," I said. "We really don't."

"Yes, you do. We could take care of Blake and whoever he's told."

"What about Dawson?" I asked quietly.

She didn't answer for a long time. "I know I should be able to put aside how I feel about Blake for him, but I can't. It's wrong. I know. But I can't."

I nodded. "I don't expect you to, but I don't want things to be like this between us. There's got to be a way…" Pride went out the window. "I miss you, Dee, and I hate that we haven't been talking and that you're upset with me. I want to get past this."

"I'm sorry," she whispered.

Tears burned the back of my throat. "What can I do to fix this?"

"You can't. And I can't, either." Dee shook her head sadly. "I can't fix Adam's death. I can't fix why you and Daemon think working with Blake is a good thing. And I can't fix our friendship. Some things are just broken."

Chapter 13

Lesa came over after school on Tuesday to help study for our bio exam the next day, which sucked, because the last thing I could concentrate on was schoolwork. Part of me expected Matthew to reschedule, since he knew what I had to do tomorrow night. I even suggested it on Monday after class, but oh no, no can do.

I rocked back in my computer chair, my barely read bio textbook in my lap. Lesa was reading her notes, and I was supposed to be listening, but I cracked open my advanced copy of a new young adult novel for my Teaser Tuesday post.

Typing up a quick post, I picked a couple of quick lines with an evil grin. '*I was his power-up—the ace up his sleeve. I was the beginning and he was the end. And together, we were everything.*' I hit post and then closed the pretty amber cover of the book.

"You are so not paying attention," Lesa said, sitting up.

"Yeah, I am." I wheeled around, fighting a grin. "You were saying something about cells and organisms."

She arched a brow. "Wow. You got this in the bag."

"I'm gonna fail." I dropped my head back, closed my eyes, and let out a long-suffering sigh. "I just can't concentrate. I'd rather read something interesting—like this." I waved toward the book I'd just posted about and then to where I knew a whole stack of other books sat. "And there's this thing I have to do tomorrow night."

"Oh! What thing? A thing with Daemon, and if you say yes, please tell me that thing starts with an *s* and ends with an *x*."

I opened my eyes and frowned. "Geez, you're worse than a dude."

Her curls bounced as she nodded. "You know it."

I threw my pen at her.

Laughing, she closed her notebook. "So, what are you doing tomorrow that has you so distracted?"

There wasn't much I could tell her, but I was full of nervous energy, and the need to talk about it snaked past my lips. "Daemon and I are going to this…club or something in Martinsburg to visit some of his friends."

"Well, that sounds like fun."

I shrugged. I'd already told my mom that I was going to the movies and, since she worked tomorrow night, curfew wasn't an issue. What was an issue was the fact that I had no idea what to wear and the stuff with Dee had put me in a huge funk.

I popped up from my seat and stalked over to my closet. "I'm supposed to wear something sexy. I don't have anything sexy."

Lesa followed. "I'm sure you have something in here."

There was a sea of jeans and sweaters, nothing like what Blake hinted at. Anger crept up my throat. With Blake being back in school, it was just messed up. He was a murderer—my lab partner was a murderer.

Queasy, I pushed a stack of jeans to the side. "Yeah, I don't know about any of this."

Lesa brushed me aside. "Let me take a look. I am the queen of smexy stuff. At least that's what Chad thinks and, well, I kinda got to give it to the boy." She flashed me a quick, saucy grin. "He's got good taste."

I leaned against the wall. "Do your magic."

Five minutes later, Lesa and I stared at the items placed on my bed as if an invisible hooker was wearing them. My cheeks were already beet red. "Uh…"

Lesa giggled. "You should see your face."

I shook my head helplessly. "Do you see what I normally wear? This—this isn't me."

"That's the fun thing about going to clubs, especially ones out of town." Her nose wrinkled. "Well, there ain't any clubs here, so everything is out of town, but anyway, you get to be someone else. Let your inner stripper come out and play."

I busted out laughing. "My inner stripper?"

She nodded. "Haven't you ever snuck into a bar or a club?"

"Yeah, but they were on beaches and everyone was dressed for summer. It's not summer."

"So?"

I rolled my eyes as I turned back to the bed. Lesa had found a denim skirt I'd ordered online last year for summer, but it had ended up being way too short. Like barely-covering-the-butt short, and I'd been too lazy to return it. Spaced above the scrap of denim was a cropped black sweater I'd usually wear over a shirt or tank. It was long sleeved, so it would cover the scars on my wrists but barely anything else. On the floor was a pair of knee-high boots I'd gotten on sale last winter.

And that was all.

Yep, that was it.

"My butt and my boobs are going to be showing."

Lesa scuffed. "Your boobs will be covered."

"Not my entire stomach!"

"You have a nice stomach; show it off." She picked up the skirt, holding it to her waist. "When you're done with this, I so want to borrow it."

"Sure." And then I frowned. "Where are you going to wear it?"

"School." She laughed at the look on my face. "I'll put some tights on underneath it, you priss."

An idea struck. "Tights!" I spun toward my dresser and started rummaging through my socks. I pulled out a pair of black opaque tights. "A-ha! I can wear these." And a jacket…maybe a mask, too.

She snatched the tights from me, tossing them across the room. "You can't wear tights."

My face fell. "No?"

"No." She peered over my shoulder and then grinned as she reached around me and pulled something else out. "But these you could wear."

My mouth dropped open. A pair of ripped tights dangled from her fingers. "That was, like, a part of a Halloween costume."

"Perfect." She placed them on the bed.

Oh, dear Mary, mother of God… I sat cross-legged on the floor. "Well, I think Daemon will approve, at least."

"Damn straight." She flopped on the bed, her grin fading. "Can I ask you something and you answer it honestly?" Warning bells went off, but I nodded. She took a deep breath. "Seriously, how good of a kisser is Daemon? Because I imagine he just makes you—"

"Lesa!"

"What? A girl's gotta know these kinds of things."

I bit my lip, flushing.

"Come on, it's sharing and caring time."

"He…he kisses like he's dying of thirst, and I'm water." I smacked my hands over my hot face. "I can't believe I just said that out loud."

Lesa giggled. "Sounds like one of those romance books you read."

"It does." I started giggling. "But, oh Lordie Lord, it's true. I'm like a puddle of mush when he kisses me. It's embarrassing. I'm so, like, 'Thank you, can I have another?' Sad."

We both broke into giggles. It was weird, because a lot of tension seeped out of my body. Giggling over boys was so amazingly normal.

"You love him, don't you?" she asked when she took a breath.

"I do." I stretched out my legs on a sigh. "I really do. What about Chad?"

She slipped off the bed and leaned against it. "I like him—a lot. But we're going to different colleges. So I'm being realistic about it."

"I'm sorry."

"Don't be. Chad and I are having fun and seriously, what's the point in anything if you ain't having fun? That's my motto in life." She paused, pushing her springy curls off her face. "I think I need to teach Dee that motto. What the hell is up with her? She still hasn't talked to me or Carissa."

All my humor vanished and I tensed up. *I can't fix our friendship.* I had tried—really tried—but the damages I inflicted on our friendship had been irreparable.

I sighed. "A lot of stuff has gone on with her—Adam and with Dawson coming home."

Lesa jumped on that. "Isn't that the strangest thing, though?"

"What do you mean?"

"Don't you think it's weird? You didn't live here then, but Beth and Dawson were like the Romeo and Juliet of West Virginia. I can't believe he hasn't heard from her."

Unease slid down my spine. "I don't know. What do you think?"

Lesa looked away, chewing on her bottom lip. "It's just weird. Like Dawson is way different now. He's all sullen and broody."

I struggled for something to say. "Well, he probably still cares for her and is upset about things not working out, and he misses Adam. You know, there's a lot going on there."

"I guess." She looked at me sideways. "Some people have been talking."

Instincts flared. "Talking about what?"

"Well, it's mostly been the usual suspects—Kimmy and them. But so many strange things have happened around here." She pushed to her feet and yanked her curls into a messy ponytail. "First, Beth and Dawson just drop off the face of the Earth. Then Sarah Butler dropped dead last summer."

Ice coated my skin. Sarah Butler had been in the wrong place at the wrong time. The night I'd been attacked by the Arum, Daemon had showed up and chased him off. Out of anger, the Arum had killed the girl.

Lesa started to pace. "And then Simon Cutters disappeared. No one has heard from him. Adam dies in a freak car accident, and then Dawson pops up out of nowhere, minus the supposed love of his life."

"It's weird," I said slowly, "but totally coincidental."

"Is it?" Her dark eyes gleamed. She shook her head. "Some of the kids—Simon's friends—think something's happened to him."

Oh, no. "Like what?"

"That he was killed." She sat beside me, her voice low as if people were listening. "And that Adam had something to do with it."

"What?" Okay, I was so not expecting that.

She nodded. "They don't think Adam's really dead. No funeral that anyone could go to and all. They think he ran off before the police could figure out he did something to Simon."

I stared. "Trust me, Adam's dead. He's really dead."

Lesa's lips pursed. "I believe you."

I didn't think she did. "Why do they think Adam had something to do with Simon?"

"Well…some people know that Simon tried something on you. And Daemon beat the crap out of him. Maybe he tried something on Dee and Adam snapped."

I laughed, more out of shock. "Adam wouldn't have snapped.

He wasn't like that."

"That's what I think, but others…" She leaned back. "Anyway, enough about this crap—you're going to look hot tomorrow night."

The conversation eventually went back to studying, but I had this icy feeling in the pit of my stomach, a piercing sensation. Like when you did something bad and knew you were about to get caught.

If people were starting to pay attention to all the weird stuff around here, how long would it take them to follow the clues back to the source of everything? Back to Daemon, his family, his kind, and to me?

Chapter 14

Martinsburg wasn't really a town, but it couldn't be called a city, either, at least not by Gainesville standards. It was on the cusp of growth, about an hour from the nation's capital. It rested right off the interstate, nestled between two mountains—a gateway to larger cities like Hagerstown and Baltimore. The south side of the town was heavily developed—shopping centers, restaurants I'd give my favorite book for Petersburg to have, and office buildings. There was even a Starbucks, and dammit if it didn't suck to have to drive past that. We were running late.

The whole trip started off badly, which didn't speak well for how the night would progress.

First off, Blake and Daemon had gotten into it before we even made it out of Petersburg. Something about the quickest way to get to the eastern panhandle of the state. Blake said to go south. Daemon said to go north. Epic argument ensued.

Daemon ended up winning, because he was driving, which made Blake pout in the backseat. Then we hit a snow squall around Deep Creek, slowing us down, and Blake had felt the need to point out that the southern roads were probably clear.

Also, the amount of obsidian I was decked out in and the lack of clothing had me all kinds of twitchy. I went with Lesa's choice in attire, much to Daemon's happiness. If he made one more comment about the length of my skirt, I was going to hurt him.

And if Blake did, Daemon was going to maim him.

I kept expecting a fleet of Arum to arrive out of the middle of nowhere and knock our vehicle off the road, but so far, the obsidian necklace, bracelet, and knife strapped inside my boot—*for crying out loud*—had stayed cool.

By the time we arrived in Martinsburg, I wanted to jump from the moving vehicle. As we neared the Falling Waters exit, Daemon asked, "Which one?"

Blake popped forward, dropping his elbows on the backs of our seats. "One more exit—Spring Mills. You're going to take a left off the exit, like you're heading back to Hedgesville or Back Creek."

Back Creek? I shook my head. We'd gone farther into civilization, but the names of some of these towns begged to differ.

About two miles off the exit, Blake said, "See the old gas station up ahead—the pumps?"

Daemon's eyes narrowed. "Yeah."

"Turn there."

I leaned forward to get a better view. Tall weeds surrounded old, worn-out pumps. There was a building—mostly a shack—behind them. "The club is in a gas station?"

Blake laughed. "No. Just drive around the building. Stay on the dirt road."

Muttering about getting Dolly dirty, Daemon followed Blake's sketchy directions. The dirt road was more like a path cleared by thousands of tires. This was so shady I wanted to demand we turn around.

The farther we went, the scarier the scenery got. Thick trees crowded the path, broken up by rundown buildings with boarded-up windows and empty black spaces where doors once stood.

"I don't know about this," I admitted. "I think I've seen all of this in *Texas Chainsaw Massacre*."

Daemon snorted. The SUV bumped over the uneven terrain, and then there were cars. Everywhere. Cars parked in haphazard lines, beside trees, crammed across a field. Beyond the endless rows of vehicles was a squat, square-shaped building with no outdoor lighting.

"Okay. I think I actually saw this in *Hostel*—One *and* Two."

"You'll be fine," Blake said. "The place is hidden so it stays off the grid, not because they kidnap and kill unsuspecting tourists."

I totally reserved the right to disagree on that.

Daemon parked as far away as he could, obviously more afraid of getting dings in Dolly's sides than us being eaten by Bigfoot.

A guy stumbled out from among a pack of cars. Moonlight glinted off his spiked collar and green Mohawk.

Or getting eaten by a goth kid.

I opened the door and climbed out, hugging my peacoat close. "What kind of place is this?"

"A very different kind of place," was Blake's answer. He slammed his door shut, and Daemon about snapped off his head. Rolling his eyes, Blake stepped around me. "You'll have to lose the jacket."

"What?" I glared at him. "It's freezing out. See my breath?"

"You're not going to freeze in the seconds it takes us to walk to the door. They're not going to let you in."

I felt like stomping my feet as I looked at Daemon helplessly. Like Blake, he was dressed in dark jeans and a shirt. Yep. That's all. Apparently, these people didn't care about the *male* dress code.

"I don't get it," I whined. My jacket was my saving grace. It was bad enough that the torn tights did nothing to hide my legs. "So not fair."

Daemon sauntered up to me, placing his hands on mine. A lock of wavy hair fell into his eyes. "We don't have to do this if you don't want to. I mean it."

"If she doesn't, then this was one huge time waster."

"Shut up," Daemon growled over his shoulder and then to me, "I'm serious. Tell me now, and we'll go home. There's got to be another way."

But there wasn't another way. Blake, God forgive me, was right. I was wasting time. Shaking my head, I stepped back and started unbuttoning my jacket. "I'm fine. Pulling on big girl undies and all that jazz."

Daemon watched quietly as I stripped away what felt like armor. My jacket off, he sucked in a low breath as I tossed it on the passenger seat. As cold as it was, my entire body somehow managed to feel like it was on fire.

"Yeah," he muttered, stepping in front of me like a shield. "I'm not so sure about this."

Over his shoulder, Blake's brows shut up. "Wow."

Daemon whipped around, arm flying out, but Blake darted to the left, narrowly missing Daemon's hand. Whitish-red sparks flew, lighting up the dark lot like firecrackers.

I crossed my arms over my bare midsection, exposed by the cropped sweater and the low-rise skirt. I felt naked, which was stupid, because I wore bathing suits. Shaking my head, I stepped around Daemon. "Let's get in there."

Blake's eyes drifted over me quickly enough to avoid certain death from the irritated alien behind me. My hand itched to smack his eyeballs out of the back of his head.

Our walk to the steel door at the corner of the building was quick. There were no windows or anything, but as we drew closer, the heavy beat of music could be felt outside.

"So do we knock—?"

Out of the shadows, a huge mother of a dude appeared. Arms like tree trunks were shown off by the torn overalls he wore. No shirt, because it was, like, a hundred degrees out here or something. The guy's hair was spiked into three sections across the center of his otherwise shaved skull. They were purple.

I liked purple.

I swallowed nervously.

Studs glinted all over his face: nose, lips, and eyebrows. Two thick bolts pierced his earlobes. He said nothing as he stopped in front of us, his dark eyes roaming over the guys and then stopping on me.

I took a step back, bumping into Daemon, who placed a hand on my shoulder.

"See something you like?" Daemon asked.

The dude was big—pro wrestler big—and he smirked like he was sizing Daemon up for dinner. And I knew Daemon was probably doing the same thing. The likelihood of us getting out of here without a massive brawl was slim.

Blake intervened. "We're here to party. That's all."

Pro Wrestler said nothing for a second and then reached for the door. Eyes fastened on Daemon, he opened the door and music blared. He gave a mocking bow. "Welcome to The Harbinger. Have fun."

The Harbinger? What a…lovely, reassuring name for a club.

Blake glanced over his shoulder and said, "I think he liked you, Daemon."

"Shut up," Daemon said.

Blake let out a low laugh and went in, and my legs carried me through a tight hallway that suddenly spilled into a different world. One full of shadowed enclaves and flashing strobe lights, and the smell alone was almost overwhelming. Not bad, but a potent mixture of sweat, perfume, and other questionable aromas. The bitter taste of alcohol was thick in the air.

Blue, red, and white lights streamed and dazzled over the teeming throng of undulating bodies in dizzying intervals. If I were prone to seizures, I'd be on the floor in a heartbeat. All the bare skin—mostly female—shimmered like the girls had been dusted with glitter. The dance floor was packed, bodies moving, some in rhythm, others just thrusting. Beyond it was a raised dance stage. A girl with long, blonde hair whirled in the center of the chaos; her slender body was short but she moved like a dancer, all graceful and fluid motions as she spun.

I couldn't take my eyes off her. She stopped spinning; her lower half still swayed in tune to the beat as she shoved the damp hair back. Her face was radiant with innocence, her smile beautiful and wide. She was young—too young to be in a place like this.

Then again, as my eyes scanned the crowd, a lot of the kids were definitely not of drinking age. Some were, but the vast majority looked like they were our age.

But the most interesting part was what was above the stage. Cages hung from the ceiling, occupied by scantily clad girls. *Go-go dancers* was what my mom would've called them. I wasn't sure what the name was now, but the chicks had on some kick-ass boots. The top halves of their faces were covered with glittery masks. All of them had hair that was all the colors of the rainbow.

I glanced down at the skin between my denim skirt and cropped sweater. Yeah, I really could've gone crazier.

Even stranger, there wasn't a table or set of chairs anywhere I could see. There were couches peeking out of the shadowed sidelines, but there was no way in hell I'd sit on those things.

Daemon's hand was firmly on my back as he bent over, speaking into my ear. "A little out of your element, Kitten?"

Funny thing was, Daemon still stood out in this crowd. He was a good head taller than most, and none of them moved like him or looked like him. "I think you should've gone with the eyeliner."

His lips quirked up. "Not ever going to happen."

Blake moved in front of us as we followed him around the dance floor, the fast techno beat easing off and another picking up, heavy on the drums.

Everyone stopped.

Fists suddenly shot into the air, followed by shouts, and my eyes widened. Was there going to be a mosh pit? A part of me kind of wanted to try that out. The angry beat may have had something to do with it. The cage girls slammed their hands against the bars. The pretty girl on the stage with all that blond hair had disappeared.

Daemon's hand slid to mine and squeezed. My ears strained to pick up the lyrics over the screams. *Safe from pain and truth and choice and other poison devils...* The yells picked up, drowning out everything except the drums.

The hair rose on the back of my neck.

There was definitely something up with this club. Not right... Not right at all.

We rounded the bar and entered a narrow hallway. People were against the walls, so close to one another I couldn't tell where one body began and another ended. A guy peered up from the neck he was busy with, and his heavily kohl-outlined eyes met mine.

He winked.

I quickly looked away. Note to self: do not make eye contact.

Before I knew it, we'd stopped at a door that read PERSONNEL ONLY, but the PERSONNEL part had been scratched out and someone had written FREAKS in permanent marker.

Nice.

Blake went to rap his knuckles on the door, but it cracked open first. I couldn't see who was behind it. I glanced over my shoulder. Kohl Eyes was still watching. Skeevy.

"We're here to see Luc," Blake said.

Whatever the mystery person behind the door said didn't look good, because Blake's spine went rigid. "Tell him it's Blake, and he owes me." There was a pause and the back of his neck flushed red. "I don't care what he's doing; I *need* to see him."

"Great," Daemon muttered, his body tensing and relaxing in

intervals. "He's friendless as usual."

Another garbled response and the door opened a little more. Then Blake growled, "Dammit, he owes me. These people are cool. Trust me. No bugs here."

Bugs? Oh, another word for implants.

Finally Blake turned to us, his brows drawn tightly. "He wants to talk to me first. Alone."

Daemon drew up to his full height. "Yeah, not gonna happen."

Blake didn't back down. "Then nothing's going to happen. Either you do as he wants and someone will come for you, or we made this trip for nothing."

I could tell Daemon wasn't cool with this, and I hadn't sat through the car ride from hell and brought out my inner stripper for nothing. Rising onto my toes, I pressed against his back. "Let's dance." Daemon turned halfway, eyes flashing. I tugged on his hand. "Come on."

He relented and as he turned completely, over his shoulder I saw the door open and Blake slid through. A bad feeling settled in my stomach, but there wasn't anything we could do now that we were here.

The drums had faded off, and a somewhat familiar song had started. Taking a deep breath, I pulled Daemon out to the floor, slipping around bodies as I searched out a spot. Finding one, I pivoted around.

He watched me curiously, almost like he was saying, *Are we really doing this?* We were. Dancing seemed crazy when so much rested on the information we'd come for, but I pushed away our reasons for coming here. Closing my eyes and drawing on courage, I stepped up to him, draped an arm around his neck, and placed my other hand on his waist.

I started to move against him, like the other dancers were, because in reality, when guys danced, they sort of just stood there and let the girls do all the work. If I remembered correctly from the few times I'd snuck off to clubs with friends in Gainesville, the girls made the guys look good.

It took a few seconds of stiffness to find the beat to the song and loosen up muscles that hadn't really seen any action recently, but when I did, the rhythm of the music resonated in my head and then through my body, my limbs. Swaying to the music, I whirled around and my shoulders moved with my hips. Daemon's arm crept around my waist, and I felt his chin graze my neck.

"Okay. I might have to thank Blake for being friendless," he said into my ear.

I smiled.

His arm tightened as the beat picked up and so did my movements. "I think I like this."

All around us, bodies were slick and shiny with sweat, as if they'd been dancing for years. That was the thing about places like this—you get caught up and hours go by but it only feels like long minutes.

Daemon spun me back to him, and I was on the tips of my boots, facing him. His head lowered, forehead pressing against mine, our lips brushing. A rush of power went through Daemon, transferring to my skin, and in the flashing lights, we were lost in this world. Our bodies surged with the beat, fitting together fluidly while others seemed to thrash beside us, never able to find the right sync.

When Daemon's lips pressed more firmly against mine, I opened up, not losing the rhythm even though he was stealing my breath. My—*our* hearts were pounding, hands grabbing, clutching, his slipping over the curve of my back, and behind my lids, I saw a pinprick of white light.

Sliding my hands across his cheeks, I kissed him back. Static flowed, cascading off our bodies in streams of reddish-white light that was hidden under the flickering strobe lights, flowing over the floor like a wave of electricity. And all around us, people danced, either oblivious to the shocks or fueled by them, but I didn't care. Daemon's hands were on my hips, tugging me closer, and we were so gonna end up like one of those ambiguous couples in the hallway.

The music may've stopped or changed or whatever, but we were still pressed together, practically devouring each other. And maybe later, tomorrow or next week, I might be embarrassed by the PDA, but not now.

A hand landed on Daemon's shoulder, and he whirled away. With a second to spare, I grabbed his arm, stopping his fist from saying hello to Blake's jaw.

Blake smiled and yelled over the blaring music, "Are you guys having sex or dancing?"

My cheeks flared. Okay, maybe right now I'd be embarrassed.

Daemon growled something and Blake took a step back, hands going up. "Sorry," he shouted. "Geez. He's ready to see us if you're done eating each other's faces."

Blake was going to get punched at some point.

Taking my hand again, I followed Daemon and Blake back through the snake-like bodies and down the hallway. My heart was still racing, my chest rising and falling too fast. That dance...

Kohl Eyes was gone and this time when Blake went to knock, the door opened all the way. I followed, hoping my face wasn't burning.

I'm not sure what I was expecting to find behind the door. Maybe a smoky, dark room with men wearing sunglasses, cracking their knuckles, or another big guy in overalls, but I wasn't expecting what I found.

The room was large and the air clean, vanilla-scented. There were several couches, one occupied by a boy with shoulder-length brown hair tucked back behind his ears. Like the girl I'd seen dancing earlier, he was young. Maybe fifteen, if that, and he had holes in his jeans the size of Mars. Around his wrist was a silver cuff that circled a strange stone. It was black, but not obsidian. In the center of the stone, there was a reddish-orange flame and below it, speckles of blue and green.

Whatever stone it was, it was beautiful and *expensive* looking.

The kid glanced up from the DS he was playing on, and I was kind of dumbstruck by his boyish beauty. Eyes the color of amethyst locked with mine briefly and then went back to the game. That kid was going to be a looker one day.

Then I realized Daemon had stiffened and was staring at a guy in a leather chair. Stacks of hundreds were splayed across the desk in front of an icy-blond guy who was staring back at Daemon, brilliant silver eyes wide with shock.

The guy was probably in his early thirties, and my God, he was gorgeous.

Daemon stepped forward. The guy stood. And my heart sped up. My worst fears spread through me like wildfire. "What's going on?" I asked. Even Blake seemed nervous.

The kid on the couch coughed out a laugh, closing his DS. "Aliens. They have this wacky internal system that lets them sniff each other out. Guess neither of them was expecting to see the other."

I turned to the kid slowly.

He sat up, swinging his legs off the couch. He would've had a baby face if it wasn't for the keen intelligence in his eyes or the experience set in the hard lines of his mouth. "So, you crazy kids want to break into the Daedalus stronghold and you want my help?"

I gaped. Luc was a mother-freaking *kid*.

Chapter 15

I waited for the kid to yell, "Psyche!" and scamper off to the nearest playground, but as the seconds stretched out, I came to accept that our messiah of information was barely a teen.

Luc smiled as if he knew what I was thinking. "Surprised? You shouldn't be. Surprised about anything, that is."

He stood, and I was shocked to discover that he was almost as tall as Daemon. "I was six when I decided to play chicken with a speeding cab. It won. Lost the coolest bike evah and a lot of blood, but lucky me, my childhood friend was an alien."

"How…how did you get away from Daedalus?" And so young, I wanted to add.

Luc moved over to the table, his steps smooth and effortless. "I was their star pupil." His grin was wicked, almost disturbing. "Never trust the one who excels. Isn't that right, Blake?"

Leaning against the wall, Blake gave a lopsided shrug. "Sounds about right."

"Why?" Luc sat on the edge of the desk. "Because eventually the pupil becomes smarter than the teacher, and I had some really,

really intelligent teachers. So." He clapped his hands together. "You must be Daemon Black."

If Daemon was surprised Luc knew his name, he didn't show it. "That would be me."

The kid's ridiculously long lashes lowered. "I've heard of you. Blake's a big fan."

Blake raised a middle finger.

Daemon said drily, "Glad to know my fan club is far reaching."

Luc cocked his head to the side. "And what a fan club—oh, my bad, I didn't introduce you to your fellow Luxen all-star. This guy goes by Paris. Why? I don't know."

Paris smiled tightly as he extended his hand toward Daemon. "Always nice to meet another not bound by old beliefs and unnecessary rules."

Daemon shook his hand. "Same. How did you fall in with him?"

Luc laughed. "Long story for a different day—if there is a different day." Those extraordinary peepers slid back to me. "Do you have any idea what they will do to you if they realize you're a fully functional hybrid?" He tipped his head down, grinning. "We are so very rare. Three of us together is actually quite amazing."

"I have a good imagination," I said.

"Do you?" Luc's brows rose. "I doubt Blake has even told you the half of it—the worst of it."

I glanced at Blake. His expression went on lockdown. An icy wind ran up my spine that had nothing to do with my lack of clothing.

"But you know that." Luc stood and stretched, like a cat after a nap. "And still you are willing to take the huge risk of going into the hornet's nest."

"We really don't have a choice." Daemon shot the quiet Blake a dark look. "So are you going to give us the codes or not?"

Luc shrugged, running his fingers over the stacks of money. "What's in it for me?"

I exhaled roughly. "Other than pissing off Daedalus, we really don't have much to offer."

"Hmm, I don't know about that." He picked up a cluster of hundreds secured with a rubber band. A second later, the edges of the bills curled inward, paper melting until the scorched scent filled the air and nothing remained.

I was envious, considering the whole using-light-for-heat-and-fire thing completely passed me over. "What can we do for you?"

"Obviously money's not an issue," Daemon added.

Luc's lips twitched. "Money isn't needed." He brushed his fingers off on his jeans. "Power isn't, either. Honestly, the only thing I need is a favor."

Blake snapped off the wall. "Luc—"

His eyes narrowed. "A favor is all I want—one that I can collect at any time. That's what I want in return, and I'll give you all you need to know."

Well, that sounded easy. "O—"

"Wait," Daemon cut me off. "You want us to agree to a favor without knowing what that favor is?"

Luc nodded. "Where's the risk if you know everything?"

"Where's the intelligence if we don't?" Daemon shot back.

The kid laughed. "I like you. A lot. But my help doesn't come without its own peril in exchange."

"God, you're like the preteen mafia," I muttered.

"Something like that." He flashed a beatific smile. "What you—all of you—don't understand is there are things much, much bigger than a brother's girlfriend or a friend...or even ending up under the man's thumb. There's change brewing behind the winds, and the winds are going to be fierce." He looked at Daemon. "The government fears the Luxen, because they represent mankind's fall from the top of the food chain. To fix that, they've created something much stronger than a Luxen. And I'm not talking about ordinary little baby hybrids."

I shivered. "What are you talking about?"

His purplish eyes met mine, but he said nothing.

Paris folded his arms. "Not to be rude, but if you're not willing to deal, there's the door."

Daemon and I exchanged looks. I honestly didn't know what to say. It seriously was like making a deal with the mafia—with a creepy kid-mafia boss.

"Guys," Blake said. "He's our only chance."

"Christ," Daemon muttered. "Fine. We owe you a favor."

Luc's eyes gleamed. "And you?"

I sighed. "Sure. Why not."

"Awesome! Paris?" He held out his hand. Paris bent down, grabbed a small MacBook Air, and handed it over. "Give me a sec."

We watched him punch away at the keyboard, brows drawn in concentration. While we waited, a door at the back of the room opened and the young girl from the stage peeked her head into the room.

Luc's head jerked up. "Not now."

The girl's frown was epic, but she closed the door. "She's the girl on—"

"Don't finish that sentence if you want me to continue. Don't even talk about her. Frankly, you've never even seen her," Luc said, eyes fastened on the screen again. "All deals will be off."

I clamped my mouth shut even though I had a thousand questions about how the two of them got away and how they were surviving virtually unprotected.

Finally, Luc placed the laptop on the desk. The screen was split into four sections, black and white, also grainy, like security film. One image contained woods. Another was of a tall fence and gate, the other a security booth, and the final one showed a man in uniform patrolling another section of fence.

"Say hello to Mount Weather—owned by FEMA, secured by Homeland Security. Nestled away in the majestic Blue Ridge

Mountains, it's used as a training facility and a stowaway for all the pretty officials in case someone bombs us," Luc said, snickering. "Also known as a complete front for the DOD and Daedalus, because underground, there are six-hundred thousand mother-effin' square feet for training and torture."

Blake stared at the screen. "You hacked into their security systems?"

He shrugged. "Like I said, star pupil and all. See this section here." He pointed to the screen where a guard patrolled the fence, almost blending into the grainy background. "This is the 'secret' entrance that doesn't exist. Very few people are aware of it— Blakey-boy is."

Luc tapped the space bar, and the camera moved to the right. A gate came into view. "Here's the dealio: Sunday evening at nine p.m. is going to be your best bet. It's a shift change and staffing is at a minimum—only two guards will be patrolling this gate. 'Cause, you know, Sunday is kind of a down day."

Paris whipped out a pad and a pen.

"This gate is your first obstacle of choice. You'll need to take out the guards, but that's a duh. I'll make sure the cameras are down between nine and nine fifteen—you know, pull a *Jurassic Park* moment. You'll have fifteen minutes to get in, get your buddies, and get the hell out. So don't let a spitting dragon take you down."

Daemon choked on a laugh.

"Fifteen minutes," Blake murmured, nodding. "Doable. Once inside the compound, the entrance leads to elevators. We can take them down to the tenth floor and go right up to the cell."

"Great." Luc tapped his finger on the gate. "The code to this gate is *Icarus*. See a trend?" He laughed. "You get inside the compound, you'll see three doors side by side."

Blake nodded again. "The middle door—I know. The code?"

"Wait. Where do the other doors take you?" I asked.

"To the great Oz," Luc said, tapping the space bar until the camera was now focused on the doors. "Actually, nowhere interesting. Just offices and actual FEMA stuff. Anyone want to guess what the code to this door is?"

"Daedalus?" I threw out.

He grinned. "Close. The code to this door is *Labyrinth*. It's a hard word to spell, I know, but make sure you do it correctly. You get one chance. Enter the wrong code and it'll get ugly. Take the elevator to the sixth floor like Blake said and then you enter the code *DAEDALUS*—all caps. *Voilà!*"

Daemon shook his head, doubtful. "There're only codes to enter? That's their security?"

"Ha!" Luc hit a few buttons and the screen went black. "I'm doing more than giving you codes and taking down cameras, my new BFF. I'm going to take down their eye recognition software. It can go down for about ten to fifteen minutes a day without raising an eyebrow."

"What happens if we're still in there and it goes back up?" I asked.

Luc raised his hands. "Uh, kind of like being on a plane that's about to crash. Stick your head between your knees and kiss 'em good-bye."

"Oh, that sounds great," I said. "So you're like a mutant hacker, too?"

He winked. "But be careful. I'm not taking down any other security precautions they may've decided to put up. *That* will raise concerns."

"Whoa." Daemon frowned. "What other security precautions could they have?"

"They rotate the codes every other day, I've discovered. Other than that, nothing but guards, but it's a shift change." Blake grinned. "We'll be fine. We got this."

Paris handed over a sheet with the codes scribbled down.

Daemon snatched it before Blake could and slipped it into his pocket. "Thank you," he said.

Returning to the couch and his DS, Luc dropped down, his smile fading. "Don't thank me yet. Actually, don't thank me at all. I don't exist, you know, not until I need my favor." He flipped open his DS. "Just remember, this Sunday at nine p.m. You have fifteen minutes and that is all."

"Okay." I drew out the word, glancing at Blake. I would love to know how these two met. "Well, I guess…"

"We'll be going," Daemon supplied, taking my hand. "It was nice, kind of, meeting you all."

"Whatevs," he said, thumbs flying over the game board. Luc's voice stopped us at the door. "You have no idea what waits for you. Be careful. I would hate for my dealing to be one-sided if you all get yourselves killed…or worse."

I shuddered. Nice way to close the conversation with a healthy dose of freak-us-out.

Daemon nodded at the other Luxen, and we headed out, Blake closing the door behind him. Only then did I realize the room was soundproof.

"Well," Blake said, smiling. "That wasn't too bad, was it?"

I rolled my eyes. "I have the feeling we just made a deal with the devil, and he's going to come back and want our firstborn child or something."

Daemon waggled his brows. "You want kids? Because you know, practice makes—"

"Shut up." I shook my head and started walking.

We hurried through the club, around the still-packed dance floor. I think all of us were ready to get out of there. As we neared the exit, I looked around Daemon and Blake, my eyes drifting over the dance floor.

Part of me wondered how many, if any, were hybrids. We were rare, but like I sensed at first, there was something different about this place. Something really different about the kid called Luc, too.

Pro Wrestler greeted us at the door. He stepped aside, massive arms folded across his chest. "Remember," he said. "You were never here."

Chapter 16

We got home late from Martinsburg, and I went straight to bed. Daemon followed, but all we did was curl up and sleep. Both of us were exhausted from everything, and it was nice with him there, a steady presence that relaxed and soothed my frazzled nerves.

I was a zombie on Thursday, and Blake's disgustingly chipper attitude in bio made me want to hurl.

"You should be happier," he whispered as I hastily scribbled down notes. No doubt I'd failed the exam yesterday. "After Sunday, everything will be over."

Everything will be over. My pen stopped. A muscle in my neck tensed. "It won't be easy."

"Yes, it will be. You just need faith."

I almost laughed. Faith in who? Blake? Or the mafia kid? I didn't trust either of them. "After Sunday, you'll be gone."

"Like the last decade," he replied.

After class, I packed up my stuff, smiled at something Lesa said, and then waited for Dawson. I didn't like to leave him alone with Blake. Not when Dawson was eyeballing the dude like he wanted to pummel information out of him.

Blake brushed past us, grinning as he switched his books to his other hand. He swaggered on down the hall, waving at a group of kids that called out his name.

"I don't like him," Dawson grumbled.

"Get in line." We headed down the hall. "But we need him until Sunday."

Dawson stared ahead. "Still don't like him." And then he asked, "He had a thing for you, didn't he?"

My cheeks burned. "What makes you think that?"

A small smile appeared. "My brother's hate for him knows no bounds."

"Well, he did kill Adam," I said in a low voice.

"Yeah, I know, but it's personal."

I frowned. "How is it more personal than that?"

"It is." Dawson pushed open the door, and we were attacked by the giggle squad on the landing.

Kimmy was captain. "Wow. Why aren't I surprised?"

I found myself moving in front of Dawson. "And why do I have no clue what you're talking about?"

Behind me, Dawson shifted his weight from one foot to the other.

"Well, it's pretty obvious." She leaned against the rail, her backpack resting on the top. Around her, the girls tittered. "One brother isn't enough for you."

Before I could react, Dawson stepped around me and spat, "You're sad and revolting."

Kimmy's smile froze, and maybe the old Dawson would've never said anything like that, because she and all her friends looked like someone just walked over their graves. Somewhere, in the back of my mind, I wanted to laugh, but I was so angry—so repulsed by the suggestion I'd be seeing two twin brothers.

I honestly don't know what happened next. A pulse of energy

left me, and the pretty pink backpack shook and then tipped over the railing. The weight jerked Kimmy. Her heeled shoes came off the floor, and in a flash I saw what was going to happen.

She was going to go right over the railing, headfirst.

A scream started in my throat and came out of Kimmy. Her friends' horrified looks were permanently etched in my memory, and my heartbeat skyrocketed.

Dawson shot forward, catching one of her flailing arms. He had her on her feet before her scream had faded from my ears. "I got you," he said, surprisingly gentle. Kimmy gulped in air, clutching Dawson's hand. "It's okay. You're okay."

He carefully pried her fingers off his and stepped back. Her friends immediately surrounded her. Then he turned to me, his eyes clouded. Cupping my elbow, he quickly steered me down the stairwell.

As soon as we were out of hearing distance, he stopped and faced me. "What was that?"

My breath caught and I looked away, confused and full of shame. Everything had happened so fast, and I'd been so furious. But it had been me—a part of me that had acted without thought or knowledge. A part of me that had known the weight of her bag would've toppled her right over the edge.

• • •

At lunch, I didn't tell Daemon about what happened with Kimmy in the stairwell, convincing myself that since Carissa and Lesa were with us, it was so not the conversation to have. It was nothing more than an excuse, but I felt as revolting as Kimmy's words. Later that day, when we were at Daemon's house, going over plans for Sunday with the crew, I told myself it still wasn't the time.

Especially when Dee was demanding to go and Daemon was having none of that.

"I need you and Ash to hang back, along with Matthew, just in case something goes wrong."

Dee folded her arms. "What, you don't think I can handle myself with you guys? That I might trip and stab Blake to death?"

Her brother shot her a bland look. "Well, now that you say it..."

She rolled her eyes. "Is Katy going in with you?"

My shoulders slumped. *Here we go.*

Daemon's body tensed. "I don't want—"

"Yes." I cut him off with a deadly look. "Only because I got most of us into this mess, and Blake won't do any of this without Daemon and me."

Ash smirked from the settee. Other than staring at Daemon like she wanted to rekindle their romance, she wasn't doing or saying much. "How valiant of you, Katy."

I ignored her. "But we do need people on the outside in case something goes wrong."

"What?" Andrew asked. "You don't trust Blake? Go figure."

Daemon sat back, running both his hands through his hair. "Anyway, we'll be in and out. Then everything...everything will be over."

His brother blinked slowly, and I knew he was thinking about Beth. Maybe even picturing her, and I wondered how long it had been since he last saw her. So I asked and surprisingly, he answered.

"I don't know. Time there was different. Weeks? Months?" He stood, shoulders rolling. "I don't think I was at that Mount place. The place was always warm and dry whenever I was taken outside."

Taken outside, like a pet or something. Wrong on so many levels.

Dawson let out a ragged breath. "I need to walk or move."

I looked around quickly. The sun had set a while ago. Not like he needed it, though. He was already out the door before anyone could say a thing.

"I'll go." It was Dee this time.

Andrew stood. "I'll follow."

"I guess I'm out of here." This from Ash.

Matthew sighed. "One of these days, we will get through everything without any drama."

Daemon laughed tiredly. "Good luck with that."

In about five minutes, everyone except Daemon was cleared out of the house. Perfect time to 'fess up to almost breaking Kimmy's neck, except there was a glint in Daemon's jade-colored eyes.

My mouth dried. "What?"

Daemon stood and stretched, flashing a slice of taut skin. "It's quiet." He offered his hand and I took it in mine. "It's never quiet around here. Not anymore."

He did have a point. I let him tug me to my feet. "It's not going to last long."

"Nope." He pulled me to him and a second later, I was in his arms and we were zooming up the stairs. He placed me on my feet in his bedroom. "Admit it. You like my method of travel."

Feeling a little dizzy, I laughed. "One of these days I'm going to be faster than you."

"Keep dreaming."

"Tool," I threw back.

Daemon's lips curved up on one side. "Trouble."

"Oh." I widened my eyes. "Harsh."

"We should make use of this quiet time." He advanced toward me, like a predator with its prey in its sight.

"Really?" Suddenly feeling way too hot, I backed up until I hit his bed.

"Really." He kicked off his shoes. "I say we have about thirty minutes before someone interrupts us."

My gaze dropped as he pulled off his shirt and tossed it. I sucked in a sharp breath. "Probably not that long."

His lips formed a wicked smile. "True. So let's say we have twenty minutes, give or take five." He stopped in front of me, his eyes hooded. "Not nearly enough time for what I'd like to do, but we can work around that."

Heat swept through my veins, and I felt dizzy again. "We can?"

"Mmm-hmm." He placed his hands on my shoulders and pressed down until I was sitting on the very edge of the bed. Running his hands to my cheeks, he knelt between my boneless legs so that we were eye level with each other.

Daemon's lashes lowered, fanning his cheeks. "I've missed you."

I wrapped my fingers around his wrists. "You've seen me every day."

"Not enough," he murmured and pressed his lips where my pulse pounded along my neck. "And we're always with someone."

God, wasn't that the truth. Last time we were alone for any considerable amount of time, we'd both slept. So these moments were precious, brief, and stolen.

I smiled as he trailed a line of kisses up my chin, stopping short of my lips. "We probably shouldn't spend it talking, then."

"Uh-huh." He kissed a corner of my lips. "Talking is such a time waster." And then he kissed the other corner. "And when we talk, we usually end up arguing."

I laughed. "Not always."

Daemon pulled back, brows raised. "Kitten…"

"Okay." I scooted back and he followed, climbing over me, his arms huge and powerful. God, I was in way over my head with him sometimes. "You might be right, but you're wasting time."

"I'm always right."

I opened my mouth to disagree, but his lips took control of mine, and his kiss reached deep down inside me, melted muscle and bone. His tongue swept over mine, and at that moment, he could have been right all he wanted as long as he kept kissing me like that.

I slid my fingers through his hair, tugging when he lifted his head. I started to protest, but he was kissing his way down my throat, over the edge of my cardigan, down the little buttons shaped like flowers, and lower still, until I couldn't keep ahold of his head. Or really keep track of where he was heading.

Daemon sat back on his haunches, going for my boots. He tugged one off, pitching it over his shoulder. It bounced off the wall with a soft *thud*. "What are these made of? Rabbit skin?"

"What?" I giggled. "No. They're faux sheepskin."

"They're so soft." He got the other one off and that too hit the wall. My socks were next. He kissed the top of my foot, and I jerked. "Not as soft as this, though." Grinning, he lifted his head. "Love the tights, by the way."

"Yeah?" My gaze fixed on the ceiling, but I really wasn't seeing a damn thing. Not when his hands moved up my calves. "Is it… because they're red?"

"That." I felt his cheek on my knee, and my hands fluttered to the bed. "And because they're so thin. And hot, but you already know that."

Hot? I felt hot. His hands traveled up my outer thighs, under the denim skirt, pushing the material up and up. I bit down on my lip, hard enough that a metallic taste sprung into my mouth. The material really was thin, a fragile almost nonexistent barrier between his skin and mine. I could feel every touch, and even the slightest was like a thousand volts of electricity.

"Kitten…"

"Hmm?" I fisted the covers.

"Just making sure you're still with me." He kissed the side of my leg, right above my knee. "Don't want you falling asleep or anything."

Like sleep was possible. Ever.

His eyes flared. "You know what. Give me two minutes. That's all I need."

"Whatever," I said. "What are you going to do with the leftover eighteen minutes?"

"Snuggle."

I started to laugh, but his fingers found the band along the top of my tights, and he pulled them down, cursing when they got tangled at my feet.

"Need help?" I offered, voice shaking.

"Got it," he muttered, balling them up. They too went flying somewhere.

Things were going further than they had before. I was nervous, but I didn't want to stop. I was too curious, and I trusted him irrevocably. And then there was nothing separating his hands from my skin or his lips and I stopped thinking, wasn't capable of forming any coherent thought. There was just him and the crazy rush of sensations he pulled forth, drew from me like an artist rendering some kind of masterpiece. Then I wasn't even me anymore, because my body couldn't shake that much. Like a balloon being pulled down and then released, I was floating and there was a soft whitish glow slipping over the walls that wasn't coming off Daemon.

When I came back down, Daemon's eyes were brilliant diamonds. He looked sort of awed, which I found strange, because he awed me.

"You glowed a little," he said, rising up. "I've only seen you do that once."

I knew the night, but I didn't want to think about that right now. I was happy where I was floating. It was good—great, even, and I really couldn't talk. My brain was mush. I had no idea *that* could be like that. Heck, I was shocked it even happened. I felt like I needed to say thank you or something.

The smile he gave me was part male pride and arrogance, like he knew he'd scrambled my brain. He stretched out beside me, tugging me close to him. He lowered his head, kissing me softly, deeply.

"Wasn't even two minutes," he said. "Told you."

My heart was somewhere in my throat. "You were right."

"Always."

Chapter 17

Sometime later, I tried to stretch and when I spoke, my voice was muffled against his chest. "I can't move."

His laugh rumbled through me as he loosened his embrace. "This is how we snuggle."

"I really should head next door soon." I yawned, not wanting to leave. I was so relaxed I couldn't feel my toes. "Mom will be home soon."

"Do you have to leave now?"

I shook my head. We had maybe an hour. I wanted to make her dinner, so another thirty or forty minutes tops. Daemon placed a finger on my chin and lifted it. "What?" I asked.

His eyes searched mine. "I wanted to talk before you leave."

Anxiety blossomed low. "About what?"

"Sunday," he said, and my anxiety turned darker. "I know you feel like you got us into this, but you know you didn't, right?"

"Daemon…" I so knew where this conversation was heading. "We are at this point because of the decisions I—"

"We," he corrected gently. "Decisions *we* made."

"If I hadn't trained with Blake and had listened to you, we wouldn't be here. Adam would be alive. Dee wouldn't hate my guts. Will wouldn't be running around doing God knows what." I squeezed my eyes shut. "I could go on and on. You get my drift."

"And if you hadn't made any of those decisions, we wouldn't have Dawson back. It was kind of a stupid-smart move."

I laughed drily. "There's that."

"You can't carry this guilt with you, Kat." The bed moved as he rose up on one elbow. "You'll end up like me."

I peeked at him. "What? An extremely tall and douchey alien?"

He smiled. "The jerky part, yes. I blamed myself for what happened to Dawson. It changed me. I'm still not back to where I was before everything happened. Don't do that to yourself."

Harder said than done, but I nodded. Last thing I wanted was for Daemon to worry about the possibility of my future therapy bills. And it was time to get to what I knew he wanted. "You don't want me going Sunday."

Daemon took a deep breath. "Hear me out, okay?" When I nodded, he continued. "I know you want to help, and I know you can. I've seen what you're capable of. You can be pretty scary when mad."

He has no idea, I thought wryly.

"But…if things go south, I don't want you involved." His gaze held mine. "I want you to be somewhere safe."

I knew where he was coming from and I wanted to reassure him, but staying behind wasn't something I could do. "I don't want *you* involved, Daemon. I want *you* somewhere safe, but I'm not asking you to stay out of it."

His brows knitted. "That's different."

I sat up, smoothing out my sweater. "How's that different? And if you say it's because you're a guy, I'm going to hurt you."

"Come on, Kitten."

My eyes narrowed.

He sighed. "It's more than that. It's because I have experience. That simple. You don't."

"Okay, you have a point, but I've also been *inside* a cage. With that intimate knowledge, I have more reason than you not to get caught."

"And that's more of a reason why I don't want you doing this." His eyes flared an intense green. A sure sign he was seconds from tapping into his protective-fueled temper. "You have no idea what went through my head when I saw you in that cage—when I hear how your voice *still* rasps when you get excited or upset. You screamed until there—"

"I don't need a reminder," I snapped, and then cursed under my breath. I tried to rein in my own temper. I put my hand on his arm. "One of the things I love about you is how protective you are, but it also drives me crazy. You can't protect me forever."

His look said he could and would try.

I exhaled roughly. "I need to do this—I need to help Dawson and Beth."

"And Blake?" he asked.

"What?" I stared at him. "Where did that come from?"

"I don't know." He moved his arm away from me. "It doesn't matter. Can—"

"Wait. It does matter. Why would I want to help Blake after what he pulled? He killed Adam! I wanted him dead. You were the one who was, like, turning over a new leaf or something."

The moment those words left my mouth, I regretted them. His expression went on lockdown.

"I'm sorry," I said, meaning it. "I know why you didn't want to…do away with Blake, but I have to do this. It'll help me get past what I caused. Like making amends or something."

"You don't—"

"I do."

Daemon turned his cheek, jaw clenching. "Can you do this for me? Please?"

My chest ached, because when Daemon said please, which was rare, I knew how much something bothered him. "I can't."

Seconds passed and his shoulders tensed. "This is stupid. You shouldn't be doing this. All I'm going to worry about is you getting hurt."

"See? That's the problem! You can't always be worried about my getting hurt."

His brow arched. "You're *always* getting hurt."

My mouth dropped open. "I am not!"

He laughed. "Yeah, try that again."

I pushed at him, but he was a wall of immovable muscle. Infuriated, I scrambled over him, even more furious when I saw the humored glint in his eyes. "God, you tick me off."

"Well, at least I got you—"

"Don't even finish that statement!" I snatched up my socks and tights. Rolling them on, I hobbled on one foot. "Ugh, I hate you sometimes."

He sat up in one fluid motion. "Not too long ago, you were really, *really* loving me."

"Shut up." I moved on to the other leg. "I'm going with you guys on Sunday. That's it. End of discussion."

Daemon stood. "I don't want you going."

I wiggled up my tights, glaring at him. "You don't get to say what I can and can't do, Daemon." I grabbed one of my boots, wondering how it got all the way over there. "I'm not a frail, helpless heroine in need of your rescue."

"This isn't a book, Kat."

I yanked on my other boot. "No, really? Crap. I was hoping you skipped to the end and would tell me what happens. I actually love spoilers."

Spinning around, I left and went downstairs. Of course, he was a step behind me, one giant shadow. We made it outside when he stopped me.

"After everything that went down with Blake, you said you wouldn't doubt me," he said. "That you would trust my decisions, but you're doing it again. Not listening to me or common sense. And when this blows up in your face *again*, what am I supposed to do then?"

I gasped, backing up. "That's… That was a low blow."

He placed his hands on his hips. "It's the truth."

Tears stung my eyes, and it took a couple of seconds to get the next words out. "I know all of this is coming from a good place, but I don't need a friendly reminder of how badly I screwed up. I totally know. And I'm trying to fix that."

"Kat, I'm not trying to be a dick."

"I know, it just comes easily to you." Headlights peeked through the fog, coming up the road. My voice was hoarse when I spoke next. "I've got to go. Mom's home."

I hurried down the steps and across the gravel and hard, frozen ground. Before I reached my own porch, Daemon appeared. Stopping short, I sputtered, "I hate when you do that."

"Think about what I said, Kat." His gaze flickered over my shoulder. Mom's car was almost here. "You have nothing to prove."

"I don't?"

Daemon said no, but it didn't seem like it when he said he expected everything to blow up in my face again.

• • •

Tossing and turning, my brain wouldn't shut down. I replayed everything that had gone down from the point I'd stopped the branch in front of Blake to the moment I found Simon's bloodied watch in his truck. How many times had there been signs that he was more than what he said he was? Too many. And how many times had Daemon stepped in and tried to talk me out of training with Blake? Too many.

I flipped onto my back, squeezing my eyes shut.

And what had he meant about Blake? Did he really think I wanted to help him and for what purpose? The last thing I wanted to do was breathe the same air as Blake. There was no way Daemon could be jealous. No. No. No. I'd have to spin kick him in the face if that was the case. And then cry, because if he doubted me...

I couldn't even think about that.

Only one good thing had come from the mess—Dawson. But everything else was... Well, it was the reason I couldn't sit back and twiddle my thumbs.

I turned onto my side, punched my pillow, and forced my eyes to stay closed.

At the crack of dawn, I drifted off for what felt like seconds to only face the sun creeping through my bedroom window a minute later. Pulling myself out of bed, I showered and changed.

A dull ache had taken up residency behind my eyes. By the time I got to school and grabbed my books out of my locker, it hadn't faded like I'd hoped. I shuffled into trig and checked my phone for the first time since last night.

No messages.

I dropped the phone back into my bag and rested my chin in my hands. Lesa was the first one in.

Her nose wrinkled when she spotted me. "Ew. You look terrible."

"Thanks," I muttered.

"You're welcome. Carissa has the bird flu or something. Hope you don't have it."

I almost laughed. Since Daemon had healed me, I hadn't even sneezed once. And according to Will, once mutated, you couldn't get sick, which was why he had tried to force Daemon to mutate him.

"Maybe," I said.

"Probably that club you went to." She shivered.

Warmth danced along my neck, and I averted my eyes like a wuss as Daemon took his seat behind me. I knew he was staring at me. He didn't say anything for about sixty-two seconds. I counted them.

He poked me in the back with his trusty pen.

I twisted around, keeping my face blank. "Hey."

A single brow arched. "You look well-rested."

He, on the other hand, looked like he normally did. Freaking perfect. "Got tons of sleep last night. You?"

Daemon popped the pen behind his ear and leaned forward. "I slept for about an hour. I think."

I lowered my gaze. I wasn't happy that last night sucked for him, too, but at least it meant he was thinking about it. I started to ask, but he shook his head. "What?" I said.

"I haven't changed my mind, Kitten. I was hoping you had." "No," I said, and the bell rang. One last meaningful look, and I turned around. Lesa shot me a weird expression, and I shrugged. Wasn't like I could explain why we were only exchanging a few syllables today. That would be an entertaining conversation.

When the bell rang, I debated on making a run for the door but reconsidered when two denim-clad legs filled my peripheral vision. I couldn't stop the tumbling my stomach did, even when I was angry with him.

I was such a loser.

Daemon didn't say anything as we left or when we parted ways, and after each class he appeared out of freaking nowhere. The same happened before bio, and he walked with me up the stairs, eyes scanning over the heads of the students.

"What are you doing?" I asked, finally tired of the silence.

He shrugged his broad shoulders. "Just thought I'd do the gentlemanly thing and walk you to your classes."

"Uh-huh."

There was no response, so I peeked at him. His eyes were narrowed and his lips pinched like he'd just eaten something sour. I went up on my tiptoes and bit back a curse. Blake was leaning against the wall next to the door, head tilted toward us, a cocky smile on his face.

"I dislike him so very much," Daemon muttered.

Blake pushed off the wall and swaggered over to us. "You guys look chipper for a Friday."

Daemon tapped a textbook on his thigh. "Do you have a reason to be standing here?"

"This is my class." He jerked his chin toward the open door. "With Katy."

Heat blew off Daemon as he took a step forward, staring down his nose at Blake. "You just love to push it, don't you?"

Blake swallowed nervously. "I don't know what you're talking about."

Daemon laughed, and it sent shivers down my spine. Sometimes I forgot how dangerous he could be. "Please. I may be a lot of things—a lot of really bad things, Biff, but stupid and blind aren't two of them."

"All right," I said, keeping my voice low. People were staring. "Time to play nice."

"I have to agree." Blake glanced around. "But this isn't a playground."

Daemon arched a brow. "You don't wanna play, Barf, because we can do that nifty freeze thing and play, right here and now."

Oh, for the love of backwoods babies everywhere, this wasn't necessary. I wrapped my fingers around Daemon's tense arm. "Come on," I whispered.

A second stretched out and static jumped from his arm to mine. Slowly, he looked at me and then he bent down, planting his lips on mine. The kiss was unexpected—deep and forceful. Stunned, I just stood there as he pulled back, nipping at my bottom lip.

"Tasty, Kitten." Then he spun, planted his right hand on Blake's shoulder, knocking him back into a locker. "See you around," he said, smirking.

"Jesus," Blake muttered, straightening. "He has anger management problems."

The faces gaping at us blurred.

Clearing his throat, Blake slid past me. "You should really head in."

I nodded, but when the warning bell rang, I was still standing there, my fingers placed against my lips.

Chapter 18

By lunch, Daemon's mood was somewhere between brooding and evil. He had half the student body frightened to death of crossing his path or breathing in the same air as him. I couldn't fathom what had his undies in a bunch. It couldn't be our argument carrying over this badly.

When he got up to grab his third helping of milk, Lesa sat back and let out a low whistle. "What is his deal?"

"I don't know," I said, pushing a lump of meat around my plate. "It must be his time of the month."

Chad barked out a laugh. "Yeah, not going there."

Lesa grinned at her boyfriend. "If you know what's wise for you, you won't."

"What's wise?" Daemon asked as he sat down.

"Nothing," the three of us said at the same time.

He frowned.

The rest of the afternoon went by way too fast and every so often the bottom of my stomach would drop. One more day—Saturday—and we were going to try the impossible. Break into

Mount Weather and rescue Beth and Chris. What were we going to do with them if we succeeded? Not *if—when* we did, I quickly corrected myself.

On the way out, my cell vibrated. A quick check left a bitter taste in my mouth. I wished Blake would lose my phone number.

We need to talk.

Gritting my teeth, I texted back: *Y*

The response was immediate: *Abt Sunday.*

"Who put that scary look on your face?" Daemon asked, out of the blue.

Squealing, I jumped. "Good God, where did you come from?"

He grinned, which would've been a good thing considering his mood all day, but it only made me wary. "I'm quiet like a cat."

I sighed, showing him my phone. "Blake. He wants to talk about Sunday."

Daemon growled. "Why is he texting you?"

"Probably because he knows you want to do him bodily harm."

"And you don't?"

I shook my head. "He's obviously less afraid of me."

"Maybe we need to change that?" He dropped an arm over my shoulders, tucking me against his side as we headed out into the bitter February wind. "Tell him we'll talk tomorrow."

My body warmed against his. "Where?"

"My house," he replied with that evil smile. "If he has balls, he'll be there."

I made a yuck face but texted it back to Blake. "Why not tonight?"

Daemon's lips pursed. "We need some quality time alone." Quality time like yesterday's quality time? Because I could so get behind that, but we really needed to talk a few things through. Before I could broach that topic, Blake responded and tomorrow evening was a go.

"Did you drive by yourself today?" I asked.

He shook his head, eyes fixed on a stand of trees. "Came in with Dee. Was hoping we could do something normal. Like an afternoon matinee."

Half of me did a happy dance. The other more responsible part put on the schoolteacher's glasses and broke out the ruler. Annoying adult Katy won. "That sounds great, but don't you think we need to talk about last night?"

"About my giving nature?"

My cheeks flamed. "Um, no... After that."

There was a flicker of a smile. "Yeah, I kind of knew that. Make you a deal. We'll do the movies, and then we'll talk, okay?"

It was a good deal, so I agreed. And honestly, I loved getting to do normal things with Daemon—like going out. It was a rarity. He let me pick the movie, and I went with a rom-com. Surprisingly, he didn't complain. Might've had something to do with the huge bucket of popcorn we were stuffing our faces with in between the buttery kisses.

It was all so divinely normal.

• • •

Divinely normal ended the moment we got to his house and he stepped out of his car, eyes narrowing. All the lights were on. Dee wasn't about conserving energy, it appeared.

"Kat, I think you should go home."

"Huh?" I closed the car door, frowning. "I thought we were going to talk? And eat ice cream—you promised ice cream."

He chuckled under his breath. "I know, but I have company."

I planted myself in front of the porch steps. "What kind of company?"

"The Luxen kind," he said, placing his hands on my shoulders. His eerily bright green eyes met mine. "Elders."

Must be nice to have a wacky internal sensing system like that.

"And I can't come in?"

"I don't think that's a good idea." He glanced as I heard a door open. "And I don't think that's an option."

I looked over my shoulder. A man stood at the door—a distinguished-looking man. Three-piece suit and all, with midnight black hair that was silver at the temples. I didn't know what I was expecting from an Elder Luxen. Maybe a guy with a white gown and bald head—they did live in a colony at the foot of Seneca.

This was totally unexpected.

Even more so was the fact that Daemon didn't drop his hands and put appropriate alien-human distance between us. Instead, he whispered in his own language and slid a hand down my back as he stepped beside me.

"Ethan," Daemon said. "I wasn't expecting you."

The man's startling violet eyes slid toward me. "I can see. Is this the *girl* that your brother and sister kindly informed me about?"

Tension tightened Daemon's frame. "Depends on what they kindly informed you of."

Air stalled in my lungs. I didn't know what to do with myself, so I stood there, trying to look as unaware as possible. The fact that I knew the guy in a suit wasn't human was a big deal. Other Luxen couldn't know I was in on the secret or that I was a hybrid.

Ethan smiled. "That you've been seeing her. I was surprised. We're practically family."

Somehow I thought it might have had more to do with the fact that they wanted him to make little alien Daemon babies with Ash than him not sending out a mass text notifying everyone that he was no longer on the market.

"You know me, Ethan; I don't like to kiss and tell the world." His thumb trailed a lazy, soothing circle along the small of my back. "Kat, this is Ethan Smith. He's like a…"

"Godfather," I said, and then I flushed, because that was the stupidest thing I could say.

But Ethan's expression said he liked the sound of it. "Yes, like a godfather." Those odd eyes settled on me, and I forced my chin up a notch. "You're not from around here, are you, Kat?"

"No, sir, I'm from Florida."

"Oh." Dark brows rose. "Is West Virginia to your agreement?"

I glanced at Daemon. "Yeah, it's nice."

"That's lovely." Ethan came down a step. "It's a pleasure to meet you." He extended a hand.

Out of habit, I reached for it, but Daemon interceded, wrapping his fingers around mine. He brought my hand to his lips and kissed my palm. Ethan noted the action with a flicker of curiosity and something I couldn't place.

"Kat, I'll come over in a little while." He let go of my hand, placing his body in between us. "I have some catching up to do, okay?"

I nodded and forced a smile for Ethan. "It was nice to meet you."

"Likewise," the man said. "I'm sure we'll meet again."

For some reason, the words settled over me with a frost-like bite. I gave Daemon a little wave and then hurried back to my car and grabbed my bag. They'd already headed inside, and I'd give my left thumb to know what they were talking about. As long as I'd known Daemon and Dee, I'd never seen another Luxen from the colony come to their home.

Kind of wigged out by Ethan's appearance, I dropped my backpack inside the hall and grabbed a glass of orange juice. Mom was asleep, so I tiptoed down the hall and shut my bedroom door. I sat on the bed, placed the glass on the table. Concentrating on my laptop, I raised my hand.

It came off the desk and moved straight to my hand. I tried not to use the alien abilities too often—maybe once or twice a day to keep the...uh, *whatever* well oiled. There was always this weird rush when I used it, like being on a roller coaster as it crests a hill, ready to fly down at eighty miles an hour—the moment when the stomach jumps and the skin tingles with awareness. It was a different feeling—not bad, kind of fun, and maybe even a little addictive.

And when I'd tapped into whatever it was the night Adam died, I'd never felt more powerful in my life. So, yeah, I could see how that power would go straight to the head. If the mutation had stuck with Will, God knew what crazy things he was doing.

I couldn't afford to think about him now, so I powered up my laptop and trolled the Internet for a half an hour, reading reviews until I shut off my computer and sent it back to my desk. Grabbing a book, I curled up, hoping to get some chapters in before Daemon swung over, but I ended up drifting off to sleep three pages in.

When I woke up, it was dark in my bedroom and upon further investigation, I discovered it was already past nine and Mom had left for work. Surprised that Daemon hadn't stopped over, I slipped on my boots and headed next door.

Dawson answered, a can of soda in one hand and a Pop-Tart in the other. "Nice sugar rush you got going on there," I said, grinning.

He glanced down. "Yeah, I guess I'm not sleeping anytime soon."

I remembered what he'd said about not sleeping at all, and I hoped that had changed. Before I could ask, though, he said, "Daemon's not here."

"Oh." I tried to hide my disappointment. "Is he still with the Elder guy?"

"God, no, Ethan was only here for about an hour. He wasn't happy. But Daemon went out with Andrew."

"Andrew?" Unexpected.

He nodded. "Yeah, Andrew and Dee and Ash wanted to grab something to eat. I didn't want to go."

"Ash?" I whispered. Okay, really unexpected. And what was totally expected was the wave of irrational jealousy that swept through me, determined to carry me into crazy-girl land.

"Yeah," he said, and then he winced. "You want to come in?"

I didn't realize I'd followed him inside until I was sitting on the couch, my knees pressed together. Daemon really went out to dinner with Ash and the others? "When did they leave?"

Dawson took a bite of his Pop-Tart. "Uh, not that long ago."

"It's almost ten at night." The Luxen had huge appetites, but come on; they didn't do dinner at night. I knew better than that.

He sat in the armchair and glanced down at his pastry. "Ethan left around five. And then Andrew, he came over around..." Dawson glanced at the wall clock, expression pinched. "He and Ash came over around six."

My stomach tumbled over itself. "And the four of them left after that to go get something to eat?"

Dawson nodded, as if speaking was too painfully awkward.

Four hours for dinner. I suddenly couldn't sit any longer. I wanted to know what restaurant they went to. I wanted to find him. I started to stand, but I tried to swallow down that god-awful burning lump in the back of my throat.

"It's not what you think," Dawson said quietly.

My head jerked toward him, and I was horrified to find tears in my eyes. The irony of it all bitch-slapped me in the face. Was this how Daemon had felt when he knew I went to dinner and then lunch with Blake? But we weren't together then. Wasn't like I'd owed him a ton of obligations at that moment.

"It isn't?" I croaked.

Dawson finished off his Pop-Tart. "No. I think he just needed to get out for a little while."

"Without me?"

He brushed a few sugary crumbs off his jeans "Maybe without you or maybe not. He's not the same brother I knew. I would've never thought he'd be with a human. No offense."

"None taken," I whispered. *Without me. Without me.* Those

words were on repeat. I wasn't one of those needy girls who had to be around her boyfriend all the time, but damn if it didn't sting.

And that sting was turned into a hot, angry knife when I pictured Dee and Andrew sitting on one side of a booth and Daemon and Ash on the other, because that's how they had to have sat when they went out to eat. It would be like old times—when Daemon and Ash were together.

Blake and I may've kissed once, but we didn't have a long-standing relationship. God, they'd probably had—

I checked myself right there.

Dawson stood, made his way around the coffee table, and sat beside me. "Ethan pissed him off. He wanted to know that Daemon's relationship with you wouldn't interfere with his loyalties to his kind." Dawson leaned forward, rubbing his palms over his bent knees. "And, well, you can imagine Daemon's response."

I wasn't so sure that I could. "What did he say?"

Dawson laughed, eyes squinting like Daemon's did. "Let's just say Daemon explained that who he was with didn't affect his loyalties, but he used different words."

I grinned a little. "Bad words?"

"Very bad words," he said, glancing at me. "They didn't expect this from him. No one did. Me? Yeah, well, they never expected much from me. Mainly because I didn't care what they thought— not that Daemon does, but…"

"I know. He's always been the one to take care of everything, right? Not the one to cause problems like this."

He nodded. "They don't know what you are, but I doubt Ethan's going to let this drop."

"They'll outcast him?" When he nodded, I shook my head. If a Luxen was outcasted, he wasn't allowed in or near Luxen communities, which meant he couldn't be near the protective cluster of beta quartz. He'd be virtually on his own against the Arum. "What is Ethan? I get he's an Elder, but so what?"

Dawson's brows pinched. "Elders are like the mayors and presidents of our communities. Ethan is our president."

My brows rose. "Sounds important."

"All those who live in the colony will listen to him. Those who don't risk the same social fallout." He leaned back, closing his eyes. "Even those who mingle with humans, like the ones who work outside the colony and whatever, are afraid of ticking off the Elders. None of us can just leave without the DOD's permission, but damn, if they wanted us out, they'd find a way to do so."

"Did they do that to you because of Beth?"

His face tensed. "They would've, but there hadn't been enough time. Not enough time for anything."

Pain sliced my chest and I placed my hand on his arm. "We're going to get Beth back."

A small smile appeared. "I know. This Sunday... Everything comes down to this Sunday."

My stomach did a topsy-turvy thing, and my pulse picked up. "What was it like in there?"

His eyes opened into thin slits. Several moments passed before he answered. "At first, it wasn't too bad. They let Beth and me see each other. They told us they were keeping us for our safety. You know, the whole 'if people find out what I did to Beth, it would get bad and we needed to be protected' bit. Daedalus was on our side. It really seemed that way for a while. I...I almost believed we'd walk out of it together."

It was the first time I heard him say *Daedalus*. The word sounded strange on his lips.

"Believing in that led to nothing but misery and eventually madness when the hope faded." His lips tipped up at the corners. "Daedalus wanted me to recreate what I had with Beth. They wanted me to *create* more like her. To help better mankind and all that BS, and when it didn't work, things...things changed."

I shifted. "How did they change?"

The line of his jaw tightened. "At first, they wouldn't let me see Beth—my punishment for failing when it seemed all too easy to them. They didn't get I didn't know how I healed and changed her. They'd bring these dying humans to me and I tried, Katy, I really tried. They just died no matter what I did."

Nausea welled up inside me, and I wished I knew what to say, but it seemed like this was one of those moments when saying nothing meant everything.

"Then they started bringing in healthy humans and doing things to them—hurting them—and I healed them. Some...some of them got better. At least they did for a little while, and it was like whatever wounds were inflicted on them came back with a vengeance. Others...others destabilized."

"Destabilized?"

Dawson's hands opened and closed on his thighs. "They'd develop some of our abilities, but something...something went wrong. This one girl—she wasn't much older than us and she was nice, very nice. They gave her some kind of pill and she was dying. I healed her. I really wanted to heal her, because she was so scared." Emerald eyes met mine. "And we thought it worked. She got sick like Beth was when they first brought us in. And then she could move just as fast as us. About a day after the sickness faded, she ran into a wall."

I frowned. "How is that so bad?"

His gaze slipped away. "We can move faster than bullets, Katy. She crashed into the wall. It was like hitting it at supersonic speed."

"Oh my God..."

"And it was like she couldn't stop herself. Sometimes I wonder if she did it on purpose. There were many, many more after her. Humans who died with my hands on them. Humans who died after I healed them. Humans who lived with no mutations but were never seen again." He looked down. "There's so much blood on my hands."

"No." I shook my head vigorously. "None of that was your fault."

"It wasn't?" Anger deepened his voice. "I have this ability to heal, but I couldn't get it right."

"But you had to want to heal them—like on a cellular level. You were being forced to do it."

"It doesn't change that so many people died." He sat forward again, antsy. "There was a period of time that I believed I deserved what they were doing to me, but never...never to Beth. She didn't deserve that."

"You didn't either, Dawson."

He stared at me a moment, then looked away. "They withheld Beth, then food, then water, and when that still didn't work, they got creative." He let out a long breath. "I guess they did the same to Beth, but I really didn't know. All I saw was what they did in front of me."

My stomach sank to the couch cushion. I had a really bad feeling about this.

"They'd hurt her just so I could heal her, and they could study the process." Dawson's jaw worked. "Each time I felt the worst kind of fear. What if it didn't work? What if I failed Beth? I'd..." He moved his neck, as if working out a kink.

He'd never be the same. Tears climbed up my throat again. I wanted to cry for him, for Beth, but most of all, for the people they once were but never would be again.

Chapter 19

After that, Dawson shut down. He talked about anything—weather, football, the Smurfs—but nothing about Daedalus or what they did to him and Beth. Part of me was grateful. I wasn't sure how much more I could handle knowing, as selfish as that sounded.

But the bad part was that once we stopped talking about serious stuff, my brain ran right back to where Daemon was and what he was doing. When it neared midnight and he still hadn't come home, I couldn't sit there any longer.

I couldn't sit anywhere.

Saying good night, I made the quick and chilly trek across the lawn. The first thing I did was check my cell. There was a text waiting and my heart stuttered.

Srry abt tnght. Tlk tmrw.

It had come in about an hour ago. Meaning he was still with Ash—er, Andrew, Dee, *and* Ash.

I glanced at the clock, like that would somehow change the time. My heart was pounding in my chest, as though I'd run from next door. Looking down at my cell, I fought the urge to throw it against the wall. I knew I was being ridiculous. Daemon was friends with them, including Ash. He could hang out with them without me. And with the fallout between Dee and me, he hadn't been spending a lot of time with her.

Ridiculous or not, my feelings were hurt. And I hated that— hated that something as stupid as this would upset me.

Taking my phone upstairs, I washed my face, brushed my teeth, and changed into my jammies, still debating on texting him back. I wanted the willpower not to, kind of like my *in your face*, but damn if that wasn't stupid considering everything that was going on.

On the flip side, I was butt sore about this. So I placed the cell on my stand and I climbed under the covers, pulling them to my chin. I stayed that way, beating myself up for not texting him back, for going out with Blake the first time, for kissing him, and for lying awake beating myself up. Finally, my brain had enough and it closed shop for the night.

Sometime later, I wasn't sure if I was dreaming or not. I was in that hazy stage where reality mixed with the subconscious. Part of it was a dream, I knew that much, because I could see Daemon in this building. I'd catch sight of his dark hair and then he drifted away. He was in one room and before I could get to him, he went to another. It was an endless maze and he kept moving around, never responding to me as I yelled his name.

Frustration swelled inside me and my chest ached. Chasing him, never reaching him in time, losing him… It wouldn't end.

And then the bed shifted and the building faded, evaporated into wisps of smoke and darkness. A heavy weight settled beside me. A hand brushed the hair back from my face, and I think I smiled, because he was here and that soothed me. I slipped back into deep sleep, where I wasn't chasing Daemon in my dreams.

• • •

When morning came, I rolled over, expecting to find Daemon. Mom worked until late morning on Saturdays and Daemon had taken to staying as long as he could, but my bed was empty.

Smoothing my hand along the extra pillow, I inhaled, expecting the outdoorsy clean scent that was uniquely his, but all I smelled was a faint trace of citrus. Had I dreamt Daemon's presence?

Geez, I was so lame if so.

Frowning, I sat up and grabbed my cell. There was a missed text that had come in around two in the morning from Daemon.

Bacon & eggs 4 breakfast. Cme over when u wake.

"Two in the morning?" I stared at the phone. Had he been out with them till then?

My heart was racing again and I flopped onto my back, groaning. Apparently I was lame and Daemon had a really late night but not with me.

Dragging myself out of bed, I showered and threw on a pair of jeans and a sweater. Numbness had settled over me as I dried my hair halfway and twisted it up into a messy bun. I headed next door and found that the door was locked.

I placed my hand on the handle and waited until I heard the locks turning over. As I opened the door, unease blossomed. It was way too easy to get in and out of people's houses, including mine.

Shaking my head, I eased the door shut and took a deep breath. The house was tomb silent. Everyone was still asleep. I went upstairs, careful of the two steps at the top that creaked. Dawson's and Dee's bedroom doors were shut, but I could hear the soft hum of music coming from Daemon's.

I cracked open Daemon's bedroom door and slipped through. My gaze went straight to the bed and I couldn't have stopped the flutter in my chest if I wanted to.

Daemon was sprawled on his back, one arm stretched across the space beside him and the other rested across his bare stomach. Sheets were twisted around his narrow hips. His face was almost angelic in sleep, chiseled lines softened and lips relaxed. Thick lashes fanned the top of his cheeks.

He looked so much younger at rest but, in a weird way, he was even more out of my league. His kind of masculine beauty was otherworldly and intimidating. Something that existed in between the pages of the books I read.

Sometimes I had a hard time convincing myself he was real.

I tiptoed over to him and sat on the edge of the bed, unable to pull my eyes away. I didn't want to wake him. So I sat there like a total creeper, watching the steady rise and fall of his chest. I wondered if I had dreamt him last night or if he had stopped in to check on me. The fluttering was back and I could almost forget the punch of anxiety of last night. Almost but not—

Daemon rolled suddenly, snaking an arm around my waist and pulling me down beside him. He kept moving, burying his face in my neck. "Good morning," he murmured.

A smile swept across my face as I placed a hand on his shoulder. His skin was hot. "Morning."

He threw a leg over mine and snuggled closer. "Where's my bacon and eggs?"

"I thought you were offering to make them."

"You mistook what I said. Get to the kitchen, woman."

"Whatever." I rolled onto my side, facing him. He lifted his head, kissed my nose, and then buried his face in the pillow. I laughed.

"It's too early," he grumbled.

"It's almost ten o'clock."

"Too early."

A stone settled in my stomach. I bit down on my lip, unsure of what I should say.

He lazily dropped an arm over my hip and turned his head so I could see his face. "You didn't respond last night."

So we *were* going to go there. "I fell asleep and I…figured you were busy."

A brow arched. "I wasn't busy."

"I stopped over last night to see you, and I waited for a little while." I fiddled with the edge of the sheet, twisting it around my fingers. "You stayed out late."

One eye opened. "So you did get my text and had time to respond."

I'd walked right into that one.

Daemon sighed. "Why did you ignore me, Kitten? My feelings are hurt."

"I'm sure Ash soothed them for you." The moment those words left my mouth, I wanted to smack myself.

Both eyes were open now, and then he did something that surprised and ticked me off: he smiled that really big one. "You're jealous."

To me, the way he said it made it sound like a good thing. I started to sit up, but his arm kept me down. "I'm not jealous."

"Kitten…"

I rolled my eyes and then a bad, bad case of verbal diarrhea occurred. "I was worried about the Elder being here, and we were supposed to talk last night. You never showed up. Instead you went out with Andrew, Dee, and *Ash*. Ash, as in the ex-girlfriend Ash, and how do I find out? Your brother. And how did those seating arrangements work out? Did Dee and Andrew sit on one side and you and Ash on the other? I bet that was real comfy."

"Kitten…"

"Don't Kitten me." I scowled, on a roll now. "You left around five or so and didn't get back till when? Past two in the morning? What were you guys doing? And get that stupid smile off your face. This isn't funny."

Daemon tried to get rid of the smile but failed. "I love when your claws come out."

"Oh, shut up." Disgusted, I pushed at his arm. "Let me go. You can call up Ash and see if she'll make you some eggs and bacon. I'm out of here."

Instead of letting me go, he shifted atop me, holding himself up with his hands planted on either side of my shoulders. Now he was grinning—that infuriating, cocky grin of his. "I just want to hear you say it: I'm jealous."

"I already said it, butt-face. I'm jealous. Why wouldn't I be?"

He cocked his head to the side. "Oh, I don't know. Maybe because I never wanted Ash, and I wanted you from the first moment I saw you—and before you get started, I know I had a bad way of showing it, but you know I wanted you. Only you. You're insane to be jealous."

"I am?" I fought back angry tears. "You guys were together."

"*Were* together."

"She probably still wants you."

"I don't want her, so it doesn't matter."

It mattered to me. "She's model beautiful."

"And you're more beautiful."

"Don't try to sweet-talk me."

"I'm not," he said.

Staring over his shoulder, I bit my lip. "You know, at first I thought I kind of deserved last night. Now I know how you felt when I went out with Blake. Like karma was schooling me, but it's not the same. You and I weren't together then and Blake and I didn't have that kind of history."

He took a deep breath. "You're right; it's not the same thing. I didn't go out with Ash on a date. Andrew stopped by and we got to talking about Ethan. Andrew was hungry, so we decided to get something to eat. Dee tagged along and Ash was there, because you know, she's his sister."

I gave a lopsided shrug. Okay, he had a point.

"And we didn't go out to eat. We ended up ordering pizza, went back to Andrew's house, and we talked about Sunday. Ash is scared to death that she's going to lose Andrew, too. Dee still wants to murder Blake. I spent *hours* talking them through this. It wasn't a party you weren't invited to."

But I wasn't invited at all, I wanted to say, but I knew that was stupid. "Why didn't you tell me, at least? You could've said something. Then my imagination wouldn't have run circles around me."

He stared at me a moment, then pushed up, sitting beside me. "I meant to stop by when I got home, but it was late."

So last night *was* a dream. Lameness officially confirmed.

"Look, I didn't think about it."

"Apparently," I muttered.

Daemon rubbed the spot above his heart. "I honestly didn't think you'd get this upset. I figured you'd know better."

I was still flat on my back, too weary to move. "Know better?"

"Yeah, that you'd know if Ash pranced naked into my bedroom right now, I'd still send her packing. That you didn't have anything to worry about."

"Thanks for that image you implanted into my brain forever."

He shook his head, huffing out a dry laugh. "This insecurity thing ticks me off, Kat."

My mouth dropped open and I flew up, coming to rest on my knees. "Excuse me? Are you the only one who's allowed to be insecure?"

"What?" He smirked. "Why would I be insecure?"

"Good question, but what do you call your little episode with Blake yesterday in the hallway? And that stupid question about me wanting to help Blake?"

He snapped his mouth shut.

"Ha! Exactly. It's even more ridiculous for you to be insecure. Let me spell it out for you." When my anger rose, the Source did, too. It skated over my skin. "I loathe Blake. He used me and was ready to turn me over to Daedalus. He killed Adam. There's only a teeny tiny bit of me that can actually tolerate him. How can you even be any bit jealous of him?"

Daemon's jaw popped. "He wants you."

"Oh, dear God, he does not."

"Whatever. I'm a guy. I know what other guys are thinking."

I threw my hands up. "It doesn't matter if he did. I. Hate. Him."

He looked away. "Okay."

"And you don't hate Ash. There's a part of you that loves her. I know you do and maybe not in the way you feel about me, but there's affection there—there's history. Sue me if I'm a little bit intimidated by that."

I pushed off the bed, wanting to stomp across the room like a toddler. Maybe even throw myself on the floor. I'd work off some energy that way.

Daemon appeared in front of me and stepped forward, cradling my cheeks. "Okay. I see your point. I should've said something. And the stuff with Blake—yeah, it's stupid, too."

"Good." I folded my arms.

His lips twitched. "But you've got to understand that you are who I want. Not Ash. Not anyone else."

"Even if the Elders want you to be with someone like her?"

He lowered his head, brushing his lips along my cheekbone. "I don't care what they want. I'm incredibly selfish like that." He kissed my temple. "Okay?"

My eyes drifted shut. "Okay."

"We're good then?"

"If you promise not to give me any crap about going with you tomorrow."

He pressed his forehead against mine. "You drive a hard bargain."

"I do."

"I don't want you going, Kitten." He sighed, wrapping his arms around me. "But I can't stop you. Promise you'll stay close to me."

My smile was hidden against his chest. "I promise."

Daemon kissed the top of my head. "You always get your way, don't you?"

"Not always." I placed my hands on his sides, drawing in his warmth. If I had my way, none of this would be happening. But that was the thing about all of this. I wondered if any of us would get our way.

His arms tightened, and I felt a sigh shudder through him. "Come on. Let's get the bacon and eggs going. I need all my strength for today."

"What, for…" I trailed off, realizing what he was saying. "Oh, yeah…Blake."

"Yeah." He kissed me softly. "It's going to take a lot for me not to commit bodily harm. You know that, right? So extra bacon for me."

Chapter 20

Dee was perched on the bottom step like a demented pixie about to unleash holy hell. Her hair was pulled back sharply, her eyes a bright and feverish green. A thin slash formed on her lips. Her fingers curled over her knees like razor-sharp claws ready to dig in.

"He's here," she said, gaze focused on the window beside the door.

I glanced at Daemon. A wolfish smile spread across his face. He wasn't at all concerned about his sister's murderous desires. Perhaps having Blake come here wasn't a good idea.

She sprung from the step, throwing open the door before Blake even knocked. No one stopped her or even moved forward.

Surprised, Blake lowered his hand. "Uh, hi—"

Dee cocked back a slender arm and slammed her fist right into Blake's jaw. The impact knocked him back a good three feet.

My mouth dropped open.

Andrew laughed.

Spinning around, she let out a long breath. "Okay. I'm done."

I watched her move toward the armchair and sit, shaking her

hand.

"I promised her one good hit," Daemon said, chuckling. "She'll behave now."

I stared at him.

Blake staggered through the door, rubbing his jaw. "Okay," he said, wincing. "I deserved that."

"You deserve far worse than that," Andrew said. "Keep that in mind."

He nodded and looked around the room. Six Luxen and a baby hybrid stared back at him. He had the sense to look nervous, even afraid. The animosity in the room was palpable.

Blake moved so that his back was against the wall. Smart guy. Slowly, he reached into his back pocket and pulled out a rolled-up paper. "I guess we should get this over with quickly."

"I guess so," Daemon said, snatching the paper from him. "What's this?"

"A map," he answered. "The route we need to take is outlined in red. It's a fire access road and will lead up to the back entrance of Mount Weather."

Daemon unrolled the map on the coffee table. Dawson peered over his brother's shoulder, running his finger along the wiggling red line. "How long will it take to get up this road?"

"About twenty minutes by car, but there's no way we're going to get a car up there unnoticed." He took a timid step forward, eyeing Dee, who was eyeballing him back. A red mark marred his right cheek. That was gonna bruise. "We're going to do it by foot and fast."

"How fast are we talking?" Matthew asked from his post by the dining room door.

"As fast as inhumanly possible," Blake responded. "We need to move at the light-speed thing. Luc's giving us fifteen minutes and we can't hang around Mount Weather, waiting for nine. We need to get there about five minutes before and hit this road as fast as possible."

I sat back. Only once did I hit the speeds necessary for what they were talking about. That's when I'd been chasing Blake's ass down.

Daemon glanced up. "Can you do this?"

"Yes." Given the reasons, I was sure I could do it. Hopefully.

Shaking her head, Dee stood. "How fast can they really run?"

"Damn fast when need be," Blake said. "Come at me again, and I'll show you how fast I can run."

Dee snickered. "I bet I'll still catch you."

"Perhaps," he murmured and then said, "You need to practice all day tomorrow. Maybe even tonight. We can't have anyone slowing us down."

It took me a second to realize he was talking to me. "I'm not going to slow anyone down."

"Just making sure." His eyes churned as they met mine.

I looked away quickly. The fact that I was obviously the weakest link burned me. Dee or Ash would probably be a better choice for this, but I knew I could do it.

"She's not your problem to worry about," Daemon snapped.

Matthew came forward, fitting in between Daemon and Blake. "Okay. We know we have this road to go up, but you want us to remain back where?"

Daemon folded his arms, eyes narrowed. "At the bottom of the access road, this should give you a running chance to get out if something goes wrong."

"Nothing's going to go wrong," Ash said, watching Daemon. "We'll wait there for you."

"Of course," Daemon said, smiling reassuringly. "We'll be fine, Ash."

I pinched my thigh. *He doesn't want her. He doesn't want her. He doesn't want her.* That helped.

"I trust you," Ash said, eyes latched to his adoringly. Like

Daemon was a saint or something.

I pinched my thigh harder. *I'm going to hit her. I'm going to hit her. I'm going to hit her.* That didn't help.

Blake cleared his throat. "Anyway, Luc said there's an old farm at the bottom of the access road. We should be able to park the cars there."

"Sounds good." Dawson stepped back, placing his hands on his hips. A lock of hair fell forward. "Once we're there, we have fifteen minutes, right?"

Daemon nodded. "According to the tween mafia leader, Luc, that's what we have."

"And this kid is trustworthy?" Matthew asked.

"I can speak for him."

I looked at Blake. "That's a ringing endorsement."

His cheeks flushed. "He's trustworthy."

"Do you think it's enough time?" Dawson asked his brother. "To get in there, get to Beth and Chris, and get out?"

"It should be." Daemon folded up the map and slid it into his back pocket. "You'll get Beth and dipshit here will get Chris."

Blake rolled his eyes.

"Andrew, Kat, and I are going to cover them. This shouldn't even take fifteen minutes." Daemon sat beside me and leveled a pointed glare at Blake. "And then you will take Chris and get the hell out of here. You have no reason to come back."

"And what if he does?" Dee asked. "What if he finds another excuse to blackmail you into helping you?"

"I won't," Blake said, and I felt his stare. "I don't have a reason to come back."

Daemon went taut. "If you do, you're going to make me do something I don't want to do—I'll probably enjoy it, but I don't want to."

Blake jerked his chin. "I got you."

"Okay then," Matthew said, addressing the room. "We meet

here at six thirty tomorrow. Do you have things covered, Katy?"

I nodded. "Mom thinks I'm doing a sleepover with Lesa. She works anyway."

"She always works," Ash said, staring at her nails. "Does she even like to be home?"

Unsure if that was a dig or not, I kept my temper in check. "She's paying for a mortgage, food, bills, and all my expenses by herself. She has to work a lot."

"Maybe you should get a job," she suggested, her eyes flicking up. "Like something after school that takes about twenty hours or so of your life."

I folded my arms, lips pursed. "Why are you suggesting that, pray tell?"

A catlike smile appeared as her attention slid to beside me. "I just think if you were concerned about your mom making ends meet, you would help out."

"I'm sure that's why." I relaxed when Daemon slid a hand across my back.

Ash noticed the gesture and got a sour pinch to her lips.

Take that.

"There's only one thing we have to worry about," Blake said, as if it really was only *one thing* that could go wrong. "They have emergency doors that shut every so many feet when alarms are sounded. Those doors also have a defensive weapon. Don't go near the blue lights. They're lasers. Rip you right apart."

All of us stared. Wow, yeah, that was a big problem.

Blake smiled. "But they shouldn't be a problem. We should be in and out without being seen."

"Okay," Andrew said slowly. "Anything else? Like an onyx net we have to worry about?"

Blake laughed. "No, that should cover it."

Dee wanted Blake out once the plans were underway. Without protest, he headed to the door and stopped as if he were going to say something. I felt his gaze once more, but then he left. Our group disbanded, leaving the siblings behind.

I clasped my hands together. "I want to practice the speed thing. I mean, I know I can do it as fast as you guys, but I just want to practice."

Dee focused on the arm of the couch, drawing in a deep breath.

"We can do that." Dawson smiled crookedly. "I could use the practice myself."

Daemon stretched back, wrapping an arm around my waist. "It's a little dark right now. You'll probably end up breaking your neck, but we can do it tomorrow."

"Thanks for the vote of confidence."

"You got it."

I elbowed him as I turned to Dee. She was still staring at the furniture like it held the answer to something. Here goes nothing. "Will...will you help?"

She opened her mouth and then closed it, shaking her head. Then, without saying a word, she pivoted around and headed upstairs. I deflated.

"She'll come around," Daemon said, giving me a little squeeze. "I know she will."

Doubted that, but I nodded. Dee was never going to *come around*. I don't know why I even bothered.

Dawson sat on my other side, confusion marking his expression. "I don't know what happened to her while I was gone. I don't understand."

I pressed my lips together. *I* happened.

"We all changed, brother." Daemon tugged me back so I was against his side. "But things... Things are going to get back to normal soon."

He watched us, brows drawn tight. Sorrow crept into his eyes, dulling their vibrant color. I wondered what he thought when he saw us together. Memories of him and Beth cuddled together on the couch? Then he blinked and a wan smile appeared. "*Ghost Investigators* marathon?"

"You do not have to ask me twice." Daemon raised his hand and the remote control shot toward him. "I have, like, six hours saved up. Popcorn? We need popcorn."

"And ice cream." Dawson stood. "I get the munchies."

The wall clock read seven thirty. It was going to be a long night, but as I settled in next to Daemon, I realized I didn't want to be any place else.

Daemon brushed his lips along my cheek as he reached behind us, tugging a blanket off the back of the couch. He draped it over both of us, allowing most of the blanket to swallow me. "He's coming around, isn't he?"

I turned to him, smiling. "Yeah, he is."

His eyes met mine. "Let's just make sure tomorrow doesn't make it all for nothing."

• • •

By one o'clock the following day, I was covered in mud and sweating like a pig in hell. I'd done better than I feared, able to keep up easily with Dawson and I only fell, like…four times. The terrain was unforgiving.

I walked past Daemon, and he made a swipe for me. I shot him a level look, which he returned with a mischievous grin.

"You have dirt on your cheek," he said. "Cute."

As usual, he looked perfect. Hadn't even broken a sweat for crying out loud. "Is he always this annoyingly good?"

Dawson, who looked as rough as I did, nodded. "Yeah, he's the best at this kind of stuff—fighting, running, physical stuff."

His brother beamed as I knocked the mud off my sneakers and said, "You suck."

Daemon laughed.

I stuck my tongue out and returned to stand next to the brothers. We were at the edge of the woods that ran up to my front yard. I took a couple of deep breaths and welcomed the Source rushing through me. That roller-coaster feeling was back and my muscles locked up.

"Get ready," Daemon said, hands curling at his sides. "Go!"

Pushing off, I dug my feet into the ground, then raced against the brothers. Air whipped around me as I picked up speed. Now that I knew to watch out for rotted branches and stones, I kept my eyes trained on the ground and my surroundings. The wind bit at my cheeks, but it was a good kind of sting. It meant I was fast.

Trees blurred as I darted around them and under low-hanging branches. Jumping over bushes and boulders, I moved ahead of Dawson. The speed tore at my hair, pulling it free from my ponytail. A laugh escaped my throat. As I ran, I forgot about the stupid jealousy, the lingering issue of Will, and even what we had to do later that night.

Running like this, as fast as the wind, was freeing.

Daemon blew past us, reaching the stream a good ten seconds before we did. Slowing down was an issue. You couldn't just stop, not at this speed. You'd face-plant into the ground in seconds. So I dug my feet in, kicking up sediment and loose rock as I slid the last few inches.

Daemon's arm shot out, wrapping around my waist so I didn't end up in the lake. Laughing, I spun around and reached up, kissing his cheek.

He grinned. "Your eyes are glowing."

"Really—like yours do? The whole diamond shining thing?"

Dawson stopped, knocking the mop of hair off his forehead. "Nah, just the color's luminous. It's pretty."

"It's beautiful," Daemon corrected. "But you better be careful not to do that in front of people." When I nodded, he walked over to his brother, clapping him on his back. "Why don't we call it quits? Both of you are good to go, and I'm starving."

A thrill of pride sparked inside me until I remembered how important tonight would be. I couldn't be the weakest link. "You guys go ahead and head back. I'm going to do some more runs."

"You sure?"

"Yep. I want to run circles around you."

"Never going to happen, Kitten." He swaggered up to me and kissed my cheek. "You might as well give it up."

I pushed at his chest playfully. "One of these days you're going to eat crow."

"I doubt any of us will be around to see that." Dawson grinned at his brother.

My heart stopped when I saw the two of them joking, and I forced my expression to remain the same, although I saw Daemon falter a little. Unaware of the importance of the exchange, Dawson knocked his hair back again and started toward the house.

"Race you, brother," Dawson called.

Go, I mouthed at Daemon.

He sent me a quick smile and then trotted up to his brother. "You know you're going to lose."

"Probably, but hey, it's good for your ego, right?"

Like he needed help with that, but I smiled and felt all warm and fuzzy as they joked and then took off. I waited a few minutes, cleared my thoughts, and then jogged back toward the house. At normal speed, it took about five minutes if I was adding correctly. Once at the tree line, I spun around and got ready. Feeling the Source snap loose, I launched forward.

Two minutes.

I did it again and timed it.

A minute and thirty seconds the second trip back. I did it again and again, until my muscles burned along with my lungs and the five-minute jog took me fifty seconds. I didn't think I could get any better than that.

And the funny thing was that even though my muscles were shaky, they didn't hurt. Like I'd been running this way for years, and I pretty much ran from the front of the bookstore to the new release section and that was all.

Stretching, I watched the sun filter through the trees and bounce off the partially frozen creek. Spring wasn't too far away. I pushed at my hair, tucked it over one shoulder. That was, if we all made it out of Mount Weather tonight.

"I was wrong. You really don't need practice."

I whirled at the sound of Blake's voice. Standing several feet away, he leaned against a thick tree, hands in his pockets. Unease and discord balled in my stomach.

"What are you doing here?" I demanded, keeping my voice even.

Blake shrugged. "Watching."

"Yeah, that's not creepy or anything."

He smiled tightly. "I probably should have thought of a better way of phrasing that. I was watching you all run. You guys are good—you're great. Daedalus would love to have you on board."

The ball in my stomach grew. "Is that a threat?"

"No." He blinked, cheeks flushing. "God, no, I just meant that you're that good. You're what they want in a hybrid."

"Like you?"

His gaze dropped to the ground. "Yeah, like me."

This was awkward and breathing the same air as Blake irritated me. Normally, I didn't hold grudges, but I made an exception with him. I started heading back to the house.

"Are you worried about tonight?"

"I don't want to talk to you."

He was beside me quickly. "Why not?"

Why not? Seriously? *Why not?* That question enraged me. Without thinking, I snapped around and slammed my fist into his solar plexus. Air expelled from him in a rush and giddy satisfaction planted a smile on my face.

"God!" he grunted, doubling over. "What is up with you chicks hitting me?"

"You deserve much worse than that." I pivoted around before I hit him again and restarted my trek back. "Why don't I want to talk to you? Why don't we ask Adam?"

"Okay." He caught up with me, rubbing his stomach. "You're right. But I've said I'm sorry."

"Sorry doesn't fix things like this." I took a breath, squinting at the harsh glare of the sun cutting through the branches. I couldn't believe I was having this conversation.

"I'm trying to make up for it."

I laughed at the ridiculous notion that he could make up for all that he had done. Ever since the night Adam died, a part of me understood capital punishment and why it was created. Maybe not a life for a life, but I got the whole life-in-prison thing.

I stopped. "Why are you really here right now? You know Daemon is probably going to be ticked off, and he hits harder than Dee or me."

"I wanted to talk to you." His gaze tipped upward. "And there was a time that you used to like talking to me."

Yeah, before he turned out to be the devil incarnate, he was a pretty cool guy. "I hate you," I said, and I meant it. The level of animosity that I felt for this boy was a chart topper.

Blake flinched but didn't look away. Wind roared through the trees, whipping my hair around my face and causing his to stand straight up. "I never wanted you to hate me."

I barked out a short laugh and started walking again. "You suck at the whole not-making-me-hate-you part."

"I know." He fell in step beside me. "And I know I can't change that. I'm not even sure I would if I had a chance to do it again." I cut him a hateful glare. "At least you're honest, right? Whatever."

He shoved his hands into his jeans. "You would do the same if you were in my shoes—if that was Daemon you needed to protect."

A shiver tiptoed down my spine as my jaw locked into place.

"You would," he insisted quietly. "You would do just as I did. And that's what bothers you more than anything. We're more alike than you want to admit."

"We're nothing alike!" My stomach seized up, though, because deep down, like I'd told Daemon before, I was a lot like Blake. Knowing that didn't mean I was going to give him the pleasure of admitting it, especially since what he'd done had changed me.

My hands curled into fists as I stomped over branches and shrubs. "You're a monster, Blake. A real live, breathing monster—I don't want to be that."

He didn't say anything for a moment. "You're not a monster."

My jaw ached from how hard I was grinding my teeth.

"You're like me, Katy, you really are, but you're better than me." There was a pause and then he said, "I've liked you from the moment we met. Even though I knew it was stupid to like you, I do."

Dumbstruck, I stopped and looked at him. "What?"

The tips of his cheeks burned red. "I like you, Katy. A lot. And I know you hate me, and you love Daemon. I get that, but I just wanted to get that out there in case the shit hits the fan tonight. Not that it will, but you know… Whatever."

I couldn't even process what he was saying. There was no way. I turned and started back to the house that was now in sight, shaking my head. He liked me. *A lot.* That's why he betrayed my friends and me. Killed Adam and then returned to blackmail us. A hysterical laugh formed in my throat and once I started laughing, I couldn't stop.

"Thanks," he muttered. "I put it out there, and you laugh at me."

"You should be glad I'm laughing. Because the other option is hitting you again, which is still up—"

Blake slammed into my back, throwing me to the ground. Air flew from my lungs in a rush and his weight immediately primed my body for a fight.

"Don't," he whispered in my ear, his hands wrapping around my upper arms. "We have company—and not the good kind."

Chapter 21

My heart leaped into my throat. As I managed to lift my head, I expected to see a fleet of DOD officers converging on us.

I saw nothing.

"What are you talking about?" I asked in a hushed voice. "I don't see—"

"Quiet."

I bristled but remained quiet. After a few seconds, though, I was convinced he was just getting a cheap thrill or something. "If you don't get off me, I'm going to really hurt—"

And then I saw what he was talking about. Creeping along the side of my house was a man in a black suit. Something about his appearance looked familiar, and then I remembered where I'd seen him before.

He had been with Nancy Husher the day the DOD showed up, while Daemon and I had been at the field where we'd fought Baruck.

Officer Lane.

Then I saw his Expedition parked farther down the street.

I swallowed thickly. "What is he doing here?"

"I don't know." Blake's breath was warm against my cheek, and I gritted my teeth. "But he's obviously looking for something." A second or so later, movement at Daemon's house caught my eyes. The front door opened, and Daemon stepped outside. To the human eye, he vanished from the front porch and reappeared in my driveway, a few feet from Officer Lane. But he just moved so quickly that he couldn't be tracked.

"Is there something I can help you with, Lane?" His voice carried over the distance, even and without emotion.

Surprised by his sudden appearance, Lane took a step back and pressed his hand to his chest. "Daemon, God, I hate when you do that."

Daemon didn't smile and whatever the Officer saw in Daemon's eyes got him straight down to business. "I'm doing an investigation."

"Okay."

Lane reached into the breast pocket of his suit and pulled out a small notebook, flipping it open. His jacket got stuck on his gun holster. I wasn't sure if it was on purpose or not. "Officer Brian Vaughn has been missing since before New Year's. I'm checking all possible leads."

"Crap," I muttered.

Daemon folded his arms. "Why would I know what happened to him or care?"

"When was the last time you saw him?"

"I haven't seen him since the day you guys showed up to do your check-in and you all wanted to eat at the disgusting Chinese buffet," Daemon responded, his voice so convincing that I almost believed him. "I still haven't recovered from that."

Lane gave a reluctant grin. "Yes, the food was terrible." He scribbled something down and then slid his notebook back into his pocket. "So you haven't seen Vaughn at all?"

"Nope," he said.

The other man nodded. "I know you two weren't big fans of each other. I didn't figure he'd make any unauthorized visits, but we have to check every avenue at this point."

"Understandable." Daemon's gaze landed on the trees we were hidden behind. "Why were you checking out the neighbor's house?"

"I was checking out all the houses," he replied. "You still friends with the girl we saw you with?"

Oh, no.

Daemon said nothing, but even from my prone position, I could see the way his eyes narrowed on the Officer.

Lane laughed. "Daemon, when are you ever going to loosen up?" He clapped him on the shoulder as he headed past him. "I don't care who you...spend your time with. I'm just doing my job."

Daemon followed the Officer's movements, twisting toward him. "So, if I decided to exclusively date humans and settle down with one, you wouldn't report me?"

"As long as I don't see undeniable evidence, I don't care. This is just a job with a good retirement, and I hope to make it to that point." He started for his vehicle but stopped, facing Daemon. "There's a difference between evidence and my gut. For example, my gut told me that your brother was in a serious relationship with the human he disappeared with, but there wasn't any evidence."

And of course, we knew how the DOD found out about Beth and Dawson: Will. But was this guy insinuating that he knew nothing about Dawson?

Daemon leaned against Lane's SUV. "Did you see my brother's body when they found him?"

A tense moment followed, and Lane lowered his chin. "I wasn't there when they said they found his body along with the girl's. I was only told what happened. I'm just an Officer." He raised his head. "And I haven't been told any differently. I'm nothing in the big scheme of things, but I'm not blind."

I held my breath. I felt Blake do the same.

"What are you saying?" Daemon asked.

Lane smiled tightly. "I know who's in your house, Daemon. I know that I was lied to—a lot of us have been lied to and have no idea what's really going on. We just have jobs. We do them, and we keep our heads down."

Daemon nodded. "And you're keeping your head down now?"

"I was told to check on Vaughn's possible whereabouts and that was about it." He motioned at his car door, and Daemon stepped away from it. "I know not to address anything unless told so. I really want that retirement plan." He climbed in, closing the car door. "You take care."

Daemon moved back. "See you around, Lane."

Tires wheeled and kicked up gravel as the Expedition pulled back onto the road, puffing out exhaust.

What the heck just happened? Better yet, why was Blake still on top of me?

Throwing my elbow back, it connected with his stomach and a grunt followed. "Get off me."

He rolled to his feet, eyes sparkling. "You like to hit."

I scrambled up, glaring. "You need to get out of here. Right now, we don't need to deal with you."

"Good point." He backed off, his grin fading. "See you later tonight."

"Whatever," I muttered, turning back to where Daemon was walking up the driveway. I trotted out of the woods and over to his side. "Is everything okay?"

Daemon nodded. "Did you hear any of that?"

"Yeah, I was heading back when I saw him." I figured if Daemon didn't know about Blake being all Creepy McCreepsters before we raided Mount Weather, it was a good thing. "Do you believe him?"

"I don't know." He dropped his arm over my shoulders, steering me toward his house. "Lane has always been a decent guy, but this doesn't sit well with me."

I wrapped an arm around his waist and leaned into him. "Which part?"

"All of it—this whole scenario," he said, sitting down on the step one from the top. He tugged me into his lap, keeping his arms around me. "The fact that the DOD—even Lane—knows damn well that Dawson's back, and that they have to realize we know they lied. And they're doing nothing." He closed his eyes as I pressed my cheek to his. "And what we're doing tonight—it can work, but it's so insane. Part of me wonders if they already know we're coming."

Smoothing my thumb along his jaw, I pressed a kiss against his cheek, wishing there was something I could do. "Do you think we're walking into a trap?"

"I think we've been inside the trap the entire time and we're just waiting for it to spring closed." He captured my dirty hand in his and held on.

A breath shuddered through me. "And we're going to still do this?"

The determined set of his shoulders was answer enough. "You don't have to."

"Neither do you," I reasoned softly. "But we both are."

Daemon tilted his head back, eyes meeting mine. "That we are."

We weren't doing this because we had a death wish or that we were stupid, but because there were two lives at stake, probably more, that were worth as much as ours. Perhaps this whole endeavor was sacrificial, but if we didn't go through with it, we'd lose Beth, Chris, and Dawson. Blake was an acceptable loss.

A tendril of panic seized my chest, though. I was scared— frightened out of my mind. Who wouldn't be? But I'd gotten us to this point and now it was bigger than me, bigger than my fear.

Drawing in a shaky breath, I dipped my head and kissed his lips. "I think I'm going to spend some time with my mom before we leave." My throat felt thick. "She should be awake soon."

He kissed me back, his lips lingering. The touch was part yearning with a hint of desperation and acceptance. If things went badly tonight, there really hadn't been enough time for us. Maybe there'd never be enough time, though.

Finally, he said in a rough, raw voice, "That's a good idea, Kitten."

• • •

When the time came to pile into Daemon's SUV and start the drive to the Blue Ridge Mountains, the mood was strained. And for once, it really had nothing to do with Blake's presence.

There were outbursts of laughter and curses, but everyone was on pins and needles.

Ash was getting into the passenger seat of Matthew's vehicle. She was decked out in all black—black tights, black sneakers, and a skintight black turtleneck. She looked like a ninja. Next to her, Dee was in pink. Apparently Dee had gotten the memo about staying in the vehicle. Unless Ash planned to blend in with the seat cushions, I wasn't sure why she was dressed that way.

Other than the fact she looked insanely hot.

On the other hand, I wore dark sweats and a black thermal that no longer fit Daemon. It must've been from his preteen years, because it wouldn't even fit over his head now, and I looked like I was going to the gym.

I was a total fail next to Ash, but Daemon said something about me wearing his clothes that sent blood rushing to every part of my body and I didn't care if I looked like a hunchback next to her.

Dawson and Blake were riding with us, the rest with Matthew.

As we pulled out of the driveway, my eyes were glued to my house until it faded out of sight. The few hours I had spent with Mom had been great…really great.

The first thirty minutes of the trip wasn't bad. Blake stayed quiet, but when he started talking, things went downhill from there. A few times I thought Daemon was going to stop the vehicle and throttle him.

I didn't think Dawson or I would've stopped him.

Dawson shifted, dropping his head into his hand. "Do you ever stop talking?"

"When I'm sleeping," Blake replied.

"And when you're dead," Daemon threw back. "You'll stop talking when you're dead."

Blake's lips thinned. "Point taken."

"Good." Daemon focused on the road. "Try shutting up for a while."

I hid my smile as I twisted around. "What are you going to do when you see Beth?"

Awe crept across Dawson's features, and he shook his head slowly. "Oh, man, I don't know. Breathe—I'll finally be able to breathe."

Moved to tears, I gave him a watery smile. "I'm sure she'll feel the same way." At least, I hoped so. The last time I had seen Beth, she wasn't all there in the head. But if I knew anything about Dawson, I knew he could handle it, because he loved her—he had my mom and dad's kind of love.

Out of the corner of my eyes, I saw Daemon's lips tip up at the corners. Something deep in my chest fluttered.

Sucking in a soft breath, I focused on Blake. The side of his head was against the window as he stared out into the dark night. "What about you?"

His gaze slid to mine. For several seconds, he didn't answer. "We'll leave here and head west. And the first thing we're going to do is go surfing. He really used to dig the sea."

I turned around, staring at my hands. Sometimes it was hard to hate without feeling sorry. And I did feel sorry for his friend. I even felt sorry for Blake. "That's…that's good."

None of us spoke after that, and at first, the mood was somber and heavy with memories and probably a thousand what ifs and a dozen scenarios of what tonight would be like for Dawson and Blake, but as we passed Winchester and crossed over the river and could see the darker shades of the Blue Ridge up ahead, the mood shifted.

The boys were tense, throwing off testosterone in buckets. Antsy and ready to just do this, I glanced at the time. Twenty till nine.

"How much longer?" Dawson asked.

"We've got time."

The SUV slipped into a lower gear as we started up the mountain. Behind us, Matthew followed closely. He knew the directions. The access road was supposedly about a half a mile before the main entrance. Daemon had typed it into his GPS, but it pretty much spewed the request back out.

A cell phone dinged and Blake pulled out his cell. "It's from Luc. He wants to make sure we're on schedule."

"We are," Daemon answered.

His brother popped between the front seats. "Are we sure?"

Daemon rolled his eyes. "Yes. I'm sure."

"Just checking," Dawson grumbled, sitting back.

Now Blake was between the seats. "All right, Luc's ready to do this. He wanted to remind us we've only got fifteen minutes. Anything goes wrong, we get out and try again later."

"I don't want to try again later," Dawson protested. "Once we get in, we've got to keep going."

Blake frowned. "I want to get them out just as badly as you, man, but we have a limited gap of time. That's all."

"We stick to the plan." Daemon's gaze met his brother's in the window. "That's it, Dawson. I'm not losing you again."

"Nothing's going to go wrong, anyway," I interjected before it turned into a royal rumble in the car. "Everything will go as planned."

I focused on the road. The highway was four lanes and heavy trees crowded the roads on the south and north lanes. It was a blur of shadows. I had no idea how Daemon would find this road, but he started to slow down and merged into the left lane.

Pressure settled on my chest as he turned onto a barely visible road. There were no markings—nothing signaling that there was even a road there. Two headlights followed us up the narrow opening that was more dirt and gravel than pavement. About two hundred feet in, under the pale moonlight, an old farmhouse sat to the right. Half the roof was missing. Weeds choked the front and sides.

"Creepy," I murmured. "I bet your ghost guys would say this place is haunted."

Daemon chuckled. "They say every place is haunted. That's why I love them."

"Ain't that the truth," Dawson said as we parked and Matthew pulled in beside us.

Both cars killed the lights and engines and with no other source of light, it was black as oil. My stomach pitched. Five till nine. There was no backing out now.

Blake's cell went off again. "He's just making sure we're ready."

"God, he's an annoying little kid," Daemon muttered, facing where Matthew parked. "We're getting ready to do this. Andrew?"

He slipped out, murmuring something to Dee and his sister. Then he turned, throwing up what I'd swear were gang signals. "I'm ready steady."

"Geez," Blake muttered.

"We stick to the plan. At no time do *any* of us"—Daemon directed this at his brother—"deviate from the plan. All of us are coming back tonight."

There were murmurs of agreement. With my pulse racing into cardiac arrest territory, I opened the door.

Daemon placed his hand on my arm. "Stick close to me."

My vocal chords seemed to have stopped working, so I nodded. Then the four of us were out of the car, breathing in the chilled mountain air. Everything was dark—with slices of moonlight cutting across the access road. I was probably standing next to a bear and had no idea.

I moved around the front of the vehicle and stood next to Daemon. Another moved beside me and I realized it was Blake.

"Time," Daemon said.

There was a quick flash of cell phone light, and Blake said, "One minute."

I drew in a shallow gasp, but it got stuck. I could feel my heartbeat in every part of my body. Out of the darkness, Daemon found my hand and squeezed.

We can do this, I told myself. *We can do this. We will do this.*

"Thirty seconds," Blake said.

I worked on my mantra, because I remembered reading something about the laws of the universe and believing in something will make it happen. God, I hoped they were right.

"Ten seconds."

Daemon gave one more squeeze, and I realized he wasn't going to let go. I would slow him down, but there was no time to protest it. A shudder rolled through my arms. I felt the Source rattle and wake up. My weight shifted back and forth.

Beside me, Blake bent forward. "Three, two, go!"

I kicked off, letting the Source rush through, expanding each cell with light. None of the guys were glowing, but we all were running, practically flying. My sneakers skidded over the road. Up we climbed, sticking to the side of the road, avoiding the streams of light. In the back of my head, I realized that keeping up with them had never been the issue.

It was seeing where to go.

But Daemon's hand remained in mine and he wasn't pulling me, more like guiding me through the night, around potholes the size of craters, and up the twisting mountain road.

Seventy-five seconds later, because I counted, a twenty-foot-tall fence came into view under spotlights. We slowed down, coming to a complete stop behind the last stand of trees.

I dragged in air, eyes wide. Red and white signs marked the fence as being electrical. Beyond them was a football-field length of open space and then a massive structure.

"Time?" Daemon asked.

"One minute after nine." Blake ran a hand through his spiky hair. "Okay, I got one guard at the gate. Do you see any others?"

We waited for about another minute to see if any were patrolling, but as Luc had said, it was shift change. Only the gate was covered. We couldn't wait any longer.

"Give me a second," Andrew said, slipping away from the trees, creeping toward the guard dressed in black.

I was just about to ask what the hell he was doing when I saw him dip and place his hand on the ground. Blue sparks flew and the guard started to twist toward him, but the surge of electricity reached him.

A violent tremor ran up the man's body, and he dropped the gun. A second later, he was lying beside it. The boys headed forward and I followed, sneaking a glance at the guard. His chest moved and fell, but he was out cold.

"He doesn't know what hit him." Andrew grinned as he blew a breath over his fingers. "He'll be out for about twenty or so minutes."

"Nice," Dawson said. "I'd have fried his brain if I tried that."

My eyes widened.

Daemon was on the move, approaching the gate. The white

keypad looked unassuming, but it was the first test. We could only hope Luc took the cameras down and had given us the right codes.

"Icarus," Blake said quietly.

Nodding, Daemon's shoulders tensed as he quickly typed in the code. There was a mechanical clicking, a low hum followed, and then the gate shuddered. It swung open, beckoning us like a rolled-out red carpet.

Daemon motioned us forward. We sped across the field, taking a couple of heartbeats to reach the doors Luc and Blake had confirmed. I came up behind Daemon as they searched the wall.

"Where's the damn keypad?" Dawson demanded, pacing between the doors.

I stepped back and forced my gaze to move left to right slowly. "There." I pointed toward the right. The pad was small, stuck back behind the overlay.

Andrew jogged to it, glancing over his shoulder. "Ready?"

Dawson glanced down at me and then at the middle door in front of us. "Yes."

"Labyrinth," Daemon murmured from behind us. "And please, God, spell it correctly."

Andrew snickered and keyed in the code. I wanted to squeeze my eyes shut just in case we ended up with a dozen guns leveled at our faces. The door before us slid open, revealing the space beyond inch by inch.

No guns. No people.

I let out the breath I was holding.

Beyond the door was a wide orange tunnel and at the end were the elevators. Not even a hundred feet and all we had to do was get to those elevators and go down six floors. Blake knew the cells.

We were seriously going to do this.

The door was wide enough for two people to move through at once, but Dawson stepped forward first. Understandable, considering what he had to gain by night's end. I followed behind.

As he moved under the doorframe, there was a sound of air releasing, a small puffing noise.

Dawson dropped like he'd been shot, but there'd been no blast. One second he was standing in the doorway and the next he was on the other side, withering on the floor, his mouth opened in a silent scream.

"No one moves," Andrew ordered.

Time stopped. The hair on the back of my neck rose. I looked up. A row of tiny nozzles, barely even noticeable, faced down. Too late, I realized in horror. The puffing sound came again.

Red-hot pain seared through my skin, as if a thousand tiny knives were slicing me apart from the inside, attacking every cell. Every part of my body erupted as I dragged in a scorching breath. My legs crumbled and I went down, unable to even ease the fall. My cheek smacked off the concrete, that flash of pain nothing compared to the fire ravaging my body.

Brain cells were scrambled and twisted. Muscles locked up in panic and pain. My eyelids were peeled open. Lungs tried to expand, to drag in air, but there was something wrong with the air—it scalded my mouth and throat. Somewhere, in the distant part of me that could still function, I knew what this was.

Onyx—airborne, weaponized onyx.

Chapter 22

My body spasmed uncontrollably as waves of pain rocked through me. Distantly, I could hear panicked voices, and I tried to process what they were saying. Nothing made sense but the deep, slicing agony of the onyx.

Strong hands gripped my arms and the anguish skyrocketed. My mouth opened and a hoarse gasp escaped. Then I was lifted up, my face pressed against something warm and solid. I recognized the fresh scent.

Then we were flying.

We had to be, because we were moving so fast that the wind howled and roared in my ears. My eyes were open, but everything was dark as my skin felt like it was being flayed open with tiny razors.

When we slowed down, I thought I heard Dee's shocked cry and then someone said *river*. We were flying again, and I didn't know where Dawson was or if they had gotten to him on the other side of the door.

All I knew was the pain pumping through my body, the racing

of my pulse and thundering heart.

It felt like hours before we stopped again, but I knew it had to be only minutes. Damp, cold air that smelled musky blew over us.

"Hold on to me." Daemon's voice was harsh in my ears. "It's going to be cold, but the onyx is all over your clothes and hair. Just hold on, okay?"

I couldn't answer, and I thought that if it was all over me, it had to be on Daemon. It had to be on him the whole way from Mount Weather to the river, which was miles. He had to be hurting.

Daemon stepped forward, slid a few feet down, and then let out a muttered curse. Moments later, the shock of icy water hit my legs and even through the pain, I tried to scramble up Daemon's body to escape, but he kept going out farther and the ice lapped up my waist.

"Hold on," he said again. "Just hold on for me."

Then we slipped under and my breath was stolen again. Shaking my head vigorously, sediment was stirred in the murky water and my hair floated around my face, blinding me. But the fire of the onyx… It was fading.

Arms tightened around me, and then we were propelled up. As my head broke the surface, I dragged in air by the lungful. Stars cartwheeled and blurred, and Daemon moved us out of the water to the bank.

Water splashed a few feet away and as my vision cleared, Blake and Andrew dragged Dawson out of the water, laying him on the bank. Blake sat down next to him, thrusting his hands through his soaked hair.

My heart dropped. Was he…?

Dawson flung an arm over his face as he bent one leg. "Crap."

Relief made my knees weak. I felt Daemon's hands on my cheeks and then he turned my face to his. Bright green eyes met mine.

"Are you okay?" he asked. "Say something, Kitten. Please."

I forced my chilled lips to move. "Wow."

His brows lowered as he shook his head, confounded, and then he threw his arms around me, squeezing me so tightly I squealed.

"God, I don't even know..." He cupped the back of my head as he twisted away from the group, lowering his voice. "I was scared to death."

"I'm okay." My voice was muffled. "What about you? You had to have—"

"It's all off me. Don't even worry about that." A shudder rocked him. "Damn, Kitten..."

I kept quiet as he squeezed me again, patted me down like he was checking to make sure I still had arms and fingers. When he kissed my eyelids, though, I thought I would cry, because his hands were trembling.

Four sets of headlights bore down on us and then there was a stream of voices and questions. Dee was the first on the scene. She dropped beside Dawson, grabbing his hand.

"What happened?" she demanded. "Someone tell us what happened."

Matthew and Ash appeared, curious and concerned. It was Andrew who spoke up. "I don't know. They had something that came out of the doors when they opened. It was some kind of spray, but it had no smell and we couldn't see it."

"It hurt like a bitch." Dawson sat up, rubbing his arms. "And there's only one thing that feels like that. Onyx."

Of course he'd also know what it was. I shuddered. God knows how many times it had been used against him.

"But I've never seen it like that before," he continued, slowly climbing to his feet with Ash's and Dee's help. "It was airborne. Insane. I think I swallowed some."

"Are you okay? Katy?" Matthew asked.

We both nodded. My skin ached a little, but the worst of it had passed. "How did you know to get us to the river?"

Daemon brushed wet curls off his forehead. "I guessed it was onyx when I didn't see any visible wounds, figured it was on your clothes and skin. I remembered passing the river. Thought it was the best place to go."

"Good thinking," Matthew said. "Hell..."

"We didn't even make it past the first set of doors." Andrew barked out a laugh. "What the hell were we thinking? They have that place wired against Luxen and, apparently, hybrids."

Daemon disentangled his arms from me and stalked over to where the rest stood. He stopped behind Blake. "You've been to Mount Weather before, right?"

Slowly, Blake pushed to his feet. His cheeks were pale in the silvery moonlight. "Yeah, but nothing—"

Daemon was like a cobra striking. His fist came out, slamming into Blake's jaw. Blake stumbled back and fell, hitting the ground on his butt. Leaning over, he spit out a mouthful of blood. "I didn't know—I didn't know they had something like that!"

"I'm finding that hard to believe." Daemon stalked the boy's movements.

Blake lifted his head. "You have to believe me! Nothing like that ever happened before. I don't understand."

"Bullshit," Andrew said. "You set us up."

"No. No way." Blake stood with his back to the calm river. He placed a hand to his jaw. "Why would I set you guys up? My friend is—"

"I don't care about your friend!" Andrew shouted. "You've been there! How could you not know they had the doors rigged with that stuff?"

Blake turned to me. "You have got to believe me. I had no idea that was going to happen. I wouldn't lead you guys into a trap."

I stared at the river, unsure of what to believe. It seemed stupid for him to set us up this way and if he had, wouldn't the DOD be surrounding us now? Something wasn't right. "And Luc didn't know?"

"If he did, he would've told us. Katy—"

"Don't," Daemon warned and his voice was so low it caught my attention. The lines of his body shimmered. "Don't talk to her. Don't even talk to any of us right now."

Blake opened his mouth but nothing came out. He shook his head as he stalked back to the cars.

There was a gap of silence and then Ash asked, "What do we do now?"

"I don't know." Half of Daemon's face was shadowed as he watched his brother pace. "I really don't know."

Dee rose. "This sucks. This *sucks* donkey butt."

"We're back at square one," Andrew said. "Hell, we're at negative one."

Dawson whipped toward his brother. "We can't give up. Promise me we won't give up."

"We won't." Daemon was quick to reassure him. "We're not giving up."

I didn't even realize I was shaking until Matthew draped a blanket over my shoulders. He met my eyes and then focused on the headlight beams. "I always carry a blanket just in case."

Teeth chattering, I hunkered down in the blanket. "Thank you."

He nodded as he placed a hand on my shoulder. "Come on. Let's get you in the car where it's warm. We're done for the night."

I let him steer me toward Daemon's SUV and the welcoming blast of heat felt wonderful, but there wasn't anything to rejoice in. Disappointment swelled. Unless we figured out a way around the onyx, we weren't just done for the night.

We were circling the drain. We were done period.

• • •

In Dee's words, the ride home sucked donkey butt. It was near midnight when we pulled into the driveway. Blake said nothing as he slipped out of the SUV and headed toward his truck. The engine roared and tires peeled as he pulled out of the driveway.

I started toward my own house, but Daemon cut me off and guided me toward his. "You're not leaving yet," he said.

My brows rose at that and the glint in his eyes, but I wasn't in the mood to argue. It was late, school was tomorrow, and tonight had been one giant fail boat.

I went into their house, still shrouded in Matthew's blanket. My skin was so chilled underneath my damp clothes that I was numb. Exhausted, my legs shook to keep me standing, but everyone was talking—Dee, Andrew, Ash, and Dawson. Matthew was trying to keep them calm, but that wasn't happening. Everyone was hyped up on anger and residual adrenaline, and I think Dawson kept talking because if he stopped then he had to deal with what happened tonight.

Beth was still with Daedalus.

"Let's get you into some dry clothes," Daemon said quietly, taking my hand.

At the bottom of the stairs, Daemon went to pick me up, but I waved him off. "I'm fine."

He made a sound in the back of his throat that reminded me of a disgruntled lion, but he followed my slow ascension. Once inside his bedroom, he closed his door. Determination seeped from his pores.

I sighed. Tonight had been a tragedy. "We kind of deserved this."

He prowled over to me, catching the edges of the blanket, pulling it off. Then he took ahold of my borrowed thermal. "How so?"

It seemed obvious to me. "We're a bunch of teenagers, and we thought we could break into a facility run by Homeland Security and the DOD? I mean, come on. This was bound to go wrong—

Wait!" The thermal was halfway up my stomach. My chilled fingers circled his wrists. "What are you doing?"

"Getting you naked."

My mouth dropped open at the same time my heart did a backflip. A heady warmth cascaded through my veins. "Uh, wow. Way to cut to the point."

A lopsided grin teased his lips. "Your shirt and pants are soaked and cold. And there are probably traces of onyx still on them. You need to get out of your clothes."

I smacked his hands away. "I can do that myself."

Daemon leaned in, speaking into my ear. "Where's the fun in that?" He let go, though, and headed for his dresser. "You really think we were doomed to fail?"

Since he'd turned his back, I made haste with removing my clothes. *Everything* beside the cold piece of obsidian hanging around my neck was ruined and had to come off. The clothing smelled like musky river water. Shivering, I folded my arms across my chest. "Don't…don't turn around."

His shoulders shook with silent laughter as he rummaged around for something for me to wear. Hopefully.

"I don't know," I said, finally answering his question. "It was a huge undertaking for trained spies. We're in over our heads."

"But we were fine until we hit those doors." He pulled out a shirt. "I hate to say this, but I really don't think Blake knew about them. The look on his face when you and Dawson went down—it was too real."

"Then why did you punch him in the face?"

"I wanted to." He turned around, one hand over his eyes as he offered me a shirt. "Here you go."

I snatched it away and quickly tugged it over my head. The soft, worn material billowed around me, ending at my thighs. When I glanced up, I saw his fingers split over his eyes. "You were peeking."

"Maybe." He took my hand, pulling me toward his bed. "Get in.

I'm going to check on Dawson and I'll be back."

I really should have headed next door to my own bed, but I reasoned that tonight was different. Besides, Mom wouldn't be home before school started and I didn't want to be alone. Doing as he requested, I climbed in and yanked the comforter up to my chin. It smelled of fresh linen and Daemon. He wasn't gone long, but in that short time, my lids fluttered shut. The onyx had zapped most of my energy, as it was meant to. We'd been so damn lucky to even make it out of there before the guard came to.

Daemon returned, moving around the room silently, and I was feeling way too lazy to open my eyes and see what he was up to. Clothing rustled to the floor and my temperature went up a degree. Another drawer opened and then he was tugging back the covers, sliding in.

Lying on his side, he wrapped an arm around my waist and tucked me against his bare chest. The flannel of his pajama bottoms teased my legs, and I let out a contented sigh.

"How's Dawson?" I asked, wiggling closer so I was pretty much plastered to him.

"He's doing okay." Daemon brushed the hair back from my cheek, his hand lingering. "He's not a happy camper, though."

I could imagine. We'd come so close to Beth only to have to turn around. That is, if Beth had really been there. Blake may've not known about the onyx defense system from hell, but I didn't trust him. None of us did.

"Thank you for getting us out of there." I tilted my head back, searching out his face in the darkness. His eyes glowed softly.

"I had help." He pressed his lips against my forehead and his arm tightened around me. "You feeling okay?"

"I feel fine. Stop worrying about me."

His eyes met mine. "Don't ever walk through a door first again, okay? And don't argue with me about it or accuse me of being chauvinistic. I don't ever want to see you in that kind of pain again."

Instead of arguing, I twisted in his embrace and placed my lips on his, kissing him softly. His lashes lowered, shielding his eyes. He returned the kiss and it was sweet and tender and so perfect that there was a good chance I'd start bawling like a baby.

But then the kisses, well, they changed. They deepened as I rolled onto my back and he followed, his weight a delicious feeling against my legs, and these kisses were anything but sweet. They scorched deep inside me, washing away the events of the last couple of hours like the river had taken away the unholy burn of the onyx. When he kissed like this, every muscle in his body coiling into a tight spring, he undid me.

His hand smoothed the shirt down, baring a shoulder, and his mouth followed. Static built in the air and a tremble coursed through his body. In that moment, after everything that happened, I wanted the feel of him against me with no barriers, nothing getting in the way. Lifting up, I raised my arms and Daemon didn't hesitate. He took what was offered. With nothing there, his hands were everywhere, tracing the slender piece of obsidian, smoothing down the curve of my stomach, over my hips, and I was pretty sure there would be no other moment as perfect as this.

Or maybe it was how close we came to losing it all tonight that propelled us both? I didn't know, nor was I sure how we'd come to this point, but all that mattered was we were both here and ready. Really ready. And when his clothing joined mine on the floor, there was no going back.

"Don't stop," I said, just in case he had any doubts about what I wanted.

There was a flash of a grin, and then he kissed me again and I was drowning in the rawness of what was building between us. Electricity coursed over our skin, throwing dancing shadows over the walls as he reared up, reaching for the small bedside table beside us.

I flushed, realizing what he was going for. When he sat up and our eyes met, I started to giggle. A wide, beautiful smile broke out across his face, softening lines that held a harsh beauty.

Daemon spoke in his language. The lyrical quality of his words made no sense to me, but they were beautiful, like spoken music that the alien part of me danced to.

"What did you say?" I asked.

He peered up through thick lashes, the foil package in his fist. "There's really no translation for it," he said, "but the closest human words would be, you are beautiful to me."

I sucked in a sharp breath and our gazes locked. Tears built in my eyes. I reached for him, sinking my fingers into his silky hair. My heart was pounding fast, and I knew his was, too.

This was it. And it was right. Perfect without the dinner, movies, and flowers, because how could you really plan something like this? You couldn't.

Daemon sat back—

A fist pounded on the door, and Andrew's voice intruded. "Daemon, are you awake?"

We stared at each other in disbelief. "If I ignore him," he whispered, "do you think he'll go away?"

My hands dropped to my sides. "Maybe."

The pounding came again. "Daemon, I really need you downstairs. Dawson is ready to go back to Mount Weather. Nothing Dee or I are saying to him is making a bit of difference. He's like a suicidal Energizer bunny."

Daemon squeezed his eyes shut. "Son of a bitch…"

"It's okay." I started to sit up. "He needs you."

He let out a ragged sigh. "Stay here and get some rest. I'll talk—or beat some sense into him." He kissed me briefly and then gently pushed me back down. "I'll be back."

Settling in, I smiled. "Try not to kill him."

"No promises." He stood, pulled on his pajama bottoms, and headed for the door. Stopping short, he looked over his shoulder, his intense gaze melting my bones. "Dammit."

A few seconds after he stepped out into the hallway and closed the door behind him, there was a fleshly smack and then Andrew yelling, "Ouch. What in the hell was that for?"

"Your timing sucks on an epic level," Daemon shot back.

Smiling sleepily, I rolled onto my side and ordered myself to stay awake, but as my breathing returned to normal, sleep dragged me under. Sometime later, I heard the door open and then Daemon was beside me, pulling me back against him. It wasn't long before the steady rise and fall of his chest lulled me back into the rhythm of sleep. Every so often I'd wake up when his arms clenched around me, his embrace so tight I thought he'd cut off my circulation, holding me as if even in his sleep he was haunted by the fear of losing me.

Chapter 23

Daemon and I rode together to school on Monday. The car still carried a musty, wet scent to it, a painful reminder of where our mission had ended—in a river. On the way, Daemon was convinced that his brother had been talked down from bum-rushing Mount Weather, but I knew we needed to come up with another way to get to Beth and Chris. Dawson couldn't wait forever, and I could understand that. If it were Daemon locked up, I don't think anyone would be able to stop me.

As soon as we stepped out, I saw Blake leaning against his truck a few spaces down. He pushed off and trotted over the moment he spotted us.

Daemon groaned. "He is not who I want to see as soon as I get to school."

"Agreed," I said, wrapping my hand around Daemon's. "Just remember we are in public."

"No fun."

Blake slowed as he reached us, his gaze dipping to our joined hands and then quickly sweeping up. "We all need to talk."

We kept walking—or Daemon kept walking. "Talking to you is the last thing I want to do."

"I can understand that." He caught up to us. "But I seriously didn't know about the onyx shields in the doors. I had no idea."

"I believe you," Daemon said.

Blake's step faltered. "You punched me."

"That's because he wanted to," I answered for Daemon, earning a wink from him. "Look, I don't trust you, but maybe you didn't know about the shields. It doesn't change the fact that we're not going to be able to get in there."

"I talked to Luc last night. He didn't know about the shields, either." Blake shoved his hands into his pockets and stopped in front of us. He was lucky Daemon didn't lay him out right there. "He's willing to do it again—take down the cameras and stuff."

Daemon blew out a long breath. "And what good does that do us? We can't get past those doors."

"Or if every door is set up like that," I added, shivering. I couldn't imagine going through that three or four times. Sure, I'd been in that cage longer, but the airborne onyx had covered everything.

The three of us were huddled along the fence surrounding the track, careful of keeping our voices low so other students didn't overhear us and wonder what the heck.

"Well, I was thinking about that," Blake said, shifting from one foot to the other. "While I was with Daedalus, they used to expose us to this stone each day. Our forks and silverware were encased in it. A lot of stuff was, almost everything we came into contact with. Burned like holy hell to touch, but we didn't have any other choice. I've walked through the doors before and recently. Nothing happened."

Daemon laughed as he looked away from Blake. "And you now just thought this was a good thing to tell us?"

"I didn't know what it was. None of us did." Blake's gaze

pleaded with mine. "I didn't think much about it."

Dumbfounded, I realized they'd been conditioning Blake. Probably exposing him and others to the onyx over and over but like last night, something wasn't right. Why would they expose them to it? Sick and twisted punishment or for tolerance? And why would they want Luxen or hybrids to develop a tolerance to the one weapon that could be used against them?

"You can't tell me you never knew about the onyx and what it could do," I said.

He met me dead-on. "I didn't know that it could incapacitate us."

I pressed my lips together. "You know, there's so much we have to just trust you with. That you really are working against Daedalus and not for them. That Beth and Chris are where you're saying they are, and now, that you didn't really know about onyx."

"I know how this looks."

"I don't think you do," Daemon said, letting go of my hand as he propped his hip against the fence. "We have no reason to trust you."

"And you've blackmailed us into helping you," I added.

Blake exhaled roughly. "Okay. I don't have a glowing history, but I want nothing more than to get my friend away from them. That's why I'm here."

"And why are you here right this instant?" Daemon asked, obviously at his patience threshold.

"I think we can get around the onyx," he said, pulling his hands out of his pockets and holding them in front of him. "Now, hear me out. This is going to sound crazy."

"Oh, goodie," Daemon muttered.

"I think we need to build up a tolerance. If that was what Daedalus was doing, then that makes sense. Hybrids have to go in and out of those doors. If we expose ourselves to it—"

"Are you insane?" Daemon turned around, running his hand

through his hair, clasping the back of his neck. "You want us to expose ourselves to onyx?"

"Do you see any other option?"

Yeah, there was one—we didn't go back. But was it really an option? Daemon was starting to pace. Not a good sign. "Can we do this later? We're going to be late."

"Sure." He sidestepped Daemon. "After school?"

"Maybe," I said, focusing on Daemon. "We'll talk later."

Taking the hint, Blake skedaddled out of there. I had no idea what to say to any of this. "Expose ourselves to onyx?"

Daemon huffed. "He's insane."

He was. "Do you think it would work?"

"You're not…?"

"I don't know." I switched my backpack to the other shoulder and we started toward the school. "I really don't know. We can't give up, but what other options do we have?"

"We don't even know if it will work."

"But if Blake really is sort of immune to it, then we can test it out on him."

A wide grin spread across his face. "I like the sound of that."

I laughed. "Why doesn't that surprise me? But seriously, if he has a tolerance to it, then shouldn't we be able to? It's something. We'd just need to figure out how to get some." Daemon was quiet for a few seconds "What?" I asked.

He squinted. "I think I have the onyx part covered."

"What do you mean?" I stopped again, ignoring the faint warning bell.

"After Will got you and a couple of days after Dawson came back, I returned to the warehouse and stripped most of the onyx from the outside."

My jaw hit the ground. "What?"

"Yeah, I don't know why I did it. Kind of like my big FU to the establishment." He laughed. "Imagine their faces when they went back and saw it was all gone."

I was speechless.

He tweaked my nose. I smacked his hand away. "You're insane. You could've gotten caught!"

"But I didn't."

I smacked him again, this time harder. "You're crazy."

"But you love my craziness." He leaned down, kissing the corner of my lip. "Come on, we're late. The last thing we need is detention."

I snorted. "Yeah, like *that* would be the biggest of our problems."

• • •

Carissa still hadn't returned to school on Monday. The flu must've been kicking her butt. Lesa seemed a bit jealous over the whole thing. "I'm, like, five pounds from my goal weight," she said before trig started. "Why can't I come down with something? Geesh."

I giggled and we moved on to some gossip. For a little while, I forgot about everything. It was nice and much needed downtime even though we were in school. The morning blew by and when Blake entered bio, I refused to let him ruin my mood.

But then he opened his mouth and the big "what the hell" statement came out. "You didn't tell Daemon about what I said to you in the woods? About me liking you?"

Ah, what the frig, man? "Um, no. He'd kill you."

Blake laughed.

I frowned. "I'm being serious."

"Oh." His smile faded and he paled. I imagined that he was playing that scenario out in his head: me telling Daemon about his dirty little secret and Daemon going ape poo poo over it. He came to the same conclusion as me. "Yeah, good call.

"Anyway," he continued. "About what I said this morning—"

"Not now." I opened my notebook. "I really don't want to talk about that right now."

I smiled when Lesa sat down and luckily, Blake respected my request. He chatted it up with Lesa like a normal person would. He was good at that—pretending.

A knot formed in my stomach as I looked at him sharply. He was telling Lesa about different kinds of surfing techniques. I was pretty sure she wasn't even listening, considering her gaze was trained on how his shirt strained over his biceps.

He laughed easily, blending in perfectly. Like a good implant would, and I knew from previous experience that Blake was skilled at faking it. There really was no way of telling what side Blake was truly on, and it was stupid to even guess.

At the front of the class, Matthew pulled out his roll book. His eyes met mine briefly and then shifted to the boy beside me. I wondered how Matthew did it—kept calm all the time. How he stayed the glue that kept everyone together.

• • •

I stopped at my locker and grabbed my US history text at the end of the day. The chances of a pop quiz tomorrow were high. Mrs. Kerns had a schedule, which really didn't make the quiz a big surprise. I closed my locker door and turned, shoving my book into the bag. The crowd was thinning out as everyone rushed to get out of the school. I wasn't sure if I wanted to rush or not. Blake had already texted me during gym about getting everyone together to talk about the onyx situation, and I really didn't want to.

I wanted one day to go home and do nothing—no plotting or dealing with alien shenanigans. Books needed reading and reviewing and my poor blog could really use a makeover. I couldn't think of a better way to finish out a Monday.

But it was probably not going to happen.

Stepping outside, I trailed behind the last group of students heading to the parking lot. From my vantage point, I could hear Kimmy's high-pitched voice from the front.

"My daddy said that Simon's father has been talking to the FBI. He's demanding a full investigation and won't stop until Simon comes home."

I wondered if the FBI knew about the aliens. Images of *The X-Files* flew through my head.

"I heard on TV that the longer a person is missing, the less likely it is for them to turn up alive," one of her friends said.

"But look at Dawson. He was gone for over a year, and he's back," another said.

Tommy Cruz rubbed a beefy hand along the back of his neck. "And isn't that strange? He's gone forever. The one Thompson kid bites it and then Dawson shows up? Something insane with that."

I'd heard enough. Going between cars, I put distance between the group and me. I doubted their suspicious would go anywhere, but I wasn't trolling for new things to worry about. We had enough.

Daemon waited by his car. Long legs crossed at the ankles. He smiled when he saw me and pushed off the side of the vehicle. "I was beginning to wonder if you were going to stay here."

"Sorry." He opened the passenger door and bowed. Grinning, I jumped in. I waited until he was behind the wheel. "Blake wants to talk tonight."

"Yeah, I know. He apparently got ahold of Dawson and already told him about the whole onyx tolerance thing." He backed out, hand on the gear shifter. Anger lit up his eyes. "And of course, Dawson is all about that. It was like handing him a winning lottery ticket."

"Great." I tilted my head back against the seat. Dawson really was a suicidal Energizer bunny.

And suddenly it struck me. This was my life—all of this craziness. The ups and downs, the near-death moments and those far worse, the lies and the fact I probably wouldn't be able to trust anyone who befriended me without worrying if they were an implant. And hell, how could I really befriend anyone normal? Like Daemon in the beginning—he'd stayed away and wanted Dee to do the same so I wouldn't be caught in their world.

It would be the same with anyone I met.

My life wasn't my own. Every moment was like waiting for the other shoe to drop. I sank back against the seat, weighted down, and sighed. "There go my reviewing and reading plans."

"Shouldn't it be reading and then reviewing?"

"Whatever," I muttered.

Daemon coasted the SUV out onto the road. "Why can't you still do that?"

"If Blake wants to talk tonight, then that's going to soak up all my time." I really wanted to pout. Maybe even kick my feet.

With one hand on the wheel and the other arm thrown over the back of my seat, he cast me a half smile. "You don't need to be there, Kitten. We can talk to him without you."

"Yeah right." I laughed. "There's a good chance someone will kill Blake without me there."

"And would you really be torn up about that?"

I made a face. "Well…"

Daemon laughed.

"And the fact that upon his untimely death, there's a letter delivered to Nancy Husher. So, we kind of need him alive."

"True," he said, catching a strand of my hair between his fingers. "But we can keep it short. You'll have a normal Monday evening full of normal suck and not extraterrestrial suckage."

Shame burned my cheeks as I bit down on my lip. As crazy as everything had turned out, I could admit that things could be worse. "That's really selfish of me."

"What?" He tugged on my hair gently. "It's not selfish, Kitten. Your whole life can't revolve around this crap. It won't."

Straightening my fingers, I smiled. "You sound so determined."

"And you know what happens when I get determined."

"You get your way." He raised his brows at me, and I laughed. "But what about you—your life can't revolve around this crap."

He pulled his hand back, resting it on his thigh. "I was born into this. I'm used to it, and besides, it's all about time management. Say, like time management last night. We did our mission thing—"

"And failed."

"There's that, but the rest of last night?" One side of his lips curled up and I felt my cheeks heat for a totally different reason. "We had the bad—the not-normal. And then we had the good—the normal. Granted, the good was interrupted by the bad, but there was time management there."

"You make it sound so easy." I stretched out my legs, relaxing.

"It is that easy, Kat. You just need to know when to draw the line, when you've had enough." There was a pause as he slowed and turned onto the lonely road leading up to our houses. "And if you've had enough for today, you have. Nothing to feel guilty about or to worry about."

Daemon coasted to a stop in his driveway and killed the engine. "And no one will kill Bill."

I laughed softly as I unbuckled the seat belt. "Blake. His name is Blake."

Daemon pulled the keys out and leaned back, his eyes glimmering with amusement. "He's whatever I decide to call him."

"You're terrible." Crossing the distance between us, I kissed him. As I pulled away, he reached for me and I giggled, opening the door. "And by the way, I haven't had enough today. I just needed a kick in the pants. But I do need to be home by seven."

I shut the door and turned. Daemon stood before me. He stepped forward and there was nowhere for me to go if I wanted to. And I didn't.

"You haven't had enough?" he asked.

Recognizing the tone of his voice, my bones melted in response. "No, not nearly enough."

"Good." His hands were on my hips, tugging me forward. "That's what I like to hear."

Placing my hands on his chest, I tilted my head back. This was totally an exercise in time management. Our lips brushed and warmth cascaded through me. It was a really fun exercise. I rose onto the tips of my toes and slid my hands up the hard plane of his chest, marveled at the way it rose unsteadily.

Daemon whispered something and then the soft kiss, which wasn't much more than a butterfly touch, strengthened me and unraveled him. His arms swept around me, and I could feel his heart pounding in tandem with mine.

"Hey!" Dawson yelled from the front door. "I think Dee caught the microwave on fire. Again. And I tried popping some popcorn with my hands and it kind of went wrong. Like really, really wrong."

Daemon pressed his forehead against mine and growled. *"Dammit."*

I couldn't help but laugh. "Time management, right?"

"Time management," he muttered.

. . .

Surprisingly, pretty much everyone was on board with the onyx thing. I was convinced we had an invasion of the body snatchers or something, because even Matthew was nodding like exposing yourself to the hellishly painful onyx was a good thing.

I had a feeling that would change the first time he came in contact with it.

"This is so insane," Dee said, and I had to agree. "This is tantamount to self-mutilation."

Ah, she kind of had a point.

Dawson's head dropped back, and he sighed. "That's a little

extreme."

"I remember what you looked like when they brought you back down the mountain." She twisted her hair around her hand. "And Katy lost her voice for a while from screaming. Who signs up for that?"

"Crazy people." Daemon sighed. "Dee, I don't want you doing this."

Her expression was clearly a *no duh* one. "No offense, Dawson, I love you and want you to see Beth and to hold her, because I wish…" Her voice cracked, but her spine straightened. "But I don't want to do this."

Dawson shot forward, placing a hand on her arm. "It's okay. I don't expect you to do this."

"I want to help." Her voice was wobbly. "But I can't…"

"It's fine." Dawson smiled and there was a moment between the siblings, as if he were saying more with just that gesture alone. Whatever it was, it worked, because Dee relaxed. "Not all of us need to do this."

"Then who's in?" Blake's eyes touched on all of us. "If we are going to do this, we need to start, like, yesterday, because I don't know how long it'll take to build a tolerance."

Antsy, Dawson stood. "It can't take that long."

Blake let out a surprised laugh. "I've been with Daedalus for years, so there's no telling at what point I built a tolerance…or if I really even have one."

"We've got to test that out, then." I grinned.

He frowned. "Wow. Kind of excited about that?"

I nodded.

Dee twisted around, eyeing Blake. "Can I test it out, too?"

"I'm pretty sure everyone will get a round." Daemon's sinister twist of the lips was actually kind of frightening. "Anyway, back to the basics. Who's in?"

Matthew raised his hand. "I want to be in on this. No offense,

Andrew, but I prefer to take your place this time."

Andrew nodded his head. "No problem. I can wait with Dee and Ash."

Ash, who hadn't said more than two words, just nodded. I realized that half of the room was staring at me. "Oh," I said. "Yeah, I'm in." Beside me, Daemon gave me a look that said, *You are so out of your mind*. I folded my arms. "Don't start with me. I'm in. Nothing you can say will change that."

The next look translated into, *This is going to turn into a conversation—argument—in private*. Blake watched with approval—a ringing endorsement I didn't want or need. Frankly, it made my skin crawl, since it reminded me of when I had killed the Arum he'd practically thrown at me.

God, I wanted to hit him again.

Plans were made to meet after school and, weather permitting, we'd head out to the lake to basically start causing ourselves an obscene amount of pain. Whee.

Since there were some hours left before bedtime, I said my good-byes and left to get some studying in and hopefully a dang review.

Daemon walked me over and I knew it wasn't a gentlemanly act, but I let him in and offered him his favorite: milk.

He downed the drink in five seconds flat. "Can we talk about this?"

I hopped up on the counter and opened my bag, pulling out my history book. "Nope."

"Kat."

"Hmm?" I flipped open to the chapter we'd been reading in class.

He stalked over, placing his hands on either side of my crossed legs. "I can't watch you get hurt over and over again."

I dug out a Highlighter.

"Seeing what happened last night and when Will had you

handcuffed in that stuff? And I'm supposed to just stand there— Are you listening to me?"

Halfway through the sentence I'd highlighted, I stopped. "I'm listening."

"Then look at me."

I lifted my lashes. "I'm looking at you."

Daemon scowled.

Sighing, I put the cap back on the Highlighter. "Okay. I don't want to see you in pain."

"Kat—"

"No. Don't interrupt. I don't want to see you in pain and just thinking about you going through what that feels like makes me want to hurl."

"I can handle it."

Our eyes locked. "I know you can, but that doesn't change how horrible it's going to be to see you go through that, but I'm not asking you not to do it."

He pushed off and pivoted around, thrusting his fingers through his hair. Tension and frustration settled over the kitchen like a well-worn blanket.

Setting my stuff aside, I hopped down. "I don't want to argue with you, Daemon, but you can't say it's okay for me to watch you go through this and not you."

I made my way over to him and wrapped my arms around his waist. He stiffened. "I know this is coming from a good place, but just because it's getting ugly, I can't back out. And you know you're not going to. It's only fair."

"I hate your logic." He placed his hands on mine, though, and I pressed against his back, smiling. "And I'm really going to hate this."

Squeezing him like my favorite teddy bear, I knew how hard this was for him to give on. This was monumental, actually. He twisted in my arms, lowered his head, and I thought, *Wow, this is how adults do things.* They may not agree on stuff all the time, they may argue, but in the end, they work it out and they love.

Like my mom and dad.

A lump formed in my throat. Crying so wouldn't be the right thing to do, but it was hard to keep those tears back.

"The only good thing is that I'm going to hold Buff down and make him kiss onyx over and over again," he said.

I choked out a laugh. "You're sadistic."

"And you need to study, right? It's school time management— not Daemon time management, which blows, because we're alone and it requires more effort for them to interrupt us over here."

Disappointed, I pulled free. "Yeah, I need to study."

He pouted and it was incredibly sexy on him. Wrong. "All right, I'm leaving."

I followed him to the door. "I'll text when I'm done and you can come over and tuck me in."

"'Kay," he said, kissing the top of my head. "I'll be waiting."

And knowing that had me all warm and fuzzy. Wiggling my fingers at him, I closed the door and went back to the kitchen, grabbed my stuff and a glass of OJ. Happy that an all-out brouhaha was avoided with Daemon, I went upstairs and bumped open my door.

I came to a complete stop.

A girl sat on my bed, hands folded primly in her lap. It took me a moment to recognize her, because her hair hung in limp strands around her pale face and her almond-shaped eyes weren't hidden behind purple or pink glasses.

"Carissa," I said, stunned. "How…how did you get in here?"

She stood wordlessly. Her hands extended out. The overhead light reflected off a bracelet I also recognized—black stone with fire inside.

What the hell…? Luc had that stone. Why would—?

Static crackled in the air and there was a smell of burned ozone a second before whitish-blue light radiated from Carissa's hands. The bracelet was no longer a concern.

Shocked into a stupor, I stared at my friend in disbelief. "Crap."

Carissa attacked.

Chapter 24

The bolt of energy slammed into my history textbook, burning a hole right through. It fizzled out before it could touch me, but the book casualty told me what I needed to know.

Carissa was not a friendly.

And that little display of the Source was not a warning.

I dropped the book and darted to the left as she lunged at me. OJ sloshed over the side of my glass, covering my fingers. Why was I still holding it? My brain was so not catching up to this turn of events.

She shot toward me, and I did the only thing I could think of in that moment. I threw the glass at her face. Glass shattered as she stumbled back, raising her hands to her eyes. Sticky liquid and glass coursed down her cheeks, mixing with tiny flecks of blood.

I bet that stung like a bitch.

"Carissa," I said, backing up. "I have no idea how this happened, but I'm a friend—I can help you! Just calm down. Okay?"

She wiped at her eyes, flinging liquid against the walls. When her gaze met mine, there wasn't an ounce of recognition in it. Her eyes were frighteningly empty and vast. Like months had been washed away, and I was nothing to her. There was zilch going on behind those eyes.

My eyes had to be deceiving me or I was dreaming, because she was definitely a hybrid and that didn't make sense. Carissa didn't know about aliens. She was just a normal girl. Quiet and maybe a little bit shy.

But she'd been out with the *flu*…

Oh, dear baby kittens… She'd been mutated.

Her head cocked to the side, eyes narrowing.

"Carissa, please, it's me. Katy. You know me," I pleaded. My back hit the desk as I eyed the open door behind her. "We're friends. You don't want to do this."

She stalked toward me, like that freaky female terminator after John Connor.

And I was so John Connor.

I drew in a breath, but it got stuck. "We go to school together— we have trig and we eat lunch together. You wear glasses—really funky glasses." I didn't know what to say, but I kept babbling, hoping to somehow reach her, because the last thing I wanted to do was hurt her. "Carissa, *please*."

But she apparently had no qualms over doing some damage to me.

The air charged with static again. I lurched to the side as she let go of the Source again. The tail end of it singed my sweater. A smell of burned hair and cotton wafted into the air as I spun toward my desk. There was a low whine from the desk and then smoke billowed out of my closed laptop.

I gaped.

My precious, perfectly brand new laptop I cherished like one would a small child.

Son of a mother…

Friend or not, it was so on.

I lunged at Carissa, taking her down to my bedroom floor. My hands went around her hair and lifted. A stream of dark strands billowed, and then I slammed her head down. There was a satisfactory *thud* and she let out a low squeal of pain.

"You stupid—" Carissa tilted her pelvis up, wrapped her legs around my hips and rolled, gaining the upper hand in seconds. She was like a damn ninja—who knew? She slammed my head back much harder and damn, did paybacks suck. Starbursts clouded my vision. Sharp pain exploded along my jaw, momentarily startling me.

And then something inside me snapped.

Blistering rage welled up, coating my skin, setting a fire to every cell in my body. There was a heady rush of power centered in my chest. It flowed like lava through my veins, reaching the tips of my fingers. A veil of whitish-red fell over my eyes.

Time was slowing down again to an infinite crawl. Heat from the vents blew the curtains out, and the flimsy material reached toward us and then stopped, suspending in air. The small puffs of gray and white smoke froze. And in the back of my mind, I realized that they weren't really frozen, but I was moving so fast that everything appeared to have been stopped.

I didn't want to hurt her but I *was* going to stop her.

Arching back, I slammed both hands into her chest. Carissa flew into my dresser. Bottles of lotion rattled and fell over, clunking off her head.

I leaped to my feet, breathing heavily. The Source raged in me, demanded to be tapped into, to be used again. Holding back was like daring not to breathe.

"Okay," I gasped. "Let's just take a moment and calm down. We can talk this out, figure out what's going on."

Slowly, painfully, Carissa climbed to her feet. Our eyes locked and the absent look in hers sent shivers to my very core.

"Don't," I warned. "I don't want to hurt—"

Her hand snaked out, lightning quick, caught my cheek, and spun me around. I hit the bed on my hip and slid to the floor. A metallic taste burst into my mouth. My lip stung and ears rang.

Carissa grabbed a handful of my hair and yanked me to my feet. Fire burned my scalp, and I let out a hoarse scream. She forced me on my back, wrapping her hands around my neck. Slender fingers dug into my windpipe, cutting off air. The moment I couldn't breathe brought me back to my very first run-in with the Arum, reviving the sense of desperation and helplessness as my lungs were starved for oxygen.

I wasn't the same girl as then, too afraid to put up a fight.

Screw that.

Letting the Source build inside me, I let it go. Stars exploded in my room, dazzling in their effect as the blast knocked Carissa back into the wall. Plaster cracked but she remained on her feet. Wisps of smoke streamed from her charred sweater.

Good God, the chick wouldn't go down.

I rolled onto my feet, trying one more time to reach her. "Carissa, we are friends. You don't want to do this. Please listen to me. *Please*."

Energy crackled over her knuckles, forming a ball, and in any other situation, I'd be jealous of how easily she'd mastered the ability in what seemed like a nanosecond, because last week...last week she'd been normal.

And now I didn't know what or who stood in front of me.

Ice filled the pit of my stomach, forming shards around my insides. There was no reasoning with her. No chance whatsoever, and the realization cost me. Distracted, I didn't move fast enough when she released the ball of energy.

I raised my hands and screamed, "Stop!" Throwing everything I had into the single word, picturing the tiny light particles in the air responding to my call, forming a barrier.

Air shimmered around me as if a tub of glitter had been dumped in a perfect line. Each speck glowed with the power of a thousand suns. And in the back of my mind, I knew that whatever was going on should've been able to stop the ball.

But it broke through, shattering the glimmering wall, slowing it down but not stopping it.

The energy smacked into my shoulder and pain exploded, momentarily robbing me of sight and sound as it knocked me down, my legs over my head. I landed on my stomach on the bed with a loud *oomph*. Air rushed from my lungs, but I knew I didn't have time to let the pain sink through.

I lifted my head, peering through strands of tangled hair.

Carissa stalked forward; her movements were fluid and then… not so much. Her left leg started to tremble and then quake violently. The shudder rolled up the left side of her body and *only* the left side of her body. Her arm flailed and half her face spasmed.

I pushed up on weak arms, scooting across my bed until I toppled off the side. "Carissa?"

Her entire body began to quiver like the earth shook only for her. I thought maybe she was having a seizure, and I stood.

Sparks flew from her skin. The stink of burning cloth and skin singed my nostrils. She kept shaking, her head flopping on her boneless neck.

I clamped my hand over my mouth as I took a step toward her. I needed to help her, but I didn't know how.

"Carissa, I—"

The air around her imploded.

A shock wave tore through my room. The computer chair overturned; the bed lifted up on one side, suspended; and the wave kept coming. Clothing flew from my closet. Papers swirled and fell like sheets of snow.

When the wave reached me, it lifted me off my feet and flung me back like I weighed nothing more than one of the floating papers. I hit the wall beside the little stand next to my bed, and I hung there as the shock wave surged.

I couldn't move or breathe.

And Carissa… Oh my God, Carissa…

Her skin and bones sunk in as if someone had hooked up a vacuum to the back of her and kicked it on. Inch by inch she shrank until a burst of light with the power of a solar storm lit the room—lit the entire house and probably the entire street, blinding me.

A loud, deafening *pop* sounded and as the light receded, so did the shock wave. I slipped to the floor, a heap among piles of clothing and papers, dragging in air. I couldn't get enough oxygen, because the room was empty.

I stared at the area where Carissa had once stood. There was nothing but a darkened spot on the floor, like what Baruck had left behind when he was killed.

There was nothing, absolutely nothing of the girl—of my friend.

Nothing.

Chapter 25

I felt the warm tingle on the back of my neck numbly, and then Daemon stood in the doorway, brows lifted and his mouth hanging open.

"I can't leave you alone for two seconds, Kitten."

I sprung from the mess of clothing and threw myself in his arms. All of it came out in an incoherent babble of words and run-on sentences. Several times he slowed me down and asked me to repeat myself before he got the general gist of what went down.

He took me downstairs and sat beside me on the couch, his fingers moving over my bottom lip as his eyes narrowed in concentration. Healing warmth spread along my lips and across my aching cheeks.

"I don't understand what happened," I said, tracking his movements. "She was normal last week. Daemon, you saw her. How did we not know this?"

His jaw tightened. "I think the better question is, why did she come after you?"

The knot that had been in my stomach moved upward, settling

on my chest and making it hard to breathe. "I don't know."

I didn't know anything anymore. I kept rewinding every conversation with Carissa, from the first time I met her up until she was out of school with the "flu." Where were the clues, the red herring? I couldn't find one that stood out.

Daemon frowned. "She could've known a Luxen—known the truth and knew not to tell anyone. I mean, no one inside of the colony knows that you're aware of the truth."

"But there's no other Luxen around our age," I said.

His gaze flicked up. "None outside the colony, but there are a few who are only a couple years older or younger than us *in* the colony."

It was possible that Carissa had always known and we didn't. I'd never told her or Lesa, so it took no leap of the imagination to think that Carissa knew but never told anyone. But why did she try and kill me?

Entirely possible that I wasn't the only person around here who knew what lived among us, but dear God, what went wrong? Had she been hurt and a Luxen tried to heal her? "You don't think…" I couldn't finish the question. It was too sickening, but Daemon knew where I was going with it.

"That Daedalus took her and forced a Luxen to heal her like with Dawson?" Anger darkened the green hue. "I seriously pray that's not the case. If so, it's just…"

"Revolting," I said hoarsely. My hands shook so I shoved them between my knees. "She wasn't there. Not even a flicker of her personality. She was like a zombie, you know? Just freaking crazed. Is that what instability does?"

Daemon moved his hands away and the healing warmth ebbed off. When it did, so did the barrier that had kept the truth of everything from really breaking free and consuming me. "God, she…she died. Does that mean…?" I swallowed, but the lump was pushing its way up my throat.

Daemon's arms tightened. "If it were one of the Luxen here, then I'll hear about it, but we don't know if the mutation held. Blake has said that sometimes the mutation is unstable and that sounded pretty damn unstable. The bonding only happens if it's a stable mutation, I believe."

"We need to talk to Blake," I said, and a shudder rolled through me. I blinked, but my vision blurred even more. I took a breath and choked. "Oh…oh, God, Daemon…that was Carissa. That was Carissa and that wasn't right."

Another shudder racked my shoulders and before I knew what was happening, I was crying—those big, breath-stealing sobs. Vaguely, I realized that Daemon had pulled me over to him and cradled my head to his chest.

I'm not sure how long the tears came, but every part of me ached in a way that couldn't by repaired by Daemon. Carissa was wholly innocent in all of this, or at least I believed her to be, and maybe that's what made this whole thing worse. I didn't know how deep Carissa was involved, and how would I ever find out?

The tears…they flowed, practically soaking Daemon's shirt, but he didn't pull away. If anything, he held me tighter and he whispered in that lyrical voice of his in a language I could never understand but felt drawn to nonetheless. The unknown words soothed me and I wondered if long ago someone, a parent maybe, had held him and whispered the same words to him. And how many times had he done it for his siblings? Even with all the bark *and* bite he carried, he was a natural at this.

It calmed the dark abyss, dulled the edges of the sharp blow.

Carissa… Carissa was gone, and I didn't know how to deal with that. Or with the fact that her last act had been to try to take me out, which was so, so unlike her.

When the tears finally subsided, I sniffled and wiped at my face with my sleeves. The one on my right was charred from the energy blast and was rough against my cheek. The scratchy feeling poked a memory free.

I lifted my head. "She had a bracelet I'd never seen her wear before. The same kind of bracelet that Luc had on."

"Are you sure?" When I nodded, he leaned back against the couch, keeping me in his embrace. "This is even more suspicious."

"Yeah."

"We need to talk to Luc without our unwanted sidekick first." He tipped his chin up, letting out a long sigh. Worry touched his face, roughened his voice. "I'll let the others know." I started to speak, but he shook his head. "I don't want you to have to go through telling them what happened."

I lowered my cheek to his shoulder. "Thank you."

"And I'll take care of your bedroom. We'll get it cleaned up."

Relief coursed through me. Cleaning up that room, seeing the spot on the floor, was the last thing I wanted to do. "You're perfect, you know."

"Sometimes," he murmured, brushing his chin along my cheek. "I'm sorry, Kat. I'm sorry about Carissa. She was a good girl and didn't deserve this."

My lips trembled. "No, she didn't."

"And you didn't deserve to have to go through that with her."

I didn't say anything to that, because I wasn't so sure what I deserved anymore. Sometimes I didn't think I even deserved Daemon.

We made plans to go to Martinsburg on Wednesday, which meant we'd be missing our second day of onyx training, but I couldn't think about that right now. Finding out how Carissa ended up a hybrid and in possession of the same kind of bracelet Luc wore was paramount. If I could figure out what happened to her, then there would be some kind of justice.

I had no idea what I was supposed to say at school when Carissa never came back and the inevitable questions began. I didn't think I had it in me to pretend to be clueless and tell more lies. Another kid missing...

Oh, God, Lesa... What would Lesa do? They'd been best friends since grade school.

I squeezed my eyes tight and curled up against Daemon. The aches of the fight had long faded, but I was weary to the core, mentally and physically drained. It was ironic that I'd spent the last month avoiding the living room and now it would be my bedroom. I was running out of rooms to hide from.

Daemon kept up talking in his beautiful language, a streaming melody, until I drifted off in his arms. I was only a little aware of him placing me on the couch and drawing the afghan over me.

Hours later, I opened my eyes and saw Dee sitting in the recliner, legs tucked against her chest, reading one of my books. A favorite YA paranormal of mine—about a demon-hunting girl living in Atlanta.

But what was Dee doing here?

I sat up, pushing my hair out of my face. The clock below the TV, an old-fashioned windup one that my mom loved, read a quarter till midnight.

Dee closed the book. "Daemon went to Walmart in Moorefield. So that will take an absurd amount of time, but it's the only place open that has throw rugs."

"Throw rugs?"

Her features tightened. "For your bedroom... There weren't any extra ones in the house and he didn't want your mom looking for one and finding the spot, thinking you were trying to burn down the house."

The spot...? Sleep faded away completely as the last couple of hours resurfaced. The spot on my bedroom floor where Carissa had basically self-destructed.

"Oh, God...." I threw my legs off the couch, but they shook too much to stand. Tears welled behind my eyes. "I didn't... I didn't kill her."

I don't know why I said that. Maybe it was because deep down I wondered if Dee would automatically assume I was responsible for what happened to Carissa.

"I know. Daemon told me everything." She unfurled her legs, lashes lowered, fanning her cheeks. "I can't…"

"You can't believe this happened?" She nodded, and I tucked my legs up, wrapping my arms around them. "I can't, either. I just can't even wrap my brain around it."

Dee was silent for a moment. "I haven't talked to her since… well, since everything." She tipped her head down and her hair slipped over her shoulders, shielding her face. "I liked her and I was a complete bitch to her."

I started to tell her that she hadn't been, but Dee looked up, a wry smile on her lips. "Don't lie to make me feel better. I appreciate it, but it doesn't change the fact. I don't think I even said two words to her since Adam…died, and now…"

And now she was dead, too.

I wanted to comfort her, but there was a gulf and a ten-foot wall topped with barbed wire between Dee and me. The electrical fence surrounding the wall had disappeared, but there wasn't any level of ease between us, and right now, that hurt more than anything.

Rubbing a kink in my neck, I closed my eyes. My brain was sluggish and I wasn't sure what I should be doing right now. All I wanted to do was mourn my friend, but how was I supposed to grieve someone who no one in the outside would knew had passed?

Dee cleared her throat. "Daemon and I cleaned up your bedroom. Um, there are a few things that weren't salvageable. Some clothing that was burned or torn I threw away. I…I hung a picture over the crack in the wall." She peeked up as if gauging my reaction. "Your laptop… It's not…in functioning shape."

My shoulders slumped. The laptop was the least of tonight's causalities, but I had no idea how I was going to explain that to my mom.

"Thank you," I said finally, voice thick. "I don't think I could've done that."

Dee twisted a strand of hair around her finger. Minutes passed in silence and then, "Are you okay, Katy? Like, really okay?"

Shock caused me to take a few seconds to respond. "No, I'm not," I said truthfully.

"I didn't think so." She paused, wiping under her eyes with the palm of her hand. "I really liked Carissa."

"Me, too," I whispered, and there was nothing else to be said.

Everything that came before tonight and everything we'd been so focused on seemed almost unimportant, which those issues weren't, but a friend was dead—another friend. Her death and her life was a mystery. I'd known her for six months, but I hadn't known her at all.

Chapter 26

Playing sick on Tuesday, I stayed home and vegetated on the couch. I couldn't do the school thing. See Lesa and know her best friend was dead and pretend I didn't know a thing. I just couldn't do it yet.

Every so often, I saw Carissa's face. There were two versions: before last night and afterward. When I saw her and her funky glasses in my memories, my chest ached, and when I saw those vastly empty eyes, I wanted to cry all over again.

And I did.

Mom didn't push it. For one thing, I rarely skipped school. And secondly, I looked like crap. Being sick didn't take a leap of faith. She spent the better part of the morning coddling me and I soaked it up, needing my mom more than she could ever know.

Later, after she went upstairs to get some sleep, Daemon showed up unexpectedly. Wearing a black cap pulled down low, he came in and closed the door behind him.

"What are you doing here?" It was only one in the afternoon.

He took my hand, pulling me into the living room. "Nice jammies."

I ignored that. "Shouldn't you be in school?"

"You shouldn't be alone right now." He twisted his cap around.

"I'm all right."

Daemon shot me a knowing look. Admittedly, I was happy that he was here, because I did need someone who knew what was really going on. All day I'd been ripped apart, caught by guilt and confusion, tossed around by sorrow I couldn't really even grasp.

Wordlessly, he led me to the couch and stretched out, tucking me against his side. His heavy arm around my waist had a soothing weight. Keeping our voices low, we talked about normal things—safe things that didn't slice through him or me.

After a while, I twisted in his arms so that our noses brushed. We didn't kiss. There wasn't one shenanigan going on between us. We held each other, though, and that was more intimate than anything else we could've done. Daemon's presence eased me. At some point, we dozed off, our breaths mixing.

My mom had to have come downstairs at some point and seen us together on the couch, just the way we were when I woke: Daemon's head resting atop mine, my hand balled around his shirt. It was the scent of the coffee that roused me just around five.

Reluctantly, I pulled out of his embrace and smoothed my hands through my hair. Mom stood in the doorway, one leg crossed over her ankle as she leaned against the frame. A steaming cup of coffee was in her hands.

Mom was wearing Lucky Charms pajamas.

Oh, holy Houdini. "Where did you get them?" I asked.

"What?" She took a sip.

"Those…hideous pajamas," I said.

She shrugged. "I like them."

"They're cute," Daemon said, taking off his hat and running his hand through his messy hair. I elbowed him, and he gave me a cheeky grin. "I'm sorry, Miss Swartz, I didn't mean to fall asleep with—"

"It's okay." She waved him off. "Katy hasn't been feeling well, and I'm glad you wanted to be here for her, but I hope you don't get what she has."

He cast me a sideways look. "I hope you didn't give me cooties."

I huffed. If anyone was spreading alien cooties, it was Daemon.

Mom's cell went off, and she dug it out of her pajama pocket, sloshing coffee onto the floor. Her face lit up, the way it always did when Will called her. My heart dropped as she turned and headed into the kitchen.

"Will," I whispered, standing before I realized it.

Daemon was right behind me. "You don't know that for sure."

"I do. It's in her eyes—he makes her glow." I wanted to barf, like, seriously. Suddenly, I saw Mom on the bedroom floor, lifeless, gone like Carissa. Panic blossomed and took root. "I need to tell her why Will got close to her."

"Tell her what?" He blocked me. "That he was here to get close to you—that he used her? I don't think that's going to lessen any blows."

I opened my mouth, but he had a point.

He placed his hands on my shoulders. "We don't know if it was him calling or what's happened to him. Look at Carissa," he said, keeping his voice low. "Her mutation was unstable. It didn't take long for it…to do what it did."

"Then that means it held." He wasn't making me feel better about anything right now.

"Or it means it faded off." He tried again. "We can't do anything until we know what we're dealing with."

I shifted my weight restlessly, watching over his shoulder. Stress built in me like a seven-ton ball that settled on my shoulders. There was so much to deal with.

"One at a time," Daemon said, as if he read my thoughts. "We're going to deal with things one at a time. That's all we can do."

Nodding, I took a deep breath and let it out slowly. My heart still raced. "I'm going to see if it was him."

He let go and stepped aside, and I hurried to the door.

"I like your pajamas better," he said, and I turned. Daemon grinned at me, that lopsided one that hinted at laughter.

My jammies weren't much better than Mom's. They had, like, a thousand pink and purple polka dots on them. "Shut up," I said.

Daemon returned to the couch. "I'll be waiting."

I went to the kitchen just as Mom was getting off the phone, her features pinched. The weight on my shoulders increased. "What's wrong?"

She blinked and forced a smile. "Oh, nothing, honey."

Grabbing a towel, I wiped up the spilled sugar. "Doesn't look like nothing." In fact, it looked like a whole lot of something.

Mom grimaced. "It was Will. He's still out west. He thinks he came down with something traveling. He's going to stay out there until he feels better."

I froze. *Liar*, I wanted to scream.

She dumped her coffee and rinsed out her cup. "I didn't tell you this, honey, because I didn't want to drag up bad memories, but Will…well, he was sick once, like your father."

My mouth dropped open.

Mistaking my surprise, she said, "I know. It seems cosmically unfair, doesn't it? But Will has been in remission. His cancer was completely curable."

I had nothing to say. Nothing. Will had told her he'd been sick.

"But of course, I worry." She placed the cup in the dishwasher, but she didn't close the door all the way. I shut it out of habit. "Useless to worry over something like that, I know." She stopped in front of me, placing her hand on my forehead. "You don't feel warm. Are you feeling better?"

The change in conversation threw me. "Yeah, I feel fine."

"Good." Mom smiled then and it wasn't forced. "Don't worry

about Will, honey. He'll be fine and back before we know it. Everything will be okay."

My heart tripped up. "Mom?"

"Yes?"

I came so close to telling her everything, but I froze. Daemon was right. What could I say? I shook my head. "I'm sure…Will's okay."

She bent quickly, kissing my cheek. "He'd be happy to know you were concerned."

A hysterical laugh crept up my throat. I was sure he would be.

• • •

Later that day, after Mom had left for work, I stood beside the lake, staring at a pile of glittering onyx.

Matthew and Daemon hadn't said much since we arrived, and even Blake was abnormally quiet. They all knew what had happened last night with Carissa. Daemon had spoken to Blake earlier in the day; the entire conversation had gone down between the two without fists being thrown and I'd missed it. Apparently Blake had never witnessed an unstable hybrid with his own eyes. He'd only heard about them.

But Dawson had.

He'd seen people who'd been brought to him, had been normal Joes before the mutation and then snapped days later. Violent outbursts were common right before they went into self-destruction mode. All of them had been given the serum I'd been given. Without it, according to Blake, the mutation could hold, but it was rare and in most cases, the mutations faded.

Since I arrived at the lake, Dawson had stayed close to my side while Daemon and Matthew handled the onyx carefully.

"I had to do it once," Dawson said quietly, focused on the overcast sky.

"Do what?"

"Watch a hybrid die like that." He took a breath, squinting. "The guy just went crazy, and no one could stop him. He took out one of the officers and then there was a flash of light. Sort of like spontaneous combustion, because when the light faded, he was gone. Nothing was left. It happened so fast, he couldn't have felt a thing."

I remembered how Carissa was shaking, and I knew she *had* to feel that. Feeling nauseous, I focused on Daemon. The onyx was in a hole, and he knelt in front of it, talking quietly to Matthew. I was glad the rest of the group wasn't there.

"Did the people they brought to you know why they were there?" I asked.

"Some did, like they signed up for it. Others were sedated. They didn't have a clue. I think they were homeless people."

That was sickening. Unable to stay still, I headed toward the bank of the lake. The water wasn't frozen over anymore, but it was still and calm. Completely at odds with how I felt inside.

Dawson followed. "Carissa was a good person. She didn't deserve this. Do we even know why they chose her?"

I shook my head. I'd spent a good part of the day thinking about everything. Even if Carissa had known about the Luxen and had been healed by one, Daedalus was involved. I knew it. But the hows and whys were the mysteries. As was the stone I'd seen around her wrist.

"Did you ever see anything on the hybrids there? Like a weird black stone that looked like it had fire inside it?"

His brows knitted. "None of mine made it except Beth. They didn't have anything like that on them. I never saw the others."

Terrible… It was just terrible.

I swallowed thickly, but my throat felt tight. A soft breeze stirred the lake, and a wave rippled from one bank to the next. Like a shock wave…

"Guys?" Daemon called, and we turned. "Are you ready?"

Were we ready to step into the house of pain? Uh, no. But we walked over to them. Daemon stood, holding a circular piece of onyx in his gloved hand.

He turned to Blake. "This is your show."

Blake took a deep breath and nodded. "I think the first thing to test out is if I do have a tolerance to onyx. If I do, then that gives us a starting point, right? At least then we know that we can build up a tolerance."

Across from him, Daemon glanced down at the onyx he held and shrugged. Without preamble, he shot forward, placing the onyx against Blake's cheek.

My jaw hit the ground.

Matthew stepped back. "God."

Beside me, Dawson laughed under his breath.

But nothing happened for several moments. Finally, Blake knocked the onyx away, his nostrils flaring. "What the hell?"

Disappointed, Daemon tossed the rock in the pile. "Well, apparently you have a tolerance to onyx and here I was hoping you didn't."

I clamped my hand over my mouth, stifling a giggle. He was such an asshole, and I loved him.

Blake stared. "What if I didn't have a tolerance to it? Good God, I kind of wanted to prepare myself for that."

"I know." Daemon smirked.

Matthew shook his head. "Okay, back on track, boys. How do you suggest doing this?"

Stalking over to the pile of onyx, Blake picked one up. There was a slight ripple of unease this time, but he held on. "I suggest Daemon goes first. We hold it to the skin until you drop. No longer."

"Oh, dear Lord," I muttered.

Daemon took off his gloves and held out his arms. "Bring it."

There wasn't a moment of hesitation. Blake stepped forward

and pressed that onyx against Daemon's palm. Immediately, his face contorted and he appeared to try to step back, but the onyx held him in place. A tremor started in his arm and traveled through his body.

Dawson and I both stepped forward. Neither of us could help it. Standing here, watching the pain harshen his beautiful face, was too much. Panic shot through me.

But then Blake pulled back and Daemon dropped to his knees, slamming his hands onto the ground before him. "Crap…"

I rushed forward, touching his shoulders. "Are you okay?"

"He's fine," Blake said, placing the onyx on the ground. His right hand shook as our eyes met. "It started to burn. There must be a limit to my tolerance…"

Daemon stood unsteadily, and I followed. "I'm okay." Then he said to his brother, who was eyeballing Blake like he wanted to toss him through a window, "I'm fine, Dawson."

"How do we know this will work?" Matthew demanded. "Touching onyx is completely different than being sprayed all over with it."

"I've walked out of those doors before and nothing happened. And it's not like they've sprayed onyx in my face before. This has to be it."

I remembered how he said everything he touched had been encased in the shiny jewel. "Okay. Let's do this."

Daemon opened his mouth, but I cut him off with a glare. He wasn't going to talk me out of this.

Picking up a glove, Blake handled the onyx differently now. He didn't come to me but to Matthew. The same thing happened with the older Luxen. He was on his knees, gasping for air, and then it was Dawson's turn.

It took a little longer for him, which made sense. He'd been exposed to the spray like me and had been tortured by the stuff off and on. But after about ten seconds, he went down and his brother massacred the English language.

Then it was my turn.

Squaring my shoulders, I nodded. I was ready for this, wasn't I? Heck no. Who was I fooling? This was going to *hurt*.

Blake winced and moved forward, but Daemon stopped him. Using the glove, he took the onyx from him and stood in front of me.

"No," I said. "I don't want you to do this."

The determined set to his jaw infuriated me. "I'm not letting him do it."

"Then let someone else do it." There was no way he could be the one who placed the onyx on me. "Please." Daemon shook his head, and I wanted to punch him. "This isn't right."

"It's either me or no one."

And then I understood. He was trying to get his way. Taking a breath, I met him head-on. "Do it."

Surprise flickered in his bottle-green eyes and then anger deepened them. "I hate this," he said, loudly enough for only me to hear.

"I do, too." Anxiety climbed up my throat. "Just do it."

He didn't look away, but I could tell he wanted to. Whatever pain I knew I was about to feel would be symbiotic. He would feel it—not the physical, but the anguish would travel to him, as if it were his own. It was the same when Daemon was in pain.

I closed my eyes, thinking that would help him. It seemed to, because maybe ten seconds later, I felt the coolness of the onyx against my hand and the roughness of his glove. Nothing happened immediately, but then it did.

A rapidly growing burn traveled across my hand and then shot up my arm. A thousand tiny pricks of pain radiated across my body. I bit down on my lip, stifling my scream. It didn't take long after that before I hit the ground, gulping in air as I waited for the burn to ease off.

My body shuddered. "All right... Okay... Not too bad."

"Bull," Daemon said, hauling me onto my feet. "Kat—"

I tugged free, taking more deep breaths. "Really, I'm okay. We need to keep going."

Daemon looked like he wanted to toss me over his shoulder and run off like a caveman, but we moved on. Over and over again, each of us touched the onyx, holding on until our body refused to cooperate. None of us increased in time, but we were just getting started.

"It's like getting hit with a Taser," Matthew said as he dropped a sheet of plywood over the onyx, then placed two heavy rocks on the board. It was late and all of us were twitchy. Even Blake. "Not that I've ever been Tased, but I image that's how it feels."

I wondered if there'd be any long-term effects from this. Like messed-up heart rhythms or post-traumatic stress. The one good thing that came out of this was that between the mind-blowing pain and watching other people succumb to it, I really hadn't been capable of thinking about anything else.

As we finished up and began to limp back to the house, Blake slowed down until he was beside me. "I'm sorry," he said.

I said nothing.

He shoved his hands into his jeans. "I liked Carissa. I wish..."

"If wishes were fishes, we'd all throw nets, right? Isn't that what they say?" Bitterness sharpened my tone.

"Yeah, that's what they say." He paused. "Things are gonna get crazy at school."

"Why do you care? You're going to leave as soon as you get Chris. You'll just be another one of those kids who vanished into thin air."

He stopped, head cocked to the side. "I would stay if I could. I can't, though."

Frowning, I glanced ahead. Daemon had slowed down, no doubt doing his best not to physically put more distance between

Blake and me. For a second, I considered asking Blake about the stone. He'd have to know, since he worked for Daedalus—still did. But it was too tricky. Blake claimed to be playing double agent. Key word: *claimed*.

I wrapped my arms around my waist. Overhead, the branches cracked against one another like a low, steady drum.

"I would stay," he said again, placing a hand on my shoulder. "I—"

Daemon was there in an instant, prying Blake's fingers off my shoulder. "Don't touch her."

Blake paled as he pulled his hand free and stepped back. "Dude, I wasn't doing anything. Overprotective much?"

Implanting himself in between us, Daemon said, "I thought we had an understanding. You're here because we don't have a choice. You're still alive because she is better than me. You're not here to comfort her. Got that?"

Blake's jaw popped. "Whatever. I'll see you guys later."

I watched Blake stalk past Matthew and Dawson. "That was a little overprotective."

"I don't like him touching you," he growled. His eyes started doing that glowing-orb thing. "I don't like him even being in the same time zone as you. I don't trust him."

Rising up, I kissed Daemon's cheek. "No one trusts him, but you can't threaten him every five seconds."

"Yes, I can."

I laughed and stepped in, wrapping my arms around his waist. Under my cheek, his heart beat steadily. His hands slid down my back as his head bent close to mine. "Do you really want to do more days like this?" he asked. "An endless stretch of days filled with pain?"

It wasn't on the top of my to-do list. "It serves a pretty good distraction, and I need that right now."

I expected him to argue, but he didn't. Instead, he kissed the top of my head. We stood like that for a little while. When we pulled apart, Dawson and Matthew were gone. Moonlight started to peek through the branches. Holding hands, we walked back to our houses, and he went to his to clean up.

My house was dark and silent, and as I stood at the base of the stairs, I struggled to breathe. I couldn't be afraid of my bedroom. That was just stupid. I placed my hand on the banister and took one step.

Muscles locked up.

It was just a bedroom. I couldn't sleep on the couch forever, and I couldn't run in and out of my bedroom as if an Arum were chasing me.

Each step up was a fight when my natural response was to turn and run in the opposite direction, but I continued until I stood in the doorway, my hands clasped under my chin.

Daemon and Dee had cleaned up everything like they said. My bed was made. Clothing put away and all the papers were stacked on my desk. My destroyed laptop was gone. And there was a neat little circular rug over the spot Carissa had stood. It was a muted, soft brown. Daemon knew I wasn't big on flashy color, not like Dee. Other than that, the room looked normal.

Holding my breath, I forced myself to go in. I moved around, picking up books and placing them back in the order I had them in, keeping my mind blank. Sometime later, I changed into an old shirt and knee-high socks, then I tunneled under the blankets and rolled onto my side.

Beyond my bedroom window, scattered stars broke up the dark blue of the sky. One fell, leaving a short stream of light behind as it crashed to Earth. Curling my fingers around the blanket, I wondered if it were a falling star or something else. All the Luxen were here, weren't they?

I forced my eyes closed and focused on tomorrow. After school, Daemon and I were heading to Martinsburg in an attempt to find Luc. The group thought we were just getting away for the night. Hopefully after our visit, we'd know a little more about what happened to Carissa.

I slept fitfully that night. It had to be late when I felt Daemon settle in beside me, his arm firmly around my waist. Half asleep, I decided he needed to be more careful. If my mom caught him in my bed again, things would get ugly. But I was content in his arms and settled back against him, lulled to sleep by his warm breath along the back of my neck.

"I love you," I think I said. It may have been a dream, but his arm tightened and his leg slid around mine. Maybe this was just a dream, because there was a surreal quality to it. Even if it was, it was enough.

Chapter 27

Lesa practically tackled me the moment I stepped into school the following day. I hadn't even made it to my locker. Grabbing my arm, she tugged me into the alcove near the trophy case.

I knew from the moment I saw her that somehow she knew something bad had happened. Her face was pale, eyes shadowed, and her lower lip trembled. I'd never seen her so upset.

"What's wrong?" I forced my voice even.

Her fingers bit into my arm. "Carissa's missing."

I felt the blood drain from my face and croaked out a, "What?"

Eyes shiny, she nodded. "She had the flu, right? And apparently she got really sick in the last couple of days, running a high temperature. Her mom and dad took her to the hospital. They thought she had meningitis or something."

She let out a shuddering breath. "I didn't know anything until her parents called me this morning asking if I'd seen or talked to her. And I was like, 'No. Why? She's been too sick to get on the phone and all.' And they told me she disappeared a couple of nights ago from the hospital room. Her parents have been looking for her and the police wouldn't file a missing person's report until she was gone for forty-eight hours."

The horror that whiplashed through me wasn't faked. I said a few things and I really didn't know what. Lesa wasn't processing anything anyway.

"They think she walked out of the hospital—that she was that sick and she's probably out there somewhere, lost and confused." Her voice trembled. "How could no one see and stop her?"

"I don't know," I whispered.

Lesa circled her arms around herself. "This isn't happening, is it? It can't be. Not Carissa."

My heart felt like it was cracking. Most times I wanted to tell the truth and confide in Lesa, but this was one of those moments when nothing in this world could have made me want to be the bearer of this news.

There wasn't anything I could say, but I wrapped my arms around her and held on until the first bell rang. We headed straight to class without our textbooks. It didn't matter. News of Carissa's disappearance had begun to spread, and no one was paying attention in class.

Kimmy announced at the end of class that the police were organizing a search party after school. She and Carissa hadn't been friends, but that wasn't important, I realized. Too many kids had disappeared, and it was touching everyone's lives. I glanced over my shoulder at Daemon and he gave me a reassuring smile. It did little to soothe me. I was a bundle of nerves. When class ended, Lesa waited for me.

"I think I'm going home," she said, blinking rapidly. "I don't... I just can't be here right now."

"Do you want me to go with you?" I asked, not wanting to leave her alone if she felt she needed someone.

Lesa shook her head. "No. But thank you."

I gave her a quick hug and then watched her hurry from class, my heart heavy.

Daemon said nothing as he pressed a kiss to my temple. He knew there wasn't anything to say. "Do you think we have time to join the search party before we leave?" I asked.

Both of us knew it was pointless, but it seemed a dishonor to her memory to not give her this respect. Or was it wrong to do it knowing what really happened? I didn't know.

Daemon didn't seem to know, either, but he agreed. "Of course."

I wanted to leave the school, too. Especially since everyone was talking about Carissa and finding her. People were in high hopes that she *would* be found, because it seemed impossible that she'd end up like Simon.

Guilt and anger warred inside me, and throughout the day, I tipped into each side. Sitting in class seemed pointless when so many things hung in the balance. These people—these kids—had no idea what was going on around them. They lived in this blissful bubble of ignorance and not even the disappearances burst it. Only tiny holes were pricked by each disappearance and I was waiting for everyone to finally pop.

At lunch, for the first time, we all sat together. Even Blake joined us. My lack of appetite had nothing to do with the mystery food occupying my plate.

"Are you guys going to the search party?" Andrew asked.

I nodded. "But we're still doing our own thing afterward."

Blake scowled. "I really think you guys should wait."

"Why?" I asked before Daemon could snap his head off his shoulders.

"You need to be working on building up a tolerance, not date night." Across from him, Ash nodded in agreement. "That's not what's important right now."

Daemon looked at him. "Shut up."

Cheeks flushing, Blake leaned on the table. "We need every day that we can get if we have any hopes of doing this soon."

A muscle flexed in Daemon's jaw. "One day isn't going to change anything. You guys can still practice or not. I don't care."

Blake started to protest, but Dawson stepped in. "Let them go. They need this. We'll be fine."

I picked up my fork, feeling my cheeks flame. Everyone thought I needed to get away, take some downtime, and I didn't want them feeling sorry for or worrying about me. But tonight wasn't date night. What Daemon and I had to do was going to be as tricky as playing with onyx.

As if he sensed my dark thoughts, he twisted beside me and his hand found mine under the table. He squeezed and for some reason I felt like crying. I was turning into such a wuss and it was all his fault.

I might have dreamed him up last night, because in the light of morning, he'd been gone and the pillow beside me didn't carry that scent I could place anywhere. But I liked to think it was real. That I hadn't dreamt him holding me close, his warm hands on my hips or his lips trailing down my neck.

If I had imagined that... Oh boy, my dreams were realistic. I couldn't ask him, because that would be way too embarrassing, not to mention Daemon's ego did not need to be stroked by the knowledge I was dreaming about him.

Thinking about his reaction to that, which would bring a whole lot of smugness to the table, I grinned a little. Daemon caught sight of it and my heart skipped a beat, because his heart had jumped first.

Sometimes the whole bizarro alien connection thing had its perks. Like it told me that I affected Daemon just as much as he affected me, and on days like this, I needed whatever pick-me-upper there was.

Chapter 28

The search party was just like the ones I'd seen on TV and in movies. People milled through fields in a direct, horizontal line behind the policemen and their search dogs. Everything was a clue to the inexperienced—a disturbed pile of leaves; a torn, old piece of clothing; faded footprints.

It was a sad affair.

Mainly because there was so much hope—hope that Carissa would be found, that she would be okay if not a little worse for wear, and everything would go back to normal. She wouldn't be the latest missing person's case, because her situation was different. She seemingly walked out of a hospital.

However, I had a hard time believing that.

Will had been an implant in the local medical center, and I didn't have to be an investigator to figure out that he wasn't the only one. My guess was Carissa had *help* leaving that hospital.

Daemon and I left after five, heading back to our houses. I went inside to get changed for our "date night." I wasn't going all out like I did last time. I settled on a pair of skinny jeans, heels, and an Lesa-approved skintight sweater that flashed a little bit of stomach.

Mom was in the kitchen making an omelet. My eyes bugged as I tugged the hem of my sweater down. She glanced over her shoulder, tossing the eggs and missing most of the frying pan.

She took Hell's Kitchen to a new extreme.

"Are you going out tonight with Daemon?"

"Yeah," I said, grabbing a paper towel. I scooped up the eggs before the burnt smell could reach my gag reflex. "We're going to do dinner and then a movie."

"Remember your curfew. It's a school night."

"I know." I threw the towel away and held onto my sweater with one hand. "Did you hear about Carissa?"

Mom nodded. "I wasn't working at Grant when she was admitted or for the last two days, but the hospital is crawling with police and the heads are doing their own investigations."

She'd been pulling her shifts in Winchester. "So, they think she really just walked out of there?"

"From what I hear, she was being treated for meningitis and that can come along with a high fever. People do strange things when they are that sick. It's why I was so worried about you when you got sick in November." She turned off the stove. "But there is no excuse for what happened. Someone should've stopped the poor girl. Those night-shift nurses will have a lot of explaining to do. Without meds, Carissa..." She clamped up, focusing on dumping the eggs onto her plate. A few pieces splattered across the floor. I sighed. "Honey, they'll find Carissa."

No, they won't, I wanted to rage.

"She couldn't have gone far," Mom continued as I picked up the yellow clumps stuffed with peppers and onions. "And those nurses won't allow something as careless as this to happen again."

I doubted it was an act of carelessness. They probably turned their cheek or helped. The desire to get even or at least walk into that hospital and smack a bunch of people in their faces was almost too hard to ignore.

Saying good-bye to Mom and promising not to stay out past curfew, I kissed her cheek and then grabbed my sweater jacket and purse. Daemon was alone next door. Everyone was down by the lake, either putting themselves through untold pain or watching it.

He swaggered up to me, his eyes dropping right to the tiny flash of skin…and something moved over his face. "I like this better than the other outfit."

"Really?" I felt exposed when he looked at me like he was staring at a piece of art commissioned just for him. "I thought you liked the skirt."

"I do, but this…?" He tugged on my belt loop and made a deep sound in the back of his throat. "I really like this."

A dizzying warmth swept through me, making my knees weak.

Shaking his head, he dropped his hand and pulled his keys out of his pocket. "We need to get going. You hungry? You didn't eat any lunch."

It took me a moment to collect myself. "I could do a Happy Meal."

He laughed as we headed outside. "A Happy Meal?"

"What's wrong with that?" I tugged my sweater coat on. "It's perfect."

"It's the toy, isn't it?"

I grinned as I stopped at the passenger side. "The boys get better toys."

Daemon turned suddenly, placing his hands on my hips and lifting me against him. Startled, I dropped my purse as I groped his arms.

"What—?"

He silenced me with a kiss that reached a deep place inside that both thrilled and frightened me. When he kissed me, it was like he was reaching for my soul.

Funny thing was, he already had that and my heart in his hands.

Slowly, he let me slide down him and placed me on my feet. Dazed, I stared up at him. "What was that for?"

"You smiled." His fingers trailed along my cheek, then down my throat. He buttoned up my sweater quickly. "You haven't been smiling much. I missed it, so I decided to reward you for doing it."

"Reward me?" I laughed. "God, only you would think kissing someone is a reward."

"You know it is. My lips change lives, baby." Daemon bent, grabbing my purse off the ground. "Ready?"

Taking the purse, I hopped into his car on wobbly knees. Once beside me, he revved the engine, and we were heading into town, stopping by the local fast-food joint so I could get my Happy Meal.

He got me a boy one, too.

His dinner included three hamburgers and two orders of fries. I had no idea where those calories went. To his ego, maybe? It seemed likely after that last comment about his lips. I was hungry more often after the mutation, but not like Daemon.

On the way to Martinsburg, we started out with a game of I Spy, but Daemon cheated and I didn't want to play anymore.

He laughed deeply, the sound pleasing. "How can I cheat at I Spy?"

"You keep picking things that no human in this world can see!" I fought back a grin at his offended expression. "Or you pick *c*— you keep picking *c*. I spy with my little eye, something that starts with a *c*!"

"Car," he said, smiling. "Cat. Coat. Church." He paused, casting me a wicked sidelong glance. "Chest."

"Shut up." I smacked him on the arm. A few moments of silence later, and I was desperate to find another game. This nonsense was keeping my mind blank. We moved onto the license plate game, and I swear he pulled up on cars so I couldn't see the plates. He had a mean competitive streak.

Before we knew it, we were heading off the exit and neither of us was in the playing mood anymore. "Do you think we'll get in?"

"Yes."

I shot him a look. "That bouncer was really big."

His lips quirked. "Oh, Kitten, see, I try to not say bad things."

"What?"

The grin spread. "I would say size doesn't matter, but it does. I would know." He winked, and I let out a disgusted groan. He laughed. "Sorry, you walked into that one. Seriously, though, the bouncer won't be a problem. I think he liked me."

"W-w-what?"

He eased the SUV around the curves. "I think he liked me, like, really liked me."

"Your ego knows no limit, you know that?"

"You'll see. I know these kinds of things."

From what I recalled, the bouncer looked like he wanted to kill Daemon. Shaking my head, I sat back and started nibbling on my thumbnail. Gross habit, but nerves were getting the best of me.

The abandoned gas station loomed up ahead. The SUV bumped over the uneven road and I gripped the door handle. Cars lined the field in front of the club, as expected. Once again, Daemon parked Dolly far away from other cars.

I knew to get rid of my sweater this time around. I wrapped it around my purse and sat it on the floorboard. We made our way around the cars. Stopping at the first row, I bent over and tossed my hair over my head, shaking it out.

"This reminds me of a Whitesnake video," Daemon said.

"Huh?" I ran my hands through my hair, hoping for the sexy look and not the "I had my head out of the car" look.

"If you start climbing on car hoods, I think I might marry you."

I rolled my eyes and straightened, giving my head one more shake. "Done."

He stared at me. "You're cute."

"You're weird." I rose up and gave him a quick kiss on the

cheek before I teetered through the knee-high grass. Heels—so not a good idea.

The lumberjack bouncer appeared out of nowhere, still in those overalls. Barrel-sized arms folded across his chest. "I thought I told ya two to forget this place?"

Daemon moved in front of me. "We need to see Luc."

"I need a lot of things in life. Like I wish I could find a decent stock trader who wouldn't lose half of my money."

Oookay. I cleared my throat. "We won't be here long, but please, we really need to see him."

"Sorry," the bouncer said.

Daemon tipped his head to the side. "There's got to be something we can do to convince you."

Oh, man, please tell me he wasn't...

The bouncer raised a brow and waited.

Daemon smiled—that sexy quirk of his lips that had every girl at school stumbling over themselves, and I...I wanted to crawl under a car.

Before I could die from embarrassment, the bouncer's cell went off, and he pulled it out of his front pocket. "What's up?"

I took the moment to elbow Daemon.

"What?" he said. "It was working."

The bouncer laughed. "I ain't doin' much. Just talkin' to a douche and a pretty lady."

"Excuse me?" Daemon said, surprised.

I choked on my laugh.

There was a toothy grin, and then the bouncer sighed. "Yep, they're here for ya." There was a pause. "Sure."

He clicked the phone shut. "Luc will see you. Go in and head straight to him. No dancing tonight, or whatever it was the two of ya did last time."

Awkward. I lowered my head and slipped past the bouncer. At the door, he stopped Daemon. I looked over my shoulder.

The bouncer winked at Daemon as he handed him what looked like a business card. "Ya not normally my type, but I can make an exception."

My mouth dropped open.

Daemon took the card with a smile and then opened the door. "Told you," he said to me.

I refused to give him the benefit of a response, instead focusing on the club. Nothing had changed from the last time. The dance floor was packed. Accompanied cages hung from the ceiling, swaying from the movements inside. People grinded to the heavy beat. A different, strange world tucked away in the epicenter of normalcy.

And the place was still alluring to me in a weird way.

Down the shadowy hallway, a tall man waited at the door for us. Paris—the blond Luxen we'd met last time. He nodded at Daemon, opened the door, and then stepped aside.

I expected to see Luc sprawled on the couch, playing DS like last time, so I was shocked when I discovered him at the desk, pecking away at a laptop, his face screwed in concentration.

The stacks of hundreds were gone.

Luc didn't look up. "Please sit." He waved at the nearby couch, all businesslike.

Glancing at Daemon, I moved with him to the couch and sat. In the corner, a tall yellow candle spread a peaches scent throughout the room. That was all the decoration. Did the door behind the desk lead to another room? Did Luc live here?

"Heard you guys didn't get very far at Mount Weather last time." He closed the laptop and folded his hands under his chin.

"About that," Daemon said, leaning forward. "You didn't know about the onyx shields?"

The boy, the little mini mogul/mafia kingpin/whatever he was became very still. Tension filled the room. I waited for something to blow up. Hopefully not one of us.

"I warned you that there may be things I'm unaware of," he said. "Even I don't know everything about Daedalus. But I think Blake's on the right track. He is right about everything being encased in a shiny blackish-red material. Perhaps we did build a tolerance so we were not affected by the onyx shields."

"And what if that's not it?" I asked, hating the icy feeling slushing through my veins.

Luc's amethyst gaze was concentrated. "What if it's not? I have a feeling that's not going to stop you from trying again. It's a risk and everything has risks. You're lucky you got out of there last time before anyone realized what happened. You get another chance. Most people don't."

Talking to this kid was weird, because he had the mannerisms and speech patterns of a well-educated adult. "You're right," I said. "We're still going to try."

"But knowing all the perils ahead seems unfair?" He tucked back a strand of brown hair, his angelic face impassive. "Life's not fair, babe."

Daemon stiffened beside me. "Why do I have a feeling there's a lot you're not telling us?"

Luc's lips formed a half smile. "Anyway, you came here for a reason other than those onyx shields? Let's get to the point."

Annoyance flashed across Daemon's face. "An unstable hybrid attacked Kat."

"That's what unstable people do, hybrid or not."

I bit back a snappy retort. "Yeah, we figured that much, but she was my friend. She gave no indication that she knew anything about the Luxen. She was fine, got sick, and then came to my house and went nuts."

"You didn't give any indication you know ET didn't phone home."

What a little brat. I took a deep breath. "I get that, but this was out of the blue."

Luc leaned back in his chair, kicking his legs onto the desk. He crossed them at the ankles. "I don't know what to tell you about that. She may've known about the Luxen, gotten hurt, and some poor sap tried and failed to heal her. Or the Man pulled her off the street like they do at times. And unless you know some darn good torture techniques and are willing to employ them on an Officer of Daedalus, I don't see how you'll ever know."

"I refuse to accept that," I whispered. Knowing would bring some kind of closure and justice.

He shrugged. "What happened to her?" Curiosity colored his tone.

My breath caught in my throat as I balled my hands into fists. "She's no longer…"

"Ah," Luc murmured. "She did the whole spontaneous combustion thing?" The look on my face must've been answer enough because he sighed sadly. "Sick. Sorry about that. A twisted history lesson for you—you know all those unexplained cases of spontaneous combustion throughout history?"

Daemon grimaced. "I'm afraid to ask."

"Funny how there's not many cases known, but they do happen out in the noob world." He spread his arms wide to indicate the world outside this office. "Hybrids—my theory at least, and it makes sense if you think about it—most do the self-destruction thing in the facilities, but a few do it outside. That's why the occurrence is rare to humans."

All of this was good and a little disturbing to think about, but it wasn't why we were here. "My friend was wearing a bracelet—"

"Tiffany's?" he asked and smirked.

"No." I smiled tightly. "It was just like the one you're wearing."

Surprise rolled over Luc's face like a wave. The little punk dropped his legs onto the floor and sat straight. "Not good."

Foreboding chills skated over my skin as Daemon zeroed in on Luc. "Why is that not good?"

He seemed to debate whether he should talk about it and then went with a, "Oh, what the hell. You'll owe me, hope you realize. But what you see here?" Luc flicked a finger along the stone. "It's a black opal—so rare that only a few mines can even unearth these babies. And it's only *these* kinds."

"The ones that look like they have fire in them?" I asked, leaning forward to get a better look. It really did look like a black orb with a flame inside. "Where are they mined?"

"Australia, usually. There's something in the composition of a black opal that's like a power booster. You know, like Mario gets when he hits a mushroom. Imagine that sound. That's what a black opal does."

"What kind of composition?" Daemon asked, eyes sharp with interest.

Luc unhooked the bracelet and held it up in the dim light. "Opals have this remarkable ability to refract and reflect specific wavelengths of light."

"No way," Daemon breathed, and apparently that was super cool. I was still lost on the whole stone and light thing.

"Yes." Luc smiled at the stone, like a father smiles at his prodigal son. "I don't know who discovered it. Someone in Daedalus, I'm sure. Once they figured out what it could do, they kept it away from the Luxen and ones like us."

"Why?" I felt stupid for asking, mainly because both of them looked at me like I was. "What? I don't have a degree in alien mineralogy. Geez."

Daemon patted my thigh. "It's okay. Refracting and reflecting wavelengths of lights affects us, like the obsidian affects Arum and onyx affects us."

"Okay," I said slowly.

Luc's purple eyes glimmered. "Refracting light changes the direction and speed. Our friendly neighborhood aliens are made of light—well, made of more than that, but let me explain it this way: let's say their DNA is light. And let's say that once a human is mutated, their DNA is now encased in wavelengths of light."

I remembered Daemon trying to explain this before. "And onyx disrupts those wavelengths of light, right? Kind of makes them bounce around and go crazy."

Luc nodded. "Opal's ability to refract allows a Luxen or a hybrid to be more powerful—it enhances our ability to refract light."

"And the reflection part—wow." Awed, Daemon grinned.

I got the whole refraction thing. Sure, super speed, ability to pull on the Source more easily, and probably a slew of other benefits, but reflection? I waited.

Daemon nudged me with his elbow. "We flicker or fade sometimes because we move fast. And sometimes you see us fade in and out—it's just reflection. Something all of us have to work at to control when we're younger."

"And it's hard when you're excited or upset?"

He nodded. "Among other things, but to control reflection?" He fixed on Luc. "Are you saying you can do what I think you can?"

Laughing, Luc hooked the bracelet around his wrist and sat back, dropping his legs on the desk again. "Hybrids are good. We can move faster than humans, but with the obesity rates nowadays, turtles can move faster than most humans. Sometimes we're even stronger than the average Luxen when it comes to the Source—it's the mixture of human and alien DNA that can create something powerful, but that's not standard." A self-fulfilled smile stretched Luc's lips. "But give a Luxen one of these, and they can completely reflect light."

My heart skipped a beat. "You mean...like, invisible?"

"So cool," Daemon said, staring at the stone. "We can change the way we look, but become invisible? Yeah, that's new."

Confounded, I shook my head. "Can we be invisible?"

"No. Our human DNA gets in the way of that, but it makes us

just as powerful as the strongest Luxen and then some." He wiggled a little in his seat. "So you can imagine that they wouldn't want any of us having these...especially one that hasn't been proven to be stable, unless..."

A cold breath of air shot over my neck. "Unless what?"

Some of the enthusiasm faded from his face. "Unless they didn't care what kind of damage the hybrid caused. Maybe your friend was a test run for a bigger incident."

"What?" Daemon tensed. "You think they did this on purpose? Hooked up an unstable hybrid and sent her out into the wild to see what happens?"

"Paris thinks I'm a conspiracy theorist with a hint of schizophrenic paranoia." He shrugged. "But you can't tell me that Daedalus doesn't have a master plan up their sleeves. I wouldn't put a single thing past them."

"But why would she come after me? Blake says they don't know the mutation held. So it wasn't like they'd send her after me." I paused. "And, well, that's if Blake's telling the truth."

"I'm sure he is about the mutation," Luc responded. "If he wasn't, you wouldn't be sitting here. See, I'm not sure even Daedalus knows everything that this stone is capable of and how it affects us. I'm still learning."

"And what have you learned?" Daemon asked.

"For starters, before I got my grubby paws on one of these, I couldn't pick out another hybrid if one did a jig in front of me. I knew the moment you and Blake arrived in Martinsburg, Katy. It was weird, like a breath washing over my entire body. Your friend probably sensed you. That's the least terrible probability."

Daemon blew out a long breath and then looked away for a moment. "Do you know if it can enhance the Arum's abilities?"

"I imagine it could if they were bloated on a Luxen's powers."

Overwhelmed, I sat back and then shot forward. "Do you think the opal can, like, counteract the onyx?"

"It's possible, but I don't know. Haven't hugged any onyx recently."

I ignored the sarcastic tone. "Where can we get some of the opal?"

Luc laughed and I wanted to kick his legs off the desk. "Unless you have about thirty thousand dollars lying around and know someone who mines opals, or you want to ask Daedalus for some, you're out of luck. And I'm not giving you mine."

My shoulders slumped. Yippee, another dead end. We couldn't catch a break if it slapped us upside the face.

"Anyway, it's about time for you guys to hit the road." He tipped his head back, closing his eyes. "I'm assuming I won't hear from you two again until you're ready to go to Mount Weather?"

Ah, we'd been dismissed. As I stood, I debated on bum-rushing Luc and grabbing his bracelet. The way his eyes opened into thin slits warned me to forget that idea.

"Is there anything else you can tell me?" Daemon prodded.

"Sure, I have something else." Luc lifted those long lashes. "You really shouldn't trust a soul in this game. Not when everyone has something to gain or lose."

Chapter 29

Over the course of several weeks, interviews given by local law enforcement and tearful pleas from Carissa's parents appeared on the nightly news, candlelight vigils were held, and reporters from all around came, drawn in by morbid curiosity. How could such a little town have so many children who just disappeared? Some even speculated that a serial killer had targeted the sleepy town in West Virginia.

Being at school, listening to everyone talk about Carissa, Simon, and even Adam and Beth was hard to do. Not just for me, but for all of us who knew the truth.

These kids didn't disappear.

Adam and Carissa were dead, most likely Simon, too. Beth was being held against her will in a government facility.

A dark, somber mood settled, creeping into every part of us, and there was no shaking it. Of course suspicion blossomed along with the spring grass and tiny buds at school, because only one of the kids had reappeared and that had been Dawson. But his reappearance had signaled the disappearance of others.

There were whispers in the hall and long looks passed among students whenever Dawson or Daemon was around. Possibly because very few could tell them apart, but both brothers acted like they didn't hear it. Or maybe they just didn't care.

Even Lesa had changed. Losing a friend would do that, as would the inability to find any closure. There was never a reason for why Carissa had disappeared, at least not for Lesa. She, like so many others, would spend a lifetime wondering why and how it happened. And not knowing created this powerlessness to move on. Even though the seasons were changing and spring was well on its way, Lesa was stuck on the day before she found out her best friend had vanished and the day after. She was the same girl in some ways: moments where she'd say something wholly inappropriate and she would laugh, and then others when she didn't think I was looking, her eyes would cloud with misgiving.

Carissa wasn't the only newsworthy case, though.

Dr. William Michaels, aka Mom's boyfriend and all-around douche canoe, was reported missing by his sister about three weeks after Carissa dropped off the radar. A frenzied storm descended once again. Mom had been questioned and she… She had been a wreck. Especially when she learned that Will had never signed in at any conference in the west, and no one had seen or heard from him since he left Petersburg.

Officials suspected that foul play might have been involved. Others whispered that he had to have something to do with what happened to Carissa and Simon. A prominent doctor just didn't simply cease to exist.

But Daemon and I were still alive, so all we could assume was that the mutation had held and since he had gotten what he wanted, he was in hiding. Worst-case scenario, Daedalus had picked him up somewhere. Didn't bode well for us if that happened, but hey, it served him right if *he* was locked in a cage somewhere.

All in all I wasn't torn up over the fact that for right now, Will was a nonissue, but I hated seeing Mom go through this again. And I hated Will even more for putting her through it. She hit every stage of the grieving process: disbelief; sorrow; that horrible, lingering lost feeling; and then anger.

I had no idea what to do for her. The best I could was spend the evenings with her on her days off, after I finished with the onyx stuff. Keeping her company and distracted seemed to help.

As weeks passed and there was no sign of Carissa or anyone else that had held the little town captive, the inevitable happened. People didn't forget, but the reporters went away and then other things occupied the nightly news. By mid-April, everyone for the most part was back to doing their own thing.

I'd asked Daemon one evening as we walked back from the lake, enjoying the warmer temperatures, how could people forget so easily? A bitter sensation had taken up residence in my tummy. Would that happen to me one day if we didn't come back from Mount Weather? People would just get over it?

Daemon had squeezed my hand and said, "It's the human condition, Kitten. The unknown isn't something that sits well. They'd rather push it away—not completely, but just enough that it's not always shadowing their every thought and action."

"And that's okay?"

"Not saying that it is." He'd stopped, placing his hands on my upper arms. "But not having the answers to something can be scary. People can't focus on that forever. Just like you couldn't focus on why it was your dad who had to get sick and pass away. That's the big unknown. You had to let it go eventually."

I'd stared up at him, his striking features highlighted in the waning light. "I can't believe you can sound so wise."

Daemon had chuckled, running his hands up and down my arms. Promising chills followed. "I'm more than looks, Kitten. You should know that."

And I did. Daemon was ridiculously supportive most of the

time. He still hated that I was taking part in the onyx training, but he wasn't pushing it and I appreciated that.

I threw myself into training with the onyx, which left little time for anything other than going to school. Onyx stripped away energy and after every session, all of us were quick to pass out. And we were so wrapped up in building our tolerance, watching out for officers and implants that we hadn't even celebrated Valentine's Day besides the flowers he'd bought me and the card I'd given him.

We kept planning to make up for it, to do the dinner thing, but time got away from us or someone got in between us. Either it was Dawson impatient to save Beth and a hairbreadth from storming Mount Weather, Dee wanting to murder someone, or Blake demanding that we do the onyx thing every day. I'd forgotten what it felt like when it was just Daemon and me.

I really began to think his sporadic late-night visits really were a product of my overactive imagination, because at the end of the night, he was just as whipped as I was. Every morning it seemed like a vivid dream and since Daemon never mentioned it, I let it go while looking forward to it. Dream Daemon was better than no Daemon, I guessed.

But by the beginning of May, the five of us could handle the onyx for about fifty seconds without losing control of our muscle functions. Didn't seem like a lot of time to the others, but it was progress to us.

Halfway through today's practice, we gained an audience that included Ash and Dee. Those two were becoming real bosom buddies of late, while I was basically friendless with the exception of Lesa on good days.

Bad days were when she missed Carissa and no one could replace that lost friendship.

Watching Ash teeter around on her ridiculous heels, I had to wonder how Ash and Dee were even getting along. Besides their obsession with fashion, they had little in common.

Then I realized what probably had bonded them together: their grief. And here I was, begrudging them of that. I could be such a tool.

Matthew was in the process of picking himself off the ground as Ash tottered over to the onyx, frowning. "It can't be that bad. I have to try it."

I bit back a mad grin. I was *so* not going to stop her.

"Uh, Ash, I really wouldn't suggest doing that," Daemon began.

Party pooper, I thought, but Ash was a determined little alien. So I sat down, stretched out my legs, and waited for the show to begin.

I didn't have to wait long.

Bending over gracefully, she picked up one of the shiny blackish-red jewels while I held my breath. Not even a second later, she shrieked, dropped the onyx as if it were a snake, and stumbled backward, falling flat on her butt.

"Yep, not bad at all," Dawson commented drily.

Ash's eyes were wide, mouth gulping like a fish's. "What...what was that?"

"Onyx," I responded, lying on my back. Bright blue skies and a touch of sun warmed the air. I'd already had three rounds with it today. I couldn't feel my fingers. "It sucks."

"It felt... It felt like my skin was ripping apart," she said. Shock roughened her voice. "Why would you guys put yourselves through this for months?"

Dawson cleared his throat. "You know why, Ash."

"But she's..."

Oh, no.

"She's what?" Dawson was on his feet. "She's my girlfriend."

"I didn't mean anything." Ash looked around for help, but she was alone on this one. Standing carefully, she took an unsteady step toward Dawson. "I'm sorry. It's just...that hurt."

Dawson said nothing as he brushed past Daemon, disappearing

into the thicket. Daemon's eyes met mine, then he sighed and trotted off after his brother.

"Ash, you need to learn a tad bit more sensitivity," Matthew said, brushing loose dirt off his jeans.

Her face fell and then crumbled. "I'm sorry. I didn't mean anything by it."

I couldn't believe it. A rarity was to see Ash show any emotion other than bitchiness. Dee went to her side and the two walked off, Matthew following after them, looking like he needed a vacation or a bottle of whiskey.

Which left me alone with Blake.

Groaning, I closed my eyes and lay back down. My body felt heavy, like I could sink through the ground. In a couple of weeks, I'd sprout flowers.

"Are you feeling okay?" Blake asked.

Several snarky responses lined up on my tongue like little soldiers, but all I said was, "I'm just tired."

There was a pregnant pause, and then I heard his footsteps move closer. Blake sat down beside me. "Onyx is killer, isn't it? I never really thought about it, but when I was first *inducted* into Daedalus, I was always tired."

I didn't know what to say so I kept quiet and for a while, so did he. Blake was probably the hardest person to be around. Because deep down, he wasn't a horrible person, maybe not even a monster. He was a desperate person and desperation can make people do crazy things.

He brought forth conflicted feelings. Over the last couple of months, I had grown, like the others, to tolerate him but not trust him, because I remembered Luc's parting words—*You really shouldn't trust a soul in this game. Not when everyone has something to gain or lose.* I couldn't help but wonder if he'd meant Blake. I didn't want to go easy on him because of what he did to Adam, and I didn't want to feel sorry for him, but I did at times. He was a product of his environment. Wasn't a justification of any sorts, but Blake didn't do what he did all by himself. There had been several factors. The strangest thing of all had been at lunch, seeing him sitting at the same table with the siblings of the boy he'd killed.

I honestly didn't think anyone knew how to handle Blake.

Finally, he said, "I know what you're thinking."

"I thought you couldn't read other hybrids' minds."

He laughed. "I can't, but it's obvious. You're uncomfortable with my being here with you, but you're too tired and it's too nice to get up."

Blake was right on all accounts. "And yet you're still here."

"Yeah, about that... I don't think sleeping out here is the safest thing to do. Besides the bears and coyotes, the DOD or Daedalus could always come around."

I opened my eyes, sighing. "And what would be suspicious about my being out here?"

"Well, besides that it's a little early in May and late in the day for sunbathing... They know I still talk to you. Keeping up appearances and all."

I tilted my head toward him. Each of the Luxen took turns scouting the area while we practiced, making sure no one was watching. Seemed odd Blake would be concerned about that now. "Really," I said.

He bent his knees, resting his arms over them as he stared out over the peaceful lake. There was another gap of silence and then, "I know you and Daemon went to see Luc back in February."

I opened my mouth but then shook my head. I sure as hell didn't need to explain why to him.

Blake sighed. "I know you don't and won't ever trust me, but I could've saved you a trip. I knew what the black opal does. Seen Luc pull off some crazy-insane stuff because of it."

Irritation flared. "And you didn't think to tell us about it?"

"I didn't think it would be an issue," he said. "That kind of opal is damn near impossible to get ahold of and the last thing I expected was for Daedalus to be outfitting hybrids with it. Hell, I haven't even thought of it."

Here I was, in the same position with Blake as usual: to believe or to not believe him. I crossed my legs at the ankles and watched a thick, fluffy cloud shuttle across the sky.

"Okay," I said, because honestly, there was no way to prove if he was lying or not. I bet if we hooked him up to a lie detector the results would be inconclusive.

Blake seemed surprised. "I wish things were different, Katy."

I snorted. "Me, too, and probably a hundred other people."

"I know." He dug through the soil, finding a pebble. He turned it over in his hand slowly. "I've been thinking lately, about what I'm going to do when this is all over. There's a good chance that Chris... He won't be right, you know? We have to go somewhere and disappear, but what if he can't blend in? If he's...different?"

Not right, like Beth had been when I'd seen her. "You've said he likes the beach. So do you. That's where you should go."

"Sounds like a plan..." He glanced at me. "What are you guys going to do with Beth? Hell, what are you going to do after you get her back? Daedalus is going to be looking for her."

"I know." I sighed, wanting to sink through the ground. "We're going to have to hide her, I guess. See how she is. Cross that bridge when we get there, that kind of thing, but as long as everyone is together, we'll figure something out."

"Yeah..." He stopped, lips thinning. Swinging his arm to the side, he tossed the pebble out into the lake. It skipped three times before sinking under. Then he stood. "I'll leave you alone, but I'll be nearby."

Before I could respond, he stood and jogged off. Frowning, I arched my back so I could see him The bank around the lake was empty, with the exception of a few robins hopping on the ground near a tree.

Now that was an odd conversation.

Settling back down, I closed my eyes and forced my mind blank. The moment I was alone and it was silent, a thousand things came from every direction inside me. Falling asleep was difficult, so I had this habit of picturing this beach in Florida that Dad liked to go to. Creating the image of frothy waves lapping blue-green foam against the shore as they crested and receded, I kept that scene going on a loop. Nothing else but that image snuck into the recesses of my thoughts. I hadn't really been planning on dozing off out here, but as exhausted as I was, I fell asleep pretty fast.

I'm not sure what woke me, but as I blinked my eyes open I found myself staring into a pair of bright green eyes. I smiled. "Hey," I murmured.

One side of his full lips tipped up. "Hey there, sleeping beauty…"

Over his shoulder, the sky had deepened to a denim blue. "Did you kiss me awake?"

"I did." Daemon was propped on his side, using his arm to support his head. He placed his hand on my stomach and my chest fluttered in response. "Told you, my lips have mystical powers."

My shoulders moved in a silent laugh. "How long have you been here?"

"Not long." His eyes searched mine. "I found Blake sulking around the woods. He didn't want to leave while you were out here."

I rolled my eyes.

"As much as it bothers me, I'm glad he didn't."

"Wow. Pigs are flying." When he narrowed his eyes, I lifted my hand, running my fingers through the soft waves that fell over his forehead. His eyes drifted shut and my breath caught. "How's Dawson?"

"Calmed down. How's Kitten?"

"Sleepy."

"And?"

Slowly, I trailed my fingers down the side of his face, along his broad cheek and down the hard line of his jaw. He turned into my palm, pressing his lips to it. "Happy you're here."

His fingers made quick work of the light cardigan I was wearing, separating the thin flaps of material. His knuckles brushed against the tank top I had on underneath. "And?"

"And glad I didn't get eaten by a bear or coyote."

He arched a brow. "What?"

I grinned. "Apparently they're a problem around here."

Daemon shook his head. "Back to talking about me."

Instead of telling him, I showed. As Daemon would say, it was the book lover in me. Showing was so much better than telling. My fingers smoothed over his bottom lip and then I moved my hand to his chest. I lifted my head and he met me halfway.

The kiss started off tentative and smooth. Silky kisses created a yearning that was becoming all too familiar. The sensation of his lips against mine, the knowledge of what I wanted, sparked deep inside us and our hearts picked up together, beating heavily and fast. I let myself fall into that kiss, drown in it, become it. The swelling wave of feelings was hard to process. At once both exhilarating and frightening. I was ready, had been ready, and yet I knew I was scared, because like Daemon had said before: humans were afraid of the unknown. And Daemon and I had been hovering on the verge of the unknown for a while.

He pressed down until I was flat on my back, and he was above me, his weight perfect and crazy. His hand slid up, bunching the material, his fingers grazing. The touch was too much and not enough. My chest rose and fell rapidly as his leg moved over mine, between mine. When he broke away, I gasped for air, for control I was quickly losing.

"I need to stop," he said roughly, eyes closing tightly, lashes fanning the tips of his cheeks. "Like, right now."

I threaded my fingers through the curls at the back of his neck, hoping he didn't notice how badly my hand shook. "Yeah, we should."

He nodded, but then he lowered his head and kissed me again. Good to see he had the same amount of willpower as I did, which was zilch. My hands slid down his back, digging into the shirt he wore, finding their way under it, splaying across his warm skin. I curled my leg around his. We were close, so close that even if our hearts hadn't beat in tandem before, it wouldn't have mattered, because they would've found each other and joined now.

Our breaths were coming fast. This was insane. Perfect. His hand crept under my shirt, moving up and up, and every part of me wanted to press the stop button on the world and then hit repeat so I could feel this way over and over again.

Daemon stiffened.

"Oh, dear God and baby Jesus in the manger, my eyes!" Dee shrieked. "My eyes!"

My own eyes snapped open. Daemon lifted his head, eyes luminous. Then I realized my hands were still up his shirt. I yanked them out.

"Oh my God," I whispered, mortified.

Daemon said something that burned my ears. "Dee, you didn't see anything." And then he added much lower, "Because you have impeccable timing."

"You were on…her and your mouths were doing this." I could just imagine her hand signals at that point. She went on. "And that's more than I want to see. Like, ever."

I pushed at Daemon's chest, and he rolled off. I sat up and twisted around, keeping my head low so my hair could hide my burning cheeks. I caught sight of Dee and even though you'd think she'd caught us buck naked in the act, instead of making out, she was grinning.

"What do you want, Dee?" Daemon said.

She huffed, pressing her hands on her hips. "Well, I don't want anything from *you*. I wanted to talk to Katy."

My head jerked up, embarrassment be damned. "You do?"

"Ash and I were going to this new little shop in Moorefield Saturday afternoon. They sell vintage dresses. For prom," she added as I continued to stare at her.

"Prom?" I didn't get it.

"Yeah, prom's at the end of the month." She glanced at her brother, her cheeks turning rosy. "Most of the dresses are going to be gone. And I don't know if the place has anything, but Ash heard about it and you know how she is with clothes, so she's in the know. Like, a couple of days ago, she found this really cute cropped sweater that—"

"Dee," Daemon said, a small grin tugging his lips.

"What? I'm not talking to you." She faced me, exasperated. "Anyway, would you like to go with us? Or have you already gotten a dress? Because if you have gotten a dress, then I guess the trip is pointless, but you could still—"

"No. I haven't gotten a dress." I couldn't believe she was asking me to do something with her. I was stunned and hopeful and stunned some more.

"Good!" She grinned. "Then we can go on Saturday. I thought about asking Lesa if she wanted to go…"

I had to be dreaming. She wanted to ask Lesa, too? What did I miss? I glanced at Daemon as his sister chattered on and he grinned. "Wait," I said. "I wasn't planning on prom."

"What?" Dee's mouth dropped open. "It's senior prom."

"I know, but with everything going on…I haven't really thought about it." A lie, because you couldn't step anywhere at school and not see flyers and banners about it.

Dee's incredulous expression grew. "It's *senior* prom."

"But…" I tucked my hair back and glanced at Daemon. "You haven't even asked me to go."

He smiled. "I didn't think I needed to ask. I assumed we would go."

"Well, you know what they say about people who assume," Dee said, rocking back on the balls of her feet.

He ignored her, his grin fading. "What, Kitten?"

I blinked. "How can we go to prom with everything going on? We're so close to having enough tolerance to go back to Mount Weather and—"

"And prom is on a Saturday," he said, pulling my hand away from my hair. "So let's say that in two weeks when we're ready to go, it will be Sunday."

Dee shot forward, hobbling from one foot to the other like her feet were playing hot potato. "And it's only a few hours. You guys can halt the self-mutilation for a few hours."

The problem wasn't the time or really even the onyx. It didn't seem right to go to prom after everything, after Carissa...

Daemon slipped his arm around me as he leaned, his voice low as he spoke. "It's not wrong, Kat. You deserve this."

I closed my eyes. "Why should we get to celebrate when she can't?"

He rested his cheek against mine. "We're still here and we deserve to be, to do normal things every once in a while."

Did we?

"It's not your fault," he whispered, and then kissed my temple. He pulled back, eyes searching mine. "Will you go to prom with me, Kat?"

Dee shifted some more. "You should really say yes, so we can go dress shopping and so I don't have to witness a really awkward moment of you turning down my brother. Even though he deserves to be knocked down a peg or two."

I laughed, glancing at her. Dee gave me a tentative smile, and that hope was springing back. "Okay." I took a deep breath. "I'll go to prom—only because I don't want this conversation to get awkward."

Daemon tweaked my nose. "I'll take what I can get for as long as I can get it."

A cloud passed over the sun and seemed to halt. The temperature dropped significantly.

My smile started to falter as a chill snaked down my spine. This was a happy moment—a good moment. There was hope for Dee's and my relationship. And prom was a big deal. Daemon in a tux and all would be a pretty awesome sight. We were going to be normal teenagers for the night, but the shadow over us had somehow slipped inside me.

"What is it?" Daemon asked, concerned.

"Nothing," I said, but it was something. I just didn't know what.

Chapter 30

One of the first things I did the next day was invite Lesa. I was thrilled when she perked up and agreed. It made me feel a lot better about my decision to go. Like Carissa's best friend approved and that went a long way.

Like me, she was a tad wary of going shopping with Ash, and a glimmer of her old personality shone through when she started making cracks.

"I bet she'll get something ridiculously tight and short and make the rest of us feel like unattractive Oompa Loompas." She sighed pitifully. "No. Scratch that. She'll probably just go to the dress store and parade in front of the mirror naked."

I laughed. "No doubt, but I'm happy Dee invited us."

"Me, too," she said seriously. "I miss her, especially after... Yeah, I just miss her."

My smile was a bit wobbly. Whenever Carissa came up in conversation, I never knew how to handle it. Luckily, for today, we were interrupted by Daemon, who decided to tug on my ponytail like a six-year-old.

He sat behind me and then poked me in the back with his trusty pen.

I rolled my eyes at Lesa and then turned around. "You and that damn pen."

"You love it." He leaned over his desk, tapping it off my chin. "Anyway, I thought I could catch a ride home with you after school. That *thing* we've got to do later was delayed for about an hour. And your mom's already at Winchester by then, right?"

A low hum of excitement thrummed through my veins. I knew where he was going with this. No Mom. An hour or so of time alone and without interruption—hopefully.

I couldn't stop my dreamy sigh. "That would be perfect."

"Thought so." He took his pen and sat back, eyeing me. "Can't wait."

Oxygen fled my brain while blood rushed everywhere. Feeling a bit out of it, I nodded and turned around. The look on Lesa's face told me she so overheard the conversation.

Her eyebrows waggled suggestively, and I felt my face burn. Oh, dear God…

After trig, the rest of the morning crept by in a slow procession. The cosmos were against me. Like they knew I was bouncing with energy and excitement. A little part of me was nervous. Who wouldn't be? If we actually had time alone and we weren't interrupted and stuff fell into place…

Stuff fell into place?

I smothered a giggle.

Blake looked up from his bio text and frowned. "What?"

"Nothing." I grinned. "Nothing."

He arched a brow. "Did Daemon tell you that Matthew has some after-school meeting with a kid's parents?"

I giggled again, earning a weird look from him. "Yeah, he did."

Blake stared at me a second and then placed his pen down. Without any warning, he reached over and picked a piece of lint out of my hair. I jerked back at the same time he pulled his arm away, which put my nose right at the perfect angle to get a sniff of his wrist.

The clean, citrusy scent sparked a muggy, uncomfortable feeling inside me. Like when you've done something stupid and you were about to face public humiliation. Pins and needles spread across my flesh.

A memory was wiggling loose. That smell... I'd smelled it before.

"You okay?" he asked.

I tilted my head to the side, like that helped my smelling abilities. Where did I know that scent? Obviously I'd smelled it on Blake before. No doubt it was one of those expensive colognes, but it was more than that.

Like when you hear an actor's voice but don't see his face. The answer was on the tip of my tongue and I couldn't shake the nagging feeling.

Why did that scent feel achingly familiar? Daemon's face popped in my head, but that wasn't right. He smelled earthy, like the outdoors and the wind. And his scent lingered long after he was gone, on my clothes, the pillow...

The pillow...

My heart stuttered and then skipped a beat. It sunk in and threatened to pull me through the seat. Shock washed over me, quickly followed by a bolt of anger so fierce I jerked forward.

I couldn't sit here. I couldn't breathe.

Static crackled under my shirt. Tiny hairs rose over my body. Burned ozone filled the air. At the front of the class, Matthew looked up. His gaze went to Dawson first, because hey, if anyone were going to lose it, it would be him. But Dawson was also glancing around the room, searching for the source of the increased friction and static in the air.

It was coming from me.

I was going to blow.

Snapping into action, I shut my book and shoved it into my messenger bag. Wasting no time, I stood on shaky legs. My skin felt like it was humming. And maybe it was at a low frequency. Violent energy rolled through me. Only once before had I felt this way and that was when Blake...

I headed past Matthew, unable to answer his look of concern, and ignored the curious stares. Hurrying from the room, I dragged in several deep breaths to try to calm down. Gray lockers blurred around me. Conversations were muted and sounded so very far away.

Where was I going? What was I going to do? Going to Daemon was out of the question, because right now, on top of everything, it was the last thing we needed.

I started forward, my fingers clenched tightly around my bag's strap. I felt...I felt like I was going to hurl. Anger and nausea roiled. I headed toward the girls' restroom at the end of the hall.

"Katy! Are you okay? Wait up?"

The floor dropped out from underneath me, but I kept walking.

Blake caught up with me, catching my arm. "Katy—"

"Don't touch me!" I wrenched my arm free, horrified...just horrified. "Don't ever touch me."

He stared at me, anger tightening the lines of his face. "What is your problem?"

A terrible, ugly feeling clawed its way through my insides. "I know, Blake. I *know*."

"Know what?" He looked confounded. "Katy, your eyes are starting to glow. You've got to chill out."

I stepped forward but forced myself to stop. I was so close to losing it. "You—you are a freak."

His brows shot up. "All right, you're going to have to give me a better explanation than that, because I have no idea what I've done to tick you off."

The hallway was empty for now, but this was no place to get into this kind of conversation. I turned, heading to the stairwell. Blake followed and once the door swung shut behind us, I whirled on him.

It wasn't my fist that hit him.

A blast of energy, probably what felt like a hit from a Taser, smacked him in the chest. Blake stumbled back into the door, mouth dropping open as his legs and arms twitched.

"What," he gasped. "What was that for?"

Static crackled over my fingers. I wanted to do it again. "You've been sleeping in my bed."

Blake straightened, rubbing a hand over his chest. The faint light coming from the window in the landing danced over his face. "Katy, I—"

"Don't lie about it. I know you've been. I smelled your cologne. It's been on my pillows." Bile filled the back of my throat and the urge to lash out hit me hard. "How could you? How could you do something so revolting and creepy?"

Something flickered in his eyes. Hurt? Anger? I didn't know or care. What he did was so wrong on so many levels that restraining orders were usually issued in response.

Blake thrust his fingers through his hair. "It's not what you think."

"It's not." I barked out a short laugh. "I don't know what else it could be. You came into my house and my bedroom uninvited and you…you got into bed with me, you sick son of a—"

"It's not what you think!" he practically shouted and the Source inside me perked even more, responding to the outburst. I expected teachers to rush the stairwell, but they didn't. "I've been keeping an eye on everything at night because of Daedalus. I patrol the area just like Daemon and the other Luxen do."

I scoffed. "They don't climb into my bed, Blake."

He stared back at me so blatantly I wanted to smack him.

"I know. Like I said, that...was never my intention. It was an accident."

My mouth dropped open. "Did you slip and fall on my bed? Because I don't understand how you've accidentally ended up there."

Red stained the tips of his cheeks. "I check the outside, and then I check the inside just to be sure. Hybrids can get into your house, Katy, as you already know. So could Daedalus if they wanted."

What would he have done if Daemon had been there? Then it struck me and I felt sick all over again. "How long do you watch at night?"

He shrugged. "A couple of hours."

So he'd have known if Daemon had come over most of the time, and the rest was just sheer dumb luck. Part of me wished he'd tried it just once when Daemon was there. He wouldn't be walking right for months.

There was a good chance he may leave this stairwell with a limp.

Blake seemed to sense where my mind went. "After I checked inside your house, I...I don't know what happened. You have bad dreams."

I wondered why. I had perverts sleeping in the bed with me.

"I just wanted to comfort you. That's all." He leaned against the wall, below the window, closing his eyes. "I guess I fell asleep."

"This wasn't a onetime thing. Not that once would be okay. Do you understand that?"

"I do." His eyes opened into thin slits. "Are you going to tell Daemon?"

I shook my head. I could handle this. I *would* handle this. "He would kill you on the spot and then we'd end up in Daedalus's hands."

Relief loosened his body. "Katy, I'm sorry. It's not as creepy as it—"

"Not as creepy? Are you serious? No, don't answer. I don't care." I stepped forward, my voice shaking. "I don't care if you were just worried and keeping an eye on me. I don't care if my house is on fire. You do not come in there again. And you sure as hell don't sleep in my bed again. You kissed…" I sucked in a sharp breath. The raw, ugly black feeling was back, crawling up my throat. "I don't care. I don't want to be near you any more than I have to be. Okay? I want you to stay away from me. No more watching or anything."

Hurt flashed in his churning eyes, and he looked like he'd protest for a long moment. "Okay."

I turned back to the door, my entire body shaking. I stopped and faced him. He stood under the opaque windows, his head lowered. He ran a hand through his spiky hair, clasping the back of his neck.

"If you do again what you've been doing, I will hurt you." Emotion clogged my throat. "I don't care what happens. I will hurt you."

• • •

Shaking off my discovery was hard to do. I alternated between wanting to take a scalding hot shower and anger so potent I could taste it the rest of the day. Luckily, I was able to convince Matthew that Blake had just ticked me off because he was Blake, which was believable and explained why Blake would follow me. I convinced Lesa I wasn't feeling well and that was why I rushed out of class, which she pointed out would put a damper on my afternoon plans.

Those had already been tainted.

I had no intention of bringing this up with Daemon. He would lose his ever-loving mind and as much as I hated it, we needed Blake. We had come too far to end up being captured by them because of whatever letter he had hanging over our heads. I also wasn't willing to risk not rescuing Beth.

Whenever I thought about it throughout the day, my skin crawled. I'd thought it had either been Daemon all of those times or a dream, but I should've known. Not once did I feel the warmth that our connection gave as warning whenever Daemon was near.

I should've known that Blake was a bigger freak than I could ever imagine.

On the way home, I swung by the post office. Daemon hopped out of the car and followed me in. Three steps from the door, he caught me around the waist from behind and lifted me up. He spun me around so fast my legs were like little windmills.

A woman and her child came out of the post office, narrowly avoiding being taken out by my legs. She laughed and I was sure it had something to do with the smile I knew Daemon was sporting.

When he placed me on my feet and let go, I swayed unsteadily through the door. He laughed. "You look a little drunk."

"No thanks to you."

He dropped an arm over my shoulder, apparently in a playful mood. We stopped at my mom's PO box and dug out the packages. A few were media mail and the rest a bunch of junk mail.

Daemon snatched the yellow packages from my hands. "Oh! Books! You have books!"

I laughed as several people waiting in line looked over their shoulders. "Hand them over."

He clutched them to his chest, making moony eyes. "My life is now complete."

"My life would be complete if I could actually post a review on something other than the school library computers."

I did that about twice a week since my latest laptop went to the big computer heaven in the sky. Daemon always went with me. In his words, he was there to "proof" my posts. In other words, he served as a huge distraction.

Taking the rest of the mail from me, he kissed my cheek.

"Wouldn't that be nice? But I think you've exhausted your mom's allowance for laptops."

"Neither was my fault." I'd been hiding my recently destroyed laptop from her. She'd go postal if she found it.

"True." He held open the door for a little old lady and then let me shimmy past. "But I bet you go to bed every night dreaming and thinking about a shiny new laptop."

A warm breeze blew a strand of hair across my face as I stopped at my car. "Besides dreaming about you?"

"In between dreaming about me," he corrected, placing my mail on the backseat. "What's the first thing you'd do if you got a new laptop?"

Letting him take the keys from me, I went to the passenger side and thought about it. "I don't know. I'd probably hug it and promise it that I'd never let anything bad happen to it."

He laughed again, eyes twinkling. "Okay, other than that?"

"Make a vlog thanking the laptop gods for bestowing one upon me." I sighed then, because that would be the only way I'd get one. "I need to get a job."

"What you need to do is apply for college."

"You haven't," I pointed out.

He cast me a sidelong glance. "I've been waiting on you."

"Colorado," I said, and when he nodded, my mom's horrified expression loomed in my head. "Mom would freak."

"I think she'd be happy with the fact that you're going to college."

He had a point, but the whole college thing seemed up in the air at this point. I had no idea what next week would hold for us, let alone a few months down the road. But I had good grades and I had looked into scholarships for next year's spring enrollment.

In Colorado...and I knew Daemon had seen the pamphlet from the university. The prospect of going away to college with Daemon like normal teenagers was appealing. The problem was that getting my hopes up and not being able to do something like that would suck too much.

My house was silent and a little warm. I opened a window in the living room while Daemon helped himself to a glass of milk. When I walked into the kitchen, he was running the back of his hand over his mouth, his hair a mess of waves and eyes as green as spring grass. The movement pulled his shirt taut over his biceps and chest.

I bit back a sigh. Milk did a body good.

His smile was just as wicked. Putting the glass on the counter, he moved so fast I didn't see him until he was standing in front of me, taking my cheeks in his hands. I loved that he was able to be real around me. I used to think the freaky alien speed thing was to annoy me, but it was just his natural state. Slowing down to human speed actually caused him to use more energy.

But then he kissed me, and he tasted of milk and something richer, lush and smooth. I didn't realize he was guiding me backward and that we were at the bottom of the stairs until he lifted me up without breaking the kiss.

I thought the whole thing with Blake would ruin this afternoon, but I had underestimated the magnetism of Daemon and his kisses. I wrapped my legs around his waist, reveling in the feel of his muscles under my hands.

He didn't stop at the top of the stairs but kept going and kissing and my heart was pounding. Turning, he gently kicked my door open and then my heart was doing the skipping thing, because we were in my bedroom and there was no one around to interrupt us. Nervous excitement enveloped me.

Daemon lifted his head. A lopsided grin appeared on his lips and I slid down, breathing fast. I watched in a daze as he moved back and sat on the edge of my bed, his fingers slowly letting go of mine, trailing across my palm. I felt the tingles all the way up my arm.

Then he looked at my desk.

My gaze followed his and I blinked, thinking a mirage had appeared in my bedroom, because I couldn't be seeing what I was.

Resting on my desk was a MacBook Air in a cherry red sleeve.

"I…" I didn't know what to say. My brain emptied. Were we in the right house? I took in the familiar surroundings and decided that we were.

I took a step toward the desk and stopped. "Is that for me?"

A slow, beautiful smile crept across his face, filling his eyes. "Well, it is on your desk, so…"

My heart stuttered. "But I don't understand."

"See, there's this place called an Apple Store and I went there, picked one out. They didn't have any stock." He paused as if to make sure I was following him, and all I could do was stare. "So I ordered one. Meanwhile, I ordered a sleeve. I did take some liberties, since I prefer red."

"But why?"

He laughed softly. "Man, I wish you could see your face."

I clasped my hands over my cheeks. "Why?"

"You didn't have one and I know how much blogging and that stuff means to you. Using the school computer isn't doing it for you." He shrugged. "And we really didn't do the Valentine's thing. So…here we are."

It hit me then that he'd been planning this all day. "When did you put it here?"

"This morning, after you left for school."

I took a deep breath. I was about five seconds from full fangirl mode. "And you got this for me? A MacBook Air? Those things cost a lot of money."

"Thank the taxpayers. Their money funds the DOD who then turns over the money to us." He laughed at my expression. "And I save money. I have a small fortune stashed."

"Daemon, it's too much."

"It's yours."

My gaze was drawn back to the Mac like it was my own personal mecca. How many times since I could spell *laptop* had I dreamt of a MacBook?

I wanted to laugh and cry at the same time. "I can't believe you did this."

He shrugged again. "You deserve it."

Something deep inside me snapped. I tackled Daemon, and he laughed, sweeping his arms around my waist. "Thank you. Thank you," I said over and over again, in between raining quick kisses all over his face.

He tipped his head back on the comforter, laughing. "Wow. You're pretty strong when you're excited."

I sat up, grinning down at him. His face blurred a little. "I can't believe you did this."

Smugness filled his expression. "You had no idea, did you?"

"No, but that's why you kept bringing up the blog stuff." I smacked his chest playfully. "You are…"

He folded his arms under his head. "I'm what?"

"Amazing." I leaned forward, kissing him. "You're amazing."

"That's what I've been saying for years."

I laughed against his mouth. "Seriously, though, you shouldn't have."

"I wanted to."

I didn't know what to say, other than scream from the top of my lungs. Getting a MacBook was like Christmas and Halloween rolled into one.

He lowered his lashes. "It's okay. I know what you want to do. Go play."

"You sure?" My fingers itched to explore.

"Yes."

Squealing, I kissed him again and then rolled off, diving for the laptop. Carrying the super-lightweight book to my bed, I sat beside

Daemon and placed it in my lap. Over the next hour, I familiarized myself with the programs and went through several phases of feeling extraordinarily cool and smart for having a Mac Book Air.

Daemon leaned over my shoulder, pointing out certain features. "There's the webcam."

I squeaked and then grinned when our faces appeared on the screen. "You should do your first vlog right now," he said.

Giddy, I hit record and shrieked, "I have a MacBook Air!"

Daemon laughed as he buried his head in my hair. "You dork."

I hit the stop button and noticed the time. Powering down the laptop, I placed it beside us and threw my arms around him once more. "Thank you."

He pulled me down and reached up, tucking the hair behind my ear. His hand lingered. "I like it when you're happy, and if I can do something small, then I will."

"Something small?" Shock heightened my tone. "That's not something small. That had to have cost — "

"It doesn't matter. You're happy. I'm happy."

My chest swelled. "I love you. You know that, right?"

A cocky grin appeared. "I know."

I waited. Nothing. Rolling my eyes, I sat up on the other side of him and kicked off my shoes. Glancing out the bedroom window, I saw nothing but beautiful blue skies. It was nice enough for flip-flops. Flip-flops!

"You're never going to say it, are you?"

"Say what?" The bed shifted as he sat up, placing his hands on my hips.

I looked over my shoulder. Thick lashes shielded his eyes. "You know what."

"Hmm?" He slid his hands up my sides, distracting as usual.

It might bother some girls that their boyfriends never said the four-letter word. With any other guy, it might've bothered me, too, to be honest, but with Daemon, well, those words would never be easy for him to say, even though he had no problem showing it.

And I was okay with it. Didn't mean I wouldn't tease him about it, though.

He pressed a kiss to my cheek and slid off the bed. "I'm glad you like it."

"I *love* it."

Daemon raised an eyebrow.

"Seriously, I do love it. I can't thank you enough."

Now he waggled that brow. "I'm sure you can."

I stood and pushed him lightly as I scanned my bedroom floor for my flip-flops. I hadn't really looked for anything since the night Carissa had been here. I was still finding stuff they'd put away in odd places. Dipping down, I lifted up the edge of my polka-dotted comforter and peered into the no-man's-land under my bed.

Several loose sheets of notebook paper cluttered the floor. Rolled socks were everywhere. One sneaker was near the top, next to a couple of magazines. The other sneaker was nowhere to be found and appeared to have run off with half the socks, since none of them looked like a match.

The flip-flops were halfway in the middle. I lay down and stretched, smacking at the floor.

"What are you doing?" Daemon asked.

"Trying to get my flip-flops."

"Is it really that hard?"

Ignoring him, I concentrated on the shoes and willed them toward me. A second later, one hit my hand and when the second pair hit, something warm and smooth-feeling bounced off my palm.

"What the...?"

Tossing the flip-flops aside, I felt around until my hand landed on the object. I wiggled out from under the bed and sat up, opening my palm.

"Oh my God," I said.

"What?" Daemon knelt beside me and sucked in a sharp

breath. "Is that what I think it is?"

Resting in my palm was a shiny black stone with red streaked through the center, like a vibrant red flame. It must've been Carissa's and although the bracelet portion wasn't attached and must've been destroyed along with her body, this survived.

I was holding a piece of opal.

Chapter 31

We sort of stared at each other like two doofuses, and then we both sprang into action. Taking the stone that was a little bigger than a nickel, we went downstairs. Our heart rates picked up.

I handed him the stone. "Try something—like that reflection thing."

Daemon, who'd probably been jonesing for a piece of opal since he learned what they could do, didn't refuse. He wrapped his palm around it, and concentration tightened the line of his mouth.

At first nothing happened, and then a faint shimmer surrounded the outline of his body. Like when Dee got excited and her arm would glimmer and fade, but then the shine spread over his body and he disappeared.

Completely disappeared.

"Daemon?" A soft chuckle came from the vicinity of the couch. My eyes narrowed. "I can't see you at all."

"Not at all?"

I shook my head. Weird. He was here, but I couldn't see him. Stepping back, I forced myself to focus on the couch. Then I noticed the difference. In front of the middle cushion and behind the coffee table, the space was distorted. Sort of wavy, like looking at water through glass, and I knew he had to be standing there, blending in like a chameleon.

"Oh my God, you're totally like the *Predator*."

There was a pause and then, "This is so cool." Moments later he reappeared, grinning like a kid who just got his first video game. "God, I am so going to sneak into your bathroom like the Invisible Man."

I rolled my eyes. "Give me the opal."

Laughing, he handed it over. The stone was body temperature, which I thought was weird. "Want to hear something crazier than me being completely invisible? It barely took any energy away. I feel fine."

"Wow." I turned the stone over. "We need to test this out."

Taking the stone, Daemon and I headed to the lake. We had about fifteen minutes before anyone else showed.

"You try it," Daemon said.

Holding the opal in my palm, I wasn't sure what to try. The hardest thing and the one that took the most strength was using the Source as a weapon. So I decided to go with that. I concentrated on the rush and it felt different this time—potent and consuming. Tapping into it came faster, easier, and within seconds, a ball of whitish-red light appeared over my free hand.

"Wow," I said, smiling. "This is…different."

Daemon nodded. "Do you feel tired or anything?"

"No." And usually this wiped me out pretty darn quickly, so the opal really did have an impact. Then I got an idea. Letting the Source fizzle out, I searched the ground and found a small branch.

Taking it to the bank of the lake, I squeezed the opal in one hand. "I could never do the heat-to-fire thing. Burned my fingers pretty badly the last time I tried it."

"Should you be trying it now, then?"

Ah, good point. "But you're here to heal me."

Daemon frowned. "Worst logic ever, Kitten."

I grinned as I focused on the branch. The Source flared once again, traveling along the slender, crooked twig of a branch, encasing it whole. A second later, the stick collapsed into an ash replica, and as the whitish-red light receded, the branch fell apart.

"Uh," I said.

"That wasn't fire, but it was pretty damn close."

I'd never done anything like that before. Had to be the opal-enhanced alien coolness, because I just turned a stick into Pompeii.

"Let me have it," Daemon said. "I want to see if it has any effect on the onyx."

Handing it over, I followed him to the pile of onyx, wiping the ash off my fingers. Holding the opal in one hand, he uncovered the stones and, jaw clenching, he picked one up.

Nothing happened. All of us had grown a tolerance to the rocks, but there was usually a gasp or flinch of pain.

"What's happening?" I asked.

Daemon lifted his chin. "Nothing—I don't feel anything."

"Let me try." We switched off and he was right. The bite of onyx wasn't there. We stared at each other. "Holy crap."

Footsteps and voices carried into the clearing. Daemon swiped the opal, sliding it in his pocket. "I don't think we should let Blake see this."

"No doubt," I agreed.

We turned as Matthew, Dawson, and Blake appeared at the edge of the woods. It would be interesting to see if the opal had any affect in Daemon's pocket or if we had to be physically touching it.

"I talked to Luc," Blake announced while we were all standing around the onyx. "He's good for this Sunday, and I think we'll be ready by then."

"You think?" Dawson said.

He nodded. "It's either going to work or not."

Failure wasn't an option. "So the Sunday after prom?"

"You guys are going to prom?" Blake asked, scowling.

"Why not?" I said defensively.

Blake's eyes darkened. "Just seems like a stupid thing to do the night before. We should be spending Saturday training."

"No one asked for your opinion," Daemon said, hands curving into fists.

Dawson shifted closer to his brother. "One night isn't going to hurt anything."

"And I have prom duty," Matthew said, sounding absolutely disgusted with the idea.

Outnumbered, Blake let out a disgruntled mumble. "Fine. Whatever."

We got started then, and I kept my eyes trained on Daemon when it came to his turn. When he touched the onyx, he immediately flinched but held on. Unless he was faking it, the opal had to be touching flesh. Good to know.

Over the next couple of hours, we did our rounds with the onyx. I was seriously beginning to think my fingers and muscle control would never be the same again. Blake kept the required ten feet distance and didn't try to talk to me. I liked to think my come-to-Jesus discussion had gotten through to him.

If not…then, well, I doubted I'd be able to control myself.

As we broke apart for the night, I lingered back with Daemon. "It didn't work in your pocket, did it?"

"No." He dug the thing out. "I'm going to hide this somewhere. Right now, I don't think we need anyone fighting over it or it getting into the wrong hands."

I agreed. "Do you think we're ready for this Sunday?" My stomach dropped thinking about it, no matter how long I'd known that this day was coming.

Daemon slipped the opal back into his pocket and then gathered me in his arms. Anytime he held me, it always felt unbelievably right and I wondered how I could've denied it for so long.

"We're going to be as ready as we ever will be." He brushed his cheek along mine and I shivered, closing my eyes. "And I don't think we can keep Dawson off much longer."

I nodded and wrapped my arms around him. Now or never. Oddly, in that moment, I felt like we didn't have enough time, even though we'd been practicing for months. Maybe it wasn't that.

Maybe I just felt we didn't have enough time together.

• • •

On Saturday, Lesa and I piled into the back of Dee's Jetta. Windows rolled down, we enjoyed the seasonably warm temps. Dee seemed different today, too. It wasn't the pretty pink summer dress she'd worn, paired with a black cardigan and strappy sandals. Her hair was pulled up in a loose ponytail and her thick hair cascaded down her back, revealing a perfectly symmetrical face that bore an easy grin—not the one I was so familiar with and missed painfully, but *almost*. She was lighter somehow, her shoulders less tense.

Right now, she hummed along to a rock song on the radio, speeding around cars like a Nascar driver.

Today was a turning point.

Lesa grasped the back of Ash's seat, face pale. "Uh, Dee, you do realize this is a no passing zone, right?"

Dee grinned in the rearview mirror. "I think it's a suggestion, not a rule."

"I think it's a rule," Lesa advised.

Ash snorted. "Dee thinks yield signs are a suggestion, too." I laughed, wondering how I could've forgotten Dee's terrifying driving. Normally I'd be clutching a seat or handle too, but today I couldn't care as long as she got us to the shop in one piece.

And she did.

And we only narrowly avoided wiping out a family of four plus a religious tour bus once.

The shop was downtown, occupying an old row house. Ash's pert little nose wrinkled as her heels touched the gravel we parked on. "I know it looks less than savory from the outside, but it's really not bad. They have cool dresses."

Lesa studied the old brick building, doubtful. "Are you sure?"

Sashaying past her, Ash cast a mischievous grin over her shoulder. "When it comes to clothing, I'll never steer you wrong." Then she frowned and reached out, flicking green-painted nails along Lesa's shirt. "We need to go shopping one day."

Lesa's mouth dropped open as Ash spun and headed toward the back door that bore an OPEN sign written in elegant calligraphy.

"I'm going to hit her," Lesa said under her breath. "You just watch. I'm gonna break that pretty nose of hers."

"I'd try to resist that urge if I were you."

She smirked. "I could take her."

Ah, no, she couldn't.

Finding dresses didn't take very long. Ash went with one that barely covered her ass, and I found a really great red dress I just knew Daemon would go gaga for. Afterward, we headed to Smoke Hole Diner.

Going out to eat with Lesa felt good, and Dee being there was like the proverbial icing on the cake. Ash? I wasn't so sure about that part.

I ordered a hamburger while Ash and Dee ordered practically everything on the menu. Lesa went with a grilled cheese sandwich and something I found entirely gross. "I don't know why you drink cold coffee. You can just get regular coffee and let it grow cold."

"So not the same," Dee answered as the waitress put our sodas down. "Tell them, Ash."

The blonde Luxen peered up from ridiculously long eyelashes.

"Chilled coffee is more sophisticated."

I made a face. "I'll be uncivilized with my warm coffee."

"Why doesn't that surprise me?" Ash arched a brow and then turned her attention back to her cellphone.

Sticking my tongue at her, I smothered a giggle when Lesa elbowed me. "I still think I should've gotten the transparent wings for my dress."

Dee smiled. "They were cute."

I nodded, thinking Daemon would've loved them.

Lesa tugged her curls out of her face. "You guys are lucky you found dresses on this short notice."

Since her and Chad had made plans to go like ordinary people months ago, she had gotten her dress from some shop in Virginia. She had gone mostly along for the ride.

As conversation picked up and Dee started talking about her dress, I sat back against the booth. Sadness trickled through me, followed by bittersweet memories. I thought I'd known Carissa, but I really hadn't. Had she known a Luxen? Or had she been picked up by Daedalus and used? Months had passed and there had been no answers; the only reminder was the piece of opal I had discovered under my bed.

Some days I'd felt nothing but anger, but today, I let it slip off my shoulders with a deep breath. What had become of Carissa couldn't tarnish her memory forever.

Ash smiled. "I'm thinking my dress will be a hit."

Lesa sighed. "I don't know why you don't just go naked. That little black dress you found is little and nothing else."

"Don't tempt her," Dee said, grinning as our food was delivered to the table.

"Naked?" Ash scuffed. "These goods aren't showed off for free."

"Surprising," Lesa muttered under her breath.

It was my turn to elbow her.

"So, are you going to the prom with anyone?" Lesa asked, ignoring me as she waved her grilled cheese sandwich at Dee. "Or are you going solo?"

Dee shrugged one shoulder. "I wasn't going to go, you know, because of... Adam, but it's my last year, so... I wanted to go." There was a pause as she pushed her chicken tender around her basket. "I'm going with Andrew."

I almost choked on my bun. Lesa gaped. We stared at her.

Her brows rose. "What?"

"You're not...like, going out with Andrew, are you?" Lesa's cheeks flamed—*Lesa's*. "I mean, if you are, cool and what not."

Dee laughed. "No—God, no. That would be way too weird for the both of us. We're friends."

"Andrew's a douche," Lesa said what I was thinking.

Ash snorted. "Andrew has taste. Of course you would think he's a douche."

"Andrew has changed a lot. He was there for me and vice versa." And Dee was right. Andrew had simmered down a bit. Everyone had changed. "We're just going as friends."

Thank God, because even though I didn't want to judge, Dee hooking up with Adam's brother would be way too weird. And then Ash dropped the bomb of all bombs as I munched on a thick french fry. "I have a date," she said.

I think I might've developed a hearing problem. "With who?"

One delicate eyebrow arched. "No one you would know."

"Is he..." I caught myself. "Is he from around here?"

Dee bit down on her lip. "He's a freshman at Frostburg. She met him at the mall in Cumberland a few weeks back."

But that didn't answer the question burning to be asked. Was he human? Dee must've read what I was dying to know in my eyes, because she nodded and grinned.

I almost dropped my soda.

Holy country roads take me home, because this was an

alternate reality if Ash was going to prom with a human—a subpar, ordinary old human.

Ash rolled cerulean eyes. "I don't know why you guys are staring at me like you're on the wrong side of special." She popped another fry into her mouth. "I would never go to the prom alone. For example—"

"Ash," Dee said, eyes narrowing.

"I went with Daemon to the prom last year," she went on, and my stomach twisted into knots, which was made worse by the secretive smile that graced her full lips. "That was a night I'll never forget."

I wanted to punch her.

Taking a deep breath, I forced a smile. "Funny because Daemon hasn't mentioned that night."

Ash's eyes flashed in warning. "He isn't the kiss and tell type, dear."

My smile turned brittle. "*That* I know."

She got my message and that conversation was thankfully dropped and Dee started talking about some TV show she was watching, which somehow sparked another argument between Ash and Lesa over who was the hottest guy on the show. I'm pretty sure those two would argue over the color of the sky.

I took Lesa's side.

In the car ride back, Lesa turned to me. "So, are you and Daemon getting a hotel room or anything?"

"Uh, no. Do people really do that?"

Lesa leaned back and laughed. "Yes. Chad and I are getting one at Fort Hill."

In the front passenger seat, Ash snickered.

"What are you doing, Ash?" Lesa asked, her eyes sharpening. "Planning to stay at prom and beat up the prom queen?"

Ash laughed in her seat but said nothing.

"Anyway," Lesa drawled. "You and Daemon haven't done it

yet, right? Prom—"

"Hey!" Dee shrieked, startling us. "I'm sitting here, remember? I don't want to hear about this."

"Neither do I," Ash muttered.

Oblivious to them, Lesa stared and waited. There was no way I was answering that question. If I lied and said yes, I'd scar Dee for life and if I told the truth, I was sure Ash would go into a detailed synopsis of their past sexual activities.

Finally Lesa dropped it, but it was all I thought about thanks to her. I sighed, staring out the window. It wasn't like we weren't ready. I guess. I mean, how do you know you're really ready? I don't think anyone seriously does. Sex wasn't something you could plan. It either happened or it didn't.

Getting a hotel room with the expectation of having sex? Hotels were so…so skeevy.

Part of me wondered if I'd been living in a cave or something, but I hadn't. At school, in-between classes, I'd heard other girls talking about the things they hoped and planned to happen after prom. I'd heard guys talking, too. But I had my mind on other things, I supposed.

And who was I to judge? A few days ago I'd really believed the reason Daemon wanted to come over to my house afterschool was to…do it. But heck, at the rate we were going, we'd be fifty before anything like that happened.

Pushing the whole subject out of my mind by the time we got home, I said goodbye to Lesa and even Ash. I couldn't wait until I saw this human college boy.

Dee and I were left alone.

She started toward her house while I stood there like an idiot, unsure of what to say. But she stopped and then turned around. Her lashes were lowered as she fidgeted with the edges of her hair. "I had fun today. I'm glad you came."

"Me, too."

She shifted her weight. "Daemon's going to love that dress."

"You think?" I lifted up the garment bag.

"It *is* red." She smiled, taking a step back. "Maybe before prom we can get together and get ready…like with Homecoming?"

"I'd love that." My smile spread so fast I bet I looked a little crazy.

She nodded, and I wanted to run up and hug her, but I wasn't sure if we were there yet. With a little wave, she spun around and headed up her porch. For a moment, I stood there with my dress and let out a happy sigh.

This was progress. Maybe things would never be like they were, but this was really good.

Heading inside, I hugged my dress bag close and kicked the door shut. Mom had already left for work, so as I took my dress upstairs and hung it on my closet door. I wondered what I was going to make myself for dinner.

Pulling out my cell phone, I sent Daemon a quick text. *What R U doing?*

He responded a few moments later. *With Andrew & Matthew, getting dinner. Want smthing?*

I glanced at the bag, recalling how flirty the dress was. Feeling naughty, I texted him: *You.*

The response was lightning quick, and I laughed. *Really?* And then, *Of course, I alrdy knew that.* And before I could respond, my phone rang. It was Daemon.

I answered, grinning like an idiot. "Hey."

"I wish I were home," he said, and a car honked. "I can be there in seconds."

Heading down the steps, I stopped and leaned against the wall. "No. You rarely get guy time. Stay with them."

"I don't need guy time. I need Kitten time."

My face flushed. "Well, you can get Kitten time when you come home."

He grumbled and then, "Did you get a dress?"

"Yes."

"Will I like it?"

I smiled and then rolled my eyes when I realized I was twirling my hair. "It's red, so I think so."

"Hot damn." Someone yelled his name—sounded like Andrew—and he sighed. "Okay. I'm going back in. Want me to pick you up anything? Andrew, Dawson, and I are going to Smoke Hole."

I thought about the hamburger I just ate. I'd be hungry later. "Do they have chicken fried steak?"

"Yes."

"With homemade gravy?" I inquired, starting back down the steps.

Daemon's laugh was husky. "The best gravy around."

"Perfect. I want that."

He promised to bring me home a hungry man's portion and then hung up. I went into the living room first and dropped my cell on the coffee table. Then I swiped up one of the books I'd gotten this past week for review and headed to the kitchen for something to drink.

Flipping over the book, I read the blurb and had to slow down because I almost walked into a wall. Laughing at myself, I stepped through the doorway and looked up.

Will sat at the kitchen table.

Chapter 32

The book slipped from my lifeless fingers, falling to the floor. The *smack* reverberated inside me, all around me. I sucked in a breath but it got stuck around my heart pounding off my ribs.

My eyes had to be deceiving me. He couldn't be here. And he couldn't look the way he did. It was Will... It was but it *wasn't*. Something was dreadfully wrong with the man.

Will sat hunched over the table with his back to the fridge. The last time I'd seen him, his dark brown hair had been thick and wavy, with a hint of gray at the temples. Patches of his skull shone under a thin layer of mousy hair now.

Will... Will had been a handsome man, but this man who sat before me had aged dramatically. His skin was sallow and drawn tight across his face. No fat or form whatsoever, and he reminded me of the skeleton decorations used to scare children at Halloween. Some sort of rash affected his forehead, looking like a blotch of raspberries. His lips were incredibly thin, as were his arms and his shoulders.

Only his eyes were what I remembered. Pale blue, full of

strength and determination, they fixed on mine. Something else sharpened them. Resolve? Hatred? I wasn't sure, but what shone deep in them was more frightening than staring down a horde of Arum.

Will let out a dry, painful-sounding laugh. "I'm a sight for sore eyes, aren't I?"

I didn't know what to do or say. As scary as hell as it was that he was here, he was in no shape to do a thing to me. That gave me a little confidence.

He sat back against the chair; the movement looked like it hurt and winded him.

"What happened to you?" I asked.

Will stared back a long moment before sliding a hand over the table. "You're smarter than that, Katy. It's obvious. The mutation didn't hold."

That I got, but it didn't explain why he looked like the crypt keeper.

"I did plan on coming back here after a few weeks. I knew the sickness would be rough—I knew I needed time to get control of it. Then I'd come and we'd be one big, happy family."

I choked. "There would be no way I'd let that happen."

"Your mother wanted that."

My hands curled into fists.

"It seemed to hold at first." A cough racked his frail body and I almost expected him to topple over. "Weeks went by and the things I could do…" A weak, brittle smile split his dry lips. "Moving objects with a wave of my hand, running miles without breaking a sweat…I felt better than I ever had. Everything had fallen into place just like I planned, just like I *paid* for."

My horrified gaze flickered over his sunken chest. "Then what happened to you?"

His left arm twitched. "The mutation didn't hold, but that doesn't mean it didn't change me on a cellular level. Something I'd wanted to prevent ended up being...propelled by the mutation. My cancer," he said, lip curling. "My cancer was in remission. The statistics of a complete recovery were high, but when the mutation faded, this..." He waved a weak hand around himself. "This happened."

I blinked, stunned. "Your cancer came back?"

"With a vengeance," he said, laughing that terrible, fragile laugh. "There's nothing that can be done. My blood is like a toxin. My organs are failing at an abnormal rate. Apparently, the whole theory of cancer being linked to DNA may have some basis to it."

Each word he spoke seemed to exhaust him and there was no doubt he was one step, maybe two, away from death. Reluctant sympathy flooded me. How crappy was it that everything he'd done to secure his health had ultimately led to his death?

I shook my head. Irony was such a witch. "If you had just left everything alone, you'd be fine."

His eyes met mine. "You want to rub that in?"

"No." And I really didn't. If anything, I was sickened by this. "It's just sad, really sad."

He stiffened. "I don't want your pity."

Okay. I crossed my arms. "Then what do you want?"

"I want revenge."

My brows shot up. "For what? You brought this on yourself."

"I did everything right!" He slammed his fist down on the table, rattling it and surprising me. Well, he was stronger than he looked. "I did everything right. It was him—Daemon. He didn't do what he was supposed to."

"He healed you like you wanted."

"Yes! He healed me! And that gave me a temporary mutation." Another fit of coughing stole his words. "He...he didn't mutate me. What he did...was he gave himself what he wanted and enough time for him to think he got away with it."

I stared at him. "The whole healing and mutation thing isn't an exact science."

"You're correct. The DOD has dedicated entire organizations to discovering how a successful hybrid is created." No big announcement there. "But Daemon is the strongest. There was no reason why it wouldn't have held."

"There's no way of knowing what would've happened."

"Don't pretend that you don't know," he spat. "That punk knew what he was doing. I saw it in his eyes. I just didn't know what it meant then."

I looked away and then faced him. "There has to be a true want behind the healing for it to work. Anything else won't do the job... or at least that's what we've learned."

"That's mystical BS."

"Is it?" My gaze drifted over him. Yeah, I was being a bitch, but he locked me in a cage, tortured me, and had slept with my mom to get what he wanted. I felt sympathy for the guy, but in a twisted way, he'd gotten what he deserved. "Sure doesn't seem that way."

"You're so cocky, Katy. The last I saw of you, you were screaming your head off." He smiled again, his head wobbling on his neck.

And there went my sympathy. "What do you want, Will?"

"I told you." He stood awkwardly, swaying to the left of the table. "I want revenge."

I arched a brow. "Not sure how you're going to pull that off."

He placed one hand on the counter, supporting himself. "This is your fault—Daemon's fault. I made a deal. I held up my end of the bargain."

"Dawson wasn't where you said he was."

"No. I had him released from the office building." His smug smile came off as a grimace. "I had to give myself more time to get away. I knew Daemon would come after me."

"No. He wouldn't have, because he really didn't know if it worked or not. If so..." I stopped.

"We'd be joined, and there'd be nothing he could do?" he supplied. "That's what I hoped."

I watched him place a hand on his bony hip, all at once grateful that Mom would never see him like this. Will would remind her of Dad. Part of me felt like I should help Will sit down or something.

He bared yellow teeth. "But you two are joined, right? One life split into two. One of you dies, so does the other."

I snapped to attention. My stomach lurched.

He caught my reaction. "If I had to pick what I'd want to accomplish here, it would be to make him suffer, to live on without the thing he cherishes most, but...he's not going to die instantaneously, right? He'll know—and those seconds of him knowing..."

His intentions sunk in slowly. A buzzing filled my ears and my mouth dried. He wanted to kill us. With what? His evil-eye power?

Will pulled a gun out from underneath his loose shirt.

Oh, yeah, that would do it.

"You can't be serious," I said, shaking my head.

"I'm as serious as they come." He took a breath, and his chest rattled a death sound. "And then I'm going to sit here and wait for your pretty mom to come home. She's going to see your dead body first and then she'll see the business end of my gun."

My heart tripped up. Ice water slipped over my skin. The buzzing roared now. Like a switch being thrown inside me, something else took over. It wasn't timid, gullible Katy who followed him into a car. It wasn't the one who stood in the kitchen seconds ago feeling sorry for him.

This was the girl who stood before Vaughn and watched the life seep out of him.

Maybe later I would be bothered by how quickly the change came over me. How easy it was for me to go from the girl who'd just bought her prom dress and flirted with her boyfriend to this stranger who now occupied my body, ready to do anything to protect those I loved.

But right now, I didn't care.

"You're not going to hurt Daemon. You're not going to hurt me," I said. "And you are sure as hell not going to hurt my mother."

Will lifted the gun. The metal looked too heavy for his feeble hand. "What are you going to do, Katy?"

"What do you think?" I took a bold step forward, my brain and mouth propelled by this stranger. "Come on, Will, you're smart enough to figure it out on your own."

"You don't have it in you."

Calmness settled over me, and I felt my lips spread into a smile. "You don't know what I'm capable of."

Up until then, I hadn't known what I was capable of, not truly, but seeing Will, staring down the barrel of that gun, I knew exactly what I *was* capable of. And as wrong as it may be, I was okay with what I was going to have to do.

Completely accepting of it.

There was a part of me that was scared of how easy that acceptance was and I wanted to cling to the old Katy, because she would've had a problem with this. She would've been sickened by this and the words I was saying.

"You do look a little ill, Will. You might want to get checked out. Oh, wait." I widened my eyes innocently. "You can't go to a regular doctor because even though the mutation *obviously* didn't stick, I'm sure it changed you and you can't go to the DOD, because that would be like suicide."

The hand around the gun trembled. "You think you're so smart and brave, don't you, little girl?"

I shrugged. "Perhaps, but I do know I'm completely healthy. What about you, Will?"

"Shut up," he hissed.

Stepping next to the kitchen table, I eyed the gun. If I could distract him, then I could take him out. I really didn't want to test the whole stopping-a-bullet theory.

"Just think of all that money you paid, and it didn't even work out in the end," I said. "And you've lost everything—your career, your money, my mom, and your health. Karma's a tool, isn't it?"

"You stupid bitch." Spittle flew from between his chapped lips. "I'm going to kill you, and you'll die knowing that your precious freak will be dead, too. And then I'm going to sit here and wait for your mother to come home."

My humanity clicked off. I was *so* done with this.

Will smiled. "Where's your smart mouth now?"

My gaze dropped to the gun, and I felt the Source soar over my skin. My fingers splayed, their tips already tingling. Drawing in the power, I focused on the gun. His hand shook again. The muzzle of the gun swayed to the left. The trigger finger twitched.

Will's throat spasmed as he swallowed. "What… What are you doing?"

I lifted my gaze, and I smiled.

His bloodshot eyes widened. "You—"

I waved my hand to the left and several things happened next. There was a popping sound, like a cork being pulled from a champagne bottle, but the sound and everything else was lost in the roar of electricity that flowed outward and then the gun flew from his hand.

It was like a bolt of lightning—pure and raw.

The stream of whitish-red light arced across the room, slamming into Will's chest. Maybe—maybe if he wasn't so ill, it wouldn't have done much, but the man was weak and I wasn't.

He flew backward, bouncing off the wall next to the fridge, his head flopping on his neck like a rag doll. He made no sound as he hit the floor in a boneless heap. That was it—it was over. No more wondering about Will or where he was, what he was doing. This part of our lives was closed.

My house is like the killing fields, I thought.

I exhaled and something—I don't know, something went wrong. Air was stuck in my throat, in my lungs, but when I dragged in a breath, there was this burning pain I hadn't noticed before. But as the Source receded back into me, the burning grew across my chest, spread over my stomach.

I looked down.

A red inkblot had formed on the pale blue shirt and it spread... larger and larger, an irregular circle that bled.

I pressed my hands against the circle—it was damp, warm, and sticky. Blood. It was blood—my blood. My head swam.

"Daemon," I whispered.

Chapter 33

I don't remember falling, but I was staring at the ceiling, trying to keep my hands pressed to the gunshot wound, because I'd seen people do that on TV, but I couldn't feel my hands, so I wasn't sure if they were there or by my sides.

My face was wet.

I was going to die in minutes, maybe sooner, and I'd failed Daemon and my mom. Failed them, because Daemon would die, too, and my mom—oh, God, my mom would come home to find this. She wouldn't survive this, not after Dad.

A shudder rolled through my body and my chest labored for breath. I didn't want to die alone on the cold, hard floor. I didn't want to die at all. I blinked and when I reopened my eyes, the ceiling was fuzzy.

Nothing really hurt, though. Books got that right. There was a point where there was so much pain I couldn't process it or I was beyond it. Probably beyond it...

The front door opened and a familiar voice called out, "Katy? Where are you? Something's wrong with Daemon..."

My lips worked, but there was no sound. I tried again. "Dee?"

Footsteps crept closer and then, "Oh my God...oh my God."

Dee was suddenly in my line of sight, her face fuzzy around the edges. "Katy—holy crap, Katy...hold on." She moved my bloodstained hands away and placed hers over the wound as she looked up, seeing Will crumpled beside the fridge. "God..."

I worked to get out one word. "Daemon..."

She blinked rapidly, her form fading out for a second and then her face was in front of mine, her eyes glowing like diamonds, and I couldn't look away. Her eyes, her words, consumed me. "Andrew is bringing him over. He's okay. He's going to be okay, because you're going to be okay. Got that?"

I coughed out a response and something wet and warm covered my lips. It had to be bad—blood—because Dee's face paled even more as she placed both of her hands over the wound and closed her eyes.

My lids seemed way too heavy and the sudden warmth radiating from hers ebbed and flowed through me. Her shape faded out and she was in her true form—bright and lustrous like an angel—and I thought if I were to die, then at least I saw something as beautiful as this before the end.

But I had to hang on, because it wasn't just my life that hung in the balance. It was Daemon's. So I forced my eyes open, kept them trained on Dee, watching as her light flickered over the walls, bathing the room. If she healed me, would we be linked? The three of us? I couldn't wrap my head around that. And it wouldn't be fair to Dee.

And then there were voices. I recognized Andrew's and Dawson's. There was a *thud* beside my head and then *he* was there, his beautiful face pale and strained. I'd never seen him so pale, and if I concentrated, I could feel his heart laboring like mine. His hands were shaking as they touched my cheeks, smooth under my parted lips.

"Daemon…"

"Shh," he said, smiling. "Don't talk. It's okay. Everything is okay."

He turned to his sister, gently pulling her stained hands back. "You can stop now."

She must've responded directly to him, because Daemon shook his hand. "We can't risk you doing this. You have to stop."

Someone, it sounded like Andrew, said, "Man, you're too weak to do this." And then I realized it was him, and he was on my other side. I think he held my hand. I may've been hallucinating, though, because I saw two Daemons.

Wait. The second one was Dawson. He was holding Daemon, keeping him in an upright position. Daemon never needed help. He was the strongest—*is* the strongest. Panic blossomed.

"Let Dee do this," Andrew urged.

Daemon shook his head and after what seemed like forever, Dee pulled back and took on her human form. She scrambled out of the way, arms shaking.

"He's crazy," she said. "He's absolutely crazy."

When Daemon slipped into his true form and placed his hands on me, there was only him then. The rest of the room slipped away. I didn't want him to heal me if he was already weak, but I got why he didn't want Dee to do it. Too risky, not knowing how or if it would link the three of us together.

Heat flowed through me and then I wasn't really thinking. Daemon's voice was in my thoughts, murmuring reassurances over and over again. I felt light, airy, and complete.

Daemon… I said his name over and over again. I don't know why, but it was grounding to just hear his name.

And when I closed my eyes, they didn't reopen. The renewing warmth was in every cell, easing through my veins, settling into my muscles and bones. Heat and safety pulled me under and the last thing I heard was Daemon's voice.

You can let go now.
I did.

• • •

When I opened my eyes again, a candle somewhere in the room flickered and danced in the shadows. I couldn't move my arms and I didn't know where I was for a second, but as I dragged in a deep breath, an earthy scent surrounded me.

"Daemon?" My voice was hoarse, dry from panic.

The bed—I was in a bed—dipped and out of the darkness came Daemon. Half of his face was bathed in shadows. His eyes glowed like diamonds.

"I'm here," he said. "Right beside you."

I swallowed, keeping my gaze fixed on him. "I can't move my arms."

There was a deep, throaty chuckle and I thought it was terrible that he would laugh when my arms couldn't move. "Here, let me fix that for you."

Daemon's hands felt around me, finding the edges of the blankets. He loosened them. "There you go."

"Oh." I wiggled my fingers and then slipped my arms out. A second later, I realized I was nude—completely nude under the blankets. Fire swept over my face and down my neck. Did we…? What the heck was I not remembering?

I clasped the edge of the blanket, wincing as skin pulled over my chest. "Why am I naked?"

Daemon stared back at me. One second passed and then two, three. "You don't remember?"

It took a moment or so for my brain to process everything and when it did, I sat up and started to jerk the blanket away. Daemon stopped me with his hand. "You're fine. There's just a tiny mark—a scar, but it's really faint," he said, his large hand surrounding mine.

"Honestly, I doubt anyone would notice it unless they were looking really close, and I'd be perturbed if anyone was looking that close."

My mouth worked without sound. Around us, the candle threw shadows along the wall. It was Daemon's bedroom, because my bed wasn't nearly as comfortable or as big as his.

Will had come back. He had shot me—*shot me* right in the chest and I...I couldn't finish that thought.

"Dee helped get you cleaned up. So did Ash." His eyes searched my face. "They put you in the bed. I didn't...help them."

Ash saw me naked? Stupidly, out of everything, that made me want to crawl back under the covers. Man, I needed to get my priorities straight.

"Are you sure you're okay?" He reached to touch me but stopped, his hand lingering an inch or so from my cheek.

I nodded. I'd been shot—shot in the chest. That thought was on repeat. I'd come close to death once before, when we'd fought Baruck, but to be shot was a whole different ballpark. It was going to take me a few moments to fully comprehend that, especially since it didn't seem real.

"I shouldn't be sitting up and talking to you," I said dumbly, peering through my lashes. "This is..."

"I know. It's a lot." He touched me then, placing the tips of his fingers on my lips reverently. He let out a shaky breath. "It's really a lot."

I closed my eyes for a moment, soaking in the low hum and warmth his touch brought. "How did you know?"

"I felt short of breath all of a sudden," he said, dropping his hand and inching closer. "And there was this red-hot feeling in my chest. My muscles wouldn't work right. I knew something had happened. Luckily, Andrew and Dawson were able to get me outside without causing a scene. Sorry, no chicken fried steak."

I didn't think I'd ever eat again.

A smile appeared on his lips. "I'd never been so scared in my life. I had Dawson call Dee to check on you. I…was too weak to get here myself."

I recalled how pale he'd looked and that Dawson had been supporting him. "How do you feel now?"

"Perfect." He tilted his head to the side. "You?"

"I feel fine." Only a dull soreness lingered, but it was nothing. "You saved my life—our lives."

"It was nothing."

I gaped. Only Daemon would think something like this was nothing. And then another new concern rose. Twisting on the bed, I searched out the bedside clock in the dark. Digital green lights showed that it was only a little past one in the morning. I'd slept for about six hours.

"I have to go home," I said, gathering the blanket around me. "There has to be blood and when my mom comes home in the morning, I don't—"

"It's all been taken care of." He stilled me. "They took care of Will and the house is fine. When your mom comes home, she won't know anything happened."

Relief was potent and I relaxed, but it didn't last long. An image surfaced of standing in the kitchen, smiling at Will and goading him, sending a shudder through me. Silence fell between us as I stared into the darkened room, replaying the evening over and over. I kept getting caught on how calm I had become, how cold I'd felt when that part of me decided I was going to have to…have to kill Will.

And I had.

A bitter taste filled the back of my throat. I had killed people and that was even counting the Arum. A life was a life, Daemon had said. So how many had I killed? Three? So I'd killed four living creatures.

My breath rose and got stuck around the quickly rising lump in my throat. What was worse than the knowledge that I had taken lives was my acceptance of doing so. I'd had no qualms about what I did when it happened and that wasn't me—that couldn't be me.

"Kat," he said softly. "Kitten, what are you thinking?"

"I killed him." Tears welled up and spilled down my cheeks before I could stop them. "I killed him, and I didn't care at all."

He placed his hands on my bare shoulders. "You did what you had to do, Kat."

"No. You don't understand." My throat tightened and I struggled for breath. "I didn't *care*. And I should care about these kinds of things." I laughed hoarsely. "Oh, God…"

Pain flickered in his bright gaze. "Kat—"

"What's wrong with me? Something *is* wrong with me. I could've just disarmed him and stopped him. I didn't have to—"

"Kat, he tried to kill you. He shot you. You acted out of self-defense."

It all sounded reasonable to him. But had I? The man was weak and frail. Instead of goading him, I could've disarmed him and that was it. But I killed him…

My control slipped and broke. I felt twisted inside, balling up into so many knots I thought I'd never be straightened out again. This whole time I had been so convinced that I could do what was necessary, that I could easily kill and when it came down to it, I *had* killed, but Daemon had been right. Killing wasn't the hard part. It was what came afterward—the guilt. It was too much. All the ghosts of those who'd died by my own hand and those who had passed on who were tied to me appeared, surrounding me and choking me until the only sound I could make was a hoarse cry.

Daemon made a sound in the back of his throat and pulled me into his arms, blankets and all. The tears came, they kept coming, and he rocked me, holding me close. And it didn't seem right or fair that he'd comfort me. He didn't know how easy it had been for me to throw that switch, to become someone else. I wasn't the same girl. Not the Katy who had changed him and inspired him to be different.

I wasn't *her*.

I struggled to pull free, but he held on and I hated that—hated that he didn't see what I saw. "I'm a monster. I'm like Blake."

"What?" Disbelief thickened his tone. "You are nothing like him, Kat. How can you say that?"

Tears streaked down my cheeks. "But I am. Blake—he killed because he was desperate. How is what I did any different? It's not!"

He shook his head. "It's not the same."

I dragged in air by the lungful. "I'd do it again. I swear I would. If anyone threatened my mom or you, I would. And I knew that after everything that had happened with Blake and Adam. That's not how people react—it's not right."

"There's nothing wrong with protecting those you love," he argued. "Do you think I've enjoyed killing those I have? I haven't. But I wouldn't go back and change those things."

I wiped at my cheeks as my shoulders shook. "Daemon, it's different."

"How is it?" He grasped my face in his hands, forcing me to look at him through tear-soaked lashes. "Remember when I took out those two DOD officers at the warehouse? I hated that I did it, but I had no other choice. If they reported back that they'd seen us, it would all be over and I wasn't going to let them take you."

His fingers chased after the tears and he dipped his head, catching my gaze when I tried to look away. "And I hated what I have done—I hated every time I've taken a life, Arum or human, but sometimes, there is no other choice. You don't accept it. You don't become okay with it, but you do come to understand it."

I grasped his wrists. They were so thick that my fingers barely met. "But what...what if I was okay with it?"

"You're not okay with it, Kat." His belief in that statement, in me, rang true in his voice, and I couldn't understand that blind faith.

"I know you're not."

"How can you be so sure?" I whispered.

Daemon smiled a little. Not a full breathtaking kind of smile, but it still reached down into me, wrapping around my heart. "I know you're good inside. You're warmth and light and everything I don't deserve, but you—you believe that I deserve you. Knowing all that I have done in my past to other people and to you, you still believe I deserve you."

"I—"

"And that's because you're good inside—you've always been and will be." His hands slipped down my throat, to curve around my shoulders. "There is nothing you can say or do that will change that. So grieve what you *had* to do. Mourn it, but never, ever blame yourself for things that are beyond your control."

I didn't know what to say.

His smile slipped into that smug half grin that infuriated and thrilled me. "Now get the rest of that crap out of your head, because you're so much better than that; you're more than that."

His words, well, they may not have washed away everything and they may not have changed the part in me that wasn't as perfect as he thought, but they wrapped around me like a soft down comforter. They were enough for that moment to…to understand what I had done and that was important, that was enough. There weren't any words for how much I appreciated what he said and what he had done. A thank-you wasn't enough.

Still shaking, my hands balled up into those tiny knots, I leaned forward and pressed my lips against his. His fingers tightened around my shoulders as his chest rose sharply. I tasted my own salty tears on his lips and as the kiss deepened, I tasted my own fear.

But there was more.

There was our love—there was our hope that we'd walk out of this with a future. There was our acceptance of each other—the good, the bad, and the downright ugly. There was so much pent-up longing. So much emotion that it packed a sucker punch straight to my soul and his, I knew it, because I could feel his heart rate picking up. Mine matched his—made for his. All of that was in a simple kiss and it was too much, not enough, and just perfect.

I pulled back, drawing in a sharp breath. Our eyes locked. A wealth of emotion shone in his brilliant green eyes. He cupped my cheek with one hand tenderly, and he spoke in his lovely language. It sounded like three lyrical words—a short, beautiful verse.

"What did you say?" I asked, my fingers loosening around the cover.

His smile was secretive and then his lips were on mine again and my eyes drifted shut. I let go of the blanket, felt it slip away, pool around my hips, and I felt Daemon stop breathing for a moment.

He guided me back, and I wrapped my arms around him. We kissed for what felt like an eternity and that wasn't long enough. I could keep going, never stop, because in that moment, we created a world where nothing else existed. We lost ourselves in each other for a while and time, it sped and crept by in the same instance. We kissed until I was breathless, pausing only to explore each other. We were warm and flushed, twisting against each other. My body arched against his and when I moaned, he stilled.

He lifted his head but said nothing. Stared for so long and so hard that every point in my body seemed stretched too far. My chest squeezed. I reached up, placing my trembling hand on his cheek.

His head dipped against my cheek, and his voice was rough and raw. "Tell me to stop and I will."

I wasn't going to. Not now. Not after everything. There was nothing to deny anymore, and my answer was to kiss him, and without words, he understood.

He settled over me, not touching, not quite. The electricity between us snapped and pulled. A wild feeling pulsed through me.

I lifted my hands, sinking them into his hair, pulling him closer. I swept my lips over his, and his body trembled. His fiery eyes drifted shut as my thumb moved on his bottom lip. My hands were on the move, slipping over the thick cords in his neck and back, around his chest and down. Lower, over the hard planes of his stomach. He sucked in a sharp breath.

The edges of his body started to glow, casting the room in a soft light. Heat rolled off his body. Daemon's eyes snapped open and he sat up, pulling me into his lap. His eyes were no longer green, just orbs of pure light. My heart tripped over itself. A fire started in my stomach, spreading through me like a wave of lava.

His hands trembled on my hips and the sudden onslaught of fresh, unbridled power washed over me. It was like touching fire or being hit by a thousand volts of electricity. It was exhilarating.

I'd never been more excited, more ready.

When his lips met mine, a thousand emotions erupted in me. His taste was delicious and addictive. I pressed against him, our kisses deepening until I was swimming in heady sensations that beat against every pore in my body. Everywhere we touched my skin came alive. His lips trailed a fiery path from mine to the column of my throat. All around us, his light flickered, like a thousand stars lining the walls, fading in and out.

Our hands were everywhere. His fingers were on my stomach, moving up, between my ribs. There seemed to be something slower about this. Each touch was measured and precise. Breathing became difficult as our explorations grew. This was definitely not his first time at any of this, but he didn't rush and he shook as much as I did.

His jeans ended up somewhere on his floor and our bodies were flush. Hands delving lower and lower. Daemon took his time even when I was pushing him to go faster. He slowed it down, made it last for what felt like forever...until neither of us could wait any longer. I remembered what Dee had said about her first time. There was no awkwardness here. Most things were expected. Daemon had protection and there was *discomfort*…at first. Okay. It hurt, but Daemon… He made it *better*. And then we were moving against each other.

Being this way with him was like tapping into the Source but more powerful. The roller-coaster feeling was there, but different and deeper, and he was right there with me. It was more than perfect and beautiful.

After what felt like hours later and honestly could've been, Daemon kissed me softly, deeply. "Are you okay?"

My bones felt like mush in a totally good way. "I'm perfect." And then I yawned, right in his face. How romantic.

Daemon busted into laughter, and I turned my cheek into the pillow, trying to hide. He didn't let me, though. As if I expected anything less. He rolled onto his side, pulling me against him, tilting my head toward his.

His eyes searched mine. "Thank you."

"For what?" I loved the feel of his arms around me and how I fit against him, hard against soft.

He trailed his fingers over my arm, and I was amazed by how he could make me shiver. "For everything," he said.

Elation swelled inside my chest, and as we lay in each other's arms, our breaths coming out ragged, our bodies tangled together, we still couldn't get enough of each other. We kissed. We talked. We *lived*.

Chapter 34

When I left Daemon's house early Sunday morning, he stayed with me until he heard my mom's car pull up the driveway. Then he did that freaky, super speed alien thing and got out without being seen. But while he'd lay there in bed beside me, apparent that he didn't want to leave me alone after what happened with Will, I never felt safer in my life. Sex had nothing to do with that, but when he came back in the afternoon and we left to get lunch for us and my mom, every small look and brush of our skin meant something infinitely more—a tender and knowing quality that had been there before, but was emphasized.

I didn't look any different. Part of me thought it would be posted on my forehead or something and I was half afraid that my mom would somehow guess and then we'd have that mortifying birds and the bees' conversation again, but she didn't.

Life went on and for a little while. It was the same... a little better in some areas, but over the next week, Daemon and I had very little time together. No one talked about Will with the exception of asking if I was okay. Even Andrew had asked and sounded genuine. Other than that, it was like that event never happened. There was a really good chance that Daemon had something to do with that.

Our practices had increased with Dawson, Matthew, and Blake, and they also included the rest of our crew. Everyone knew their plan. Everyone also knew that we wouldn't get another chance after Sunday if we failed.

We were already pushing our luck.

Blake stood apart from the group. He'd been that way since I'd confronted him about his creepy, stalkerish behavior... Thank God. "The time frame is still the same. We have fifteen minutes to get in and get out with them."

"And if anything goes wrong?" Dee asked, nervously twirling her hair around her faded fingers.

Daemon picked up a piece of Onyx. All of us at this point could handle it for about a minute and twenty seconds. And with the tiny piece of opal, it didn't even bother Daemon and I.

"We'll be fine with the onyx shields." He tossed the rock back into the pile. "Each of us can withstand it long enough."

"But it's not being sprayed in your faces," Dee protested, eyes wide. "You're just handling it."

Blake inched closer. "It was never sprayed in my face. All I did was handle it over and over again. It's the only logical explanation."

"No. It's not." She let go of her hair and faced her brothers. "Handling onyx and having a tolerance is one thing. Having it sprayed in your face is totally different."

Dee had a point, but it was all we could do.

Dawson smiled for her and it was always strange to me when he did smile, because it was so rare to see a real one, and it transformed his face. "We're going to be okay, Dee. I promise."

"And the lasers—you have the lasers to watch out for," Andrew threw in, grimacing."

"No doubt," Blake said. "But they shouldn't be an issue. The emergency doors are activated only when the alarm goes off and if everything goes smoothly, we'll be fine."

"That's a big if," Dee muttered.

Heck ya, it was a huge if, but we were in this to the end. Just looking at Dawson reaffirmed why we were about to put our lives on the line again. Because I knew beyond a doubt, if it were Daemon locked in Mount Weather, I'd take as many risks as there were to free him.

Part of Dawson was missing and the other half was Beth. None of us could expect him to walk away from this. And all of us would go to the end of the earth for the ones we loved.

After another grueling session with the onyx, we called it a night and gimped back to the houses. Matthew and the Thompsons left, as did Blake. Dee went inside while the three of us lingered and finally Dawson disappeared somewhere around the side of the house.

Daemon took my hand and sat on the third step up, pulling me down between his legs, so that my back was against his chest. "You feeling okay?"

"Yes," I said. It was the same question he asked every, single time after practice. And yeah, I sort of loved him for that. "You?"

"You don't need to worry about me."

I rolled my eyes, but leaned back, liking the feel of his chest and the way his arms circled me. He dipped his head, pressing his lips against my pulse. I could tell where his mind was going and I was on board that train.

Dawson reappeared, the fading sun casting a halo around him. That train came to a crashing halt. He shoved his hands into his jeans and rocked back on heels, not saying a word.

Daemon sighed and straightened. "What is it?"

"Nothing," he said, eyes squinting at the rapidly darkening sky. "I was just thinking."

We waited quietly, because we both knew that Dawson couldn't be rushed. He'd say whatever it was he wanted to say when he was ready. Again, I found myself wondering what he was like before all this terrible stuff had happened to him.

Finally, Dawson said, "You guys don't need to do this on Sunday."

Daemon's arms fell away. "What?"

"You guys shouldn't have to do this. Dee's right. It's too much of a risk. We don't know if we really are going to be able to walk past those onyx shields. Who knows what Blake's deal is really? This doesn't involve you all."

Dawson looked at us then, expression full of sincerity. "You shouldn't be doing this. Let Blake and I go in. It's our risks to take."

Daemon fell silent for several moments. "You're my brother, Dawson, so whatever risk is yours, it is mine."

I smiled, tipping my head back. "And whatever risk is Daemon's, is mine."

"*That* I don't agree with, but you get what we're saying?" Daemon placed his hands on my shoulders. "We're in this together, for the good and the downright crappy."

Dawson's lashes lowered. "I don't want to see either two of you get hurt. I don't think I could live with that."

"We're not going to get hurt," Daemon said, so strongly that there was no doubt in my mind that he believed this to be true. His hands landed on my shoulders, gently rubbing the tensed muscles. "All of us are going to walk out of there, along with Beth and Chris."

Pulling his hands out of his pocket, Dawson thrust them through his hair. "Thank you." His lips twitched as he lowered his hands. "You know, I'm going... I'm going to have to leave afterward? Maybe... I can finish out the semester, but Beth and I will have to leave."

Daemon's hands stilled and I felt his heart trip over itself, but then his hands started up again. "I know, brother. We'll make sure that Beth is hidden until you're ready to leave. It's going to suck, but... but I know what you have to do."

His brother nodded. "We'll stay in touch."

"Of course," Daemon said.

Lowering my gaze, I bit my lip. Man, I sort of wanted to start balling. Their family shouldn't be split up again. All of this because of what they were and none of them brought this on themselves. It wasn't fair.

Worst of all, it didn't seem like there was anything we could do about it.

• • •

Thursday evening, after another skin-numbing training session, Daemon and I caved to our mad sugar need by hitting up the local fast-food joint—sweet tea for the win. Instead of going in, he lowered the latch on the back of his SUV and we chilled out.

The skies were clear and the glimmering stars started to fill up the heavens. Whenever I looked at the stars, I thought of Daemon and his kind.

He elbowed me playfully. "What are you thinking?"

I grinned around the straw. "Sometimes I forget what you are, but then I see those stars, and I remember."

"Do you forget what you are?"

Laughing, I lowered my cup. "Yeah, I guess I do."

"Nice."

I swung my feet back and forth. "But seriously, I really do. I think that if the public knew about you guys, they'd get used to the Luxen."

"Really?" He sounded shocked.

I shrugged. "You guys really aren't any different."

"Besides the whole glowworm thing," he teased.

"Yeah, besides that."

He chuckled and leaned in, rubbing his chin along my shoulder like a big cat. Thinking he'd like the idea of him being compared to a lion or something, I grinned. "I want you to carry the opal on you on Sunday," he said.

"What?" I pulled away and twisted toward him. "Why? You're the stronger one out of all of us."

A cocky grin appeared. "And that's why I don't need the opal."

"Daemon." I sighed, handing over the rest of the tea. He took it. "Your logic fails. Because you are stronger, the opal will do more for you than any of us."

He sipped the tea, his eyes practically twinkling. "I want you to wear the opal in case anything goes wrong. I'm not arguing with you."

"Whatever." I crossed my arms.

"And if you don't agree, I'll tie you up—and not in the fun way—and lock you in your bedroom."

My mouth dropped open.

"Okay, maybe in the fun way. Like later, after everything is done, I'll come back and—"

I cut him off. "I'd like to see you try to tie me up."

His eyebrow arched. "I bet you would."

"Shut up," I growled. "I'm being serious."

"So am I. You're wearing the opal."

I scowled. "This makes no sense."

"It makes perfect sense." He kissed my cheek. "Because I'm perfect."

"Oh, dear God." I elbowed him, and he laughed. I turned my gaze back to the starry sky and then it hit me like a cement truck. How could we have not thought about this before? "I have an idea!"

"Does it involve getting naked?"

I elbowed Daemon. "God. No. You're such a perv. It involves the opal. What if we can break it up into pieces and share it between us?"

His brows furrowed in concentration. "It could work, but it's a huge risk. What if we shatter the rock? I doubt it would work in powder form. And even if we did manage to break it into pieces, will it still be effective?"

All good questions. "I don't know, but can't we try? Then everyone is protected, at least some."

He didn't say anything for a long moment. "It's so much of a risk. I'd rather know that you're protected instead of hoping that you are. And I know that makes me sound selfish, but I am. I am *incredibly* selfish when it comes to you."

"But Dawson...?"

Daemon looked at me. "Like I said, I'm incredibly selfish when it comes to you."

I honestly didn't know what to say.

He sighed as he rubbed his palm along his jaw. "If we ended up destroying the piece of opal, then you go in there with nothing backing you up. Matthew, Dawson, and I are Luxen. We are going to be stronger than you. We won't tire as easily. We don't need the piece of opal, not like you do."

"But—"

"I'm not willing to risk it. If breaking up the opal weakens it, then how does it really help you out?" He shook his head. "We don't need the extra boost. You do."

My shoulders slumped at the finality in his words. Frustration swelled inside me. It wasn't that I didn't get what he was saying, we just didn't agree.

Later on, Daemon retrieved the opal from wherever his hidey-hole was and pressed it into my palm, wrapping his hand around mine as we stood on my porch. Night birds sung out around us, a canopy of chirps and calls. The spring roses I'd planted after school a week before filled the air with a clean, fresh scent.

It would be romantic if I didn't want to punch him in the face.

"I know you're mad." His eyes met mine. "But this makes me feel better about everything. Okay?"

"A few days ago you told Dawson that nothing was going to go wrong."

"I did, but just in case... I want you to be able to get out no matter what."

My heart stuttered. "What...what are you saying?"

He smiled, but it was forced and I hated it. "If something goes wrong, I want you to get out of there. If you have to leave this damn town or state, do it. And if for whatever reason I can't get out of there, you don't stop. Do you understand?"

Air rushed out of my lungs painfully. "You want me to leave you?"

Daemon's eyes were brilliant as he nodded. "Yes."

"No," I cried out, wrenching away. "I will never leave you behind, Daemon."

He clasped my cheeks, holding me still. "I know—"

"No you don't!" I grasped his wrists, my fingers biting into his skin. "Would you leave me behind if something happened to me?"

"No." His face twisted into a fierce scowl. "I would never do that."

"Then how can you ask me to do the same?" I was close to tears, mainly because I couldn't bear the idea of Daemon being captured, suffering what his brother had. "You can't."

"I'm sorry." The lines of his face softened and he bent his head, quickly kissing me. "You're right. I shouldn't have asked you to do that."

I blinked furiously. "How could you even consider asking me to do something like that?" Now I really wanted to sock him, because my heart was racing and terrible, horrific images were in my head. But then...then I realized something.

"You caved pretty easily," I whispered, distrustful.

He laughed, sliding his arms around my shoulders, pulling me against him. "I just understand what you mean."

Uh, yeah, this was odd. I tipped my head back, searching his face for a telltale sign. But all I saw was tenderness and a bit of the smug self-assurance that was always there. I didn't bother asking him if he was hiding anything, because I doubted he'd 'fess up, and I wanted to believe that he'd seen the error of his ways.

But I wasn't stupid.

Chapter 35

On the afternoon before prom, Dee stood in my bedroom, twisting my hair around a medium-barrel curling iron. While the conversation started off a bit awkward, it eased up about halfway through the styling process. The conversation was light and easy by the time she'd pinned my hair up in an intricate design that showed off all her hard work.

I was applying my own eye makeup when she sat on the edge of my bed, her hands clasped in her lap. She'd gone with a simple twist—a ponytail with her hair wrapped around it in a thick bun, a classic look that showed off her angular face perfectly.

Rubbing my pinkie under my eye, I blended the brown eyeliner. "Are you excited about tonight?"

She shrugged. "I just want to do it, because, you know, it's our last year. It's probably going to be our last year together—all of us—and I want to experience it. I know Adam would want me to go and have fun."

I placed the eyeliner in my bag and rooted around for my mascara. "He would," I said, glancing back into the bedroom. "He seemed like the kind of guy who would want the best for you, no matter what it meant for him."

A smile flickered and faded. "He was."

With a sense of sadness, I turned back to the mirror and my gaze dropped to the golden tube. She should be with Adam tonight. "Dee, I'm—"

"I know." One second she was on the bed and the next she was standing in the doorway. Her lower half faded out and wow, was that weird to see. "I know you're sorry. I know you never intended for Adam to die."

I turned toward her, twisting the piece of obsidian between my fingers. "I would change everything if I could."

Her gaze flickered away from me, settling over my shoulder. "Are you scared about tomorrow night?"

Facing the mirror once more, I blinked back tears. For a moment, it had felt like we'd come so far, but then the door had been slammed in my face. Okay, maybe we had come somewhere, but not as far as I wanted to.

So, stop being a wussy, I ordered myself. *That's a lot of makeup to waste.*

"Katy?"

"I'm scared," I admitted with a little laugh. "Who wouldn't be? But I'm trying not to think about it. That's what I did last time, and I was so freaked out."

"I would be freaked out no matter what—I *am* freaked out, actually, and all I'm doing is waiting by the car." She disappeared from the doorway in a flash and reappeared by the closet. She lovingly unwrapped my prom dress. "Just be careful and keep my brothers safe. Okay?"

My heart tripped and I didn't hesitate. "Okay."

Switching places, she finished with her makeup, and I slipped on my dress. Mom appeared in my bedroom, camera in hand, and here we went again. She snapped pictures of Dee and me, got all teary eyed, talking about how I used to play dress-up in her shoes and run around the house naked, and that was all before Dee left and Daemon arrived.

It could only get worse from there.

But when Daemon stepped into the living room where I waited, fiddling with a small clutch Mom had given me, I was struck speechless.

Daemon looked good in just about anything—jeans, sweats, a lumberjack outfit—but in a black tux tailored to his broad shoulders and narrow hips, he was absolutely amazing.

Dark waves fell across his forehead, swept to the right. He held a pretty corsage in one hand. As he straightened his tie, his gaze started at the tips of my shoes and made the slow perusal up, lingering in a few spots I hoped my mom didn't notice. His fingers stilled around the tie, and I flushed, feeling the intensity in his gaze and his approval.

Daemon did like the color red.

My cheeks had to match my dress by then.

He walked up to me with that rock-star swagger and stopped a foot before me, bent his head, and whispered, "You look beautiful."

A deep flutter started in my stomach and spread. "Thank you. You don't look so bad yourself."

Mom fluttered around like an erratic little bird, taking pictures and fussing over us. Whenever she looked at Daemon, she got the doe-eyed look on her face. She was totally smitten with him.

She took a lot of pictures of him taking the corsage out and tying it to my wrist. The corsage was a simple rose in full bloom surrounded by green leaves and baby's breath. Beautiful. We posed for Mom's pictures and the whole process was natural, nothing like Simon and homecoming. My thoughts wandered to Simon as we did a couple more pictures and Daemon swapped out the camera so we could do some of the mother-and-daughter bit.

Was Simon alive? Blake had sworn that the last he'd seen

Simon, the boy had been alive as the DOD carted him away. Whatever happened to Simon was because he had seen me lose control of the Source. Another possible death linked to me, and Simon *had* to be dead, because what would the DOD or Daedalus want with him alive? He was just human…

I thought of Carissa.

Daemon placed his hand on my lower back. "Where are you at?"

I blinked, drawn back into the present. "I'm here, right with you."

"I hope so."

Mom came up, pulling me into a hug. "Baby, you look so beautiful—you two look so beautiful together."

Daemon stepped away, grinning at me over her shoulder.

"I just can't believe this is it. Your senior prom," she said, sniffling as she backed up, facing Daemon. "It was just yesterday when she was running through our house, tearing off her diapers—"

"Mom," I snapped, finally jumping into the conversation. Her telling any baby Katy stories was bad enough. Anyone hearing them was mortifying. But with Daemon it was about a thousand times more horrifying.

Daemon's eyes lit up with interest. "Do you have pictures? *Please* tell me you have pictures."

Her face broke out in a wide smile. "Actually, I do!" She spun toward a bookcase in the corner, stock full of humiliating pictures. "I chronicled every—"

"Oh, look at the time." I grabbed Daemon's arm and pulled. He didn't budge. "We really need to go."

"There's always tomorrow," he said to my mom, winking. "Right?"

"I don't go to work until five." She grinned.

That was so not happening. On the way out, she stopped and gave me another hug. "You do look beautiful, baby. I mean it."

"Thank you." I squeezed her back.

She held on like she was never going to let go and I didn't mind, because after tomorrow night, there was a chance that I may not come back. So I needed my mommy's hug and I wasn't too proud to admit that.

"I'm happy for you," she whispered. "He's a good boy."

I gave a watery smile. "I know."

"Good." She pulled back, patting my arms with both hands. "Curfew?"

"I—"

"You have none tonight." To my shock, she smiled. "Just behave and don't do anything you'll regret in the morning." Her gaze drifted over my shoulder, and she muttered, "Wouldn't be much."

"Mom!"

Laughing, she gave me a light shove. "I'm old, not dead. Now get going and have fun."

I left as fast as I could. "You didn't hear that last part, right?"

Daemon grinned.

"Oh, God…"

Tipping his head back, he laughed as he took my hand. "Come, milady, your chariot awaits."

I laughed as I climbed into Dolly and once he was inside, we argued over the radio until we were halfway to the school and Daemon sent me a sideways glance. "You really do look beautiful, Kitten. I mean it."

I smiled, running my fingers over the beads on my clutch. "Thank you."

There was a pause. "I thought you looked beautiful homecoming night, too."

My head snapped toward him, clutch forgotten. "Really?"

"Hells yeah. I hated that you were with someone else." He laughed at my expression and then refocused on the dark road.

The easy grin tugged at my heart. "When I saw you with Simon? I wanted to beat the ever-loving crap out of him and snatch you away."

I laughed. Sometimes I forgot that during those tumultuous first months of knowing each other, a teeny tiny part of him may have liked me.

"So, yeah, I thought you were beautiful then."

I bit my lip and then hoped I hadn't smeared my lip gloss. "I always thought you were…" *Beautiful* wasn't exactly a manly descriptor, so I went with, "Very handsome."

"What you mean is that you always thought I was incredibly hot and you couldn't take your eyes off me."

"We really need to work on your modesty." The woods blurred outside the windows, and I could see my grin in the reflection. "But God, did you ever tick me off."

"It's a part of my charm."

I snorted.

The prom was held the same place homecoming was—the high school gymnasium. Real fancy here. The parking lot was packed and because we were running a little late, we had to leave Dolly in the nosebleed section.

Daemon took my hand as we strolled up to the school. The air was warm with just a hint of coolness. The nights were still pretty cold here in May, but I didn't need a shawl or anything, not with Daemon beside me. He always blew off an incredible amount of heat.

At homecoming, the gymnasium had been transformed by all the fall festive decorations, but for prom, white lights had been strung along the ceiling and down the closed bleachers, forming a dazzling waterfall effect. Large, leafy potted plants had been brought in, surrounding the white-linen-covered tables sitting at the edge of the matted dance floor.

Music was loud, and I could barely hear what Daemon was

saying to me as he tugged me forward. Lesa appeared out of nowhere, taking my hand and pulling me toward the floor. She looked awesome in a deep blue trumpet dress that flattered her hourglass curves. Out on the floor other girls surrounded us. Laughter mingled with the beat and I thought of the club in Martinsburg and the cages.

Totally different worlds.

Daemon reappeared, stealing me away from the girls. It was a slow dance and his arm fit perfectly around my waist. I rested my cheek on his shoulder, glad that he and Dee had convinced me into doing the prom thing. Getting out and doing this felt great, like a seven-ton weight was lifted from my shoulders.

Daemon hummed along with the song, his chin brushing my cheek every so often. I liked the way his chest thrummed against mine, reminding me of the natural way his body felt.

Toward the end of the song, I opened my eyes and they locked with Blake's.

I sucked in a sharp breath. Hadn't expected him to be here, so seeing Blake caused quite a bit of shock to shoot through me. Was he with someone? No girl was near him, but that didn't mean anything. Something about the way he stood there watching us was above the acceptable creep factor for my taste.

A couple moved in, laughing as the boy pawed at her hips. When they passed on, Blake was gone, but a weird, icky feeling had popped up in my stomach. The feeling I got whenever I saw Blake, which meant I tried not to think about him at all.

Seeing him made me think of someone else, though. I lifted my head. "Dawson didn't come?"

Daemon shook his head. "Nah, I think he'd feel like he was betraying Beth if he did."

"Wow," I whispered, unsure of what to think of that. His dedication to Beth was more than admirable—it was sort of awe-inspiring. Maybe it was the alien DNA.

Daemon's arm tightened and the tux pulled taut across his shoulders.

Yes, definitely the alien DNA at work on many, many aspects.

After the slow dance, Andrew and Dee joined us. She looked as divine as I thought she would in her dress and fresh, clean look. I noted that Dee and Andrew kept a discreet distance between each other. To me, it was clear they were just friends—more only because they shared something they lost.

When Daemon left to find something to drink, I was blindsided by Ash and her human date…and her little black dress.

Ash grinned like a cat that ate an entire family of canaries. "David, this is Katy. Don't worry about remembering her name. You'll probably forget."

I ignored her and offered a hand. "Nice to meet you."

David was handsome—very handsome—and could easily hold his own with the Luxen. He had curly brown hair and his warm whiskey-colored eyes were friendly, too.

He gave a good handshake. "My pleasure."

And polite. What was he doing with Ash?

"I have certain talents," she whispered in my ear, as if she read my thoughts, and I frowned at her. "Ask Daemon. He can tell you all about them." Straightening, she laughed.

Instead of hitting her, which was something I really wanted to do—and I could feel the Source begging me to be used—I smiled sweetly as I brushed past her and placed my hand on the exposed length of her slender back. A high-charged electric surge passed from my hand to her skin.

Letting out a low shriek, Ash jumped and spun around. "You…"

Beside her, David looked confused, but behind him, Dee busted out laughing. I kept smiling, giving Ash a little wink before turning around. Daemon stood there with two cups, one eyebrow arched.

"Bad little Kitten," he murmured.

Grinning, I stretched up and kissed him. It was an innocent one—or maybe it was on my end, but Daemon totally took it *there*. When we parted, I was breathless.

Leaving the group behind, we danced again, so closely that I kept waiting for a teacher to come around and break us apart. Several times I danced with Lesa and even Dee joined in once. We all looked ridiculous, flailing around and having fun.

By the time I was back in Daemon's arms, we'd been at the prom for about two hours. Some of the kids were already leaving, heading out to the notorious field parties held on farms.

"You ready to leave yet?" he said.

"Do you have something planned?" Oh gosh, did my mind go wild then.

"I do." He smiled mischievously. "I have a surprise."

And my mind went far, far south at that point. Daemon and the word *surprise* in the same sentence usually was an entertaining adventure.

"All right," I said, hoping I sounded adult and cool while my heart was doing the stupid happy-girl dance.

Finding Lesa, I told her we were leaving and gave her a hug. "Did you guys get a hotel room?" she asked, eyes glittering in the white lights.

I slapped her arm. "No. God. Well…I don't think so. He says he has a surprise for me."

"Totally the hotel room," she yelled. "Oh my God, you guys are going to have, you know, the three-letter word."

I smiled.

Lesa's eyes narrowed and then flew open. "Wait. Did you guys—"

"I've got to go." I started to pull away, but she followed.

"You have to tell me! I need to know." Behind her, Chad watched on curiously.

Getting away, I shook my head. "I really need to go. I'll talk to you later. Have fun."

"Oh, we'd better talk later. I demand it."

Promising to call her, I then looked for Dee but all I found was Ash, and after I zapped her earlier, she was looking like she wanted payback. I veered in the other direction, scanning the floor for the willowy raven-haired girl.

I gave up when I saw Daemon again. "Have you seen Dee?"

He nodded. "I think she left with Andrew. They decided to go to the diner or something and eat."

I stared.

Daemon shrugged.

Now I was unsure about my earlier conviction when it came to their relationship. Adam and Dee were notorious for doing things like that. Then again, Luxen liked to eat...all the time. "You don't think they're...?"

"I don't even want to know."

Me neither, I decided. Taking his offered hand, we headed back out of the steamy gymnasium and down the streamer-laden hallway. The temps had dropped outside, but the cold air felt good against my flushed skin.

"Are you going to tell me about the surprise?"

"If I did, then it won't be a surprise," he replied.

I pouted. "But it's a surprise now."

"Nice try." He laughed, opening the door for me. "Get in and behave yourself."

"Whatever." But I climbed in, primly crossing my legs. Daemon laughed again as he loped around the front of his car and got in.

Casting me a glance, he shook his head. "You're dying to know, aren't you?"

"Yes. You should tell me."

He said nothing and remained quiet the whole way home, much to my surprise. Nervous excitement built inside me. There'd only been a few minutes here and there of being alone together since that fateful Saturday night.

Strange how something so terrible and so beautiful could happen in one night—the best and the worst day of my life, I realized.

I didn't want to think of Will.

Daemon parked the car in his driveway. The living room light was on in his house. "Stay in the car, okay?"

When I nodded, he got out and disappeared—gone in a flash. Curious, I twisted around in the seat, but I didn't see him or anyone. What could he be up to?

Suddenly, my car door opened and Daemon extended his hand. "Ready?"

A little knocked off-kilter by his reappearance, I gave him my hand and let him swoop me out of the SUV. "So my surprise…?"

"You'll see."

Hand in hand, we started walking. I thought he was going to lead me to his house, but he didn't, and when we passed mine and made our way down the road, I had no idea what he had planned. That was, until I saw that we were heading to the main road and when we stopped there, I was taken back several months to the first time I learned about Daemon's kind.

I'd walked out in front of a truck.

Yeah, idiotic move, but I'd been upset and hadn't been thinking. Douche-version of Daemon had been to blame.

Crossing the road, I got a general idea of where we were heading. The lake. Squeezing Daemon's hand, I fought back a stupid grin.

"Do you think you can walk in those heels?" he asked, frowning as if he'd just thought of it.

Doubtful, but I didn't want to ruin any of this for him. "Yeah, I'll be fine."

He took it slowly anyway, making sure I didn't fall flat on my face or break my neck. Incredibly sweet, actually, as he made sure to get all the low-hanging branches out of the way and at one point, he even let a part of his true form take hold. White light surrounded his hand, casting over the uneven ground.

Who needed a flashlight when you had Daemon?

It took a little longer than normal to get to the lake, but I enjoyed the walk and his company. And when we stepped out of the last stand of trees and the scene before me unfolded, I couldn't believe what I was seeing.

Moonlight reflected off the calm waters and several feet away from the bank, next to the white wildflowers that had started to bloom, were several blankets spread out and piled atop one another, creating a comfy-looking sitting area. There were a few pillows and a large cooler. A fire crackled closer to the lake, surrounded by large stones.

There were no words.

The whole setup was exceptionally romantic, sweet, awesome, and so, so perfect that I wondered if I were dreaming. I knew Daemon was capable of surprising me—he always did, but this…? My heart swelled so quickly I was sure I would float away.

"Surprise," he said, stepping ahead, his back to the fire. "I thought this would be better than a party or whatever. And you like the lake. So do I."

I blinked back tears. God, I needed to stop crying all the time, especially tonight, because I had loaded my lashes with mascara. "It's perfect, Daemon. Oh my God, it's wonderful."

"Really?" A bit of vulnerability crept into his voice. "You really like it?"

I couldn't believe he had to ask. "I love it." And then I started to laugh, which was better than crying. "I really love this."

Daemon smiled.

I launched myself at him, wrapping my arms and legs around him like a demented monkey-girl.

Laughing, he caught me and didn't stumble. "You really love it," he said, walking backward. "I'm glad."

So many emotions were running through me that I couldn't settle on one thing, but they were all good. When he put me down, I kicked off my shoes and moved to the blankets. They were soft under my toes, luxurious.

Sitting down, I tucked my legs under me. "What's in the cooler?"

"Ah, the good stuff." He flashed out and appeared beside the cooler, kneeling down. He cracked it open, pulled out a bottle of wine and two glasses. "Wine cooler—strawberry. Your favorite."

I laughed. "Oh my God."

He popped the cork with some kind of weird alien-mind-Source-Jedi power and poured each of us a glass. I took it and sipped the fizzy liquid. I liked the wine cooler because it didn't taste like alcohol and I was really a lightweight.

"What else?" I asked, leaning over.

Out came a canister and he carefully peeled the lid off and tilted it toward me. Chocolate-covered strawberries rolled temptingly.

My mouth watered. "Did you make them?"

"Ha. No."

"Uh…did Dee make them?"

That got a laugh. "I ordered them from the candy shop in town. Try one?"

I did and I think my mouth died and went to heaven. I may've even drooled on myself. "They are so good."

"There's more." He pulled out a plastic container full of sliced cheese and crackers. "Also pre-made from the store, because *I* am not a cook or whatever."

Who cared how he got the stuff? He did this—this was all him.

There were also cucumber sandwiches and a veggie pizza. Perfect munchie food, and we dug in, laughing and eating while the fire slowly died off.

"When did you do all of this?" I asked, reaching for my fifth or so slice of veggie pizza.

He picked up a strawberry, inspecting it with narrowed eyes. "I had the stuff in the cooler down here and the blankets wrapped in canvas. All I did when we got back was come down here real quick, spread the stuff out, and start the fire."

I finished off my slice. "You're amazing."

"I know it didn't take you this long to realize that."

"No. I've always known it." I watched him root around for another strawberry. "Maybe not in the beginning…"

He peeked up. "My awesomeness is all about the stealth."

"Is it?" The temp had dropped and I huddled closer to Daemon and the dying fire, shivering but not anywhere near ready to head back.

"Uh-huh." He grinned, closing the bowl and placing the rest of the food back in the cooler. Tossing me a soda, he cleaned everything up. We'd moved on past the wine coolers a while ago. "I can't show all my dynamic sides at once."

"Of course not. Where's the mystery in that?"

He picked up a throw blanket. "There is none." Draping it over my shoulders, he then settled back down next to me.

"Thank you." I pulled the soft material close. "I think the general public would be shocked to know how deep your sweetness runs."

Daemon stretched out, resting on his side. "They can never know."

Grinning, I leaned forward and kissed his lips. "I'll take the secret to my grave."

"Good." He patted the spot next to him. "We can go back whenever you want."

"I don't want to leave."

"Then get your happy little hybrid butt over here."

Scooting over the remaining space, I laid down beside him. Daemon moved a pillow down so that it was under my head. Snuggled close to him, it would take an army of Arum to split us apart.

We talked about the dance, school, and even the university in Colorado. We talked well beyond midnight.

"Are you worried about tomorrow at all?" I asked, running the tips of my fingers along the curve of his jaw.

"I'm worried—but I'd be insane not to be." He kissed my finger when it drifted too close to his lips. "But not about what you think."

"What, then?" My hand drifted down his neck, over his shirt. He'd taken off the jacket a while ago. His skin was warm and hard underneath the thin material.

Daemon shifted closer. "I worry that Beth won't be like Dawson remembered."

"Me, too."

"I know he can handle it, though." He joined in, his hand sliding under the blanket, curving on my bare shoulder. "I just want the best for him. He deserves it."

"He does." I held my breath as his hand traveled south, over the dip in my waist then the flare of my hip. "I hope she's okay—that everyone is okay, even Chris."

He nodded and gently eased me onto my back. His hand smoothed over the skirt of my dress to my knee. I shivered. He smiled. "Something else is bothering you." When I thought about tomorrow and what the future might hold, a lot of things were bothering me. "I don't want anything to happen to you." My voice broke. "I don't want anything to happen to anyone."

"Shh." He kissed me gently. "Nothing will happen to me or anyone."

I balled my hands around his shirt, holding him, as if I could somehow stop the worst-case scenario from coming to fruition just by keeping him close. Silly, I knew, but holding him there kept the most horrific of fears at bay.

That I would walk out of Mount Weather, but Daemon wouldn't.

"What happens if we do succeed tomorrow night?"

"You mean *when* we do?" His leg brushed over mine, settling in between. "We go back to school on Monday—boring, I know. Then we hopefully pass our classes, which we will. Then we graduate. And then we have all summer…"

His weight did wicked things to my thoughts, but panic loomed too close. "Daedalus will come looking for Beth and Chris."

"And they won't find them." His lips pressed against my temple and then the curve of my brow. "That is, if they get close enough."

My stomach churned. "Daemon…"

"It'll be okay. Don't worry."

I wanted to believe. More like I needed to.

"Let's not think about tomorrow," he whispered, his lips grazing my cheek and then my jaw. "Let's not think about next week or the next night. It's just us right now and nothing else."

Heart racing, I tipped my head back and closed my eyes. It seemed impossible to forget all that was coming, but as his hand traveled over my knee and up under the hem of my dress, it really was only us and nothing else.

Chapter 36

Like the last time we made our trip to Mount Weather, I spent the bulk of Sunday with my mom. We went to a late breakfast and I filled her in on all the prom details. She was misty-eyed when I told her about Daemon's surprise by the lake. Heck, I got misty-eyed and my chest fluttered as I told her.

Daemon and I had stayed out there until the stars had faded from the night and the sky had turned dark blue. It had been simply perfect and the things we'd done in those late hours still made my toes curl.

"You're in love," Mom said, chasing a piece of cantaloupe across her plate with her fork. "That's not a question. I can see it in your eyes."

Red swept across my cheeks. "Yeah, I am."

She smiled. "You grew up too fast, baby."

Didn't always feel that way, especially this morning when I couldn't find my other flip-flop and I'd been, like, two seconds from kicking a fit.

Then her voice lowered so that the packed church crowd

couldn't hear. "You're being careful, right?"

Oddly, I wasn't embarrassed by the change in conversation. Maybe it had to do with the "naked baby Katy stripping off her diapers" comment yesterday. Either way, I was glad that she asked—that she cared enough. My mom may be busy working like most single parents, but she wasn't on the absentee list.

"Mom, I'd always be careful with that kind of stuff." I took a sip of my soda. "I don't want any baby Katys running around."

Her eyes widened with shock and then they watered again. Oh, dear… "You have grown up," she said, placing her hand over mine. "And I'm proud of you."

Hearing that felt good, because on the whole parent side of things, I wasn't sure what she could feel proud of. Sure, I went to school, stayed out of trouble—mostly—and got good grades. But I'd failed on the college thing so far, and I knew that bothered her. And everything else that I struggled and dealt with, she didn't know.

But she was still proud of me, and I didn't want to do anything to let her down.

When we arrived back home, Daemon stopped over for a little while and it took everything in me to keep Mom away from the photo albums before she went to grab a few hours of sleep, leaving Daemon and me to our own devices, which would sound like a really fun thing, but I was strung too tightly as the hours crept by.

Once I'd changed into the black sweats, Daemon asked for the opal. I handed it over.

"Don't look at me like that," he said, sitting across from me on my bed. He reached into his pocket and pulled out a thin, white string. "Instead of keeping it in your pocket, I thought I could make a necklace out of it."

"Oh. Good idea."

I watched him wrap the chord around the piece of opal, adjusting it so there was enough string left on either side to fit comfortably around my neck. I sat still why he tied it and slipped the stone under my shirt. It rested slightly above the piece of obsidian I wore.

"Thank you," I said, even though I still thought we should've risked shattering it.

He grinned. "I think we should skip out of lunch tomorrow and go to the movies."

"Huh?"

"Tomorrow—I think we should make it a half day."

Making plans to skip afternoon classes tomorrow wasn't on my priorities list and I was about to point that out when I realized what he was doing. Distracting me from the possibility there might not be a tomorrow that I wanted to see, keeping things normal and, in a way, hopeful.

I lifted my lashes and our eyes held. The green hue of his burned extraordinarily bright and then turned white as I rose to my knees, cupped his face, and kissed him—really kissed him like he was the very air I was thirsting for.

"What was that for?" he asked when I sat back. "Not that I'm complaining."

I shrugged. "Just because. And to answer your question, I think we should definitely skip and play truant for the day."

Daemon moved so fast that one second he was sitting and the next he was over me, his arms like bands of steel on either side of my head and I was on my back, staring up at him.

"Did I tell you I have a soft spot for bad girls?" he murmured. His form blurred at the edges, a soft white as if someone had taken a paintbrush and smudged an outline around him. A lock of hair fell forward, into those astonishing diamond-like eyes.

I couldn't find my breath. "Truancy does it for you?"

When he lowered his body, it thrummed with a low charge and where our bodies met, sparks flew. "*You* do it for me."

"Always?" I whispered.

His lips grazed mine. "Always."

• • •

Daemon left sometime later to meet up with Matthew and Dawson. The three of them wanted to run through things again, and Matthew, being the anal-retentive planner at heart, wanted to take a few more shots at the onyx.

I stayed back, hovering around my mom like a small child as she got ready. Feeling exceptionally needy, I even followed her outside and watched her back out of the driveway in her Prius.

Alone, my gaze went to the flowerbed skirting the porch. The faded mulch needed replacing and it could use a good weeding.

Stepping off the porch, I went to the small rose bushes and started pulling off the dead petals. I'd heard once that it could help the flowers bloom again. Wasn't sure if that was correct or not, but the monotony of carefully picking out the leaves eased my nerves.

Tomorrow, Daemon and I would skip out at lunch.

Next weekend, I would convince my mom I needed to do an overhaul on the flowerbed.

At the beginning of June, I would graduate.

Sometime that month, I would get serious about filling out the paperwork for University of Colorado and I would drop that bomb on my mom.

In July, I would spend every day with Daemon swimming in the lake and getting a Jersey Shore tan.

By the end of summer, things would be normal between Dee and me.

And come fall, I'd move on from all of this. Things wouldn't ever be mundane. I wasn't fully human anymore. My boyfriend—the guy I loved—was an alien. And there may become a point where, like Dawson and Blake, Daemon and I would have to disappear.

But there was going to be a tomorrow, a next week, month, summer, and fall.

"Only you would be out gardening right now."

I whipped around at the sound of Blake's voice. He leaned against my car, dressed in all black, ready for tonight.

This was the first time since our confrontation that Blake had come around me while I was alone, and the alien part of me responded. That roller-coaster feeling was swelling inside me. Static pricked along my skin.

I held my ground. "What do you want, Blake?"

He laughed softly as his gaze fell to the ground. "We're leaving soon, right? I'm just a little early."

And I was just a little bit of a book nerd. Yeah, right.

Brushing the dirt off my fingers, I watched him wryly. "How did you get here?"

"Parked at the end of the road at the empty house." He gestured with his chin. "The last time I parked here, I'm pretty sure someone melted the paint on the hood of my truck."

Sounded like Dee and her microwave hands. I crossed my arms. "Dee and Andrew are next door," I felt the need to point out.

"I know." He pulled a hand out, ran it through his spikey hair. "You looked really good at prom."

Unease unfurled in my belly. "Yeah, I saw you. Did you come alone?"

He nodded. "I was there only for a few minutes. Never did the high school dance thing. Kind of disappointing."

I said nothing.

Blake dropped his hand. "You worried about tonight?"

"Who wouldn't be?"

"Smart girl," he said, and smiled a little. It was more of a grimace than anything. "No one that I know of has infiltrated one of their facilities before or even gotten as far as we did last time. No Luxen or hybrid, and we can't be the first to attempt it. I bet there're a dozen Dawsons and Beths, Blakes and Chrises."

Muscles tightened in my neck and shoulders. "If this is supposed to be a pep talk, you completely fail at it." Blake laughed.

"I don't mean it that way. Just that if we do this, we're the strongest, you know. The best out of their hybrids and out of the Luxen."

Funny or maybe just ironic, I thought, that what Daedalus wanted so badly was the only ones who could go up against them.

I reached into my pocket, feeling the warm, smooth edges of the opal. "Then we're just awesome, I guess."

Another pained smile and then Blake said, "That's what I'm counting on."

• • •

We were all dressed like a ragtag group of reject ninjas. My skin sweated under the long-sleeved black thermal. The idea was that the less skin exposed, the less the onyx impacted us.

Didn't really pan out that way last time, but we weren't taking any chances tonight.

The opal was burning a hole in my pocket.

Driving to the mountains of Virginia was a quiet affair. This time around, even Blake was silent. Dawson was a ball of energy beside him. Once, luckily not when cars surrounded us, he slipped into his true form, nearly blinding all of us.

Blake's words lingered in my head. *That's what I'm counting on.* I was probably being paranoid, but they settled like sour milk. Of course he was counting on us to pull off the near impossible. He had just as much as us to gain.

And then I thought of Luc's warning: never trust those who have anything to gain or lose. But that meant we couldn't trust either him or our friends. All of us had something to gain or lose.

Daemon reached over the center console and squeezed my fidgeting hand.

Thinking these things right then wasn't the best route to travel. I was getting myself all worked up and spazzy.

I smiled at Daemon and decided to focus on our afternoon. We didn't really do anything. Just cuddled together, both of us wide awake, and somehow that was more intimate than anything else. Last night or early this morning had been a different story.

Daemon was a creative fellow.

My cheeks were stained red the rest of the trip.

The two SUVs arrived at the little farm at the bottom of the pitch-black access road with five minutes to spare. As we climbed out, Blake got his confirmation text from Luc.

Things were a go.

Instead of limbering up, we all stayed still, conserving our energy. Ash, Andrew, and Dee remained in their SUV. The rest of us moved to the edge of the overgrown field.

I hoped I didn't get infested with ticks.

With one last look at the Luxen in the vehicle, it was time to go. Letting the Source flow through my blood and bones and ripple over my skin, we took off into the darkness, without the light of the moon on the cloudy night. Like last time, Daemon stayed beside me. The last thing anyone needed was my tripping over something and rolling back down the hill.

Things were quiet and tense when we reached the edge of the woods, waited to see that only one guard manned the fence.

It was Daemon who took him out this time. Then we were at the fence, keying in the first code.

Icarus.

Taking off across the stretch of field, the five of us moved like ghosts. Visible in one's peripheral vision, but gone when looked at head-on.

At the set of three doors, Dawson entered in the second

password.

Labyrinth.

And now it was do or die time. All these months had led up to this. Did our onyx training mean a damn thing? Daemon glanced at me.

I slipped my hand into my pocket, wrapping my fingers around the opal.

Going through the onyx spray would still hurt like the fiery bowels of hell for the others, but it should be manageable if Blake had been right.

The door slid open with an airlock sound and Daemon was the first through.

Air puffed and he flinched, but one leg moved in front of the other and then he was through, on the other side. He stopped, glancing over his shoulder, and smiled that half smile.

All of us let out a collective breath.

We filed through the onyx-shielded door. Each of the guys took the spray with a wince and grimace of pain. I barely felt a thing.

Inside Mount Weather for the first time, we fell behind Blake, who knew most of the way. The tunnel was shadowed, with small lamps placed every twenty feet or so on the orange walls. I searched for those murderous emergency doors but it was too dark to see them.

Tipping my head up, I noticed something terrifying about the ceiling. It was shiny—like it was wet or something, but it wasn't liquid.

"Onyx," Blake whispered. "The whole place is covered in onyx."

Unless they did a massive remodel recently, that couldn't be something new to Blake. Feeling the opal against my skin, I pulled on the Source and waited for the extreme rush of energy as we flew down the tunnel.

There was a tiny spark of extra energy, but nothing like it

had been when Daemon and I had tested it out. My heart sunk as we neared the end of the long tunnel. It had to be all the onyx, somehow weakening the opal.

At the end of the tunnel, it split into a crossroad. Elevators were in the middle. Matthew edged toward the opening, checking the space first.

"Clear," he said, then faded out, moving so fast that when he hit the elevator button, my eyes couldn't track him until he was beside us again.

When the doors slid open, we moved at once, filling the steel elevator. Apparently the stairwells were under password and I wondered what the heck people did to get out in case of emergency.

I looked around the elevator, noting a few blackish-red shiny parts in the flickering overhead light. I half expected to be doused with onyx while we waited, but it didn't happen.

Daemon's hand brushed mine, and I looked up.

He winked.

Shaking my head, I shifted my weight restlessly. This seemed like the slowest-moving elevator in the world. I could figure out a trig formula faster.

Daemon squeezed my hand, as if he could sense my nervousness.

I stretched up on the tips of my toes and cupped Daemon's cheek, guiding his head down to mine. I kissed him deeply and without reservation.

"For good luck," I said after I pulled back, a bit breathless.

His emerald eyes glinted with a wealth of promises that sent a very different kind of chills over me. When we got home, we were so getting some one-on-one time.

Because we would get home, all of us. There could be no other outcome

Finally, the elevator doors popped open, revealing a small waiting room. White walls. White ceilings. White floors.

We'd stepped into an insane asylum.

"Lovely decorative colors," Matthew said.

Daemon smirked.

His brother moved ahead, stopping at the door. There was no way, no idea of seeing what waited for us on the other side. With this code, we were going in blind.

But we'd come this far. Excitement hummed through me.

"Careful, brother," Daemon said. "We take this slow."

He nodded. "I've never been here. Blake?"

Blake moved to his side. "Should be another tunnel, shorter and wider, and there'll be doors on the right side. Cells, really, outfitted with a bed, a TV, and a bathroom. There'll be about twenty rooms. I don't know if the others are occupied or not."

Others? I hadn't thought about others. I looked at Daemon. "We can't just leave them."

Before he could answer, Blake intervened. "We don't have time, Katy. Taking too many will slow us down, and we don't know what kind of condition they are in."

"But—"

"For once, I agree with Blake." Daemon met my shocked stare. "We can't, Kitten. Not now."

I wasn't okay with this, but I couldn't run down the hall, letting people free. We didn't plan for that and we only had a set amount of time. It sucked—sucked worse than people who pirated books, sucked more than waiting a year for the next book in a beloved series, and sucked more than a brutal cliffhanger ending. Leaving here, knowing we could possibly be leaving innocent people behind, would haunt me forever.

Blake took a deep breath and keyed in the last code.

Daedalus.

The sound of several locks sucking back into place broke the silence and a light at the top of the door, on the right, flashed green.

As Blake inched the door open, Daemon moved to stand in

front of me. Matthew was suddenly behind me and I was shielded. What the…?

"We're clear," Blake said, sounding relieved.

We went through the door, discovering another onyx shield. Now we had two more to get the others through. This wasn't going to be easy.

The tunnel was like the one above, but all white and like Blake had informed us, it was shorter and wider. Everyone was moving but me. We'd made it—we were here. My stomach lurched and my skin tingled.

I almost couldn't believe it.

Happy and anxious all at once, I felt the rush of responding Source, but it peaked and then quickly sputtered out. The amount of onyx in this building was insane.

"The third cell is hers," Blake said, rushing down the hall, toward the last cluster of doors.

Spinning back around, I held my breath as Dawson reached for the onyx-coated door handle and turned. It met no resistance.

Dawson stepped into the room, his legs shaking, his entire body trembling, and his voice cracked when he spoke. "Beth?"

That one word, that one sound was pulled from the depths of Dawson and we all stopped, our breaths holding again.

Over his shoulder, I saw a slender form on a narrow bed sit up. As she came into view, I almost cheered—I wanted to, because it was her, it was Beth…but she looked nothing like she had when I'd last seen her.

Her brown hair wasn't stringy or greasy but pulled back in a smooth ponytail. A few strands had slipped free, framing a pale but elfin face. A huge part of me feared that she wouldn't recognize Dawson, that she'd be that cracked shell of a girl I'd met. I'd been planning for the worse. That she might even attack Dawson.

But when I saw Beth's dark eyes, they weren't empty like they'd been at Vaughn's house. They also looked nothing like Carissa's frighteningly blank stare.

Recognition flared in Beth's eyes.

Time stopped for those two and then sped up. Dawson stumbled forward, and I thought he was going to drop to his knees. His hands opened and closed at his sides as if he had no control over them.

All he could say was, "Beth."

The girl scrambled off the bed, her eyes bouncing over us and then they settled and stayed on him. "Dawson? Is that... I don't understand."

They both moved as one, rushing forward, crossing the distance at the same moment. Their arms went around each other and Dawson lifted her up, burying his face in her neck. Words were traded, but their voices were thick with emotion, too low and too fast for my ears to track. They were holding onto each other in a way I knew they were never going to let go.

Dawson lifted his head and said something in his language and it sounded just as beautiful as it did when Daemon spoke it. Then he kissed her, and I felt like an interloper watching them, but I couldn't look away. There was so much beauty in their reunion, in the way he showered her upturned face with tiny kisses and the wetness that gathered on her cheeks.

Tears crept up my throat, burning the back of my eyes. Happy tears blurred my vision. I felt Matthew place his hand on my shoulder and squeeze. Sniffling, I nodded.

"Dawson." Urgency filled Daemon's tone, reminding all of us that we were running out of time.

Pulling apart, Dawson grabbed her hand and turned around as a whole boatload of questions came streaming out of Beth's mouth.

"What are you guys doing? How did you all get in here? Do they know?" And on and on she went as Dawson, who was grinning like an idiot, tried to keep her quieted down.

"Later," he said. "But we have to go through two doors and it's going to hurt—"

"Onyx shields, I know," she said.

Well, that solved that problem.

I turned as Blake came back, carrying the prone body of a dark-haired Luxen boy. A reddish stain bloomed across the teenager's jaw. "Is he okay?"

Blake nodded. The skin around his lips was drawn tight and pale. "I… He didn't recognize me. I had to keep him quiet."

A tiny crack fissured my heart. The look in Blake's eyes was so hopeless and bleak, especially when they flickered toward Dawson and Beth. Everything he had done: lied, cheated, and murdered had all been for the guy in his arms. Someone he considered a brother. Again, I hated that I felt sympathy for Blake.

But I did.

Beth looked up and her onslaught of questions faded off. "You can't—"

"We need to go." Blake cut her off and stalked past us. "We're almost out of time."

And we were. The reminder whipped through me and I gave the other girl what I hoped was a reassuring smile. "We have to leave. Now. Everything else can wait."

Beth was shaking her head vigorously. "But—"

"We need to go, Beth. We know." And she nodded at Dawson's words, but panic was building in her eyes.

Urgency kicked adrenaline into high gear and without any more delay, the five of us took off down the hall. Daemon punched the code into panel on the wall, and the door opened.

The all-white waiting room wasn't empty.

Simon Cutters stood there—missing, presumed dead Simon Cutters—as big and burly as ever. All of us were caught off guard. Daemon took a step back. Matthew came to a halt. I couldn't wrap my head around how he was alive, why he was standing there, as if he were *waiting* for us.

The tiny hairs on my arms started to rise.

"Oh shit," Daemon said.

Simon smiled. "Missed me? I missed you guys."

Then he raised an arm. Light reflected off a metal cuff he wore. A piece of opal glittered, nearly identical to the one I wore around my neck. Everything happened so fast. Simon opened his hand, and it was like being hit with gale force winds. I was lifted off my feet and thrown back through the air. I crashed into the nearest door, my hip hitting the metal door handle. Pain exploded, knocking the air out of my lungs as I hit the floor.

Oh, my God… Simon was…

My brain raced to keep up with what was happening. If Simon had a piece of opal, then that meant he had to have been mutated. He probably wouldn't have gotten us if we hadn't been so unprepared to see him. It was like with Carissa. He was the last person I expected.

Daemon was picking himself up several feet back down the hall, as was Matthew. Dawson had Beth pressed back against the wall. Blake was closer, using his body to shield Chris's.

I pushed myself up, wincing as pain arced down my leg. I tried to stand, but my leg gave out. Blake was there, catching me before I hit the floor for the second time.

Simon stepped into the room and smiled.

Daemon staggered to his feet. "Oh, you are so dead."

"Ah, I think that's my line," Simon responded. A burst of energy flew from his hand, and I yelled Daemon's name. He narrowly avoided a direct hit.

Daemon's pupils were starting to glow white. He reared back. Energy arced across the room, a whitish-red light. Simon dodged it, laughing.

"You're going to wear yourself out, Luxen." Simon sneered.

"Not before you."

Simon winked and then spun toward us, throwing his hand

out again. Blake and I skidded back. I started to fall and Blake grabbed me. Somehow his arm ended up around my neck. There was a tugging feeling and then Daemon was beside me, shoving me behind him.

"This is so not good," Blake said, edging closer to Simon. "We're running out of time."

"No shit," Daemon spat.

Dawson shot toward Simon, but he threw him back, laughing. He was like a hybrid suped up on steroids. Another blast of energy flew at Blake and then toward Matthew. Both of them dive-bombed the floor to avoid taking a hit. Simon kept advancing, still smiling. I looked up and our eyes locked. His were devoid of all human emotion. Unreal. Inhuman.

And they were so very cold.

How had he been mutated? How was it successful? And how had it turned him into this unfeeling monster. There were so many questions, and none of them mattered right now. The breath-stealing pain made it difficult to concentrate, to even keep standing.

Simon's smile spread, and a shudder rolled through me as I pulled on the Source, feeling it spark deep inside me. Before I could release it, he opened his mouth. "Want to play, Kitty Kat?"

"Oh, screw this," Daemon growled.

Daemon was just so much faster than me. He shot past Blake and Matthew, beyond Dawson and Beth. Moving so fast had to have affected him with all the onyx, but he was like lightning. Half a heartbeat later, he was in front of Simon, his hands on either side of Simon's head.

A sickening crack echoed down the hall.

Simon hit the floor.

Daemon stepped back, breathing deeply. "I never liked that punk in the first place."

I stumbled to the side, heart racing as the Source stirred restlessly inside of me. Eyes wide, I swallowed hard. "He's... He was…"

"We don't have time." Dawson pulled Beth down the hall, into the waiting room. "They have to know we're here."

Blake scooped Chris up, casting a look at Simon as he passed the prone body. He said nothing, but what was there to say?

My stomach dipped as panic threatened to take hold. Forcing myself forward, I ignored the jagged pain racing up and down my leg.

"Are you okay?" Daemon asked, his fingers threading through mine. "You took a nasty hit."

"I'm okay." I was alive and I could walk, so that had to mean I was okay. "You?"

He nodded as we entered the waiting room. Taking the elevator filled me with so much dread I thought I'd hurl, but there were no doors to stairwells. Nothing. We had no other choice.

"Come on." Matthew slipped into the elevator, his face pale. "We need to prepare for anything once these doors are open."

Daemon nodded. "How is everyone?"

"Not feeling very good," Dawson answered, his free hand open and closing. "It's the damn onyx. I don't know how much is left in me."

"What the hell was up with Simon?" Daemon turned on Blake as the elevator pitched into motion. "He barely seemed affected by the onyx."

Blake shook his head. "I don't know, man. I don't know."

Beth was babbling on about something, but I couldn't pay attention. The ball of dread was building in my stomach, spreading into my limbs. How could Blake not know? I felt Daemon shift beside me, and then his lips brushed my forehead.

"It's going to be okay. We're almost out of here. We got this," Daemon whispered into my ear, and more tension seeped out of him, out of me. Then he smiled. It was a real one, so wide and beautiful that my own lips curved to meet his. "I promise, Kitten."

I closed my eyes briefly, soaking in his words and hanging onto them. I needed to believe in them because I was seconds away from freaking out. I had to hold it together. We were a tunnel away from freedom.

"Time?" Blake asked.

Matthew checked his watch. "Two minutes."

The doors released with a suction-cup sound and the long narrow tunnel appeared, thankfully, beautifully empty and devoid of anymore freak-me-out surprises. Blake and his bundle were the first out, his strides long and quick. Daemon and I took up the flank with Matthew in front of Dawson and Beth, just in case something happened.

"Stay behind me," Daemon said.

Nodding, I kept my eyes peeled. The tunnel was a blur, we were moving that fast. The pain in my leg increased with each step. As Blake reached the middle door, he shifted Chris to over his shoulder and entered in the key. The door rattled and then slid open.

Blake stood there, swathed in the darkness of the encroaching night. In his arms, the motionless Luxen was pale and seemed barely alive, but he'd be free in seconds. Blake had finally gotten what he wanted. Our eyes met from across the distance. There was something churning in those green flecks.

A great sense of foreboding took root and spread rapidly. Immediately, I reached for the opal around my neck and all I felt was the chain the piece of obsidian hung from.

Blake's lips slowly curved up at the corners.

My heart stuttered and then my stomach fell so fast I thought I'd be sick. That smile... That smile felt like a big *gotcha*. A surge of unbridled terror turned my skin icy cold. But it couldn't be. *No. No. No. It couldn't be...*

Blake cocked his head to the side as he stepped back. He opened his free hand. The thin, white string unraveled, slipping through his fingers. The piece of opal dangled there, in his grasp. "Sorry," he said, and he truly sounded sorry. It was unbelievable. "It had to be this way."

"Son of a bitch!" roared Daemon, breaking free from me. He launched forward, going after Blake in a way I knew would end in bloody violence.

Heat flared between my breasts, unexpected and just as terrifying as an army of DOD soldiers. I reached down, yanking the obsidian from my shirt. It glowed red.

Daemon drew up short, snarling.

The darkness behind Blake thickened and stretched out, creeping into the entrance of the tunnel. The blackness seeped over the walls. Lamps sparked and went out. The shadows dropped onto the floor, rising up all around Blake. Not touching him. Not stopping him. The smoke formed pillars at first and then human forms. Their skin was like midnight oil, slick and shiny.

Arum formed all around Blake—seven of them. All dressed the same. Dark pants. Dark shirts. Eyes shielded behind sunglasses. One by one, they smiled.

They ignored Blake.

They *let* him go.

Blake disappeared into the night as the Arum flew forward.

Daemon met the first one head on, his human form flickering out as he slammed the Arum back into the wall. Dawson shoved Beth to the side as he closed line on an advancing Arum, taking him down.

Reaching down, Matthew grabbed a slender shard of Obsidian, sharpened into a fine point. He spun around, slamming it deep into the belly of the nearest Arum.

The Arum drew up, losing its human form as it rose to the low ceiling. It hung there for a second and then shattered as if it were made of nothing more than frail bone.

I snapped out of it.

Knowing that none of them, including me, would be able to rely on the Source for very long, this would be a hand to hand kind of combat. I yanked the obsidian around my neck and the chain snapped just as one of the Arums reached me. I saw my pale face in its dark sunglasses and searched for the Source inside me.

He reached forward, and whitish-red light erupted from me, throwing the Arum back and knocking it flat on its ass. The energy rushed out like an overflowing stream. The onyx had lessened the blow, and the Arum was on his feet as Daemon took out the one he was fighting. Another explosion of black smoke rocked the corridor.

The Arum I knocked down was in front of me, sunglasses gone. His eyes were the palest blue, the color of the winter sky. They were just as cold as Simon's, if not more.

I took a step back, my hand clenching the piece of obsidian.

The Arum smiled, and then he twisted to the side, swinging his leg out and catching my bad one. I yelped as my leg caved. I started to go down, but he caught me around the neck, lifted me off my feet and into the air. Beyond him, I saw Daemon spin, saw the anger building in him, saw the Arum rising up behind him.

"Daemon!" I shouted as I slammed the piece of obsidian into the chest of the Arum holding me.

The Arum dropped me as Daemon whirled, dodging the other one. I hit the cement floor for the umpteenth time as the Arum broke apart with such force it blew my hair back from my face.

Daemon grabbed ahold of the enemy closest to him by the shoulders, tossing it several feet behind me as I stood on shaky legs. My hand trembled around the heated obsidian.

"Go! We need to go!" Dawson grabbed Beth and started for the door, dodging an Arum. "Now!"

I didn't need to be told twice. This was a battle we wouldn't win. Not when we had no time left and there were four Arum still standing, obviously unaffected by the onyx.

Pushing past the pain, I started forward, taking a few steps before my leg was snatched from behind. I went down fast and hard, dropping the obsidian to save my face from smashing into the cement. The coldness of the Arum's touch soaked through my sweats, traveling up my legs as its grip on my ankle tightened.

I twisted onto my side and kicked out with my good leg, catching the Arum in the face. There was a satisfying wet crunching, sound and the Arum let go. I scrambled to my feet, gritting my teeth from the pain in my leg as I headed for Daemon. He'd turned and was coming back for me as a low hum rumbled through the building, gaining and gaining until it was all that we could hear. All of us stopped. Light flooded the tunnel and down the hall, automatic locks slamming into place. The *thump-thump-thump* went on in an endless succession.

"No," Matthew said, his eyes darting down from where we came. *"No."*

Daemon's gaze shot behind me. I turned, seeing light flaring in the tunnel, crackling and forming a wall of shimmering blue light. One after another, every ten feet or so, over and over…

The blue light came down on one of the Arum not too far behind me. It caught it, and the light flared. There was a loud cracking sound, like a fly caught in one of those traps.

"Oh my God," I whispered.

The Arum was gone—simply just gone.

Don't go near the blue light, Blake had said. *They're lasers. Rip you right apart.*

Daemon lurched forward, his hands reaching for me, but it was too late. Before he could reach me, and not even a foot from my face, a sheet of blue light appeared and heat blew off it, blowing my hair back. Daemon let out a startled scream, and I jerked back.

I couldn't believe it. Not possible. I *refused* to believe it. Daemon was on the other side of the light, closer to the exit, and I…I was on the other side, the wrong side.

Daemon's eyes met mine and the look in them, the horror

in his extraordinary green eyes cracked my heart into a million useless pieces. He understood—oh, God, he understood what was happening. I was trapped with the remaining Arum.

Shouts sounded. Booted feet pounded on the floors. They sounded like they were coming from everywhere. In front of us, from behind, and all corners. I couldn't turn, though, couldn't look behind me or away from Daemon.

"Kat," he whispered, pleaded, really.

Sirens blasted shrilly.

Daemon reacted so fast, but for once in his entire life, he wasn't fast enough. He couldn't be. Emergency doors started to slide from the top and bottom, and Daemon shot to the side, slamming his palm on a tiny control panel. Nothing was working. The doors kept sliding together. The blue light was like a stream of destruction separating us. Daemon whipped toward me. He launched toward the blue shield, and I let out a startled gasp. He'd be destroyed if he hit the lasers!

Pulling from the Source as much as I could, I held out my hand, ignoring the heat as I pushed at Daemon with the last of my strength and will, holding his straining body back from the blue lights until Matthew sprang into action, grabbing Daemon around his waist. I slid to the floor, my knees barely catching me. Daemon went wild, throwing punches and dragging Matthew as he struggled to move forward, but Matthew got him back from the light, managing to bring Daemon down to his knees.

It was too late.

"No! Please! No!" he roared, his voice cracking in a way I'd never heard before. "Kat!"

The voices and sounds of pounding feet were drawing closer, and so was the bone-chilling coldness of the Arum. I felt them along my back, but I couldn't look away from Daemon.

Our eyes locked, and I would never, ever forget the terror in his, the look of pure helplessness. Everything felt surreal on my end, like I really wasn't here. I tried to smile for him, but I'm not sure I managed one.

"It'll be okay," I whispered as tears filled my eyes. The doors were coming out of the ceiling and the floor. "It'll be all right."

Daemon's green eyes held a glassy sheen. His arm reached out, fingers splayed. They never reached the laser or the door. "I love you, Katy. Always have. Always will," he said, voice thick and hoarse with panic. "I will come back for you. I will—"

The emergency doors sealed shut with a soft *thud*. "I love you," I said, but Daemon... Daemon was gone. Gone on the other side of the doors and I was trapped—with the Arum and Daedalus. For a moment I couldn't think, couldn't breathe. I opened my mouth to scream, but terror poured into me, cutting off the sound.

I turned around slowly, lifting my head as a tear rolled down my cheek. An Arum stood there, head tilted to the side. I couldn't see his eyes behind the sunglasses, and I was glad I couldn't.

He knelt, and beyond him and the other Arums, I could see men in black uniforms. The Arum reached out, trailing an icy finger down my cheek, chasing the tear, and I recoiled away, pressing against the emergency doors.

"This is going to hurt," the Arum said. He leaned in, his face inches from mine and his breath cold against my mouth.

"Oh God," I whispered.

A burst of pain encompassed every cell in my body, and the air flew out of my lungs. Suspended there, I couldn't move away. My arms didn't work. Someone grabbed me from the side, but I couldn't feel. It felt like I was still screaming, but there was no sound.

There was no Daemon.

Acknowledgments

Thank you to the wonderful team at Entangled Teen—Liz Pelletier, Stacy Abrams, Stacey O'Neale, and Rebecca Mancini. And to my agent, Kevan Lyon, you rock as always. If it weren't for my friends and family, I'm sure I'd be a hermit living in a writing cave by now, so thank you for putting up with me when I go on a writing binge. A special thanks to Pepe Toth and Sztella Tziotziosz for being awesome cover models and joining us on our Daemon Invasion tours.

None of this would be possible if it weren't for the readers. I love you guys. I wish I could hug every one of you, but I suck at hugs, and it would just be all kinds of awkward. So trust me, this thank you is better than a hug. I promise.

Get tangled up in our Entangled Teen titles...

Gravity by Melissa West

In the future, only one rule will matter: Don't. Ever. Peek. Ari Alexander just broke that rule and saw the last person she expected hovering above her bed—arrogant Jackson Locke. Jackson issues a challenge: help him, or everyone on Earth will die. Giving Jackson the information he needs will betray her father and her country, but keeping silent will start a war.

Greta and the Goblin King by Chloe Jacobs

Four years ago, Greta fell through a portal to a world where humans are the enemy. Now a bounty hunter, she's caught the attention of the darkly enticing young Goblin King, who invades her dreams and undermines her will to escape. But Greta's not the only one looking to get out of Mylena...

Luminosity by Stephanie Thomas

Beatrice had her first vision at the age of twelve, and now the Institution depends on her to keep the City safe from the Dreamcatchers. But Beatrice has a secret that could put everyone in danger. A secret that could kill her and everyone she loves. The enemy has been coming to her in her dreams, and she might be falling in love with him.

Ward Against Death by Melanie Card

Ward de Ath expected this to be a simple job to launch his fledgling career as a necromancer. But when Ward wakes the beautiful Celia Carlyle, he gets more than he bargained for. If he could just convince his heart to give up on the infuriating beauty, he might get out of this alive...

Get tangled up in our Entangled Teen titles...

Inbetween by **Tara Fuller**

It's not easy being dead, especially for a reaper in love with Emma, a girl fate has put on his list not once, but twice. Finn will protect the girl he loves from the evil he accidentally unleashed, even if it means sacrificing the only thing he has left...his soul.

The Marked Son by **Shea Berkley**

When Dylan sees a girl in white in the woods behind his grandparents' farm, he knows he's seen her before...in his dreams. Only he can save her world from an evil lord—a world full of creatures he's only read about in horror stories. Worse, the human blood in his veins has Dylan marked for death...

My Super Sweet Sixteenth Century by **Rachel Harris**

The last thing Cat Crawford wants for her sixteenth birthday is an extravagant trip to Florence, Italy. But when her curiosity leads her to a gypsy tent, she exits . . . right into Renaissance Firenze. Cat joins up with her ancestors and soon falls for the gorgeous Lorenzo. Can she find her way back to modern times before her Italian adventure turns into an Italian forever?

All the Broken Pieces by **Cindi Madsen**

Liv comes out of a coma with no memory of her past, and not even her reflection seems familiar. But when Liv starts hanging around with Spencer, life feels complete for the first time. Can Liv rebuild the pieces of her broken past, when it means questioning not just who she is, but what she is?

Get tangled up in our Entangled Teen titles...

Conjure by Lea Nolan

Sixteen-year-old twins Emma and Jack Guthrie hope for a little summer adventure when they find an eighteenth-century message in a bottle revealing a hidden pirate treasure. Will they be able to set things right before it's too late?

Chosen Ones by Tiffany Truitt

The government, faced with humanity's extinction, created the Chosen Ones. When Tess begins work at a Chosen Ones training facility, she meets James, and the attraction is immediate in its intensity, overwhelming in its danger. Can she stand against her oppressors, even if it means giving up the only happiness in her life?

Pretty Amy by Lisa Burstein

When their dates stand them up for prom, Amy, along with the beautiful Lila and uber-cool Cassie, take matters into their own hands—earning them a night in jail. With Lila and Cassie parentally banned, Amy feels like she has nothing—like she is nothing. Navigating unlikely alliances, Amy finds that maybe getting a life only happens once you think your life is over.

Toxic by Jus Accardo

When a Six saved Kale's life the night of Sumrun, Dez was warned there would be consequences. But she never imagined she'd lose the one thing she'd give anything to keep... Dez will have to lay it all on the line if there's any hope of proving Jade's guilt before they all end up Residents of Denazen. Or worse, dead...